THE NAVIGATOR'S DREAM, VOLUME 2

THE NAVIGATOR'S DREAM,

VOLUME 2

Gulftide

Julia A. Turk

iUniverse, Inc.
Bloomington

The Navigator's Dream, Volume 2
Gulftide

This is a work of fiction. All of the characters, names, incidents, organizations, and dialogue in this novel are either the products of the author's imagination or are used fictitiously.

iUniverse books may be ordered through booksellers or by contacting:

iUniverse
1663 Liberty Drive
Bloomington, IN 47403
www.iuniverse.com
1-800-Authors (1-800-288-4677)

Because of the dynamic nature of the Internet, any web addresses or links contained in this book may have changed since publication and may no longer be valid. The views expressed in this work are solely those of the author and do not necessarily reflect the views of the publisher, and the publisher hereby disclaims any responsibility for them.

Any people depicted in stock imagery provided by Thinkstock are models, and such images are being used for illustrative purposes only.

Certain stock imagery © Thinkstock.

ISBN: 978-1-4697-4747-7 (sc)
ISBN: 978-1-4697-4748-4 (hc)
ISBN: 978-1-4697-4750-7 (e)

Library of Congress Control Number: 2012900896

Printed in the United States of America

iUniverse rev. date: 01/16/2012

Chapters

Prologue 1

1) Page of Pentacles 6

2) Knight of Pentacles 24

3) Queen of Pentacles 38

4) King of Pentacles 51

5) Page of Swords 64

6) Knight of Swords 79

7) Queen of Swords 95

8) King of Swords 107

9) Page of Cups 119

10) Knight of Cups 132

11) Queen of Cups 147

12) King of Cups 161

13) Page of Wands 173

14) Knight of Wands 189

15) Queen of Wands 205

16) King of Wands 219

17) Ace of Pentacles 232

18) Ace of Swords 244

19) Ace of Cups 260

20) Ace of Wands 276

Epilogue 291

Prologue

My Guide looked at me firmly as he spoke. "The power of the four weapons I have chosen to keep is too great for you to handle during your next experiences. You will find that all the other objects are absolutely useless, and should be left behind."

I instantly objected. "You have chosen the four most beautiful articles! Can I not have one to take with me? Why have you picked these four?" I began to sulk a little, as I admired the splendor of the weapons, and I could see Suckersie start to squirm as I did so. I promptly pulled myself together.

"I have explained that already," the old man said sternly. "These four objects hold the most energy, and if you misuse that power, evil will come to you." He passed his hand lightly over the Platter, the Cup, the Dagger and the Wand. "You must wait, and prove yourself many times before you can receive these into your hands. Now, let us move on and meet Belvedere."

I had no alternative but to agree, but I had to wonder who Belvedere was. The old fellow remained obstinately silent while opening the door in the left hand wall of the sanctuary. A handcart stood outside into which we loaded the remaining items. Suckersie sat on top, for she was tired, and we began to push the cart towards a low-lying open area several miles long with soaring cliffs visible in the distance. A shining body of water appeared on our right, rippling in bands of red, yellow and blue, merging and changing into the rainbow colors I loved so much. I was fascinated, and didn't notice at first that a squat purple tower about forty feet tall made of amethyst cubes stood in our path, barring the way as we came nearer the shimmering Lagoon. From its roof, two poles stuck out horizontally on each side and several small objects fluttered from the poles like little wind chimes. At the bottom of the tower, a small door stood open to a spiral staircase, beside which gratings were sunk into the ground. Above, a covered overlook occupied the top of the tower, and I could see a movement in the dim shade beneath it. I stepped forward and looked up. There was a face up there - a strange face that peered down at me silently. It was the face of Belvedere, which I now saw for the first time.

The face was huge, even at that distance, and crowned by a shock of curly red hair that stirred in the breeze. I couldn't see his features very well from there, except the eyes, which were dark and seemed to pop out of his head, as the whites were clearly visible all around the iris. I didn't like the look of him, and I backed off and turned to look for my Guide. "He doesn't look very friendly," I murmured indistinctly. "Who is he, anyway?"

"Belvedere is your Ego," chuckled the old man. "He rules all your entities, for you are not a single personality at the moment, but a collection of parts which make up a confusing whole. If you look up to the top of his tower, you'll see. On either side of the tower, you'll notice two extensions, each with ten hooks. See what I mean?" He pointed upward and I squinted to make out what the fluttering things were. Oh! My God! They were not wind chimes, but tiny bodies, which were attached to the pole by strings as they swung to-and-fro flaccidly.

"They look like a bunch of puppets!" I exclaimed in shock. "What are they doing there?"

"You are right," said my Guide. "They are puppets – little manikins – controlled by their puppet master, Belvedere. They are your different selves, and each one of them must be brought under your control to be transformed, or vanquished if they are too evil to be changed. While you are at the Lagoon, you will have the opportunity to adventure with all of them, those you already know and others who, in the past, controlled your lives. You may make the decision as to whether they are worth keeping, or not. Those that you choose to keep must be altered in a positive way so that they can serve you as crew on the journey you will eventually begin in the Mystic SEA. But for now, let us go upstairs and meet Belvedere himself." My Guide made a move towards the door.

I held back. "I don't want to go up there. I'd rather not know who Belvedere is and I certainly don't believe I'm made up of manikins!"

"Have you already forgotten those who accompanied you on your river journey? I am disappointed. Globdinig, Swollup, Bazoom – they mean nothing to you?" The old fellow looked disappointed.

"Well, of course not! I remember them, but they were mostly pretty annoying. I didn't like them. They kept popping up all the time, and only a couple of them turned out to be useful." I protested.

"That's the secret. However irritating they are, if they become useful, it is because your view of them is beginning to change, and you're seeing the other side of them."

"Do they have another side?" I was surprised. "I didn't see it. Do all of them have another side? There are twenty, aren't there?" I had counted the little manikins.

"All of them have an alternative presentation." The old man sighed. "But some of them have been wicked for so long that they cannot be changed, and these you must destroy."

"Which are the ones that I must get rid of?" I still hung back, refusing to move towards the door and continuing my questions. "How do I know the right ones?"

"I have already helped you with that," my Guide responded. "The puppet entities that you met on your river journey – there were twelve – might be transformed. The remaining eight are too wicked and must be removed from your aura. That will be hard, for Belvedere will do everything in his power to protect them, although you will not see him again at the Lagoon."

"I must get rid of eight? How can I do that? I don't even know who they are."

"Don't worry about that. They will present themselves as you evoke the right moods. We have to climb the tower now without further delay, so come along." The lean old man stepped forward with a long stride and disappeared through the door. I felt myself drawn forward, and as I passed the gratings beside the entrance, I looked down. In the gloom, I thought I saw a shadowy face with an eerie grin, but it disappeared before I could be sure. My heart pounding, and Paragutt hot on my heels, I began to climb the tower.

The steps of the spiral staircase up the tower looked as if they had never been used. Spiders' webs hung from every corner and brushed against my face, sending shivers down my back as I climbed. The staircase was lit by narrow slits in the wall, and from time to time I stopped to look out. There gradually emerged a better view of the Lagoon, which stretched as far as the eye could see. I could make out an island in the middle, with a white pyramid on it. Dimly I also saw four castles set at intervals along the right hand shore of the lagoon, whereas on the left, nothing was visible through the thick mist that seemed to roll in from the sea, obscuring the sandbar which must separate them. Finally, I found myself standing at the top of the stairs behind my Guide and looking up at a gigantic figure.

Belvedere must have been about nine feet tall, and he was dressed entirely in purple satin with a lace collar and cuffs, and buckled black shoes. His shoes looked dirty, but I couldn't understand why, if he never went downstairs. I didn't at first want to look at his face, but plucked up courage as my Guide pushed me forward.

"Look at him! This is your Ego who rules your life, beyond which you cannot see, and who must be brought to heel."

Belvedere laughed – a dull, booming sound like a hollow drum that reverberated throughout the tower and set the manikins dancing on their poles. He spoke in a raspy voice. "I don't think so! Brought to heel, indeed. Just try it! I have ultimate power over you, remember? And that pipsqueak …" here he looked down scornfully at the old man, who was only six feet tall, "He won't be able to help you."

I flushed with anger as Paragutt disappeared, and felt Bazoom reverberating in my pocket where he had left his hook and flown to me. "How dare you insult my Guide! He is more powerful than you think. He can do special things……" Here a nudge from the old fellow, who glared at me, silenced me.

"I know you are in control here." The old man seemed all of a sudden very meek and apologetic. "I'm just here to introduce you two, for our Navigator was not aware of your existence before now. Belvedere means beautiful view, and you certainly have an incredible lookout here." He walked over to the balustrade and gazed out, addressing me. "Why, I can see the Lagoon clearly and the four Castles of the Elements built on the eastern shore. This is where you will prove yourself. Come and have a look."

I walked over to the edge of the balustrade and looked out again. I could see the nearer shore of the Lagoon where it met the barren rocky land around the tower. A small punt was moored at a wooden dock below, and I thought I saw a dark, scurrying figure dart away from it and disappear down the grating.

"Who was that?" I exclaimed. "I saw someone. There's someone living down below, under that grating, isn't there?"

My Guide looked somber. "So you have seen her. It is she who you met before, the one with the pale horse who dragged you over the cliff. I rescued you then, but I could not destroy her. She is the Hoodwinker, who is the wife of Belvedere, but she has been shut away for years and he pretends that she no longer exists. But we know better."

"What was she doing over by the punt? I'm sure she's up to no good!" I was feeling exhausted and crushed by the information I had received. Things didn't look good for my next journey into the Lagoon. My Guide had said I had to prove myself, but twenty-one times seemed too many to cope with. I began to despair and soon found Globdinig beside me. I collapsed onto the floor, but the old man pulled me to my feet sharply.

"We will leave now," he said sternly. "Get rid of Globdinig this minute." He turned to Belvedere as I made an effort to cheer up. "I must prepare my charge for a journey to the Castle of Earth, which is the first stronghold to be visited." He led the way back down the stairs, and I was extremely glad to be out of the tower, although I glanced at the grating as I passed and caught a faint cackle of laughter.

We walked to the punt, pushing the handcart. Suckersie had remained behind and was hanging on her hook near Belvedere. Paragutt, Bazoom and Globdinig had likewise returned to their places, fluttering in the wind as Belvedere glared down at us without saying goodbye, and on the wind came twenty voices raised in a faint song:

"You aren't one so make no fuss. Many are you for we are us…"

Page of Pentacles – Rules Ten and Nine of Pentacles.

My Guide and I loaded my few belongings from the handcart into the punt moored by the wooden dock below Belvederes' tower. I observed that the tower actually blocked the way to the Lagoon, and that we must have exited by a back door in order to get down to the water. Had the tower grown bigger? Where was the path? Confused, I looked back and could just see the little manikins swaying in the wind. Twenty of them! I wondered what the twenty-first test would be and whether I would ever reach that point.

Having arranged everything in the waterproof boxes attached to the sides and bottom of the boat, with Joana the cricket in her place, my Guide pointed to the Castle of Earth and told me I would meet a young man there who was a Page at the castle. He would take me on my first adventure and it was important that I either vanquished or brought under control any puppets that I might encounter. I was extremely nervous, and was indignant that Paragutt had not come to accompany me, but for some reason all of the puppets were still hanging from the poles at the tower. It did seem unusual, for Paragutt and the others were always prompt when my moods came on. I wondered if they had become indifferent to my fate.

Nevertheless, I knew I must push off alone, and the old fellow untied the lines and gave the punt a shove out into the water. It floated off and the distance to the dock increased rapidly. I looked around for a pole, but could not see one. I panicked and yelled back to my Guide.

"Where's the pole? You forgot the pole! I don't have any way to direct the punt." I was on my feet, balancing as the boat rocked wildly.

A laugh came over the water. "You must find the pole. One of the objects you have stowed in the boat is the pole. All you have to do is find it, dip it in the water, and – there is your pole! Better hurry up and look for it before the tide sweeps you away."

H'm, I thought, so I'm in tidal waters from now on. When I had been on the river, at least I knew the flow was always in the same direction – downriver. It was typical of the old man to play a trick like this now. I hastily went through the boxes in the bottom of the punt, reasoning that the pole must be something that was long and thin. The distance between my boat and the shore was rapidly increasing, and the old man merely a dot on the horizon, yet his faint chuckle still echoed across the water. Desperately I turned to the final box and found the dead rattlesnake curled up. He was long and thin. I took him out and dangled his tail in the water and he seemed to smile at me. I felt a quiver run suddenly through his slack body, and he became rigid and began to elongate. His skin seemed to lose its sleekness and became woody and grainy. When he reached about ten feet, he stopped and said – for his head was still at the top of the pole – that he thanked me for releasing him from bondage and allowing him to be useful in his new life. I patted his neck and we poled off together, the Lagoon being relatively shallow across most of its width.

We approached the Castle of Earth, built of dark bricks made of clay baked in the sun, its somber rectangular turrets reared over square windows let into the walls. Around the outside of the castle wall was a group of small mud huts, and there was some sort of disturbance going on in the central square of this village. We pulled in and I let the rattlesnake lie down in the punt, where he coiled up for a snooze. Mooring the boat, I walked over to the huts, hearing the sound of voices raised in anger. A crowd was gathering around a young man dressed as a Page in knee-length russet pantaloons and a v-neck citrine blouse, cinched at the waist by a narrow belt. A short russet cape was around his shoulders and on it, the motif of a crossed spade and fork. He had a ruddy, strong face with bright hazel eyes and curly brown hair, and appeared to be a hard-working, conscientious person. He was ushering along a small herd of pigs, and seemed to be the butt of the villagers' wrath.

"Ignorant serf! You allowed those pigs to escape."

"You have not been watching our swine!"

"Foolhardy idiot – think you that our pigs are worth nothing?"

"You are to leave the village –go! GO! We have had enough of your dreaming."

These were some of the epithets thrown at him. Evidently, the Page had lost several pigs, and it appeared that pigs were very important here. I waited until he turned and, picking up his backpack, sadly made his way out of the village towards the shore with the four remaining pigs, dragging his wooden staff.

"Hello. Can I help you?" I asked, stepping forward.

He turned to me with relief. "Please take me away from here. I can't stand their ignorance any longer! I was studying and two of the pigs ran off. Now they are lost and it's not the first time this has happened. I've already lost eight other pigs, making a total of ten. They must be in the forest. Will you help me? Could we go there and try to find them? My name is Trid, by the way, and this is for you." He handed me a barred hawks feather and pointed to an area about a mile beyond the castle where the trees grew thickly down to the waters' edge.

"I can take you in the punt, and I see you have only four pigs left, so they will fit in too. Just mind they don't mess it up – it's new. Go ahead and jump in and the pigs should follow you."

I half-wished I hadn't offered the ride, as the bristly pigs, squealing and snuffling, slithered over the side of the punt, leaving a trail of mud and dead leaves, and milled about in the bottom. I picked up the snake, who stiffened himself again, and poled towards the wood, where we left the boat in dense reeds by the waters' edge.

Threading our way through some trees, we reached a small clearing where a gopher sat thoughtfully chewing. As we sat down for a rest, Trid told me his story. The Queen of the Castle of Earth had chosen him as a Page to serve at table, but, being ambitious, he had decided to study and learn to read and write so that he could become a Squire and eventually a Knight for the Kingdom of Earth. He also took part in weapons training, fighting with the club and pike, and was an expert with the slingshot. The peasants in the village, however, were uneducated and resented the fact that he had been singled out for favor. What is more, they relied on their pigs for their livelihood and assumed he was completely ignorant of their needs because he had let them escape. Trid told me that he had read the tea leaves and a dark stranger was supposed to help him.

That could be me, I thought. "What does the dark stranger have to do?"

"That person must prove that they can **temper acquisition with cautious moderation,**" said the Page. "I'm not sure what it means."

It sounded like a mouthful. "Where did you hear that?"

"It was in the tea leaves. I don't know what it signifies." The Page went on. "I only know I need to find the ten missing pigs, and they're probably rooting for truffles in the forest."

A bluebird flew into view and perched for a moment on a twig nearby, then flew directly towards the forest and disappeared.

"There, that's a sign." I pointed rapidly in the direction of the forest. "That bird knows where the pigs are. We'll follow it, quickly now. Leave your backpack here and we'll pick it up later." I got up and ran towards the trees and Trid followed, hoping the bluebird had not vanished, and there it was, perched a little further on as if beckoning to us. We plunged deeper and deeper into the wood, pushing through dense brambles and undergrowth, the bird keeping just ahead and the four pigs rooting noisily beside us. After pressing on for a couple of hours, we came to a cliff in which was the dark entrance to a cave. The bluebird fluttered about at the mouth of the cave but wouldn't go in.

"This must be the spot," I volunteered. "The pigs should be in that cave. It's nearly sundown and they've gone in there for the night."

"Pigs don't have to go in when it gets dark," said my companion, as he tucked the bluebird inside his shirt, where it settled down. "But we'll go in anyway and see. These pigs look as if they know something's in there."

His four muddy pigs were already snuffling at the mouth of the cave as we began to climb over the rocks at the entrance, the four pigs hurrying just ahead of us. Soon total darkness swallowed us, and we crept along, feeling our way over the damp walls and following the direction the excited pigs had taken. The passage closed in as the cave narrowed down, and we were getting claustrophobic and almost ready to turn back, when ahead of us we heard snuffling and a couple of squeals of delight, that accompanied the patter of cloven hooves. Rounding a bend, we found a narrow band of evening sunlight filtering down from a hole in the ceiling of a large cave, illuminating the missing pigs. All ten of them were there, hunkered down in a pile, snorting and flapping their ears with pleasure as the remaining four joined them.

Trid was elated. "Wonderful! We've found them. Now at least I can return them to the village. They can find someone else to do their pig-herding in future."

"Not so fast!" A nebulous voice spoke from the shadowy nether regions of the cave, as a faint shimmering green light filtered up from behind the rocks. "You have entered the realm of Persephone, goddess of the underworld and pig-lover. Have you been negligent in the care of these pigs?"

The Page was taken aback. "I-I didn't mean t-to lose them," he stammered. "I wanted to learn to read and write."

"That is just an excuse. You were responsible for the pigs and now they have led you to my territory. Before I can allow you to return with them, you must pass a test, which I will give you both. Leave the pigs in my care and come to the back of the cave." Persephones' voice commanded.

We nervously moved towards the darkened part of the cave, and with a swish, the green light brightened, revealing a misty aperture that led us away from the forest into another world – a world I recognized – for there were Lance and Gwen, my parents, standing outside their house welcoming a group of guests who were emerging from several long limousines.

I walked up to them and hugged each of them. "Hello. I didn't expect to find you here! What's going on?"

My mother looked at me, her eyes sparkling. "It's so good to see you. We thought you were gone forever. We're having our first convention for venture capitalists here. It's such a beautiful setting. Since we've become philanthropists, we've been reaching out to find others to share and work with us to benefit villages threatened by poverty in Turkey."

"What a worthwhile cause!" I exclaimed, as the Page stared, fascinated, at their mansion. "May I introduce Trid, the Page of Pentacles," I turned towards him. "This is my mother Gwen and my father Lance who parented me in a previous life."

The Page bowed respectfully. "I am Trid of the Castle of Earth, pig herder and student of grammar." He held out a grubby paw, which my mother took in her white hand rather delicately.

"We are pleased to welcome you here. Are you going to join the venture capitalist convention?" She looked him up and down doubtfully. "Everyone here has to possess a fortune of at least one billion dollars......." Her voice faded away as she regarded Trids' ragged tunic and filthy leggings.

"Don't worry, mother." I reassured her. "We're just passing through on the test that Persephone has set us, for we can't get the pigs back from her unless we complete it. Actually, she didn't tell us what the test was." Here I paused, racking my brains for an answer.

Gwen looked somewhat confused. "Who is this Persephone woman? I haven't heard of her. How do pigs come into this?"

"We don't know any more than you do. Trid has to get his herd of pigs back to the village, though." I turned to the Page. "I think we should climb that cliff at the base of the lake over there and see what's at the top. Maybe we can find out. Come on."

We wandered through a magnificent garden, as Gwen showed us the great falls that plunged into their natural lake. The foaming water was filled with gold coins, which glittered and leaped as they fell showering into the lake, where a gardener in a boat was busying himself fishing loads of cash out of the water with a large net. I felt I recognized him, as he was quite tall, about seven feet, and had an extraordinarily long nose, but I wasn't sure.

"Where is the source of this wealth?" I asked my mother, looking up at the top of the falls as a thrill of excitement shot through me. "It must come from up there."

"We don't know and we don't ask," replied Gwen somewhat slyly. "Ever since we started to give money away, the gold coins have been falling faster and faster. Now we can afford to give much more than we gave before, and yet maintain a comfortable style of living."

"That's wonderful," I heard myself saying. "You have learned to temper acquisition with cautious moderation."

Where had I heard that before? I slid a glance at Trid, but he had become mesmerized by the sight of the money. "Let's find out where the coins are coming from."

The feeling of intense excitement continued to rush through me as we said goodbye to Gwen and set off up the cliff, which was quite a scramble. I left the Page behind as I sped from rock to rock in my eagerness, finding easy finger and toe holds, my anticipation growing as I thought of finding the source of all that money.

About half-way up the cliff I heard shallow panting behind me and, thinking it was my companion, turned around. Trid was resting further down the cliff, however, and between us a wizened gnome-like figure that I had not seen before clung to a rock just below me. I showed my astonishment.

"Who are you?" I exclaimed in surprise.

The creatures' narrow mouth opened and a thin stream of saliva dripped onto the rock. "I am Aquirot, your greedy self, and I am coming with you to find the gold that you desire." The horrible entity grinned, as a furtive look crossed its cracked features.

"I don't know you. Go away!" I said crossly. "I'm not intending to share my discovery with anyone. Except maybe Trid." I added reluctantly.

Aquirots' twisted mouth opened in a leer, revealing a complete set of gold dentures. "You'll have to share with me. You have no choice. I'm your greedy self, remember? As long as your desire for the gold exists, I will be with you, and I will demand my half." She, for I had discerned a female trait in the figure, crowed harshly and waggled scrawny ears, which glittered with golden rings of every shape and size.

Well, I decided, Aquirot would have to tag along, because I wasn't going to abandon my search for the source of the coins. As long as I wanted the gold, I understood that my greed would remain unabated. I called down to Trid. "Are you OK? We have a new companion for the trip, I'm afraid."

"Yes, I'm fine. I want to be with you for this adventure, no matter what. I'm not sure where the little woman came from but maybe you'll explain later. In the meantime, it's my duty to be vigilant and look after you for you are traveling in my card. And, after all, I'm enjoying acting as your escort!" Trid sounded very determined.

"Well, I'm sorry I took off so quickly up the cliff. I'm so used to doing things on my own I didn't realize you were being left behind." I shrugged off the feeling that he was keeping an eye on me, and the three of us climbed on, the scratching of Aquirots' claws on the rocks irritating me beyond belief.

We reached the top of the cliff and found ourselves in a bleak landscape, partly desert, where a few mesquite and cactus plants struggled for survival between some large boulders surrounding a great gleaming lake. The opalescent water seemed to flash blue, then green and gold, yet there was no visible sign of the gold coins that were spilling over the waterfall. I figured the money must be hidden in a current traveling below the opaque surface of the lake. The humps of several sandbanks showed above the water in some places, as laden barges with lateen sails drifted along the shore. In the distance, I could see a canal leading into the lake and above it, on a hillside dusted with scrubby plants, a small walled town clustered about two miles from the canal. Several truncated pyramids rose up by the water.

Brushing away the slight disappointment I felt on seeing that the surface of the lake contained no sign of the coins, I reasoned that any gold would be concealed below. This didn't deter Aquirot, who was glancing around and sniffing under every boulder she could find, muttering to herself. We headed in the direction of the town, noting as we got closer several small pyramids behind the busy wharves along the canal. Donkeys drawing carts and pack mules bearing heavy burdens were loading and unloading various goods, and many people dashed about, shouting orders and urging on their servants, who staggered under huge sacks of grain.

When we reached the docks, I decided to examine the truncated pyramids, so we walked over to them. Peering up at the nearest one, I saw a window high up in the side of the structure, and within it the glint of gold. My heart began to race as Aquirot jumped up and down, opening and shutting her wizened mouth with frenzied glee and shouting hoarsely.

"There it is! The lovely stuff! I want some, I want some."

Brushing her aside, I quickly climbed onto the Pages' shoulders in order to see the treasure better. It was, indeed, pure gold! A fabulous amount of wealth was in plain view, coins and jewels spilling over each other right behind the window for anyone to see. What a strange way to hoard treasure, I thought. It would be easy to break the window and pocket some of it. I had been without money for so long, the desire to buy, buy, buy, came over me in a rush, and at the same time Aquirots' hoarse yet syrupy voice spoke close to us as I jumped down to the ground.

We turned and saw her narrowed eyes, as a calculating look chased itself across her gnarled face. "Remember me. I want that gold! Until today, you have not thought of me for a long while and I feel neglected. It is time for me to be here with you at last, and I can help you break in to the treasure, you'll see." Aquirot licked her thin lips, her tongue still dripping with saliva, which splashed onto the ground as she spoke.

How disgusting, I thought privately, but I found myself asking another question out loud. "How can we break into the pyramid? I want some of that money."

"They won't miss it. The village is rolling in dough. Everyone has money and they don't need any more. Then you can buy many trinkets at the bazaar, too. There is a market just inside the town gates with many beautiful things for sale." Aquirot cast a fleeting look up towards the walled town through yearning eyes.

I followed her glance and noted a stony path leading up to the town on which a steady stream of mules and donkeys plied their trade, and even from this distance I could see busy movement around the town gates and the faint cries of vendors on the air.

Her grating voice spoke at my elbow. "We need to wait until dark. Then there won't be anyone around, because they all go inside the walls at night. They are afraid of the nightjars that fly through the scrub during the dark hours. These birds have huge mouths that can swallow a person." Aquirot announced threateningly.

It was already early evening, so I acquiesced and we strolled around the wharves discreetly until darkness fell. People began to trickle back towards the town, and soon a three quarter moon rose in the east and the wharves became deserted except for the increasing twitter of the nightjars in the desert around us. We found a tall ladder and the three of us set it up next to the largest pyramid. "I wonder where the tops of the pyramids have gone?" I mused. "They must have them hidden somewhere."

"Never mind about that," said Aquirot hurriedly, rubbing her dry hands together with a rasping sound. "Let's break the glass and get out of here with the loot."

I let Aquirot go first up the ladder wielding a large stone, so that any broken glass would fall on her rather than myself, following her up to steady her while Trid leaned on the bottom of the ladder. Aquirot pounded on the glass with the stone, making a loud banging that vibrated on the night air.

"Quiet!" I urged. "Someone will hear us."

"They're all up in the town, remember? But… I can't break the glass – it's giving under my blows but it's not cracking. I'll try again….." Her voice trailed away as she looked down and a look of dismay crossed her shriveled face, for a heavy hand had fallen on Trids' shoulder below us. A man in purple with a silver crown stood there, his face a mask of fury.

"What are you doing here? Never mind, I can see! Trying to break into the pyramid, eh?" He burst into laughter. "You fools! You cannot raid this pyramid. The covering on the windows is completely burglar proof. Only those who know where the top of the pyramid is can open the chamber by replacing it. You are guilty as thieves, and I will punish you in our traditional manner. I am Fakoor, the chief merchant in this area and I have the authority to set any sentence without trial. I will leave you in the desert to be swallowed by the nightjars, I think…" He rubbed his hands together and snickered to himself as we climbed down, shivering with fear, and removed the ladder. Paragutt immediately appeared by my side.

"Go, now – into the wasteland." Fakoor pulled out a large baton and waved it in the air threateningly. Although Paragutt clung tearfully to my waist with his thin legs dangling down behind, his influence was tempered by the furious rage that Aquirot had fallen into. She was beside herself, thrashing through the bushes, thinking of ways to get hold of the loot, even though our lives were now threatened. It was the first time I had to deal with two entities at the same time – my greed for the money remained unabated while fear for my life clung to the pit of my stomach. We stumbled ahead of Fakoor for half an hour through the mesquite bushes, unable to see much around us, and then he turned and walked away, abruptly leaving us to our fate.

The light of the moon faintly picked out the scrubby landscape and as we stood there, a vast twittering arose and hundreds of small birds began to fly towards us, whirling and twirling as they got closer, their wings brushing across our shoulders and their huge mouths gaping open as they began to peck at our faces. We cowered and raised our arms to defend ourselves. I was thinking fast, for I now realized my greedy attitude had trapped us. Maybe this was the test that Persephone had set. I didn't want to get rid of Aquirot by taking my thoughts off the gold, for she would then reappear later in my life, and now I recalled the advice of my Guide. Here was the chance for me to destroy her and escape at the same time from her influence forever. I needed to attract the nightjars' full attention towards her, and then we might be able to slip away while they attacked and swallowed her.

Wondering how that could be done, I remembered the hawks' feather in my pocket that Trid had given me. I pulled out the barred feather, crouching low behind the scrub to protect myself from the attacking nightjars. The whirring of the birds' wings was getting even closer while the vociferous trilling of their calls drove me crazy. I took the hawks' feather in my hand, remembering my encounter with Hawkley P. Mann, and his disembodied voice came soft, but clear.

"What can I do for you? I am getting a picture of many birds. Are you under attack?"

"Yes, we are. Can you help us?" I quickly responded.

"We will gather together and come to you. All birds are afraid of hawks and they will soon disperse, don't worry. I will bring a squadron of nighthawks, as it is very dark."

"Wait a minute!" I hesitated. "First I need at least one of the nightjars to stay so that I can dispose of Aquirot, my greedy self, for I don't want her in my life. She is irredeemable."

"H'm. Then you'll have to act quickly. Capture a passing nightjar, and then you will know what to do. Remember the silver cord. We will wait close by and come at your call. But hurry!"

The hawks could save us, yet first I must take the opportunity to remove Aquirot. How could I persuade one of the nightjars to swallow the horrible woman? A faint remembrance of an entranced journey down the throat of a nightjar jogged my memory. Of course! I jumped up and grabbed one of the birds that circled around my head. A frantic twittering arose as my hand closed around the little captive, its mouth agape. I knew that to get rid of Aquirot, my greedy entity, I would have to go into that mouth myself for an instant, because she was an inseparable part of me, and she would be forced to follow. Then I must somehow get out again, giving up all thoughts of greed and desire to acquire goods and money forever, in order to leave her behind.

I gulped and gazed deeply at the pink throat in front of me, and found myself gradually drawn, trancelike, down into the birds' mouth, Aquirot reluctantly pulled down beside me. She was yelling at me to stop, her clawlike nails digging into the birds' beak, but I refused. I could hear Trid desperately shouting at me too, but I knew I had to go further. I had to find Isis.....

Concentrating, I held the little bird firmly and soon I noticed a thin, milky cord wavering in front of me. With Aquirot by my side, still protesting, for I had not yet totally rid my mind of the riches I had seen, I floated along the cord for some distance up into the sky towards a bright six-pointed star that I thought must be Sirius. Gradually the figure of a beautiful woman, clad in green draperies, appeared before us. She stood at the top of a little silver staircase in a copper boat, holding on her shoulder a vase from which flowed the milky vapor.

"I was expecting you," she said softly purring. "I see you have Aquirot by your side. You want to rid yourself of her influence, and your feelings are sincere, I can tell. I will take Aquirot to my bosom if you can sincerely give up all hopes and expectations of material riches, for I am Isis, the mother goddess, natural progenitor of all that is, and at my will I can dispose of all hellish things. Come, Aquirot – come and sit in my boat. You must stay here with me." Isis held out her hand in guidance and the wizened little woman meekly sat down, her resistance gone. The goddess turned to me. "And now you must return immediately, for your friend Trid is in grave danger. Go now, and summon the hawks."

Feeling her copper boat drift away from me, I found myself pulled rapidly backwards, as if through a vortex, landing heavily in the scrub next to the cowering Page, who was under attack and severely scratched and pecked on his head and arms. Quickly I held up the barred feather, summoning the hawks of the night, and with a great rushing noise they came in hundreds, dropping down from the dark sky directly over the circling nightjars. A vast clattering of wings and feathered confusion arose as each little bird tried to escape the predators, and within minutes the desert was silent again and the hawks sitting around us on the bushes, one or two of them thoughtfully ripping up the nightjars they had caught.

A proud, beautiful hawk near me spoke up. "I am Hawkley P. Mann, whom you met in your last life adventure. I'm happy to help you, for I know you are on a great quest. Be aware of your evil entities, for I fear that a time will soon come when you will be doubly tempted. May you go safely now, and the wishes of the Mystic Society of Enochian Anchorites be with you. You have passed the first test."

With that, and before I could clarify the content of the test, the nighthawks took off and were quickly gone.

Trid and I slowly traced our way back down towards the canal, nursing our wounds, and boarded the punt, where we slumped into a dazed sleep. I didn't even begin to wonder how the boat, which we had left in the reeds when we entered the forest near the Castle of Earth, had come to be tied up behind some bales of straw by the canal. The following morning, I awoke and looked towards the pyramid where the gold lay behind the protective glass. I felt no desire to own any of it now, but I was still curious as to where it was coming from. I gently shook Trid awake, for an idea had formed in my head.

"Trid, Trid!" I whispered quietly in his ear, for the wharves were already stirring with early morning activity. "Gwen and Lance are sending gold bullion to villages in Turkey. I wonder whether this village has received any? I must say, they don't seem to need it, but I'd like to find out. Who knows, their gift may be being misused, and since we're here, lets go up to the village and find out what's afoot."

The Page sat up slowly, taking the bluebird from his shirt, setting it down and giving it some seed out of his pocket. "Sounds like a plan. We'll have to look out for Fakoor, though. He probably thinks the nightjars have stripped our skeletons bare by now." He chuckled.

"I saw Fakoor boarding one of the barges. He often accompanies them down to the lake to trade with the miners, so he won't be around once the barge pulls away."

We waited until the barge slipped her moorings, watching Fakoor strutting around the deck, checking everything as the boat slid down the canal. "OK. We should be safe now. Nobody else saw us yesterday, so let's go." As I said this, I heard a loud chewing noise on the other side of the straw stacks, so we looked around to see what it was. There stood my friend the donkey Mandrake with another donkey beside him.

"Mandrake! It's you!" I exclaimed happily. "Can we ride you up to the town?"

"Of course. That's why I'm here. The hawks told me there were two of you, so I brought Cubit along. Jump on and we'll go."

I mounted and Trid easily vaulted onto Cubit, a small brown ass. I could see he was an expert horseman.

"You'll soon be a Squire." I called to him a little enviously.

"I hope so. I've practiced horsemanship all my life. My hope has always been to become a Knight in the service of our Queen." He soon had Cubit trotting smartly up the path to the village, and Mandrake and I followed.

We arrived at the gate after a bumpy half hour and left our mounts tied up, blending quickly into the crowd. Our plan was to find the village treasury, but first we stopped to look at the vendor's wares. Some of the objects were clearly sexual in nature and quite embarrassing, and I hesitated to face the leers of the vendors, so I turned away and as I did so, I spied a little donkey cart going by with a huge safe, barred and locked, balanced on it. I grabbed Trid's arm and we followed the cart surreptitiously as it wound through several narrow alleys, passing along a lane that I recognized. On the right side, halfway along this lane, was a closed and shuttered house with an old, torn striped purple awning hanging dismally from rusty poles. I felt I had been in that house. What was it that reminded me of a visit there, and why was the place now deserted? I racked my brains as we continued on our way, but I couldn't recall the circumstances. We stopped outside the gates of a large house near the top of the hill, which obviously belonged to the village chief or someone of rank. I soon knew who that was, as, hiding behind the gates, I heard the driver say to the gatekeeper that the safe was for Fakoor and was the regular weekly delivery.

The cart passed through the gate and we made as if we were strolling by, admiring the view, but at the same moment, I was casing the house to see a way inside. I wanted to find out more about the contents of the safe but I was wary of being caught a second time. The house was constructed of square towers at each corner, with passageways between them and an interior courtyard with a large stone turtle fountain that could be seen through the gate. The towers had windows, but the openings had bars on the lower floors, and the walls were high. I thought again of Hawkley and wondered if he could help us. I pulled out the barred feather and stroked it gently, but no answer came. I had used up the energy in the feather. Trid saw me look disappointed and made a suggestion, gently handing the little bluebird, who chirped merrily, out of his shirt.

"If the hawk doesn't come anymore, maybe the bluebird can fly into the top window of the house and check things out."

We decided to try it. The tiny bird flew up and through an open window in the nearest tower. It was gone for a while, and we waited nervously, but it reemerged with something in its beak. When it alighted, we saw the object was a gold coin that was partly melted down and still warm from the furnace. It was evident that Fakoor was processing the bullion that must be in the safe – the weekly delivery – which was almost certainly from Lance and Gwen, and turning the gold into something else – but what?

I remembered seeing the strange jewelry the vendors were selling, but almost all the settings were of silver, with diamonds in different styles. Where did the jewels come from? I thought about Fakoor going away on the barge, and remembered them loading a big chunk of what looked like gold just before he left. So gold was being melted down – then - could it be - exchanged for silver and diamonds? We could learn no more at Fakoor's house, but would have to return to the lake and trace the route of the barge to its destination.

We found Mandrake and Cubit by the town gate and rode them back to the canal. Leaving them by the straw stack, we hid in the punt until evening, then woke the rattlesnake and silently poled down the canal and out onto the lake, setting off in the direction I felt the barge had taken. All night we pressed on, and morning found us close to the end of the lake, where the entrance to a large underground quarry reared up before us, the rattle of carts filled with ore trundling out of the blackness. This was evidently the silver mine, and the diamond shaft must be close by. But, where was the melted gold on the barges to be delivered? Trid and I must search for that, for then we might get to the bottom of this mystery.

We waited until nightfall once more, concealed the punt carefully, and went to explore the deserted mine. We soon found the shaft, which, of course, was pitch black. We needed light to venture into the mine. Over the water, thousands of tiny fireflies were dancing. We managed to catch enough in a muslin bag that we tied to a stick to light our way, and set off down the passageway. We must have walked four miles into the well-timbered shaft when we came to a parting in the ways, and our direction was decided for us by the sound of metal on metal coming from the left fork in the passage. Creeping slowly, the noise grew louder and a dim light in front of us gradually grew brighter, while a foul smell of rotting garbage and burning metal overwhelmed us. Holding our noses and staying low, we came out upon a ledge high up in a great cavern with a narrow staircase descending from it, and looked down on an extraordinary sight.

In front of us, many boxes of rendered gold were being fed into a vast furnace, above which the air shimmered with heat, while several strange beings were shoveling coal into the open access. These entities gleamed as if made of different metals that had been torn apart, forming jagged shapes and interwoven with cracks and bent shards of steel. They were each different, some being bullet-shaped, other more rounded and squashed, while larger ones took the shape of bombs and cannon balls. No hair crowned their heads and their faces were masks of cruel indifference. I shuddered to see them, while from the other end of the furnace emerged a long line of golden pyramid-shaped objects, which were being stacked on the floor at the back of the cavern.

Off to one side, another operation was taking place, and the workers engaged on this project were even more horrible-looking than the first, some being either black and hairy, or brown and smooth with fissures running down their bodies, while others resembled scallop shells, nautilus shells, and other marine shell life. Each dangled a long chainlike tail behind it and their faces, when glimpsed, were indescribably repulsive. The large mint over which they toiled was turning out coins of a dark grey colored metal that looked like lead. Two of the shell-like creatures then dipped the coins in a bath of molten gold to coat them thinly. When they were cool, they were thrown into a conduit where a fast current of water boiled past and disappeared in the direction of the lake.

I turned to Trid, whose face was a mask of disgust and horror, and muttered. "My God! These creatures are terrifying! What on earth are they?"

"I didn't want to tell you about them before, but I have heard whispers of them in my village. The people dare not speak their name aloud. They call them the Qliphoth, the Shells." Trid murmured gravely. "They are the remnants of things past that live underground, some of which were used in wars to destroy people, towns and nations, while others, the ones at the coin mint, are the shards of jettisoned psychological garbage from individuals, those who ate the best parts of their lives and then discarded the rest. But they are not destroyed and live here eternally, working ceaselessly to pour out fake gold coinage, so that those who use it don't realize they are being cheated."

Well! I thought. The coins were just like the ones that were arriving at Lance and Gwens' house. Then - they were not pure gold but were merely lead made to look like the real thing. I wondered if my parents had been fooled.

"But, Trid – the riches stored in the pyramids aren't forged, are they?"

"No. They are real. Unfortunately, they are in the hands of our evil friend, Fakoor, who keeps the gold for himself instead of fairly distributing it amongst the townsfolk. I know about that. However, this village is so materialistic that all the people who live here have more than enough income without a bonus from Fakoor. In my village, many of us seek equality, but we can't achieve it. The village chiefs always hold more power, and choose how to distribute the assets. It is never fairly carried out however hard we work to obtain our share."

Shocked at this story of greed, I turned towards the other operation in the cavern and quickly put two and two together. The small golden pyramids must be the tops intended for the truncated pyramids, which held the village hoard. Only the person who was able to place these tops on the storage pyramids would be able to open them and reach the treasure. And that person was Fakoor!

Realizing the danger we were in if the Qliphoth discovered our presence, we backed silently off the ledge and returned through the passageway to the outside world, where we quickly boarded the punt, awoke the rattlesnake, and poled away from the mine. My plans were to go back down the cliff and tell Lance and Gwen of our findings, so we left the punt moored close to the waterfall and climbed down the rocky face again.

Gwen greeted us at the bottom, where the strange gardener was still fishing the coins out of their ornamental lake. I felt dreadful about telling her the truth and decided to wait for the right moment. Their generosity had been sincere, and here I was, the messenger of bad news and unbridled evil. We walked back to the mansion, and stayed for a meal of roast pork with applesauce. I noticed that Trid didn't seem hungry, but left his pork untouched by the side of his plate. I wondered why, but I was more concerned about broaching the subject of the coins. Taking a deep breath, I turned to Lance and Gwen.

"I'm sorry to bring you this news, mother and father, but I have made a shocking discovery up there." I glanced up at the cliff through the window. "We found out where the coins are coming from. It is not good news. You are, in fact, being cheated!"

I paused, and swallowed. "Your coins aren't pure gold, but lead coated with gold. They are made underground by some horrible creatures, the Qliphoth, who are unbelievably evil. I'm so sorry to have to tell you this." I stared down at my plate, aghast.

A ripple of merriment made me look up sharply. My mother and father were in fits of laughter! Rocking to-and-fro, holding their sides and guffawing. What was this very strange reaction?

"My dear," Gwen was still giggling. "We knew this all along. We have accepted it and found a way to profit from it nevertheless. Can you imagine what that is?" Her eyes seemed to narrow a little as she spoke.

"You knew already? Then, why didn't you stop us from finding out?"

I was indignant. "We traveled a long way and all the time you were deceiving us."

Lance calmly explained. "We didn't want you to know the truth about how we were making money. It was entirely your idea to climb the cliff to discover where the gold was coming from, and we didn't want to deter you. Now I guess it's time to tell you. We process the coins to remove their thin gold covering, and then melt the lead down into bullets. We have set up a large trade in armaments all around the world, and we're supplying bullets to many bands of insurgents who are fighting to free their country from the tyranny of the democratic world, including the village you just visited."

A cold shock ran over my body! I knew that one of my entities, Bardogian, was an anarchist, but....my parents as well! I rose from the table, leaning over to place my hands each side of my plate, and glared at them. "I am disgusted! Come, Trid, we must leave. Gwen and Lance, I must tell you that as long as you continue this illicit trade, I can't acknowledge our relationship any more. Please accept my thanks for the dinner and I wish you well in your choice of a livelihood." Snapping upright, I turned and, with the Page at my side, walked firmly away, my heart sunk and feeling like lead in my breast. I did not look back as the sound of their soft laughter continued.

Trid and I still had to find the entrance to Persephones' cave and collect the herd of pigs. He took the bluebird out of his blouse and set it on his arm, and the bird cocked its head and twittered, then flew off in little zigzag bursts in the general direction of a copse of trees on the estate. We entered the wood and soon saw in front of us the cave mouth, which shimmered with a green glow as we entered it.

The cavern lay in front of us and the pigs were there snorting and rooting happily. A voice rose from the darkest recesses of the cave. "So here you are! Your mission is completed, and you may have the pigs back now." It was Persephone.

"But.... what was the mission?" I asked in puzzlement. Any of our adventures could have been the answer, I thought.

"It was not the unmasking of your parents' true nature, nor was it the discovery of the hateful Qliphoth and their activities, nor the summoning of the hawks. It was the eternal banishment of Aquirot, after you realized how she was leading you astray, and had been for years in time long past. Remember – temper acquisition with cautious moderation – and you will be fine. Congratulations on a task well done." Persephone clapped her hands and from all corners of the cavern came an answering ghostly clapping from unseen listeners. "Now, you may take your pigs and go, and may Gaia be with you."

We thanked the hidden voice and made our way out of the cave and back through the forest to the village. The villagers saw us coming and crowded around the fourteen pigs with joy in their faces.

"You've found our pigs! Where were they? Trid, you are a good herder after all. Thank you," they chorused.

The Page looked solemn. "Yes, I've brought the pigs back, and I'm glad you're pleased. But now you must find another pig herder, for my companion will take me up to the Castle, where I will enter the service of the Knight as his Squire, for I have dreamed of this for many years."

The villagers slapped him on the back heartily. "That's OK. We know you're different from the rest of us. We're content to stay here where life is simple, and we're happy for you if you want to complicate yours. Go now to the Castle, and dignify yourself, but never look down on us, for these are your roots, remember."

He shook hands with the village elders and we set out for the Castle of Earth at the top of the hill. There we inquired of the gatekeeper where the Knights' lodging was and made our way towards his quarters.

Knight of Pentacles - Rules Eight and Seven of Pentacles

Trid and I stood in the courtyard of the Castle of Earth, gazing up at the adobe brick walls soaring above us, at the top of which we could catch glimpses of soldiers in russet and olive uniforms patrolling along the battlements, their crossbows fully charged. Above the turret nearest us fluttered a citrine flag with the design of a black beetle upon it. We continued on our way to the Knights' quarters, walking swiftly past the blacksmiths' forge, several chicken pens, and servants who were busy hanging out linens, before arriving at a slightly larger and neater dwelling under the castle walls. A banner, six citrine bulls' heads on a black ground, hung above the narrow doorway, and a liver chestnut charger tied to the hitching rail outside stamped his great feet, jingling the heavy armor he wore.

We knocked timidly, uncertain of what to expect. The door opened cautiously, revealing a small, sturdy man, his dark brown eyes gazing steadily at us in a rather unnerving manner. We had interrupted the Knight while he was putting on some very cumbersome black armor, and he held a breastplate in one hand. He gave the impression of steadfast self-confidence as he invited us inside. The house was small but neat, simply furnished in the way common to bachelors.

"Good day to you, Sir," said the Page solemnly. "My name is Trid and I've come from the village to seek a Squires' position serving a brave Knight. Are you in need of an efficient Squire?"

"Why, how fortunate! Yes I am!" The Knight replied. "My name is Terramud and my horse Claydung is already harnessed and saddled outside, for I'm about to leave on my next quest. I need someone who can help me with my armor, and read and write to attend to my affairs here at the castle while I'm away. Do you have your letters?"

"Sir, I have been studying my letters diligently for the past five years and I know how to read and write. I am a pig herder, but anxious to improve my status in the world, and one day I hope to be a Knight too."

"You look an honest person," mused the Knight. "I'll hire you. And who is your friend?"

Trid introduced me. "This is the Navigator with whom I have been adventuring recently. A brave and intelligent person."

I stepped forward and bent my knee to the Knight. "I am at your service, Sir."

"Wait here while Trid helps me with my armor and then I will take him up to the castle and explain his duties." Here Terramud became serious. "I have a task for you, too. Can you ride a horse?"

"Yes, I have ridden since I was a child."

"Good. For you will be riding pillion when I take off over the Abyss," Terramud said firmly. "Your task will be **to evolve competence to plan compromise.**"

Furrowing my brow, I stared at him. "What does that mean?"

"I do not know. That is the task. I have been waiting for the right person to undertake it, and I feel sure you are that person. We must jump off over the Abyss – I know nothing more than that." Turning, he strode away with Trid, who waved goodbye as he hastily followed him up to the castle.

I tried to relax in front of the fire in the Knights quarters, but my mind was in turmoil. We had to jump an Abyss? I didn't like the sound of it. As far as the task was concerned, I drew a blank. Trying to work out what the obscure words meant was impossible. I must learn to be patient while I wait and see what will happen, I thought, as my next adventure unfolded before me.

Terramud soon returned and quickly donned a black ridged helmet that covered most of his head. Clad in his shiny black armor, he looked exactly like a large beetle. I wondered if there was a connection between the design of his armor and the castle flag. He closed the door of his house, untied Claydung, and led him to a mounting block, hauling himself into the saddle with difficulty. I could see how heavy his equipment was.

"Jump up behind me, now," Terramud instructed. "And hang on."

Slithering over the horses' back, I looked for a handhold on Terramuds' cold, glinting armor, but there was none. I compromised by getting a handful of his cape, a translucent olive green with a design of windmills around its hem.

"Off we go," said Terramud, putting his heels to the horses' sides. With a great lurch, the powerful animal broke into a canter, and we headed out of the Castle gate, with me sliding and bouncing on his haunches. We rode hard for about four hours, as the countryside became more desolate and mountainous around us. We were crossing a high, flat mesa that seemed to stretch for miles in front of us when Terramud suddenly pulled his horse to a stop, and I saw that immediately in front of us the ground had opened up. A yawning crevasse dropped away beneath Claydung's hooves, and I could see nothing on the opposite side.

I heard a twittering below, and saw that one of the nightjars from our previous adventure was crouched below us. "It is where the nightjar lies camouflaged that we must take off," announced Terramud. "That is the right position. I'm going to back up so that Claydung can get a good run at it."

"B-but, we can't take off when there is nothing to land on!" Fear surged through my body and I felt Paragutt, a third passenger, hanging on behind me. The horse couldn't possibly carry three people, so I quickly pulled myself together and banished him, although he strongly objected.

"You must have faith in me, to take this leap. Don't be afraid. I have taken many risks in my lifetime. That is the only way to achieve competence. Hang on, now." Terramud turned his mount and urged him to a gallop. The wind rushed by as, with a tremendous bound, the great horse launched itself off the cliff. I gripped the cape frantically, my eyes tightly closed, for I dared not look down to see if anything lay at the bottom of the chasm.

Claydung stretched himself and flew through the air, soaring like a bird. The wind currents above the abyss were very contrary, however, and he was buffeted to-and-fro. Terramud's foot was sliding backwards out of his right stirrup, which suddenly detached itself from the saddle and fell away into the Abyss, followed by the left one. He clung on with his armored heels to the horses' sides and seemed secure, but I found it increasingly difficult to hold on. I took a nervous peek downward and saw nothing except the vertical sides of a gigantic cliff, riddled with strange roots that twisted in queer snakelike arches. That was a mistake! I found myself beginning to slide off the horses' back and, as I struggled to hold on, the Knights' cape became like a wild thing, fluttering madly in the wind and seeming almost to shake me free as if with distaste. My grip slackened and I lost my handhold. I felt myself going, going, and then, with a shriek, I was falling through the air, twisting and turning, the Knight and his horse vanishing far above me.

Although the air rushing past was buffeting my body, I managed, with careful wriggling, to turn into a sky diving position, where I had some control over my fall and could see below me. There seemed no bottom to the Abyss, which fell away below me into impenetrable darkness, and I quickly became depressed. I realized I had minimal control over my fall and no way of slowing down. After another moment, when I had sunk into despair, I caught a glimpse of something sticking out of the cliff wall far below me, and I edged over to check it out as I hurtled down towards the object. I could soon make out that it was a large, square net of the type used under a circus trapeze. If I could hit it, I reasoned, my fall would be broken and I would land in comparative safety. Leaning this way and that to steer towards the security of the net, I saw a strange creature sitting on a ledge by the net, and a gloomy voice began directing me towards it.

"Veer a little to the left. No! Not so far. Don't oversteer. Now edge to the right. Straight ahead….. Watch out for the bounce!" The figure instructed me solemnly. With a mighty whang, I hit the net, digging my fingers into its strands to contain my recoil, and crawled over to the ledge, behind which was a cave.

"Haven't I seen you somewhere before?" I asked, as I looked more closely at the two dark, bloodshot eyes in the bloated pink and blue face of a mounded figure that sat on, or rather draped itself over, the ledge.

"Alas! You have indeed. I am Globdinig, your depressed self and I live in different caves around here." The figure paused, mopping its' eyes with a bandanna on which a design of crocodiles wavered. "I'm always here when you're miserable and I think it's lucky for you that I drew your attention away from the Abyss and arrested your fall, for if you had continued, you would have hit the bottom, and that is not good." She sighed profoundly. "You must stay here with me for a few days, and together we will search into your soul to find some meaning. You rush on with your life so fast, I can never catch you and give you a chance to reflect. That's why I put out my net. You are too good to waste. And now, please accompany me into my home."

Globdinig turned and waddled into the cave, and I followed. I was already tired anyway, and didn't feel like going anywhere. In fact, I realized I could not go anywhere, since I was probably over a thousand feet down in an Abyss with no way up or down, and who knew what lay at the bottom if I fell off the narrow ledge? I wondered about the Knight. Had he continued his jump and landed somewhere? I hoped he hadn't fallen off after losing his stirrups, but I was annoyed with him for being so lacking in chivalry and not even conducting a search for me.

Globdinigs' home seemed a continuation of herself. The cavern walls were entirely swathed in blue and black sackcloth, which hung in drapes mirroring the pendulous folds of her own body. In a corner were scattered the ashes of a long-dead fire. She oozed moistly over towards the wall and reached upwards.

"Let's have some light," she said as she pulled a switch, illuminating many small, dim lights around the cavern, half-hidden in the folds of cloth and resembling bloodshot eyes that glared at me somberly. I felt as if I was being scrutinised from every angle in the faint light, and this deepened my feelings of despair. However, the lights did reveal strange touches of purple satin between the sackcloth drapes. This beautiful material wound in and out of the main curtains, and glowed with a mysterious sheen that I found intensely attractive. It would be some time in the future before I understood the reason for these purple windings.

Globdinig moved towards an ancient radio in a corner. "This is my Oracle," she murmured. "Her voice will help us to resolve your most pressing problem, which is that of indecision and lack of intention, for in this kind of mood – the feelings of despair which I represent – you cannot form a clear vision of your future." Here she paused, sobbed briefly, and buried her face in one of the many cotton bandannas which lay about the place. "You may think I am a bad person," she said in a muffled voice. "In fact, I am one of the most valuable entities you have, but you do not realize it. Through this radio, you can reach the voice of the Oracle, who will make many things known to you. This will not happen all at once, but over many encounters. I will be with you often, until you are completely at one in understanding with the Oracle."

My entity turned a knob, and a misty voice issued from the radio. I bent my head forward to catch what it was saying, and I heard my task repeated.

"Your task is to evolve competence in order to plan compromise. You will realize that compromise is difficult to achieve in life, because of the conflict between individual selves. A person who is competent and empowered by knowledge of themselves can overcome this problem. You will notice that even the word "themselves" indicates that there are many selves in a single person. Let us take the word "competence" which means to be suitable for the allotted task. You'll know, of course, that competition against an opposing team reveals the winner, the most fitting for the victors' crown. You cannot be a winner if you are convinced that you are a loser. The state in which you find yourself, and which Globdinig is a part of, renders you apathetic and unable to act or to form an intention. She will help you to reach inside yourself to discover the reason for your inability to move forward."

I turned to my entity miserably, picking out the negative remarks in the message. "The voice says I'm a loser. I'm apathetic and can't form a plan. I really feel I'm worthless – even you aren't trying to understand me and offer help." Here, I was unable to continue, and relapsed into sobs. Globdinig raised her eyes and handed me a clean bandanna. I broke down completely, my legs folded under me, and I rolled over the floor, ending up smothered in the ashes of the fireplace. She did not make any move towards me, nor did she speak, but sighed deeply.

After a while, I was able to staunch my tears and raise my head, my hair now covered with bits of charcoal. I was aware that the radio voice had started up again.

"I am not done. You chose to misunderstand the message. Listen carefully. The second half of your task is to reach a compromise. When you leave here, the adventure you will experience will test your abilities to achieve that. "Compromise" means to promise with someone else to achieve a mutual goal that must be clearly defined during the negotiations. The people that you will meet need your leadership to do this. Now I will leave you to think about your good qualities – not to dwell upon the bad. I will – l l – l r-e-tu-r…..." the voice faded and Globdinig switched off the radio.

"What a wonderful Oracle that is!" She rhapsodized. "I couldn't do anything without her. You must see how she expresses everything so logically. I can't think rationally myself, that's why I need her. Logic came into the world after emotions. It is through the path of metaphorical Death that we can connect the two and achieve balance. Now, you know that you have already helped many people on your river journey, and given them wise advice. I want you to remember that journey and change your state of mind to a positive mood. Then I will be able to disappear for now."

"What will I do here if you are gone?" I asked her nervously. "I'm not hungry but there is no food here anyway."

"I never feel like eating. I don't bother to go to the store because I tend to trip over the grocery cart and catch my folds under the wheels. It's very uncomfortable."

"So, what will happen to me?" I insisted.

"Meditate for a while to calm your mind, and the answer will come," she replied. "Now, I'm exhausted and I'm going to sleep for a while." She moved over to the curtains and disappeared behind them. I hunkered down in a corner, brushed the charcoal from my hair, and tried to meditate.

Since I had practiced meditation before, though infrequently, I was slowly able to fall into a trance. Before my inmost vision, Globdinigs' cavern seemed to dissolve, and I found myself floating over an ancient harbor in which many trading ships lay. There were ships plying up and down a wide river, which led to the sea, and then dispersing in different directions. My depression had disappeared, and I formed the intention of taking ship for a foreign port, since I had left my punt behind at the Castle of Earth. No sooner had I thought it than I was landing on the deck of a large Roman bireme loading with big clay platters, on each of which was etched the design of a five-pointed star. I stretched my legs and turned to find two identical twin brothers standing behind me, one of them holding a large telescope.

"How did you get here?" One of them asked in amazement. "You came from nowhere!"

I didn't want to reveal my astral flight, so I pretended I had crept aboard during the night and hidden in a coil of rope. "Please help me. I need to take an ocean voyage to a particular island where I recently met a parrot. Do you have that port of call in your itinerary?"

"Why, yes, we do. My name is Laurentius and my brother is Lascarius. Of course, you're not supposed to stow away, but I have a feeling you might be useful, so you can ship with us. We are trading these clay platters with the islanders for fire opals." Here he laughed. "They don't have any clay on the island, so they can't make pottery. But they have a large opal mine, and because there are so many fire opals, they don't value them at all. We are making a fortune, and I'm trying to save and invest as much money as I can." Here he turned to his brother with a wry smile. "Lascarius here wants to spend the money on the acquisition of Greek statues. He insists that they will be valuable one day. If he can't get hold of a particular statue, he hires a Greek artist to reproduce it. I think it's an unnecessary expense and we have many disagreements about it, but can't seem to come to any compromise."

Lascarius looked annoyed. "You need to look into the future and take some risks, Laurentius. You're always so conservative. It really irritates me. Your investments aren't that secure. Supposing we lose one of our ships? At least the statues won't be cruising around in dangerous waters, although…." here he smiled, "some of them have been found at the bottom of the sea."

The brothers showed me a hammock slung on deck that I could use, and within a few days, we were on our trading route, expecting to be away for several months. I wondered how Lascarius and Laurentius could leave their business office at the same time, but when I asked them, they told me they had an efficient manager who remained at the port. It was hard to tell the difference between them except by their demeanor, Lascarius being the one who always sprinted up the rigging with his telescope to scan the horizon, while Laurentius sat in their cabin working on accounts.

Days passed between calm and storm. Lascarius, thoroughly frustrated, would stride the deck when the ships' sails flapped feebly as she rolled beam to beam in the suffocating heat of a windless day in the doldrums. Urging on the oarsmen became increasingly difficult as they weakened and fell sick from scurvy and thirst. Laurentius, ignoring their moans, sunned himself on the poop, a glass of rum at his side. When the storms came, Lascarius was everywhere, urging on the crew, heaving on lines and furling sails with his men, while Laurentius crept around, a safety harness trailing behind him, checking the lifeboats for leaks, testing the fire extinguishers, and making sure the Epirb rescue beacon was still hanging upside down. I found it quite amusing to watch their widely divergent behavior.

After visiting several islands, where we took on small amounts of different goods in exchange for the platters, the ship lost her wind in the Sargasso Sea and Lascarius called the rowers once more to duty. The shimmering sea rolled under us, its hidden waves heaving gently as the ship swayed on, the dip of the oars making an even splash pattern on its smooth surface. Days went by, and each morning there were fewer oarsmen at their posts, as the bodies of those who had died were thrown overboard. We were running desperately low on food and water. Anxiously I searched through the ship for anything useful, eventually finding my food pouch hidden behind some rum casks, where it had washed up during one of the storms. I recalled the day that my Guide had given it to me, and told me it was inexhaustible, so I opened it hopefully and peered inside. I saw a jug of water, which I quickly pulled out, pouring glasses for the whole crew. The jug remained full, and I examined the pouch again. Inside there was a large barbecued chicken and a loaf of bread. These I distributed amongst the sailors, with plenty for all and some left overs, and they thanked me heartily. That night, a light wind arose and we were able to continue on our route to the next port. My bottomless food pouch had saved the remaining crew, although I wished that I had found it earlier.

One morning I saw on the horizon signs of ashy smoke and fire, belching from a large volcano. As we approached, we could see roils of molten lava snaking down the hillside and quenching themselves in the steaming sea. We found a little port close to a large beach of black lava, and while the brothers were unloading, I went for a walk along the beach. I remembered being there before and encountering a large parrot named Arty Weight who had given me the two faced Janus key, but I couldn't find him. I looked around. As it was approaching dusk, hundreds of crickets began to chirp around me, and I suddenly remembered my own cricket Joana, whom I had caught here on the beach, in her little cage slung to the bulwarks of my punt. I was worried for a moment, then realized that, as I was on an astral projection, no time would have passed in the world where I had left the punt.

Strolling back towards the port, I met an angry-looking woman wearing a belt with six green figs suspended upon it. They looked delicious and I recalled eating one very similar a long time ago. I addressed the woman, who flashed me an irritated glance.

"Good evening. How are you?" I said politely.

"I'm fed up! I've been trying to stop my brother Mea'a going to the casino every night, but he simply won't listen. A little while ago, I met a person who advised me that trying to control his habits wasn't going to help me, but I'm having a hard time stopping myself. My name is Lea – what's yours?"

I told her my name and that I had just shipped to the island. Looking into her flashing eyes, I recognized a flicker of the past. I heard the voice of Globdinigs' radio Oracle in my head, saying all that stuff about compromise. I wondered if I was competent after all, and decided that, at least in my astral self, I was totally confident in my abilities. I knew in my heart I had to help her, but how?

We walked back to the ship and I introduced Lea to the brothers. "Let's go out and eat," I urged, feeling very hungry. "Do you know a place, Lea?"

She smiled grimly. "There's only the casino. They serve really cheap meals. It's to get people in there so that they're lured into gambling, dammit!"

"We don't have to gamble if we go in," I pointed out. "We can overcome the temptation."

"I don't know about you," grumbled Laurentius, "but I know Lascarius always wants to take risks. We'll have to watch him."

"Let's go, then." I went ahead and the three of them followed, Lea very reluctantly. However, I could see that she was interested in the quiet Laurentius and wanted to spend some time with him. We had an excellent meal – grilled parrot with a black lava coating followed by chocolate covered crickets in hibiscus sauce. Lascarius disappeared to the men's room, while Lea and Laurentius chatted away until she suddenly caught sight of a familiar figure sneaking between the slot machines.

"There he is!" She yelled, jumping to her feet. "There's my brother Mea'a, gambling again."

"You have to let go of him." I advised. "You can't change his behavior."

"He promised me he hadn't been to the casino in months. He's lying! I wanted to believe him. Now I know it's not true."

"He may have convinced himself that he's not at the casino," I suggested. "Sometimes people get so accustomed to lying that they believe their own fabrications. They are caught up in their own addictions – that's the only reality they have. You need to find a compromise – you love your brother, but you have to step back and let him lead his own life, however bad his decisions may seem to you, for that is his Destiny, and it can't be changed."

Laurentius agreed, reaching forward to squeeze her hand. "My brother Lascarius is the same. He's always taking risks and it makes me nervous. I'm afraid one day we'll lose our business over his addiction to Greek antiquities. Where did he go, anyway?"

I looked around, and spied Mea'a chatting with Lascarius at the far end of the casino by the blackjack table. They soon sat down at the table with a pile of chips in front of each one. Oh, dear! I thought, that is not a good idea.

Fortunately, Lea and Laurentius were gazing into each other's eyes by this time. I left the dinner table and walked over to the blackjack game. I could see straight away that they were both on a losing streak, and, feeling concerned for the frugal Laurentius, I hastened back to his table.

"They're over there together gambling," I hissed. "And they're on a losing streak."

Laurentius rose instantly. "We have to stop them somehow. Who owns this casino, anyway? Most casinos have a barred entry policy. If a gambler requests it, the casino will stop him from entering to gamble. It's a last resort."

Lea answered him, looking shamefaced. "I hate to admit it, but my family owns the casino. My father died of a drug overdose after gambling away a fortune, but my uncle was able to keep things going. He has recouped my father's losses and made a success of the business, but he's getting old and wants to sell a half share in it."

"Then I will buy it!" Laurentius announced firmly. "It's certainly a safe investment." Here he laughed shortly. "When it's mine, I'll ban them from entering. That will settle their problems for good."

Lea looked at him fondly, a light in her eyes. "What a good idea! Can we arrange the deal tomorrow?"

"We'll do that in the morning. We can't stop them now. Let's go for a walk."

I declined to accompany them, but went back to the ship, where I fell asleep. In the morning they quickly accomplished the transfer of the casino ownership shares, and a new ban was instated against family members' entry.

Mea'a was furious. He had lost several hundred pistachios during the night, and obviously Lascarius hadn't done well either, for he was out of sight hiding in the crows' nest of the ship. I persuaded Lea not to get into a fight with her brother, and shortly afterwards we saw Mea'a putting to sea in one of their outrigger canoes, paddling furiously. Laurentius turned to Lea.

"Let him go. He has to come to terms with himself. Underneath his bravado, he feels bad about losing all that money. He's always thought he would win it back one day. Now he can't come into the casino, and it's the only one on the island. Maybe he'll find another island casino one day. There are plenty of them out there."

Lea wiped away a tear. "I'm sad, but I'm relieved that he's gone. I realize now that I'll never be able to change him. For many years I haven't felt able to focus on my own life. Now I'm ready to make a fresh start."

Laurentius held her close to him and looked down at her. "Maybe we can do that together," he said.

Realizing that Lea had achieved a compromise with herself, I didn't think I had played any part in it except that I had introduced them. Maybe that was the only thing I had to do. My part in this adventure was complete.

We persuaded a much-chastened Lascarius down from the mast and all took ship again for the Roman port, carrying a full load of fire opals. During our voyage, the happy couple were married by the ship's captain as we crossed the Equator. Lascarius learned his lesson, and he would never gamble again. He continued to make an outstanding collection of

Greek marbles, which I felt certain he would hand down through the generations.

Disembarking from the ship at their home port, I bade goodbye to the twin brothers and Lea. Then I remembered the Knight, who had disappeared while jumping the Abyss. Where was I, exactly? Oh, of course, on an astral projection. I had better get back. It was dangerous to stay out so long, at least, it seemed a long time. I sat down and began to meditate. I soon went into a deep trance, but couldn't seem to find my way. Confusing scenes flashed before me and a hooded figure leered at me from the shadows, but I didn't recognize any of the places. Where was the cave I had left my body? I began to panic, thinking that I had lost it and would be out in space forever. I must focus… Suddenly a scene flashed before me of a cavern draped in blues and blacks. With a tremendous jolt, I rejoined my body, which was sitting in a corner.

I wasn't depressed any more, but felt rejuvenated and alert. There was no sign of Globdinig, so I went out on the ledge to look around. The Abyss gaped in front of me, and over to the left of my line of sight, a tiny figure on horseback was approaching. It was the Knight, Terramud, and he had come to fetch me. Claydung landed on the ledge with a clatter of hooves, skidding to a stop in the narrow space.

"Are you ready?" asked Terramud, as if I had only stepped off his mount for a moment. "I've come to pick you up. Your task is completed and now you can continue your quest."

For a moment, I didn't think I had completed anything, but then I remembered my astral journey. That must be what he meant. I was more then anxious to climb onto the horse, but questioned him cautiously. "I tried to hold on but I slipped off. Do you have something I can grab onto this time so that I don't fall off?"

"Yes, my cape. It shook you off on purpose last time, but it won't do it again – at least, not on the earth plane. Capes are tricky and have their own agenda so you have to watch them. But, now that you have accomplished your task, the cape won't act up, I promise you."

"If you're sure, I'll climb on, then." I grasped the cape and slid onto Claydungs' back. The Knight seemed to rotate and then, like a helicopter, was flying through the air once more across the Abyss.

"Where are we going?" I yelled from my position behind him, but there was no reply. The cape, softly and capaciously, seemed to snuggle me in its embrace, and I soon fell asleep.

I woke to a gentle bump as Claydung landed after what seemed a long flight. To my surprise, we were back on the mesa at the edge of the Abyss, and swiftly heading back down to the Castle of Earth at a gallop. The cape held me firmly, and our journey did not take long. Arriving at the Castle, we dismounted and were soon sitting in front of a warm fire in the Knights' home. I was anxious to ask some questions about my experiences, but first I wanted to know where the Page was, and how he was doing.

"How's Trid? He must have been busy while we've been away."

"Well, he hasn't gotten much done so far," said the Knight. "After all, we've only been gone a few minutes."

"That's impossible! We went all the way to the Abyss; we jumped it; I fell off and met Globdinig; I had an astral adventure at a casino; you rescued me and we came back here. That must have taken days, not minutes!" I protested.

"A Knight can travel between space and time," explained Terramud, "for we are all certified initiates on the Quest. Knights are able to squeeze between atoms on the material plane and therefore are not subject to time and space constraints."

"Oh." I mulled that one over and accepted it. "Now can I ask you some more questions?"

"Of course. Go ahead. I hope I can answer them."

"The task I was given. To evolve competence to plan compromise – I didn't succeed, Lea did. I feel bad about it, but I'm sure I didn't solve the problem."

"Oh, but you did!" laughed the Knight gently. "I don't know of anything more competent than to turn a disastrous fall into the Abyss to your advantage. You were quick thinking enough to turn into a sky diving position, thus exerting some directional control. Secondly, you cleverly set up a net in which to fall, thus saving yourself from hitting the bottom of the Abyss."

"H'm. I did do the sky diving bit, but Globdinig set out the net. I was just lucky I could steer into it."

The Knight chuckled quietly. "And who is Globdinig? Isn't she a part of you? I don't think she can survive without being activated by you, can she?"

I immediately understood what Terramud meant. It was true, I had summoned my entity Globdinig as I fell by getting very depressed. Immediately, the net was there.

"I see what you mean. I stopped myself from bottoming out in the Abyss because I was able to connect with her, and she persuaded me to listen to her Oracle on the radio and follow that advice, which led to my meditation and astral journey. Is that the way to avoid reaching the depths of the Abyss?"

"It certainly is. By stopping your fall into deep depression, listening to your inner voice, and connecting with your higher self through meditation, you were able to pull out of a dangerous situation and achieve competence. Those who plunge to the bottom often destroy themselves by suicide. That is not your path. What is more," Terramud went on, "you helped those on your astral journey reach a compromise. There was no hope for Mea'a – he is addicted to gambling and will never recover, but Lea found love with Laurentius, and Lascarius was taught a lesson which he will long remember. You have accomplished your task with great success."

Surprised and pleased, I hadn't thought that the task would be done without involving rational plans. It had just worked out that way. The Knight gave me a bowl of ratcatcher soup and a piece of rye bread. "Eat now, and then you will be ready to meet the Queen. She is waiting to allot your next task, and I will take you to her soon." Terramud sat down and we ate together in harmony after our exertions.

Queen of Pentacles – Rules Five and Three of Pentacles.

The following morning Terramud and I set out to meet the Queen of Pentacles in the Castle of Earth. He led me down a long stone-flagged corridor towards the kitchens, from whence came the smells of cooking and a low murmur of voices. A hearty, rich voice soon separated itself from the rest and, as we entered the door, we saw the Queen of Pentacles addressing a group of cooks and scullions.

"I'm expecting the King to come home tonight from the campaign he's been fighting against the Viceroy of Muckabad. He'll be in a bad mood, as he's lost the last battle, and will be very hungry and tired. I asked you a moment ago if you had the roast boar and pheasant I requested yesterday on the banquet menu. Now you are telling me that we have run out of boars and that the pheasants have been chased away by foxes in the neighborhood." The queen paused, tightening her lips. "What, now, do you propose to do about replacing these dishes for the banquet?"

The Queen, a small and lively woman with long, reddish-brown hair flowing naturally down her back and a rosy look of health to her face, confronted her chief cook with the question. The cook stepped back and, bowing slightly, stammered out.

"W-well, Madam, we a-are very sorry that we can't obtain these i-items. The hunters have been out for the last ten days looking for b-boar, but none have been sighted, and the men can't understand why they have been driven from the f-forest nearby." The cook gulped, and then continued. "May I suggest a c-couple of our fat pigs instead of the b-boar?"

"I can never understand why you are always so disorganized. Of course, pigs are not the same flavor, but I suppose we'll just have to make do," grumbled the Queen. "Now, what about replacing the pheasants?"

"There is a large flock of doves up in the dovecote. We can make a delicious dove pie from them. We would need, maybe, one hundred and eleven." The cook looked hopeful.

"All right, then. But you need to hurry! The king is on his way and his messenger arrived two hours ago. Send someone to slaughter the pigs and get them on the spits. Have a scullion climb into the dovecote and capture the doves, then make a worthy pastry to enclose them." The Queen sighed. "Why is it that things never go as planned down here? I banished that gardener called Murphy, yet his influence is still rampant throughout the castle."

She turned towards us and Terramud hastened to present me. "Ma Dame, please be gracious enough to greet the Navigator, who has come here to learn of the tests required in the Castle of Earth."

I stepped forward and genuflected. "Ma Dame, I am prepared to gladly undertake any test you may wish to set me, for I have a dream that I mean to fulfil."

"That is excellent. Please call me Soyla. You are one of those for whom we have been waiting. Many aeons have passed since we got word that you would come. Welcome to our world of Earth. In due course we will leave together to complete your next test. Now, let us go upstairs and meet some of my family." With that, she led the way out of the kitchen and up a long staircase to the castle apartments.

As we climbed, I could hear the sounds of children playing from above. We soon opened the door to a large playroom, and I was taken aback by a swarming rush of ten little kids, dressed in various black and white costumes, who milled about me, their activities somewhat poorly contained by four nursemaids who hovered nervously in the background. Queen Soyla patted the two nearest children on their heads.

"My little dualists!" She murmured fondly. "What are you up to today?"

"Oh, Mother! We are playing resolution of conflicts again. It's such a great game. Will you play with us now?" They pulled at her hands expectantly.

"My beloved contestants, I can't play with you now. The Navigator has arrived and I must attend to the test that is required. I will summon my groom who will prepare my dun mare, for I must ride into my secret forest glade to perform the ceremonials. When I return, I'll spend some time with you." Soyla turned and rang a small bell and a valet popped into the room. "Take a message to my groom to saddle the dun mare Dusty immediately, for we must ride into the forest."

The valet scurried off and Soyla led us down a winding staircase to the courtyard, where, very soon, a groom led the mare and Claydung to the mounting blocks. I didn't see a horse for myself, but Terramud must have read my thoughts, for he told me to jump up behind him again. A mount awaited me in the forest, apparently. We rode for a short way along a soft, grassy track into the dense trees behind the castle, and as the forest became thicker, came to a little glade in the center of which stood a black throne, made of ebony, with a small table to the left of it. The Queen dismounted and sat down on the throne, taking up a ball of black clay that rested on the table and molding it in her hand thoughtfully. Immediately, two tiny monkeys jumped up on her shoulders and sat there, chattering busily.

"Terramud, you may leave us here now. Go back to the castle and start planning the jousting matches we are arranging to celebrate the King's safe return." The Knight bowed and rode off through the trees, leading the mare. Soyla and I were left alone in the enchanted glade, where strange animal scents drifted in the soft air. A warm and earthy feeling coursed through me and I felt like sitting down, but dared not in front of the Queen, so I looked about me. Behind the Queens' throne rose an abrupt cliff, down which trickled a small waterfall ending in a pool behind her. I saw a movement up on the cliff and narrowed my eyes sufficiently to make out a large elephant, which was browsing on some tree branches.

Soyla followed my glance and spoke. "There is our mount. The test I will set you is to **find dissatisfaction and demand action.** Take this clay ball and climb up the cliff behind me. There you will find a mossy spring in the hillside. Remove your clothes and bathe in this spring, being sure to take with you the ball of black clay. You must mould this clay into whatever form you desire, then return to me with the result."

I took the clay, which rested heavily in my hand, and began to climb the low cliff, keeping an eye on the elephant, which seemed unusually large. I wondered what the test meant, yet I was already learning from my two previous tests that I probably wouldn't discover the answer until the test was completed.

Undressing, I gave a sly glance at the elephant that seemed to have moved closer. Nervously I sank into the fresh water of the pool and allowed the clay to mould itself into a form in my hands. After a while, I returned to the bank and wrapped the little form in my bandanna, but I couldn't find my clothes. I looked over towards the cliff in time to see the two monkeys disappearing over the edge with my tunic. Running up, I saw my pants at the bottom of the cliff, while the monkeys chattered and gesticulated over my tunic, pulling on it until I was afraid it would rip apart. I yelled out and they scuttled away, dropping the tunic. Suddenly the elephant trumpeted and began to lumber towards me. I ran down the slope as fast as I could, followed by crashing, sliding noises as the heavy animal pursued me, and knelt down in front of the Queen, stark naked. I dared not look behind as I felt a long trunk stroking the back of my neck, which sent a shiver of fear through me as I gave the clay form I had molded to Soyla, who chuckled broadly as she set the figure on the table.

After hastily recovering my clothes and my equilibrium, I returned and gazed at the clay figure on the table. It was the image of a black goat. It looked rather alarming, not the sort of thing I would have voluntarily molded. Maybe it created itself? Soyla, smiling, turned to me and explained.

"Capricorn. Its the symbol of the state of being in my card. Don't worry about it. Take the statue with you and it will come in useful later. Now, we are ready to continue our journey into the forest. You will ride in the howdah on the elephant with me."

Surprised, I turned to see that the elephant now carried a howdah, decorated in tasteful earth colors, and a caparisoned headdress with tassels. On his back sat a groom with a little whip in his hand. The elephant knelt and Soyla and I climbed into the howdah and sank down in the soft cushions. I was disgruntled to note that the monkeys had also joined us and were jumping around and pulling at the tassels as, with a lurch, we were on our way. Penetrating deeper and deeper into dense jungle, the vines trailing overhead and the canopy of trees creating a moist twilight, we reached a place where we could make no further progress. The Queen told us to descend, which I was glad to do, as the monkeys were pulling my hair and biting my ears. The groom and I began to hack our way through the undergrowth with machetes, which I wielded with vigor. As soon as I started work, two other figures beside us also hacked into the bushes surrounding us. Not knowing who they were, I stopped to ask the rather angular-looking man why they were there.

"Of course we're here." Was the patronizing reply. "Don't you remember us? I'm Endevvy, your working self, and this is my assistant Little Laboria. We are your laboring entities, and each time you begin manual work, we have to be here with you." Endevvy threw down his machete and signaled to the little woman to continue cutting. "I only work enough to get her started. I have more important things to do, like timekeeping, so I let her do most of the hard labor."

I could see that the frail woman with him was old and already becoming exhausted. After a while, she fell to her knees and dropped her machete. Endevvy strode over to her, hauling her to her feet and pressing the machete back into her hand. "You're giving up already? I need more work than this out of you. Now, keep at it and don't be so lazy."

Laboria attempted to cut through some of the thick vines with a few more swings, then she collapsed onto the jungle floor, where she lay inert. Endevvy was about to stride forward and chastise her when I took his arm and held him back. "What do you think you're doing, forcing an old woman like that to work until she drops? Shame on you! Can't you see she is too decrepit for the job? Leave her alone and do the work yourself, you jerk."

"That's not my job." Endevvy insisted angrily. "I'm the time keeper, the organizer, I do all the bookwork and send out the accounts. Why should I do the manual labor too?"

"Then you'll have to change your job. If she has to work, find something lighter for her. Start a new profession – you can do it."

Endevvy pulled away from me obstinately and walked over to Laboria where she lay, addressing her with scorn.

"Get up, you old hag. You're getting me into trouble with the boss. I don't want to change my job to satisfy you. I'm quite content to oversee your work." He took her by the scruff of the neck and kicked her, hauling her to her feet where she stood swaying uncertainly as he walked away. "You dumb bitch! Now, take this machete and start hacking, or else......."

With that, he flung the blade at her in a rage. The machete whirled through the air and she put out her right hand to catch it, but missed. To my horror, the blade sliced swiftly through her arm, leaving a stump above the elbow, as the cleanly severed limb dropped to the ground. With a terrible scream, Little Laboria sank down to the forest floor beside her severed arm and fainted dead away. I rushed forward as Endevvy, realizing what he had done, stepped back in horror, his hands over his face. The whole event had happened so fast, all we could do was to save Little Laboria as quickly as possible. I made a tourniquet for her stump and picked up the arm, wrapping it in some leaves, although I knew in my heart we couldn't replace it in time. We carried her gently to the howdah and the Queen bent over her, administering some kind of soporific to dull her pain.

What a situation! We were miles from medical aid and, of course, as soon as I took my mind off work, both Endevvy and Laboria would disappear. Queen Soyla and I decided, therefore, that I should continue work until we had cut our way through to more open forest and at the same time she would stabilize Laboria's injury so that it would not progress further. I could then stop work and Laboria, as my entity, would be held in a state of suspension until we returned to the Castle for further treatment.

Deciding on this, the groom and I hastened to complete a path big enough for the elephant to pass. We soon broke through the remaining undergrowth and found ourselves in the clear and facing, ahead of us, a grove of particularly tall and magnificent trees. Here the Queen ordered a halt and we set up the royal tent for the night. Of course, since I had now stopped work, there was no sign of Endevvy or his wife, and I worried about what they would have to face when I started again. Maybe I could change my job? That would force them to change as well, of course. Little Laboria would be permanently injured but could possibly work in a library or something. I dismissed the thought for the time being. These entities were a continual problem! However, there did seem to be some hope of turning Endevvy into a useful workman if he could be brought down a peg or two. With Laboria losing her right arm, the hope of returning to manual labor was over for me. I realized that it was the fault of my workaholic self that was causing this crisis.

The following morning was bright and clear. I woke early and, wandering into the forest, a shadow flitting through the trees caught my eye. I could make out a long nose sticking out from behind a bush, and a grubby hand that dropped a hamburger wrapper on the ground before it disappeared. I went over to the bush, hoping to see the creature, but found only a golden cushion with red tassels lying on the moss. Picking it up and tucking it under my arm, I sat down on a log, noticing another pile of wrappers from a fast food restaurant at the foot of one of the tall trees. That was strange, and stranger still when, looking up, I espied two legs hanging out of the side of a giant birds' nest about forty feet up. Why would someone be up in a birds' nest eating hamburgers? I wondered who it was and decided to find out.

Queen Soyla was awake and taking coffee, so I sat down beside her and told her about the wrappers and the legs. "I think we have found Istas," she said mysteriously. "She is another who needs help. Show me the tree." With the monkeys on her shoulders, Soyla and I walked to the tree and I pointed out the nest.

"That's too high for me to climb," I quickly announced.

The Queen brushed aside my attempt to wriggle out of my duty.

"But you must climb it! We have to persuade Istas to come down. She has been in self-inflicted isolation for too long, dissatisfied with her situation and feeling guilty about her long-lost lover Satsi. What Istas doesn't yet understand is that Satsi is her other half, and she can never get rid of her, whether she is cruel to her, or kind and gentle. Istas must learn to know Satsi, take action, and then she can resolve her conflict. Now, my monkeys will help you up the tree."

The Queen spoke softly to her monkeys in a strange language. Upon hearing her, they pulled rude faces, but saluted and came over to me, each one grabbing onto my arms. Before I could gasp out, the wiry creatures were hauling me up the tree faster than I could count, bark scraping my face, my legs catching and bashing against branches as we climbed higher and higher until we were level with the person who lay there in the nest.

Inside the large structure, made of reeds cut from a nearby stream, was a young woman, clad in a leather strap outfit and holding a three-lashed whip, which she used from time to time to chastise herself. I seized the whip, jerking it away from her, and she immediately curled into a fetal position and remained immobile. Nothing I could say or do would penetrate her autistic state. At this, the monkeys became very excited, and began to jump all over her, pinching and pulling at her straps and penetrating her trance as she fought to keep them off. I bent forward and dragged her to her feet, the monkeys hanging onto her back grimly. I took one of the little beasts around the waist and pulled hard, nearly falling out of the nest in my efforts, but Istas screamed in pain as the monkeys' paws bit deep into her flesh, and I had to let go. I hit the other monkey and yanked his tail, but he merely jabbered at me, showing his teeth in a grimace.

I had to get the monkeys off her back. I remembered that I still had the gold velvet cushion with me. Maybe that would do the trick? Hastily I threw the cushion under her and pushed her down. With a great shriek, the two monkeys jumped off her shoulders and quickly ran back down the tree, their tails between their legs. Well, evidently that worked!

From down in the forest, I thought I heard a faint shout of laughter, but I dismissed it, as the next thing was to persuade Istas to come down the tree herself and with that in view, we peered over the edge of the nest. It looked awfully high up and the monkeys were obviously not going to help, so I began to weave a rope out of some thin vines that I gathered. Immediately I started work, I heard a loud groan from Laboria in the howdah below, and Endevvy appeared beside me, his hatchet face as grim as ever. I thought quickly. Maybe I could persuade Endevvy to help us out of the tree, although I knew that might be difficult.

With that in mind, I turned to Endevvy. "I need your help. It's important to get Istas down from this tree. Laboria is badly wounded, and can't do any work. It's up to you, Endevvy."

His answer came without hesitation. "That's manual labor. Not my kind of work. I keep the accounts, make your appointments and organize your life. I'm not supposed to do anything else."

I began to get irritated. "Oh! Yes, you are. You're my working self. It doesn't matter what I ask you to do – you must do it, or I can banish you. I recently banished Aquirot, my greedy entity. Do you want to go the same way?"

A blank look crossed his face. "Who is Aquirot? I never heard of her. I don't know how to do that manual work and I won't do it!"

I flared up, and instantly Bazoom, my angry entity, was sitting on my right shoulder.

"Aim me! Aim me!" He entreated. "I want to hit him!" He jumped up and down, pricking me with his spines. I didn't need his jai alai stick – it was close range. I thought of him hitting Endevvy in the gut and he immediately attacked. Endevvy doubled up with a shout, clutching his midriff.

"Ouch! Why did you do that?"

"You need to learn how to work, or be banished. You have great potential and could become very useful, if only you would do things my way. I won't have it. Make up your mind. You have already seriously wounded Little Laboria, and you could stand trial for grievious bodily harm. I can only protect you if you agree to co-operate."

"OK, OK, I'll do as you say." Endevvy rubbed his stomach ruefully. "Just keep that little shit off me." Here he spat at Bazoom, who snickered menacingly.

"Right, Endevvy." I said as Bazoom disappeared. "You can finish weaving this rope, for a start. Then cut some footholds in the tree trunk, and tie the rope firmly to this branch when you're done." Endevvy began work on the plaited rope with a very bad grace, while I turned my attention to Istas, who was still sitting on the gold cushion.

"I have a plan for you, Istas. There is a friend of mine, Shela, who is working alone on a large project, translating ancient metaphysical manuscripts into a new format. This is called the Navigators Tarot. She needs assistance with her research. I would like you to be the one to help her finish the project. Would you be interested?"

Istas hesitated. "I'm not sure I could do that, but I'd like to try. I'm still getting these bad moods – feeling guilty and wanting to punish myself. Maybe a big project like the one Shela is working on would give me a chance to gain the self respect I lost during my relationship with Satsi." She looked at me expectantly.

"I'm sure it would. That's why I suggested it. It's settled, then."

Glancing down the tree where Endevvy had finished some rough steps in the trunk and was now busy knotting the rope to a strong branch, I announced.

"I think we can start down now. Thank you, Endevvy. For the first time, you have worked independently of me and I'm proud of you. You will be a useful member of our team in future. Now, please help Istas down."

Endevvy caught hold of the rope and motioned Istas to climb on his back. He swung down the tree trunk with alacrity, and they were soon on the ground in front of the Queen, who had been watching the proceedings. I was pleased to see what Endevvy could do on his own initiative. Although Laboria was out of action and we would have to find her another activity, I felt that she would be much happier away from his influence, and he, instead of focusing on berating her, would be able to find other things to do.

Endevvy leapt at the rope and returned to the nest. He told me to get onto his back, and then we swung down, excited and free, away from the tree, landing some distance out in the clearing. "Wow! That was fun!" cried Endevvy, a smile lighting his hatchet face for the first time. "I'm going to enjoy my new role in life, after all."

Queen Soyla was also smiling as she mounted the elephant and signaled us to climb in beside her. Something held me back. That laughter in the forest – what was it? Who was the long-nosed person that was eating fast food and possibly owned the magic cushion I had found?

"Ma Dame, I earnestly request permission to remain here and seek the owner of the gold velvet cushion, who is hidden in the forest. I hope you will give your consent." I looked up at the Queen expectantly.

"I know this is important for you." She replied "Therefore you may stay here, and then you will bring the owner of the cushion to me at the castle when you find him. That is an order."

"Thank you. I will go to search for him now." I quickly turned and made off into the forest as the elephant, carrying its precious load, headed back towards the castle. I held the cushion under my arm, ready to return it to its owner. Before I gave it up, I wanted to know why the monkeys had fled from its influence in such fear.

It was fairly easy to find the direction to go in, as a trail of paper wrappers led for about half a mile deep into thick forest. The path then widened out into a small clearing, where a pup tent stood pitched in the center, a fireplace with a pile of neatly stacked logs close to it. On a tree stump, neatly laid out, was a plate and mug, knife, fork and spoon. There was no sign of the owner. I felt a bubble of laughter rise up in my throat, and thought of a trick I would play on the fellow - quite simply, to light a fire and sit by it as if I occupied the spot. I soon had a fire going and a drift of smoke rose up through the trees as I sat chuckling to myself. It wasn't long before I heard the stealthy approach of someone through the undergrowth. A long nose poked out from behind a tree. I held up the cushion, and a tall figure emerged, grinning at me, and, taking the gold cushion, sat down on it in front of the fire.

Not a word had been spoken, but I knew that this was my trickster entity, Krackenwergle. We had met before on several occasions. "So, this is where you live. Not exactly like the bazaar!" I joked.

Kracklewergen smiled thinly. "Er-a poor joke. I like it here. In the forest, I am completely, er-hem, free, and away from people who er-might try to influence me. I can't stand advice from them, especially if it's, er-hem, unsolicited, you know. The bazaar is a hotbed of gossip, and that is the greatest trickery of all."

"You're right, of course." Naturally, I agreed with him, the most powerful of my entities. "Most people have their own opinion of events. Their opinion is always colored by who they are and their conception of the truth. In fact, all truth is merely relative. You know what I mean."

"I certainly do, hmmmmm. Only Himself knows absolute er-Truth. They call me the Fool, er-hem. That is the joke on them, for the Fool knows all. He is closest to the er-reality."

There was no need to say more on that subject. Then I continued, remembering the small figurine of the clay goat in my pocket, and pulling it out to show him. "I made this – at least, I think I did. What could it be for?"

Krackenwergle smiled again. "That goat, er-hem. I expect the er-Queen told you it represented Capricorn, didn't she? Hmmmm. That is only a small part of the er-truth. The black goat is Himself, in fact, er-hem, and he also embodies the god Pan. Pan plays his pipes and the whole er-world dances. That is the dance of life, hmmmm. Without life, we can't progress, er-hem, yet the dance is as you saw it in the nest with Istas. The er-dance is the unremitting conflict, er-hem, taking place in your mind between good and evil. Hmmmm. It is a mind-thing. You were fortunate to receive the er-blessing of the black goat, for the figurine shows that you, er-hem, will be guided by Himself throughout your testing period on the Lagoon."

I looked at the small clay model. It must have incredible power. Did I want that sort of power guiding me through my tests? I wondered what had happened to my Guide, the old man, whom I hadn't seen since he initially pushed my punt into the Lagoon. I wanted his advice, but he wouldn't come to me. I thought about the cushion.

"I wondered about your gold velvet cushion. You allowed me to find it again. Why were the monkeys so afraid? And why did the cushion enable Istas to throw them off?" I leant forward, gazing at Kracklewergen's gleaming eyes in anticipation.

"It's true. The er-cushion does hold magic. It originally belonged to the Princess Marijusha, hmmmm. I won't say how I er-came by it, but I know that one day Himself will come for it, er-hem. Until then, I await that time." The trickster continued. "This gold er-cushion is the way to find truth. When a person sits on it, hmmmm, all falsehood is swept away and sincerity, er-hem, is revealed in all its' splendor."

Nodding in agreement, I reflected on his statement. "So that was why the monkeys fled! They couldn't face the truth, which set Istas free."

Krackenwergle agreed. "As for the er-monkeys, since the cushion represents Himself, hmmmm, who is the Lord of Conflicts, the er-force it emanates is able to overcome all minor conflicts. That, er-hem, includes not only the battle that Istas had with her other er-self, represented by her former partner Satsi, but also the, er-hem, irritating confusion created by the monkeys' lower er-brains. They were hit, hmmmm, by a power far greater, an evil er-power, which terrified them and made them flee. You may wonder, er-hem, how ultimate truth can be obtained through the er-Lord of Conflicts. It is quite simple. Every disagreement, er-hem, has at its roots the need to find absolute truth, and that is the er-reason for war in the world, hmmmm."

With that, Kracklewergen abruptly ended our conversation.

"You must now er-return to the Castle of Earth. You are aware, hmmmm, that you carry the black goat. It is up to you whether you keep it in your er-possession, but it is hard to get rid of. I am your trickster, er-hem, and the goat is also a trickster. As you pass through the Lagoon, you will find that er-people will play tricks on you, hmmmm, and that will tend to increase as you get near the central island, er-hem, where the White Pyramid of the four Aces sits. There lies your er-ultimate test in this phase of your initiation, er-hem. Now, I be gone." He got up, picked up the cushion, turned and vanished behind a tree, leaving me wondering how far it was to walk to the castle.

I was sitting musing on my conversation with Krackenwergle, the clay image in my pocket, when I heard a clomping in the undergrowth and a loud snort. The Knight of Pentacles, Terramud, stood before me, astride Claydung and leading the dun mare Dusty.

"Don't waste time, now. The Queen has sent her mare for you to ride swiftly to the Castle, as we have heard King Compos' advance trumpeters already in the distant hills. There will be a great banquet tonight and tomorrow the jousting will begin."

I climbed up on the dun mare, and we trotted off through the forest towards the Castle of Earth.

Queen Soyla greeted me in the kitchens and told me that I had successfully passed the test "to find dissatisfaction and demand action." Because Endevvy had freed himself from my personality, he and Little Laboria now had a separate existence. I had also removed the bad karma from Istas by thinking of seating her on the cushion. Meanwhile, Laboria was being tended by the Queen's own doctor, who soon healed her wound and fitted her with a suitable claw. The arm, regretfully, could not be replaced and was eventually dried and hung as a talisman over the Knights' front door. Laboria became the efficient head of the nursery with the four nursemaids working under her, as a reward for her hard labor. Istas, meanwhile, set out with a group of knights who were heading to the West, where she would join up with Shela to complete the tarot project. Now, we were waiting for the Kings' arrival, and the smells of roast pig and dove pie wafted in from the kitchen, making everyone very hungry.

The banqueting hall was festooned with hemp leaves interwoven with ivy and deadly nightshade. Servants were setting simple wooden platters on the long tables as the sound of the Kings' trumpeters drew near. Outside the postern gate, a long line of tramping soldiers could be seen steadily approaching, making the ground shudder beneath them. Their banner was at half-mast, indicating the loss of the campaign against the Viceroy of Muckabad. In the center of the formation rode King Compos and, as he approached, I saw a big man with lank brown hair tucked under a black helmet, having a square, ruddy countenance, a broad nose and saddened eyes under deep brows. He wore armor and a long red cloak with a design of stags' heads and snakes on it – the design reminding me also of a plough. The party reached the postern and clattered across the drawbridge, dismounting inside the courtyard, where the king removed his helmet, his long hair cascading down his back, and walked slowly into the banqueting room.

Buckets of hot water and cloths were brought to sponge his face and feet, then a three-pronged green crown was fitted to his head, and he sat down on the throne at the head of the table. Instantly we heard a loud rumbling from the seat. I hid a smile, but was astonished to see that three jets of molten lava were rising and falling gently from the points of his crown, while the earth shook underfoot.

I saw Trid, lately the Page of Pentacles, but now become the Knight's Squire, coming towards me and I greeted him happily. "Trid – it's good to see you. How are you getting along? What was that rumbling noise?"

Trid shook my hand and explained. "The Castle of Earth represents the deepest level of existence on earth. The shuddering is caused by the Kings' approach and occurs every time he moves. He can control molten lava under the surface and designates when earthquakes, eruptions and fault lines appear. King Compos is, indeed, a vigorous King and deserves volcanic respect."

"Hail to the King!" A voice rang out from the balcony. "We bless Persephone, the goddess who protected him from harm during his campaign against the wicked Viceroy of Muckabad. Let us offer sacrifices to her and much feasting. For ten days should we feast, for the King is alive and well!"

Queen Soyla was shocked, and I knew why. The castle was short of provisions and she had only arranged for one day of feasting and jousting. What would she do? After a moments' thought, Soyla leaned forward and whispered to the King. He rapped on the floor with his scepter and silence fell. In a booming voice, he responded. "We thank the bearer of this message for the King's good health. We will have the ten days of feasting. Tomorrow morning we will sacrifice to the goddess Persephone, who will bring us many boar. We order it."

Sitting between Trid and Terramud at the table below the royal spread, I hoped that the sacrifice would be successful, as the servants entered with the roast pigs and dove pie. We had a most successful evening, with a band of mummers dressed as devils, who played upon the panpipes and cymbalines, while dancers veiled in colors of russet and citrine whirled before us. I left the banquet early and went to bed, for a full ten days of jousting and feasting awaited us. The task for the cooks, I thought, would be to find sufficient food for all, since the lack of boars was a serious problem.

King of Pentacles - Rules Four and Two of Pentacles.

The following morning the Queen held a meeting in the kitchens. The subject was the provision of food for the ten days' of feasting. The cooks' faces were somber, as she explained that they were to bring a black goat to the sacrifice in order that the boar would return to the forest and allow themselves to be killed. Two scullions went after a goat, and I followed them. We found the goatherd sitting on a rock outside the castle, his goats close by. I scanned the herd. There were brown goats, grey goats, spotted goats and white goats, but no black ones. What were we to do? The situation was desperate.

Remembering the black clay goat in my pocket, I wondered if I could bring it to life and use it as the sacrifice. I walked away from the scullions, who were conferring with the goatherd, and hid behind a rock. Frantically running through my brain went the list of items that I had in the punt. Would one of them be useful? The clay image of the goat was formed in the water and then left to dry, but never baked hard in a kiln. Water should dissolve it, but I ran the risk of losing its' power, which might disperse. I needed an object made of clay to contain it, but what could I find useful?

Here I recollected my lungfish, happily hibernating in his ball of clay in the punt, moored in the reeds by the Castle wall. I hurried to the boat and found the hardened ball of mud with the lungfish inside, a small hole in the top allowing him to breathe while asleep. I widened the hole with a stick, being careful not to poke him, and inserted the goat image into the ball. I then placed the dry ball of mud in a shallow pool at my feet and waited to see what would happen, my heart in my mouth. I was dealing with unknown forces. Could they destroy me?

A few moments passed and the ball containing the lungfish started to wriggle and expand rapidly. Two moving shapes were visible struggling together inside the ball as the softened mud floated to the surface. Soon the pool became murky and I could no longer see what was going on. I peered anxiously at the surface, waiting for any result. The pool became more and more agitated, waves breaking from churning movements below, until finally the head of a black goat broke the surface and began to swim rapidly out towards the Lagoon, followed by a large ripple that cut the water behind it.

Oh, darn it! I was overjoyed that the clay goat had materialized, but now it was about to escape! The old crone Ediug, who had given me the lungfish, had told me that its function was to chase off watery predators. Now the fish was assuming the goat was a predator, and intent on chasing it away from me! I needed to get the lungfish to change direction, and the only way to do that was to take the punt out into the Lagoon quickly and place it in front of the goat. The lungfish would then think that the goat was going to attack me in the boat, and would chase it back to land, where I could catch it. I poled the punt with the stiffened rattlesnake as fast as I could across the water and passed the swimming goat, getting ahead of him. I saw the ripple made by the lungfish make a big turn and come in beside the punt. There was a skirmish, and the goat swam back towards the shore, bleating pathetically.

I poled the punt back to shore behind the fish, and was happy to see the two scullions running down the hill. The lungfish came right out of the water and chased the goat up the hill, where they caught the animal, and soon we were marching proudly back to the Castle with our black goat, while the lungfish began making a fresh ball of mud to resume his hibernation. I thanked him profoundly before I went back to the kitchens, where shouts of joy were greeting the scullions' find.

"Here comes a black goat! Marvellous! Where did you find that goat?"

"That's amazing, by gum. There aren't any in the herd, and they are banned from the countryside."

"The King has ousted them, for they are considered evil."

These remarks and many others echoed around the kitchens. The Queen had a strange look on her face – she seemed almost fatuously content, and I wondered why. In any case, there was no time to consider her attitude as the goat was prepared for the sacrifice, adorned with a necklace of meadowsweet and led out to the courtyard. In the eastern corner of the yard was an altar of stone surmounted by a five-pointed star. Some five paces in front of it a large fire was burning, with an empty spit hanging ready.

I won't go into the sacrifice, for the goat bleated sadly and, although I knew it was the image of Himself, I couldn't suppress a feeling of pity for the animal. After the sacrifice, the scullions placed its body on the spit to roast. I was somewhat surprised that the company was apparently going to eat the goat, as normally a sacrifice of this importance would have been placed at the mouth of a cave for the goddess Persephone to collect. I asked the Knight, Terramud, who was in the crowd, why the goat was to be cooked.

"This goat won't be cooked, but burnt," explained Terramud. "The burning, which will continue on the spit until the body is consumed, is the only way to exorcise the power of the black goat. The ashes will then be scattered in front of the cave, and that will satisfy the goddess as well as protecting us from any evil influence of the goat."

"But – why did the Queen pick a black goat for the sacrifice in the first place? There were many other goats. I would have thought that a white goat would have been preferable." I was puzzled.

Terramud smiled. "You have not understood. The Queen knew you had the image of a black goat in clay. She wanted to see if you had the earthly power to materialize it. It was a trick and a test at the same time. Fortunately for you, the crone Ediug was aware of a possible test, and that's why she gave you the lungfish."

"Ediug did that for me!" I thought back to the old crone that I had met on my river journey and felt a rush of affection. I wondered where Ediug was at this moment. She must know what had happened and how well the lungfish had performed. Again I felt a twinge of loneliness without my Guide and longed for his presence, but I knew he would probably only appear if I was in serious danger.

Once the sacrificial goat was reduced to a heap of ashes, a group headed by the Queen set out towards Persephones' cave to scatter the remains. The King, meanwhile, had ordered up a hunting party and was picking out his best boarhounds with meticulous care, for hunting the wild pig was his favorite sport. He asked me to join the chase mounted on Dusty, and we trotted off to the forest, there being about 21 of us. We knew that nobody had sighted boar for several weeks, the animals being extremely scarce and seeming to have left the area after an invasion of large asses had moved into the forest from the plains nearby. Neither asses nor boars were predators of each other, although it was clear they did not get along. We rode for several hours, finally having to pitch our tents for the night near a swamp from which rose a nauseous stink. I was at a loss as to how we could find the boars, since I was not familiar with the area or the method of hunting boar.

Feeling both ignorant and useless, I sat down on a rotten log and cursed my stupidity. It was true that I could not be expected to know everything, but that was humiliating for me. I soon realized that another figure was sitting beside me. I turned to examine her, finding it was a dumpy-looking female with a blank look on her face. I gave her a poke, at which she gazed at me vaguely. "Who are you?" I asked.

She licked her sagging lips slowly. "I'm – I think I'm Mithinkky. I'm your ignorant self. I don't know anything. Nothing at all, and what's more, I don't intend to find anything out. It's safer that way."

What a piece of moronic idiocy, I thought. Just when I needed some answers, she had come to burden me. "Don't you have any information? You have no thoughts about the migration of boars, for example? Or asses' habits?"

Mithinkky looked stubborn. "I don't study bores – they are boring. As for asses, they are too asinine for me to delve into."

A spark lit up in my mind. We might possibly be able to reintroduce boars to the forest by making their environment more interesting, while asses would have to be lured to the nearest sinkhole and persuaded to dive in. I sprang to my feet as Mithinkky vanished. What a great idea! I hurried to the Kings' side and begged audience of him.

"Come in, come in," said the King irritably, swatting at a horde of mosquitoes in his tent. "What a hell-hole we're in and no sign of our quarry. What do you want?"

"I have an idea, Mi Lawd. May I present it to you? It concerns the asses and the boars. I – methinks – I can get rid of the asses and entice the boars to return by making the forest more inviting for them."

"What's that? Some crazy idea of yours? How do you propose getting the asses to leave?"

"Mi Lawd, the asses are stupid. I will tell them that there is a fabulous new liquor factory near here. Most asses like to drink different liquors. They will be attracted by the idea! I will tell them that the drink is in an experimental stage and is, therefore, fermenting in sinkholes near the factory. The manufacturers need to test the buoyancy of the drink, and require volunteers to swim in the sinkholes. Those who agree will have electrodes attached to their buttocks to measure the buoyancy of the liquor. We will then see what happens." I finished proudly.

"What is supposed to happen to the asses then? It sounds stupid. Oh! well, it might work. We'll give it a try. Now, what do you propose concerning the boars?"

"Do not worry, Mi Lawd. I will think of a way to entice the boars to return. First, let's get the asses moving in the right direction."

At the King's command, therefore, we posted notices on many forest trees announcing the new factory, and soon hordes of asses were to be seen eagerly looking for the liquor. The King, his valet and I took up position on a hillside above the sinkholes. There was, of course, no factory, but we posted signs to it anyway, and then set up a large generator behind a bush with wires attached to electrodes by the hole. As the first asses arrived, servants dressed as factory workers attached the wires to their buttocks and bade them dive in. Alas, all were electrocuted, yet still they came, and when they looked down at the floating bodies in the sinkhole, they thought they were swimming in bliss, and thus dove in after them, grinning happily.

Shortly, we were able to exterminate the majority of asses, and the resulting spicy and valuable liquor would be bottled and sent into the city, where more asses eagerly awaited it. The King slapped me on the back, nearly flinging me off my horse, with a guffaw.

"My, you're cleverer than we thought. Now we'll celebrate with a dinner of chipped lizards. That's the only food available around here. Tomorrow you will come up with an idea to interest the boars. So, give it some thought tonight. And, by the way, you have inadvertently completed your task already. It was "**to take the spiritual out of the material.**" We forgot to mention it before."

I couldn't sleep that night, tossing on my pallet and wondering how to attract the boars back into the forest. At eleven o'clock, I sat up and acknowledged my lack of understanding of boars' habits. I was ignorant in that subject and again felt the gross humiliation of admitting I didn't know everything. A thump on my mattress told me that Mithinkky was back – I didn't want to turn and see her, but - she had provided me with an answer before without realizing it.

"You're back, Mithinkky, I see." I muttered shortly. "Well, what are we going to do?"

"I'm just a cornball, you know. How can you expect me to give you an answer? I never read a book in my life and I don't understand the method of luring boars. My mind is like an echoing cave – empty, and dripping with moisture from the fog of ignorance." Mithinkky sniffed sentimentally. "The only thing I pay attention to is feeding corn to my pet raccoon."

"Where is the coon now?" I asked irritably.

"He's in the forest playing with his friends." Mithinkky looked past me and I saw several little masked faces peering out from the bushes. Was there a message here? Coon – cornball – lures - corn – corn goddess – cave – Persephone. Why, that was it! Mithinkky had unwittingly given me the answer. I knew that both boars and coons loved corn, and Persephone was the goddess of corn and lived in a cave. I would find the nearest cave and beg the goddess to enlighten me. The pig was dedicated to her and she would surely have the right answer.

It was midnight when Mithinkky and I set off, stumbling through the black forest, for we had not thought to bring a light. Finding a dark cave on a moonless night would not be easy. It was up to the goddess. I fervently asked her to show me a cave near us.

No sooner had I focused on the goddess, than Mithinkky vanished and I felt myself losing my footing and falling, falling deep into the earth. A spasm of fear shot through me, but Paragutt quickly clung to my back and together we made a soft landing in some mud about twenty feet down. I stood up, covered in filth, and faced a faint green glow at the back of the cave, which I addressed with fervor.

"Oh, Persephone, goddess of the underworld, help us to find your boars and lure them back to the forest, so that Compos, the mighty King of Pentacles, may celebrate his safe return from the wars by feasting and jousting in your honor. Speak, O goddess."

A hiss came from the depths of the cave, and the goddess Persephone addressed me in a sibilant voice.

"I will help you, for you are the respected one who was able to materialize the black goat, whose ashes were given to me in reverence. You must climb out of the cave first. When you have found your way out, you will come across a heap of golden corn by the entrance. Take this corn and spread it along the route of the raccoons, for their sense of smell is acute and they will find it. The boars, who have little sense of smell, will see the coons a-feasting, and will hurry into the forest to partake of the corn. In order to lure them towards the King, I will then authorize you to tie one of my pigs to a stake and poke her with a stick." Here she laughed. "A pig in a poke, you might say. The pig will start to squeal, and that will interest the boars. They will move towards the spot where the pig is, and the King will then be able to shoot the two boars he will need for tomorrows' feast easily. His Majesty will know the two who wish to be killed, as they will present their most vulnerable spot to the Kings' arrows. Now, go, and do my bidding. In the meantime, Mithinkky, the ignorant one who is also innocent, will remain with me until the earth is new again."

The green glow faded and I found myself alone in the dark, thanking the goddess profoundly for her simple wisdom and for releasing Mithinnky from my ignorant grip.

To find a way out of the cave, I would have to wait until morning. As I had fallen straight down there must be an opening directly above me, but were there any handholds on the walls? I spent the rest of the night in a daze. Persephone had made contact with me twice. I felt blessed, and knew in my heart that, in spite of my current predicament, my journey to the Castle of Earth was successful.

At the first light of morning, I looked up and saw, to my astonishment, a rope ladder, woven of ivy, stretching up to a small shaft of light above me. I scrambled up the ladder, which was incredibly strong, and, leaping out of the cave, found a large heap of corn a few feet from the entrance. Taking my fur cloak, I filled it with the golden grains and scattered them about the forest tracks in many places, before returning to the campsite still smothered in mud.

A raucous bellow of laughter greeted me. "Ha. Ha! HA! Where have you been, my little friend? Rolling with the swine?" The King, who was already up, threw his head back and guffawed as the tiny flames in his crown flared up, and the ground trembled under my feet. "Better take a bath. You smell terrible! Here." The King turned to his valet. "Bring hot water and wash down our friend, and hurry!"

The valet scurried away and soon came back with a tub of water, in which he bathed me and then dressed me in clean clothes. I bowed to the King. "Thank you, Mi Lawd. I feel much better. I am also glad to be able to tell you that we may now move to a selected place in the forest and set up a hideaway there for you to reside while you wait for the boars, who will soon come to you."

"I don't believe it! How did you come up with an idea, and what is it?" The King leaned forward with interest, a rumbling emerging from beneath his seat.

"Mi Lawd. I was honored with audience of the goddess Persephone during the night. She graciously told me how to attract the boars. I have already arranged the first stage. All you have to do is build the hide in your chosen spot, tie a pig to a stake in the glade, and poke it with a stick. The boars will come when they hear the pigs' cries."

"Well! I don't know, I'm sure." King Compos turned to his servants. "Send men to construct a hide in yon nearby glade. Take down the tents and break camp. We will be prepared for the boars." This was no sooner said than done, and the King settled down in the hide, his bow and arrows ready and keen. The Squire Trid led a large sow to the stake and tied her firmly, then sharpened a stick. I hoped the sow wouldn't be too upset, as it was Persephones' will that she should shriek as loudly as possible.

I returned to the campsite and remained outside the forest, on a hill above the swamp with a good view of the surrounding countryside. I soon saw many raccoons loping along the forest tracks towards the corn, which they sat down and began to eat with their fingers. It wasn't long before I smelled a strong odor from the swamp, and observed the surface of the mud bubbling ominously in several places. The bubbling became louder and louder, and huge globs of mud spat out of the surface in many spots, rather like a mud geyser exploding. Then, to my amazement, I saw the muddy head of a boar appear in the center of a boiling mass of bubbles, then another, and another, until the swamp was filled with emerging boars, who shook the mud off their backs and rushed into the forest, grunting loudly.

There must have been fifty animals, many of whom had ferocious tusks, and they were huge – much bigger than the pigs that Trid and I had traveled with before, and hunks of coarse hair hung from their bellies. Trailing a dense odor behind them, they spread out through the forest, gobbling up the corn while I kept a safe distance behind. Then I heard the loud squeals of a stuck pig, and knew that Trids' stick was doing its' work in the glade. The shrieks grew louder, and some of the boars nearby stopped eating and faced the sound, grunting warmly, then started moving in the direction of the Kings' hide. Soon a dozen boars were closing in on the chosen spot and I darted around behind a tree and climbed it to watch. Trid was in the center of the glade prodding the sow, whose pink mouth stretched wide as she squealed angrily. As the first boar entered the glade, Trid ran to the tree and quickly climbed to my branch. Several boars were now milling about the glade, and we could see the King, hidden behind some branches, raise his bow and begin to take aim.

Suddenly the group of boars split apart and two great, tusked animals stood in the center. Each one faced the Kings' hide and knelt down, stretching their heads along the ground. They then dug five times into the earth, leaving small mounds of soil in front of them. Lastly, the great animals rose to their feet and solemnly turned sideways to stand motionless in front of the hideaway. With a zing, the monarchs' arrows flew straight to one animal, but bounced harmlessly off its tough hide. Compos looked annoyed and strung another arrow to his bow. A second shot failed to take down the other boar, although neither of the animals moved, but stood their ground. The King loosed a succession of arrows at them, but not one arrow could pierce their thick skins.

Here was a problem. The King was, by now, in a towering rage and his crown shot out spouts of flame ten feet high, while the ground shook with a magnitude 7.4 earthquake as the servants huddled together under a bush. I was afraid the forest would catch fire, so I quickly thought of the magic arrow that I carried in a small quiver on my back. I was loath to give it up, but maybe this was the time. I went to the Kings' hideaway and offered him the arrow, its beautiful silver shaft ending in the scintillating diamond head.

"Mi Lawd. Please take this arrow and string your bow with it. You will succeed in piercing the boars' side with it, for it is as cutting as a diamond."

King Compos grabbed the arrow from me with a snarl and fitted it to his bow, aiming at the first boar. The magic arrow flew straight, and the boar fell. At the same time, the second boar also sank down to the ground, and both lay there, their blood mingling with the soil, and a great shout arose from all around as the rest of the boars fled. The servants swarmed in, raising the dead boars up onto the backs of two ponies and carrying them back towards the Castle of Earth, followed by the crowd with King Compos rejoicing in their midst.

That very evening we sniffed the odor of roast boar, turning gently on two huge spits in the courtyard. King Compos was in an excellent mood, slapping everyone on the back and joking and telling bawdy stories to all the courtiers, who tittered politely. A small hunting party would set out again for the forest early in the morning, as the cooks would need two more boars each day of the festivities, making twenty in all, and they would have to be caught fresh each morning. Now that they had the diamond arrow, one shot would dispose of two animals at once, and many arrows would, therefore, be saved. Because of the delayed hunt, the jousting was to begin the following day, so I sought out the Knight Terramud and went with him to the lists, where some fine horses were exercising. At the lists I was surprised to see no sign of the usual shields, pikes and clubs that the Castle of Earth used as weapons. Instead, rows of platters hung on the walls, some large, some medium and others small, of all different patterns and blazons.

I turned to Terramud. "What are these platters for? Where are your pikes and clubs? How can you joust without those?"

"This is the Castle of Earth. The royal family that lives in the Castle of Fire use cannons and rifles, and those in the Castle of Air have swords and daggers. The Castle of Water uses deadly water balloons and cups of boiling tar. Each castle has its' own special weapons for jousting." Terramud explained.

"But how can you joust with platters? They look very awkward. Do you throw them or clout people on the head with them?"

"We have several different games. For one, there is clay pigeon shooting, done with crossbows. Then we have Frisbee competitions; a trial we call Whack the Platter, in which the Knight must gallop towards a hanging clay platter and break it with a club; and, best of all, we have the juggling. This year, we have two very expert jugglers who have traveled many miles over the sea to perform for us. They are pretty girl twins from the Isle of the Obelisk in the South Seas under the seven stars. Their names are Ulani and Kaula. You will meet them tomorrow and be amazed at their skill with the disks."

"I think I've met the twins before. Their names sound familiar, but from a distant time, I recall. Yes, I remember one of them was very good at the disks, and the other hopeless. She must have picked it up by now, then." I cast my mind back to the island and the great obelisk which stood in the center, with its' hidden message. Then I had another thought.

"Terramud – I saw the boars coming up out of the swamp! How could they have hidden in the swamp? They can't breathe underwater."

"Ah! As you know, they have long noses and the nostrils are right at the end. This enables them to breathe just on the surface, as they rest in the quagmire at the end of each day. What else would you expect of boars? They are always bogged down. This time, they got so bored with themselves they couldn't get up again, and only the sight of the coons stealing their corn roused them. Although the coons like corn too, they are not allied with it in the underworld. That is the boars' prerogative."

"How strange. I have another question, too, about my ignorant entity, Mithinkky. She seemed to know what to do – the answers, you know." I was puzzled.

"Ah! But it isn't always the know-alls who have the answer. Sometimes the ignoramus can simplify the problem and come up with some remarkable suggestions."

"So it's not so bad to be ignorant, after all?" I queried.

"Of course not. It is better to admit you don't know than to pretend that you do. Mithinkky knows that. But you don't want to answer every question by saying "I don't know" because that makes you look very apathetic, and that is bad for business. So, one must make an effort to say something in response." Terramud chuckled. "Now, it is soon going to be time for the banquet. Come with me to the wine cellars and we will choose a good vintage for the King and Queen."

The banquet was a grand success and minstrels from Persephones' kingdom played dirges on a stringed scythe and sistrum. The two boars were delicious, served up with a puree of root vegetables, after which we went to bed replete. The following day, the jousting began, and Terramud was able to gain first prize for Whack the Platter with ten wins. The Frisbee contest, held on horseback, was most exciting and reminded me of polo, and the clay pigeon archers scored many hits with their crossbows. As for the star show, Ulani and Kaula took the audience by storm with some amazing juggling, including up to twenty disks in the air at once. They were awarded the Order of the Boar shortly afterwards, a necklace containing boars' teeth and tusks, which was for ceremonial purposes only, as it was very heavy.

The jousting and banqueting continued unabated for ten days, and at the end, King Compos gave out the prizes. Summoning his Treasurer, he told her to bring out the golden pentacles for the winners. The young woman I recognized as Zola, the servant who had been in charge of the Fathers' treasure in the Vatican on my river journey, and by whose help Einerline and I had secured some very valuable books. She had escaped with us and I was very glad to see that she had found such a suitable profession with the royal court in the Castle of Earth.

I was eager to hear about Zolas' adventures since I had helped her escape from the Vatican. We chatted amicably as I accompanied her to the castle treasury and waited in the corridor while she secretly put in the combination for the great door. She took out four golden pentacles, and began carrying them carefully along the passageway, tiptoeing and glancing about her. I followed discreetly, feeling a very threatening atmosphere that emanated from some small holes in the walls of the corridor at eye level. We were soon beyond that section of the passage, and she sank down on a divan to rest, for the pentacles were heavy.

"That felt very uncomfortable – in the passage, I mean." I remarked. "What is behind the peep holes in the wall?"

"I will tell you. Years ago, the treasure of the King of Pentacles was mixed up with the riches that the wicked ones, the Qliphoth, had stolen. The Castle of Earth was losing power, because the Qliphoth were draining off the Kings' gold to turn into lead. He ordered his architects to design and construct a thick wall between the two areas, and for a while this prevented them from entering his vaults. They didn't give up, however, but began to drill through the wall, and eventually made holes, so that they could watch what was going on. We try to keep any treasure we are carrying below eye level, so that they can't see it, but eventually they will make the peep holes larger, and will be able to crawl through and infiltrate the treasury once more."

"Can't you block the holes?" I asked sensibly.

"We have tried that, but they pulled out the excuses and lies we used to block them. We need a long lasting method to keep them out."

"What about honesty? That comes in very compact units and is highly tenacious. It is almost impossible to penetrate once installed in the correct position."

"What a great idea!" Zola clapped her hands in glee. "Where can we get some? Would it be near here?"

"It is right in your own throat and in the throats of all who live in the castle. All they have to do is to come down to the passageway and speak the truth through each hole, until they fill them up. This will block off the evil Qliphoth for good."

"Thank you, thank you. What a simple solution. Let's start today!" Zola cried. "It's not a moment too soon." She rose and, carrying the pentacles to the Kings' chambers, spoke with him privately, and he set in motion the process whereby the evil ones were blocked from the Castle of Earth forever.

When the feasting was over, King Compos requested my presence in his chambers. Here he awarded me the sign of the Pentacle – Earth Aethyr, which was a beautiful baked clay disc on a leather thong with a pentagram in the center, which he hung around my neck. "The Pentacle is sacred to Hygeia, Goddess of Healing. You have earned our eternal gratitude. Go forth from our presence in the Castle of Earth and spread healing wherever you find those who are in need. Farewell, and may Persephone be with you."

After I had thanked the King, he called in his commanders and began to prepare his next campaign. The battle was to be against the Shriek of

Yaboo, a desert potentate who had amassed much wealth, of which King Compos was anxious to avail himself. Now it was time for me to leave the Castle of Earth, and so I said goodbye to King Compos and Queen Soyla, Terramud and Trid his Squire, and sadly walked down to my punt, which I pushed out into the still waters of the Lagoon.

Page of Swords - Rules Ten and Nine of Swords.

Waking the rattlesnake from his slumber, at which he quickly stiffened into a pole, I untied the punt and pushed out into the Lagoon at dawn. It was a dry, warm morning with the scent of turned earth in the air. I continued in a leisurely fashion for some miles, until I saw further along the coast on my right, the spires of a delicate building rise in the distance. From time to time, as I approached, swirls of mist hid the Castle, for such it was, and the air grew damper and cooler.

The building appeared larger than I thought, as it rose high above me. Out of the fog behind it I could see a range of high mountains, yet it seemed to shimmer elusively before their immensity. I knew this must be the Castle of Air, where my next series of tests would begin, and a shiver of excitement assailed me as I moored my punt close to the bank and climbed out, leaving the rattlesnake coiling himself up to wait for me. The ground rose up steeply and it was quite a struggle to reach the top of the bank, where I came out on a narrow pathway leading past the Castle. I followed this path for a while as it wound its way towards the mountains until it widened and I came out into a narrow, lush green valley hidden between the castle and the peaks. Cattle were scattered in fields along the way and many storks rose from the chimneys of little cottages, where they had made their nests.

As I wandered along, I began to notice the grass and vegetation becoming parched, and eventually there was an area of dust surrounding a small dwelling in the middle of the valley. Everything around this place was as if scorched by evil flames, and nothing grew. As I got closer, I could hear angry words from inside the cottage and the sound of slaps and cries. Although the noise of conflict put me on edge, I knocked at the door, feeling that I should find out what was happening within. No-one heard me, as the argument continued unabated, so I knocked several times more. Finally there was a long pause, and silence, then a faint shuffling towards the door, which was opened a crack, revealing a small, dry woman with a beaked, dripping nose and reddened eyes.

"What do you want? Coming here without our consent! Go away and leave us alone, you interfering scoundrel."

With that, she slammed the door in my face, but as she did so, I was able to catch sight of a young girls' appealing face just behind her, who gazed at me in desperation. The door was shut, yet I knew instinctively that I had been led here to help her escape.

The family was evidently dysfunctional, so much so that their conflict and hatred of each other had destroyed the surrounding vegetation, where nothing could flourish. I hid myself behind a small derelict barn and pondered my next move. From the sound of a male voice, there was obviously a man in the cottage, probably the girls' father. I knew they would have to sleep at some point, maybe then I could make entrance through the window and get the girl out. I would have to send her some sort of message, though, so that she would be ready.

There was a stork's nest on the chimney, and two large birds watched me from their perch. After a few minutes, one of the birds flew down and landed one or two feet from me, then gradually came closer, eyeing me sideways with care. The stork had a very large beak that it clacked as it moved forward. I was astonished to see that it opened its beak and gestured inside with its foot, and there was a small slip of paper with something written on it. Cautiously I reached in and drew it out.

The words were plain: "HELP ME! I am a prisoner here with my abusive parents. Send me word."

Quickly I wrote on the reverse side. "I will come at one o'clock in the morning. Be ready to escape through the back window." I replaced the note in the storks' beak and it flew back to the chimney. I do not know how the note reached the captive, but at one o'clock, while I waited by the window, the young girl appeared and with my aid was able to climb through, and then we ran away from that evil place towards the mountains, which we reached at dawn.

Pausing in the foothills, we sat down to rest, and I asked the girl her name. She was a pretty girl with a pale face surrounded by long black hair, a distinguished nose and finely chiseled lips. She was tall, and wore a pair of purple knee breeches and a yellow tunic, while on her shining hair rested a winged cap. Her dark eyes were huge as she gazed at me.

"I am Breata, a Page at the Castle of Air. My parents have kept me from the Castle for the last month. They are convinced I am having an affair with one of the grooms, but it isn't true. The royal family will be very upset and wonder why I haven't come in to work. My father is jealous of any influence, as I'm his only child. I can't bear it at home any longer. My dream is to become a scholar and work with the Aces on the Isle of the White Pyramid in the center of the Lagoon. But I don't know how to achieve this."

I thought for a moment. "So you are the Page of Swords, for they inhabit the Castle of Air. We can maybe arrange for you to live at the Castle. They must have servants' quarters there."

"That is where I was, until my father came yelling and dragged me away by the scruff of my neck, and threw me on his horse and rode home......"

Here Breata burst into tears and sobbed quietly for some minutes. I tried to comfort her as she murmured brokenly.

"I want to climb high into the mountains. I feel there is an answer there for me. The stork is my friend. She has told me of many things, for she sees afar. She will help me to see my future if I can climb as high as she flies. Let us go up to the highest peak and find the answer. Will you come with me?"

I wasn't too keen on the idea of a lengthy ascent up the craggy face of the nearest rocks, but I overcame my reluctance and we set out and climbed for some hours. The weather was good as it was still summer, and the snow had retreated to the highest levels. The climb got steeper and more precipitous as we moved steadily upwards, and we eventually reached a jagged ledge where we could rest. To my surprise, a triangular blue stone was balancing precariously there on a sharp rock with a sword lying on top of it. At the same time, we heard a rush of wings, and the stork flew up to us, carrying in its claws blue gentian flowers that grew nearby. I felt the stork was trying to tell us that we must pay attention to the blue stone, which Breata had now stepped upon unawares.

"Look, Breata. That stone under your foot – it isn't from here. Someone must have placed it there. And the sword, can you get hold of it?" I was clinging to a ledge nearby.

"I'll try." She leaned down cautiously and attempted to grab the hilt of the sword, but it shivered out of her grasp. Again and again she reached for it, and seemed almost to hold it, and yet it escaped her. "I can't get hold of it. It's there, but it's not, at the same time. It doesn't want me to have it."

Moving over beside her carefully and holding onto the nearest grip, I reached for the sword. Although my hand seemed to grasp the hilt, I felt no contact. It seemed like a mirage. I reached for it once more but again it eluded me, yet remained essentially in the same position.

"It's a mystery." I admitted reluctantly. "The sword must be magical, for it can change its composition at will. Let us think what to do next."

"We could try the blue stone." Breata suggested, leaning down and moving her hand close to the stone. But, as her hand approached, it seemed to pass right through the stone, and yet the lapis remained in the same position. "I can't get it. I wonder why not. What can we do now?"

The stork was perching on a nearby rock. It tapped its beak three times on the rock, and a puff of air blew in our faces, which quickly grew stronger until it became a fresh breeze. The rock below the stork began to shimmer with a yellow haze as if the sun had struck it, and a light, airy voice came to us.

"I am Eos, goddess of the winds and the cool air, and I will tell you what you must do. Listen carefully. You, the Navigator, must "**prove that martyrdom is not the result of egoism.**" That is your task. Now, you must both descend from the mountains and make your way to the Castle of Air, where I will give Breata my protection against the wrath of her father, and you will stand by her. He will be prevented from taking her back, for she has too long been the scapegoat for her parents' problems. Once you reach the Castle, you will find out how you can help the brother sword smiths Yevgeny and Yaroslav with their concerns. You may then be able to get a sword. Go now, and may the breath of Eos be with you."

The floating yellow luminescence dispersed and faded away, and the stork took off and glided down to the valley. Breata and I followed slowly down, from handhold to handhold, taking pains not to slip or let go, and reached the foothills, where we slept overnight in a windblown heap of leaves and then set foot on the trail to the Castle. We were exhausted as we arrived at the drawbridge, which glimmered like transparent glass over a grey bottomless moat of swirling fog. The wind blew constantly and the guard at the gate was forced to sound his horn loudly, before a gossamer portcullis, billowing in the breeze, drew slowly upwards and let us into the courtyard.

We were greeted by a handsome African woman who was the King of Swords' Keeper of the Records and the Castle scholar. Fola had been educated at the University of the Congo after she was rescued from a cursed toad, which was removed from her presence by a kind stranger. This person had been exiled from her tribe because of her disagreement with the hypocrisy of her elders, who were selling their fellow tribesmen down the river as slaves. She was strongly against any sort of forced labor and had been doing much work to free slaves wherever she found them. She led us into the Castle library, where the shelves were lined with printed books bound in leather, and we relaxed on couches while she explained the predicament of the brothers up the mountain.

Yevgeny and Yaroslav held territory some eight miles from the Castle itself. They were warlike and constantly preyed upon their neighbors, stealing servants and peasants for their own use and enslaving them. In recent times, they had attacked the Castle of Air and carried off the entire collection of hawks and falcons belonging to the King of Swords. This was very upsetting. In retaliation, the King was about to wage a campaign against them to get the birds back, and preparations were well on their way. The brothers had previously been allies of the Castle of Air and were expert sword smiths, producing the finest blades anywhere within one hundred leagues of the Castle, and the King had bought many fine weapons from them, so their change of heart was inexplicable.

I knew Fola from the past, and certainly I had left her toad, Oojo, on the Galapagos Islands with some iguanas in order to recover his health. He was a nuisance but I still missed the cursed fellow, so I had reluctantly taken him back when he showed up riding on a lotus leaf. Fola described how, apparently after a castigatory raid on their own peasants by a nearby Duke, they had fallen into a great quarrel between themselves, and Yevgeny had crucified Yaroslav on four swords. He would have died, had not a stranger passed by, released him, tended his wounds and suggested how they could resolve their quarrel. Yevgeny had sacrificed his right arm as penance so that Yaroslav might be restored to health, but the peace had not lasted between them, and as soon as Yaroslav was recovered, they began arguing about organizing another raiding party – this time against the very allies who had supported them for years. The question was how to find out what had turned them against King Atmos and his Queen Phere. Fola quietly told us that we had been chosen to journey to the brothers' kingdom in secret and discover the cause of their disloyalty. In order to allay their fears, we must disguise ourselves and make an excuse for the visit.

The Page was happy to be my companion on this quest, and soon we were dressed in concealing outfits and mounted on two fast ostriches heading for the brothers' territory. Breata, it turned out, was an expert swordswoman and fencer, which made me feel a little more secure. Our ostriches covered the ground in great strides and were amazingly comfortable to ride, as their feathers were bouncy and soft. However, they were inclined, from time to time, to stop dead and thrust their heads deep in the sand where they would remain for some minutes before agreeing to continue, which was very annoying.

In a couple of hours we reached a river that wound between canyon walls, and traversed the bank until we came to a steep staircase cut into the rock, where we left the birds hobbled to fend for themselves until we returned.

After a long climb up the steps, which seemed endless, we finally emerged on a level plain where stood an ancient castle, which was evidently in process of restoration, with a smithy nearby from whose chimney belched forth smoke and steam. The sound of hammers ringing on metal led us towards the brothers' workshop, where we found Yevgeny and Yaroslav hard at work tempering swords by plunging them red hot into a vat of water, and then withdrawing and hammering the metal repeatedly to create the keen edge and flexible blade needed for their exceptional weapons. They looked up as we approached, so we stood respectfully at a distance from the roaring forge.

The smaller of the two men, who was missing his right arm, stepped forward and introduced himself. "My name is Yevgeny. What are you doing here in our territory? Do you wish to order a fine sword?"

I replied, hastily making up an excuse for being there. "Yes, we would like to order two of your best swords, but we need them in a hurry. How long would it take you to make them?"

"Ah! Now a good sword requires several weeks to make. It must be thrust repeatedly into the furnace, then withdrawn, cooled, and hammered to make the metal pliable. When the sword is too stiff, the metal will shatter on the first blow, especially during jousting. On the other hand, if the sword bends too much and is soft, its edge will not be sharp enough...."

Here he suddenly lunged forward in our faces, waving his good arm.

".... to cut off your head!"

We leapt back in fright as the little man burst into merriment at his joke, which had scared us both, and set our hearts hammering.

Recovering swiftly, I asked. "Do you have accommodation for travelers at your castle? For we have come from afar and still have many miles to go. We would like to wait here while the swords are made, and can pay you handsomely for our keep."

"Well, you can stay here, although the room where you would sleep is not the best. A bit fowl, you might say. Ha! Ha!" Here he laughed briefly. "You can eat with the servants in their hall and we can set up some lessons for you in swordsmanship, if you like."

"It's a deal, then." I chuckled inwardly. This would give us plenty of time to discover the brothers' change of heart against the Castle of Air, and their servants' gossip would be invaluable. Breata, who had said little, exchanged a wink with me. We gave the brothers precise instructions for the making of the two swords, and then walked up a slope to the dilapidated castle, where we were shown into a poor shed that appeared to be a nesting place for chickens. It appeared we would have to put up with several weeks of roosting with the hens in order to accomplish our mission.

It was less than a week later, and already we were tired of quizzing the servants for information, sleepless with the effort to hang onto the perches by our toes amongst the clucking hens and sick of eating eggs, when great fortune came upon us in the shape of two figures that came trudging up one day from the canyon and went into the forge to discuss affairs with the brothers. As soon as they had disappeared, Breata drew me aside tremulously.

"Those people – they are my mother and father! What could they be doing here? I mustn't let them see me, so I shall hide. Would you creep around the smithy and try to hear what they're talking about? Please."

"Of course I will. Keep your head down here. I'll be back in a minute." I moved stealthily behind the buildings and reached the rear wall of the smithy, where I put my ear to the wall and was able to hear their conversation.

"So, she has disappeared. Just when we wanted to blame her for everything, too. We can't find her." The man was speaking. "Now our plan will come to nothing. Have you seen a young girl with black hair coming this way?"

I was glad that we had bleached Breatas' hair and fitted her with a fake moustache and goatee. She passed very well as a young swaggerer.

"No, we haven't," came Yevgenys' reply. "There are just two people here ordering swords. Are you saying now that we can't carry out the plan?" He sounded angry. "That's your fault for letting her escape. Now we will have to decide what to do."

I pressed my ear tightly to the stone wall in case I missed a word.

"We were to go to the Castle of Air and tell the King that Breata had stolen all the hunting birds, falcons and hawks, and that's why we took her from the servants' quarters to punish her and make her confess. Now we can't pin the missing birds on her and the royal family suspects that you two have the birds. Why did you involve us in this?" The mother was complaining.

"On the contrary, this was your idea." One of the brothers responded. "You know very well that the advantage of having the girl staying at the Castle was to make her the scapegoat for the missing birds, but you kidnapped her from there and took her home with you. With the blame passed to Breata, we could have taken the hawks to market far away and sold them by now. The profits were to be shared between us. Now, we are stuck with the birds, and already we have word that the King plans an attack against us to recover them. We only took the birds because you wanted revenge against the court for the seduction of your daughter. Now I'm not sure whether that really happened. You have drawn us into a trap." Yevgeny was shouting now. "We were allies with the King of Swords, and he bought many weapons from us. You led us astray with this cock-and-bull story. We should never have listened to you."

A third man, presumably Breatas' father, responded in a sly voice, pointing out. "You were easily persuaded, remember. The gold that these valuable birds would fetch was too much temptation for you. You have betrayed a good ally. It doesn't matter to us. We are enemies of the court anyway. Them and their riches! A hoity toity lot they are with low morals. I want my daughter Breata back. You'd better find her, or further misfortune will befall you and your stupid brother here. I'll give you seven days to find her, or I will cut off your heads with your own swords. Come on, wife, let's get out of here." With that threat, I heard the sound of scraping boots and retreating footsteps, so I stayed hidden until the parents had disappeared down the canyon. I then ran back and shared my story with Breata, who was horrified by the accusations.

"I always felt that my father was a mean, cunning old man, and mother just went along with it because she was afraid. He beat her and made her mean, too. Now I know how they behave to other people – not just to me."

She drew a deep breath. "My hatred of them both is justified. They are trying to implicate me in the theft of the birds. I will not be their scapegoat!"

"We can remedy this, now that we know about the conspiracy, Breata." I felt confident. "You have never put yourself forward to take the blame for others' evil actions. Nor have you thought martyrdom would raise you in the eyes of the world. No. You are humble and honest, and you've been cruelly mistreated. But don't worry, there is a way to clear your name for good with the Castle of Air."

"How can that be done? The King and Queen will never believe us."

"On the contrary, remember we were sent on this mission to find out what was going on with the brothers. Fola is the Keeper of the Records and told us to come here. We have the Kings' authorization and the court is behind us. Besides, we must get the birds back. I have a plan."

"Good. What is it? I'm so excited." Breata was jumping and clapping her hands in glee.

"Yevgeny and Yaroslav are in trouble. They have stolen the hawks and falcons and are having to feed them, which is expensive as tasty mice and voles are in short supply. King Atmos is very angry with them and plans an attack. Now your parents, who consorted with them, have also threatened them, for your father wants you back and has promised violence if you don't return home. We will go to the brothers and reveal who we truly are – emissaries of the Castle of Air, who have come in sorrow to enquire why the alliance has been broken. We will tell them that we know they have the birds and stress the importance of returning them and asking for forgiveness from the King, and to beg his indulgence. I am sure they will agree, since it will get them out of worse trouble."

"That's a great idea. Sensible. All we have to do is tell the truth. Do you think the court will give me protection from my father?"

"You are already protected, you know. The Air Goddess Eos promised that, and her safeguard is far more powerful than any other promise. Do not fear, you are Eos' chosen one, and be grateful. Now, let's go and talk to the brothers." I took her arm and we crossed to the smithy.

It goes without saying that the brothers, although surprised to see us without our disguises, were only too glad to agree to return the birds to avoid an attack by the Castle of Air, and to regain King Atmos' favor and protection against Breatas' father. We then discussed a means of forever silencing him, as it was felt by all concerned that he would never change his ways. We laid a plan, to be carried out as soon as possible.

Yaroslav, who was gentler with the birds then his tough little brother, took us over to the mews, where we found twenty pair of beautiful gyrfalcons, peregrines and hawks in their jesses. The mews was presided over by their faithful hawk, Suroh, who flew down to my hand. I recalled the advice that Suroh had given me, that saved Yaroslavs' life and liberated him from the crucifixion of the swords, as I stroked his glossy feathers.

Servants were called and placed decorated hoods on the birds, each man carrying two pair of falcons. The party mounted and rode off towards the Castle while we hurried back down the staircase and mounted our ostriches. We were easily able to outstrip the brothers, as they had to slow down with so many birds perched on them. We raced ahead to inform the King of their approach and Breata, the Page of Swords, had the honor to inform the Court of our plan. One and all, they agreed that it was the only thing to do, so they arose from their seats, mounted their ostriches and galloped out to the middle of the valley with us, surrounding the desolate area with the cottage inside. At the noise of our approach, the woman opened the door and began to shout at us, but she was soon silenced by the great numbers of people, and became afraid, darting back inside, where we heard a roar of anger and the sound of thrashing and moans, which became fainter and fainter.

Yevgeny and Yaroslav then rode up with their party and the King clapped his hands and smiled as he saw his beloved birds again. King Atmos summoned his valet, who strode to the door of the cottage and pounded on it, announcing that his Majesty desired audience of the owner. The door opened and Breatas' father stepped out, an attitude of defiance on his face. The valet closed the door behind him and went around to the back of the cottage quietly. The hoods were off five pairs of peregrine falcons and their jesses released simultaneously as they flew straight towards the man, striking him with their beaks and claws over and over again until he sank to the ground in a stupor, and even then, they did not stop. The birds left nothing of him but a tattered mass of flesh. He would never rise to trouble his daughter again.

It was hard for Breata to watch, but she took it as a Page should, and then her mother, who had been severely beaten by the dead man, was brought from the cottage and placed under guard. While this took place, we noticed the wind was rising, blowing the dust up into plumes around the building, and, as the gusts increased, the thatch began to give way and fly into the air, where it was scattered over the scorched earth, and the walls, dry as they were, crumbled into dust, and were no more. Tables, chairs, kettles and pans were caught up in a tornado that ripped across the valley, scattering for ever all trace of the evil dwelling. And over all was the voice of Eos, crying out vengeance with every gust of wind.

We returned to the Castle of Air, where Breata tended to her injured mother, who clung to her and begged forgiveness for her weakness, which the girl gave without a moments' thought. The mother was to remain at the Castle and help in the kitchens once she had recovered. Breata not only regained her position as Page of Swords, but was also honored by the gift of a tutor, Fola. She was willing to teach Breata all she needed to know to become the scholar she wanted to be, for all the royalty in the Castles knew of the Isle of the White Pyramid where the Aces ruled, and how revered was their knowledge of the Cosmos. I asked Fola if I could also join them at their studies and she agreed, but I was soon to discover that I had made a grave error in requesting this tutorial.

The first unpleasant thing that happened was that I was unable to keep up with the advanced studies that Breata, with her bright intelligence, quickly accomplished. I fell behind, and Fola lectured me on my lack of attention, the only result of her complaints being that I sank into a state of apathy and refused to attend the classes, but sat for hours by my punt, staring out into the Lagoon. I couldn't learn all that stuff – Latin, Greek and Pythagorean mathematics. The geometry especially stumped me. I found my brain going numb and did not even care to be sociable or join in the banquets and entertainments at the Castle.

The second blow was that I was called on by a vision of Eos, who informed me that I had not yet passed the test she set me, as I hadn't proved that martyrdom was not a product of egoism. It was a rough time. Fola treated me coldly and I spent many hours asleep in the punt to avoid seeing her.

One morning, when I was feeling particularly apathetic, I awoke to find a strange personage sitting in the boat with me. She was a tall, sad-looking middle-aged woman with half-closed eyes, who drooped over the thwart in melancholy fashion. At first I thought it might be a cousin of Globdinig, but the suicidal feelings of overwhelming depression were not there, rather it was a floating sensation, as if nothing really mattered anymore, neither ego demands, nor the struggle to suppress them. Her clothes were in a dreadful state and obviously hadn't been washed in weeks, and she smelt horrible. I couldn't help looking down at my own grubby tunic and unwashed feet.

"Who are you?" I mumbled half-heartedly. "Are you another one of those wretched puppets?"

She gazed vacantly into space. "Indeed, I am. Numbyling is my name. I'm not like Mithinkky. She is just plain stupid and ignorant. I am very intelligent. But I have no desire to learn. That is why I sit here with you.

You have abandoned your studies. I will stay with you until you shake off your apathy. It is caused by a challenge you can't face. That is egotistical, for you aren't humble. You are humiliated by your failures. You will not try to succeed……..." Here she trailed off and became silent, looking down at the floorboards of the boat.

I was glad she had stopped talking, for her staccato sentences were extremely upsetting. I felt angry Bazoom approach, but hastily pulled myself together. Numbyling was right – I had failed to keep up with the math, believing it to be too difficult. Sitting in the punt was not going to get me anywhere. I needed some sort of action to get me moving again, for my time at the Castle of Air was nowhere near finished and, what was worse, I had failed to pass the test set for me for the first time. What was I to do about that? I shook myself, at which Numbyling disappeared, and went back to the Castle, where I attempted to barge into the class that Fola was teaching.

That was a big mistake! Fola leapt up, fixing me with a glare, and coldly ordered me from the room while Breata shrank back in surprise. "How dare you come in here without my permission? You abandoned your studies. Before you can return, you must prove to me that you have shaken off that attitude of indifference. Now go!"

Leaving in a rage, I marched back to the punt and Bazoom jumped onto my shoulder, whispering in my ear. "She's a bitch! She knew you wanted to try again. That's why you went into the classroom. But who wants to work with a harridan like that!"

I listened to him, and I shouldn't have done, for I remembered in my anger the connection between Fola and my toad Oojo. He had belonged to her, hadn't he? I was the stranger who had agreed to take him. I looked sadly at Oojo's bag, hanging on the thwart of my punt, and to my surprise, there was something kicking about inside. It was bigger than Oojo had been, so I peeped in to see what was there.

My goodness! It was the toad. He had grown twice as big, and was almost the size of a football after his absence. Well, now he could go back to her, for all I cared. I tore open the bag that held the animal and told him where Fola was. Oojo grinned at me.

"You let me out at last! Now I don't have to put up with that daft cricket, Joana. I'm free!" With that, the toad gave a gigantic leap and hopped up the hill as fast as he could in the direction of the castle. Bazoom ground his teeth and cackled in a frenzied dance.

"That's right, Oojo. Go give it to her! Haunt that bitch forever. She hurt my friends' feelings and I want revenge."

By the time I had calmed down a little and Bazoom had gone again, I realized it was too late. What had I done? Fola had been cursed by Oojo before, and had only been absolved when I had taken the toad myself. But - I had been warned by my Guide not to keep the toad, but to take him immediately to the nearest zoo where he would be locked up safely. Instead, I had listened to Oojo's blandishments and promises of good behavior, and had kept him. He had spent some time on the Galapagos Islands, where the iguanas must have fed him well, and then mysteriously floated back to me. Now I was in real trouble. The huge, cursed toad was on his way back to Fola, who really didn't deserve it.

For a couple of hours, I hid in the bottom of the punt, but soon I heard the tramp of feet, and two soldiers appeared with their swords drawn. They dragged me out of the punt and marched me up to the Castle, where I was thrown into a dungeon beneath the courtyard, and left alone. I screamed and rattled the bars for hours, but finally sank back exhausted. The night passed, and no-one came to bring me food, and I heard the groans and smelt the filth emanating from the other wretched inmates beside me.

Two days went by in a haze. I was desperate for water, and during that time Numbyling sat beside me constantly. I sank into a doze and dreamed that my Guide had come to rescue me. When I awoke, someone pressed a cup of fresh water to my lips, and, looking up, I saw the familiar face of the old man above me, smiling grimly.

"You're in a mess because you lost your temper. Fola has gone crazy and been put into a straitjacket. They had to lock her up. But they can't get rid of the toad, who has attached himself to her throat. If they pull him off, she may die from loss of blood from the torn wound. They know where the animal came from and they will put you to the torture tomorrow if you don't remove the toad immediately. I warned you not to keep that toad – remember? But you disobeyed. You should have left Oojo at the zoo, as I told you. Now we must get you out of this situation as quickly as possible. I will bring food, and then we will go."

"How can you get me out of here?" I said frantically. "I'll do anything to get the toad back into his bag."

"You will see. Now, rest while I get food, and don't worry."

The old fellow straightened up and walked out of my cell, and yet the door never opened. He disappeared through the bars like a phantom and was gone. He soon returned with a plate of cold duck that I ate ravenously. When I had finished, he made a circle around us with a piece of chalk and took my hand. Muttering some words under his breath, I felt a sucking sensation and was lifted, as by a giant vacuum cleaner, through the roof of the dungeon and flew through the air, landing with my Guide near a grey, shimmering hut which was built on the outskirts of the Castle grounds. I felt I had been in the hut before as my Guide sat me down and wagged his finger at me.

"Now," said the old man sternly. "This is what you must do. First of all, get Joana the cricket out of her cage and take her up to the room where they are holding Fola. You will be dressed as a wandering minstrel – I will provide the disguise – and no-one will recognize you. You must take the toads' bag with you and work fast, as they will come to the prison for you early in the morning, and when they find you gone, there will be mayhem. Put Joana in at the keyhole of the room, and she should take with her this small fish hook attached to a thin line. Urge her to taunt Oojo. He hates her, so that should be easy. He will get mad and come after her, releasing Fola. Joana will back up towards the keyhole and squeeze through, and when the toad tries to follow her, she will catch him in the jaw with the hook. I will make the door open, and you can get hold of Oojo and stuff him back into the bag. We will then release Fola from her straitjacket and she will be overwhelmingly grateful for her rescue."

"Joana and I can do that." I announced. "I know you will help us. How can I make amends to Fola, though? She has gone mad."

"You have an entity close to you that can help. Numbyling is apathetic and indifferent to life in general. This attitude will calm Fola down, so your job will be to remain with Fola, keeping yourself in a detached state of mind so that she can feel Numbylings' influence. That will restore her sanity. Fortunately, she does not know that it was you who released the toad! She thinks he came out of the woods. She will take you back into her class because she is grateful for your help. You will say nothing – nothing, do you hear?"

The old man shook me by the shoulders. "This matter will be closed. However, you must study diligently with Fola and learn from her how to pass the test you were set, otherwise you can't move on to your adventure with the Knight of Swords, Typhona. Now, let us go upstairs and carry out our plan."

The old wise man and I carried out his plan, and all went smoothly. Oojo was taunted, took the bait, and was hooked and replaced in his bag, where he shook and croaked furiously for several hours. I stuffed the bag into my pocket to shut him up, put Joana back in her bag after awarding her with a tidbit, and we crept downstairs.

My Guide left me by the hut, reminding me not to get into trouble again if I could help it. I was so glad to get out of jail, I thanked him profusely.

"Don't thank me. Thank yourself. I am you, remember – your Higher Self, who knows what to do in these situations. Now, get back into your indifferent mood and evoke Numbyling, and then return to the Castle and offer to sit with Fola. You will be successful, although it will be hard to keep a detached attitude for several days. Finally, I must say goodbye until we meet again." With that, he and the hut dissolved into thin air, and I replaced the two antagonists' bags in the punt and retraced my steps to the Castle.

I humbly and deferentially knocked on Folas' apartment door. As I slipped into apathetic mode, Numbyling appeared beside me. A servant opened the door and showed us to Folas' bedroom, where she lay delirious amongst tossed and sweaty sheets. We sat down by the bed and Numbyling took her hand.

Immediately Folas' expression changed. The conflict that had been raging inside her seemed to subside, and her features became smooth and calm, as if in death. Numbyling spoke in bland tones, her voice dreary and uninspiring, and for some days continued in this manner, while Fola seemed to relax and sleep. All stimulation had been removed from her, and she rested in limbo between life and death, and yet her energy was slowly being restored.

It was hard for me to maintain my indifferent attitude in order to keep Numbyling active, but one day I realized that it was worth it, as Fola opened her eyes and gazed at me, and I saw the old brilliance of her glance and the challenge within it.

"Fola! You are restored to us." I leant forward and kissed her on the cheek, then helped her to rise from the bed. Since I was filled with excitement, Numbyling had disappeared, and Fola was unaware of her passing.

"I feel wonderful!" She smiled. "Are you here to start your studies again?"

"Yes, please. I would love to, if you will agree to teach me. I won't give up again. I am determined to learn the meaning behind Sacred Geometry. I'm ready to start whenever you wish."

"Then, let it be now." Fola moved to her desk and motioned me to sit at the table in front of a white board. "Let me explain the Cube of Space..."

Knight of Swords - Rules
Eight and Seven of Swords.

I studied diligently with Fola for some months at the Castle of Air, and learned much of Sacred Geometry, but still had not found the answer to the test question to "prove that martyrdom is not the result of egoism." I couldn't move on to my next test until I had solved this dilemma.

Finally, the Knight of Swords, Typhona, came to me and firmly told me that she wasn't willing to wait around any longer, but planned to go on her next adventure without me. I didn't want to be left behind, so I had to find the answer. All night I pondered, racking my brains, and in the middle of the night, I awoke to find my intellectual entity, Einerline, by my side.

"It was imperative for me to come," Einerline said. "Your brainwaves were so disturbed that they reached me in the library where I was deep in study. I can solve the test that you've been set, and the answer is not what you would think. I found the answer in several of the books that we stole from the Vatican – remember? Those books were ancient texts of paganism, hidden by the Father to stop them being read by the public, because of the knowledge they contained." Einerlines' transparent brain was whirring and clicking as he spoke.

"Oh, can you help me, then? What is the answer? Please, let me know, for Typhona is getting fed up, and I want to go on to my next test."

Einerline smiled faintly and raised his eyebrows. "The answer is, martyrdom is always the result of egoism, and can be no other way. Only the ego would want to destroy the body itself in order to gain favor and attention from others for a cause that it believed to be true. We know of many saints and other certain people who have made examples of themselves to promote their beliefs. That is ego speaking. What one person believes is not necessarily true for another. The test is a trick. You must go to Eos' dwelling and tell her what I have just said. She will then release you."

"Thank you, dear Einerline. That is very true, when one thinks carefully about it. I had no idea it was a trap. I have always felt that martyrs gave their lives for a cause greater than themselves. Now I understand that even the "cause" they embrace is a mere projection of their own ego." I put my hand on his shoulder. "By the way, I miss our conversations together. When will I see you again?"

"You are a silly idiot! I have been at your side every moment of your studies with Fola. But you were too busy concentrating to notice me. I am glad you went back to study, because now our talks will be even more interesting. I must go now, because Eos and Typhona are waiting for you."

With a fizzle like a damp light bulb, Einerline went out, and I jumped from my bed and left the Castle for the mountains, where I knew I would find Eos and inform her of the answer to my test.

I didn't have to go far. I was still within view of the Castle when I felt a rush of wind, and a soft voice spoke to me.

"I am Eos, goddess of the winds and the rational mind, and I can read your thoughts. The answer Einerline gave you was correct, for he is one of my beloved followers. The suit of Swords means intellect, you know, and Einerline is very clever. All the people at the Castle of Air are famous scholars and intellectuals. You will learn much from them, but you will not learn how to deal with your emotions. Those who inhabit the Castle of Water will teach you that, but those things are none of my affair. Go now, and the Knight of Swords will be waiting, for she knows you have passed the test."

Eos faded away and her cool breeze swept my brow as I turned and went back to the Castle, where I found Typhona, already mounted on a fine grey hunter with a hogged mane and neatly groomed tail.

"Ah, there you are at last." Typhona grinned. She was a tall, spindly pale woman with black cropped hair and a bright look in her dark eyes. Her mouth was narrow but had a lilting smile at the corners, and her golden armor and purple cape fitted her well.

"I was wondering how long it would take you to realize you had been tricked!"

"I know. Thank goodness for Einerline and his studies. He knows so much about theology and historical documentation of saints and martyrs." I looked at Typhona. "Why do you have a horse when everyone else at the court rides ostriches? And how can you be a Knight if you're a woman?"

"Women can be Knights too, you know. Pages are male and female, and become Squires. Everyone who lives around the Lagoon has equal opportunities. As for the horse, well, all Knights ride horses. The horse is part of their progress pattern and represents their desire to move forward – motivation, if you like. They would look pretty silly on an ostrich with all that armor, don't you think?"

Typhona patted a small pillion saddle behind her. "Jump up, now, for Eos is gathering a great storm out on the lagoon, and we must go to meet it. And, by the way, your next test is **"to learn to avoid becoming the victim of evil powers."**

That sounded scary, I thought, as I vaulted up behind her and we galloped off towards the Lagoon, followed by a huge, swooping albatross. We had only gone a few strides when I felt Typhonas' horse, Swirl, lift into the air, which was filled with racing clouds, and fly out over the surface of the Lagoon as it broke into white caps under us. We rode about fifty feet above the stormy water, bucking the gale as it rapidly grew stronger, the troughs steeper, and white crests began breaking roughly and frothing down the face of the waves. The wind continued to intensify, and I felt Swirl begin to turn in an anti-clockwise direction, whirling faster and faster as the gusts roared around us and we were thrust ever upwards, towards a blue break in the clouds far above us.

"Hang on there." Typhona yelled. "We're in the centre of a hurricane, and we'll soar up inside the eye wall to avoid the fiercest winds and escape out of the top of the storm. This is the way I must always travel, for I am the Knight of Air twice-born, once through the properties of the Sword, and once through the grace of the Sephira Hod, which rules the Air element. You once met members of the Hodian foundation when you took the rower Koorong, who had lost his oars, up to their group in the dunes to educate him. There are no emotions in Hod, but you will find them at the Castle of Water when you arrive there. For now, we are concerned to connect with Ganieda, who is facing a tough decision, and then rescuing Damalis, who is in serious danger from the Seven Shades."

"I saw what happened to Koorong." I responded in horror, remembering the ghastly event. "He exploded! It was awful. The doors blew open and he landed at my feet. He was dead, I'm sure."

Typhona laughed. "Well, he probably looked dead to you. The Hodians don't need peoples' bodies. They took his mind and that is the essence of him. Koorongs' knowledge of the Dreamland will be very important in their studies, for he is an Aborigine."

"Oh! So Koorong isn't dead, then? Only his body is discarded?"

"That's right. You will learn more and meet Koorong again when you reach the Sphere of Hod, which is in the Mystic SEA. But first you must complete several more tests here at the Lagoon."

As we rose higher through the center of the storm, I asked Typhona who the Seven Shades were. "They are the familiars of the Hoodwinker," replied the Knight seriously. "She controls them in an attempt to rule the lives of those who have become enmeshed with evil people, usually through ignorance or weakness. Damalis is one of these. She was anxious to please the Shades, and came under their influence. Now she struggles to break free. We will help her, but first we must go to find Ganieda, who also needs assistance."

By now we were so high up that I could look down and see the distant white caps of waves within the vast hurricane, as it roiled and swirled beneath us, a spiral of huge clouds that stretched for miles. I wondered if it was affecting the Castle of Air, and hoped that the Castle wouldn't be blown away as the cottage had.

"The wind - Typhona. Will it damage the Castle?"

Typhona smiled. "We are far from the Castle, further than you think. You didn't notice that we flew many, many miles away. The hurricane doesn't reach that shore, but if it did, the Castle wouldn't be affected – after all, it is the Castle of Air!"

I hadn't thought of that. We were now above the storm and traveling east at a furious pace. After a while, we saw below us an old crusader castle set on a promontory by a desert shore. This was the place I had met Hawkley P. Mann, and he had given me the barred feather, which proved so effective in summoning his allies, the nighthawks, when Trid and I were attacked by the nightjats. I looked down and could see activity in the castle courtyard below and the ominous glint of sun on metal.

At this moment, Typhona unexpectedly swung her horse Swirl into an incredibly tight turn, and I lost my balance and felt myself falling, the air rushing past me as the castle loomed up below.

The probability of sudden death threatened, and thoughts of saving myself rushed through my mind. I had to communicate with the people in the courtyard below, for, as the air rushed past me, I saw my salvation in a trapeze tied up on one of the battlements. If someone were to untie it, I could catch it in my descent and land safely. No sooner had this thought occurred, than a small figure below ran to the trapeze across the castle battlements and released it, and it swung towards me. Stretching out my arms, I was able to grab the bar, which stopped my fall with a violent jerk and swung me out fast across the courtyard. I could see below me a group of knights gathered in amazement, looking upwards and holding out a large blanket. As the trapeze slowed, I jumped from it and landed safely in the blanket, where they received me with great hospitality.

I thanked them and turned to speak to the woman who had released the trapeze.

"You're Ganieda, aren't you? You saved me, and I understand that you must be able to read my thoughts. Therefore, you are one of the few people here who can communicate fully, but your attempts at reaching an understanding are often cut short."

I expected her to reply, but instead she motioned to a small jackal beside her who wore an orange collar.

The jackal barked in a staccato voice "I Ganiedas' spokesperson… ally of Thoth, God of Intentional Thought. I speak for her. Ganieda cannot speak… Dumb… you right, she can read all thoughts… is one who always wish… communicate. You give her … advice last time. So found… different approach, she able to put… message to knights. But now things … more serious. We need your help again. She face condemnation. She insist on relaying… message she has received."

The jackal took me aside confidentially, and continued in gruff barks. "Ganieda is Court Seer here… has had vision. Knights wish to begin… great battle against infidel. Who occupy these lands. They ask to foresee outcome. There will be….terrible battle. She know they will lose…Thoth give me warning. If she tell truth, they imprison her. Go to war anyway. When they fail… she will be put to sword."

"That is a dreadful situation." I concurred. "How about informing the knights that Ganieda has been told to arbitrate a treaty with the infidel that will benefit both of them? Tell them that she has seen in visionary dreams a truce with their enemy, not another battle. The revelation is that of agreement after concessionary terms have been settled. How does that sound?"

"It's worth trying." The jackal wuffed uncertainly and ran his tongue around his narrow lips. "But Thoth tell me... bad experience... many other visionaries executed... divulging the truth. She afraid." The jackal sighed, casting a glance at Ganieda, whose face showed unease. "That often ... fate of those... who see further than most people."

"Those who have the gift of vision make that agreement." I nodded. "They know upon entry to this world that they face great opposition, but it is worth their effort."

I couldn't help thinking that a few days ago I had been told quite the opposite concerning the reasons for martyrdom, but I kept silent. It was a paradox. "Ganieda must have faith. Shall we ride into the camp of the infidel now?"

"Yes.... We make haste." The jackal moved close to Ganiedas' heel and we mounted two horses that stood nearby wearing octagonal saddlecloths. She rode without bit or reins, being a skilled horsewoman, and with the jackal running beside we set out across the desert towards the winking lights of distant camp fires, where the black tents of those we knew as infidels were pitched.

Arriving at their camp, we were graciously received. The jackal told the story and no-one seemed surprised that he could speak, for all knew the magic of the God Thoth. When all was done, their chief, the Shriek of Yaboo, spoke up.

"We will negotiate to conclude this truce. I recognize the Navigator, for whom I provided the dun mare to cross the desert to inspect my private vaults, where I lost seven camels in that disastrous cave-in. Welcome, to you, my friend."

I was pleased to see that the Shriek headed the desert army. I knew him to be an honorable man, and I couldn't imagine why there had to be war between his tribe and the knights. But he explained.

"These knights came into my lands many years ago, in search of loot and with the intention of conquering us and wiping out our religion." The Shriek said mournfully. "They wanted us to think like them, hold their beliefs. But their God is not our God, and their dogma is false to our truths. They must leave our land and return whence they came. In recompense for their retreat, we will award them many fast horses to improve the breeding stock in their land, and beautiful silk cloth for their women."

Discussing the fine points of this offer with the Shriek for some hours, we settled on a fair truce, as Ganieda and the jackal looked on. We then returned to the crusader castle with the terms of peace, hoping that we could persuade the knights to back off.

The situation at the castle was not encouraging. All the knights were already fully suited with their swords buckled on, and about to mount. I arranged a meeting in the great hall, where I put the terms that the Shriek of Yaboo had offered to them. There were many murmurings and muttered arguments among them.

"The Shriek is offering fine horses." Said a tall knight. "I need to improve my racing stock. I have the Byerley Turk and I need to cross him with the Godolphin Arabian to perfect my thoroughbreds. Let us accept his offer."

"No!" Came another voice. "I do not trust the Shriek of Yaboo. I have heard that he deliberately arranged for a camel caravan of valuable pottery to fall into his vaults. He is a swindler."

"I don't think we want war, do we?" The first speaker was begging for moderation. "Our forces are already depleted by yellow fever and we are underhorsed. Accepting this offer would allow us to save face."

"The King, and those who sent us and financed our crusade, would kill us if we returned with no prisoners or loot." A third knight spoke adamantly. "Besides, if we don't dispose of the Shriek and his minions, in a few years there will be millions of them, and they will attack us again. Kill them all now, before it is too late."

"Yea! Yea!" The crowd bawled. "The King is waiting impatiently for our return. We must bring gold, jewels and spices, not merely a few horses and womens' stuff." There was a rousing shout. "To arms, to arms, in the Kings' name."

After hearing this, their leader stood up and faced me angrily. "We do not agree to the terms that the Shriek of Yaboo has offered. He and his people are wicked infidels, and must be wiped from the face of the earth. We are determined to press on and fight this battle."

My heart sank and I glanced at Ganieda, whose face was white.

"There is nothing further we can do." I whispered telepathically. "Come, let us go to the castle battlements and conceal ourselves. We will be able to watch the outcome of the battle from there."

The unrepentant knights rode out and faced the Shrieks' army on the plains before the castle. Needless to say, the prophecy was fulfilled and they were slaughtered to a man, their armor cut off, horses taken and swords stolen with whoops of joy, as the weapons were of fine quality. Since not a single knight returned to the castle, they could not carry out their threat to Ganieda, and I brought her and the jackal to my punt. We were able to leave by sea the following day, after the Shriek had presented us with their finest silks as a gift to the Castle of Air.

We traveled northwest by boat for several days. It was hard going, as the snake that normally provided the pole for the punt couldn't touch the bottom of the sea, no matter how far he stretched himself. His disappointment showed on his face, and he drooped over the transom, whisking his rattle unhappily. Soon we noticed the punt begin to move ahead, and shortly after we were traveling at a merry clip, with the rattlesnake happy as a sandboy as he lashed his tail furiously and provided us with rotary power.

Gathering clouds began to worry me as we approached our next destination. The weather grew steadily worse and the seas began to build. Ganieda was seasick and the jackal looked very green himself. We ran out the bag with Oojo the toad in it as a sea anchor for'ard – just to punish him for his attack on Fola – and prepared to ride the storm out. But my time in the boat had run out, for with a swoosh the Knight of Swords suddenly appeared and took me up on her pillion, and we soared far up into the clouds which swirled around us, followed by a great albatross.

"Typhona! You've forgotten the others. Ganieda and her jackal, and my snake are still in the boat, and it may become swamped. What will happen to them?" I tried to look down, but the sea was blanketed by mist and I could see nothing.

"Don't worry about them." Typhona said soothingly. "We are in a different time warp. By now, they are safe on shore and looked after, for they are not needed as we go to help Damalis. In fact, it would be too risky for them to accompany us. We must go into the danger alone. Now, I must try to grasp my sword."

As the Knight leant down towards her weapon, which floated beside the horse, I noticed for the first time that she had no stirrups. At the same moment, a clattering noise sounded below us, as all Typhonas' leg armor detached itself, her greaves and boots dropped off, whirled away and were soon out of sight.

"What is happening to your armor? Typhona, your legs are exposed, and you have no stirrups." Anxiety showed in my voice. "Be careful. You might slip off Swirl and be injured. What's going on?"

"It was time for me to cast off some of my armor, which was becoming a burden. I do need help, though, because I can't quite reach my sword, which I will have to bear when I confront the Seven Shades. Please try to get it for me." Typhona sounded desperate. I leaned down to grasp the sword, but it remained just out of reach.

"I can't reach it." Again I tried, nearly falling off Swirl again, but the sword seemed to twitch itself just beyond my flailing hand. "We'll have to go on without it. Maybe we'll find another one handy."

"We are near the dwelling of the Shades now and you'll have to leave. Without my sword, I cannot fight them. You must go on alone."

"How – leave? I can't get off your horse up here."

"We must dump you again. I can't fight without my magical weapon – it would be useless. You're on your own now. Damalis is down there, bound to a stake somewhere in the village, a prisoner of the Shades. She disobeyed her Higher Self again, even though it warned her. Seek for the monk. Good luck."

With that, the Knight took Swirl into a tight turn and in spite of my attempts to hold on, I slid off his back. This time, it wasn't far to fall, and I landed safely in a bush, somewhat scratched and extremely angry. Beside me, Bazoom came out of the bush immediately. I was furious! That was a dirty trick! Typhona was a coward and I hated her. I shook my fist into the sky at the disappearing rear end of her horse.

Bazoom laughed. "Boy, you're really mad this time! You'll be extremely motivated to face the Seven Shades now."

I didn't thank him for his observations. I was alone and unarmed, and somewhere near me lurked the Shades. I felt the challenge ahead of me, but calmed down to think about a strategy. What did Typhona mean - seek for the monk, indeed! What was that supposed to signify? I wondered if there was a monastery nearby.

Climbing the cobbled streets of the small fishing village where I had landed, my steps took me firmly in a certain direction. I came to a green door with a grille in the center, and from inside I heard muffled groans. I knocked several times, but no-one came. Something inside me told me this was the correct door. The Seven Shades were inside, and they had Damalis prisoner, I was sure. I tried knocking again, seven times. Slow, shuffling steps approached the door and then paused. There was a loud sneeze and the sound of frantic scratching and grunts, then the grille opened and a horrifying masked face appeared.

"Who goes there? Friend or foe?" The mouth of the mask seemed to move as a sonorous voice rasped out. "What do you want?"

My mouth hung open and my throat was paralyzed. I couldn't speak. I couldn't take my eyes off the mask, which seemed to suck me towards it. I fought off the feeling, making an excuse.

"I'm so sorry – wrong house. Sorry to trouble you." I backed off in a cowardly fashion and quickly retraced my steps down to the harbor. A small rowing boat lay there, gently rocking, and seated with his back to me on the center thwart was a brown robed figure. I approached and tapped him on the shoulder, at which he turned. It was a monk! I stared at him, confused.

"Well, what are you waiting for?" He said gently. "Climb in and let me row you over to the monastery. You can't help Damalis yet. She will survive. You went to the right place – the Shades are there, and they have her. But we need a plan to get her back." The monk continued as he rowed. "There was a time when I thought she had shaken off their evil influence, but they lured her back with empty promises. Some people are very gullible, and she still has a lot to learn."

We reached a small rocky ledge where we moored the dinghy and began to climb some very steep steps up a narrow cleft in the rock, passing many small religious icons and paintings of stiff virgins with gold halos on each level. Finally we came out into a long, cold corridor which led into a dark armory, the walls being covered with swords of different shapes and sizes, and other weapons of many kinds. The monk led me up to a large mirror at the end of the room.

"Stand before me and gaze into the mirror," he directed. "You will see me over your shoulder on your left side. Now, do not turn around, whatever happens. Watch carefully, and you will understand what needs to be done to free Damalis."

I stared at my reflection in the mirror. I could see the monk clearly over my left shoulder, in fact, he appeared almost to be a part of my body. As I looked steadily, the monk seemed to shrink, becoming so small he could virtually be standing on my shoulder. How strange! He was standing there, right on my shoulder, and he whispered in my ear.

"Look backwards through the mirror, beyond me. Count the swords on the wall. One is missing – can you remember which one? It is the one with the emerald......"

Casting my mind back as my eyes roved over the reflection of the armory wall, I knew he was correct. There was an empty space. I focused on that spot. A vision – a memory – of a small jewel-encrusted sword came to me, and in the center of the hilt was a great green stone – the emerald that had rolled out of the dead Shades' hand... Immediately I saw again the figure of the stricken masked one as it lay on the floor of that filthy hovel, its' hand, in apparent death, revealing the missing emerald, which I had immediately picked up and given to Damalis.

I recalled the return of Damalis to the monastery, where she was to replace the emerald in its position on the sword. She had seemed so certain, so confident of herself, and the monk, who accompanied her, was well satisfied with her decision.

Now the sword was missing again. And Damalis was a prisoner. The Seven Shades had lured her back against her will and stolen the sword. What evil thoughts could do that, to change such a firm determination? Truly the world of the Swords, the world of reason, was irrational. Why, decisions could be made and changed in an instant! The rational world was illusive, after all. The tiny monk on my shoulder was smiling.

Smoothly I reported. "OK. I see that the sword with the emerald is missing again. Damalis has taken it back to the Shades, hasn't she? But how did they persuade her to alter her decision? Is she as weak as that?"

I was almost talking to myself, but the monk nodded.

"The Seven Shades wanted the sword badly. It is the weapon of Lucifer, who fell from grace. They put on a big carnival with a roller coaster, carousel, shooting booths and a contest for swordsmen. Damalis loves carnival and dressed up to go. She wanted to fight in the contest, for she is a good swordswoman, and she took her favorite sword – the one with the emerald. Of course, that was what the Shades were after. They ambushed her as she passed the booth of the bearded lady, stripped her armor, stole the sword, and bound her, dragging her off to their lair."

The monk paused, passing a tiny hand over his forehead. "I, who am her Higher Self, love her dearly. But I can only remind her quietly when she takes the wrong course, and try to protect her. I can do nothing to help her in the material world, for I am the mirrored one, who is seen and then not seen, throughout her life." The little monk sighed and lay down on my shoulder, then seemed to slip away into nothingness, and I was alone once more.

Sitting down on the floor, I cuddled my cloak around my body, for it was bitterly cold. The Gothic windows of the monastery had no glass in them, the wind swept through, and the freezing temperature was making me feel sleepy, so I lay down. Only a moment seemed to pass when I awoke again to a flutter of mighty wings and a loud croak. I sat up to look out of the window and there, perching unsteadily on the sill, was the huge albatross that had followed Typhona, the Knight.

"I caught you just in time," the bird said hoarsely. "You're suffering from hypothermia. You mustn't sleep now. Come here, and I will thaw you."

He opened his gigantic wings and I moved towards his downy breast, feeling his wings folding over me with their soft warmth as he spoke. "There, now. Relax and I will tell you of a plan. Are you ready to listen?"

"Mm..m, I'm much warmer now. Tell me what your plan is."

"I know something of the Seven Shades, for Typhona encounters them frequently. They are envious of birds, for they are part of the underworld, and cannot fly. When they appear to be flying, they are merely taking giant leaps into the air, which carries them away at amazing speed. They like to watch birds, and they'll stand for hours with their noses in the air, searching the sky with binoculars. Yes, they are great bird watchers. That's why we will put on an Air Show." The albatross looked satisfied.

"An Air Show? But planes haven't been invented yet. That's a dumb idea."

"Planes will come in their own good time. For now, we have birds. The crows can put on a mock battle by pretending to attack a passing eagle; the geese will do a low level formation flight; the kingfisher, somersaults; stormy petrels can play water polo amongst the waves and the heron give a demonstration of jabbing – the Shades would love that. I can think of many more attractions, too, for birds are extremely versatile. While the Shades are watching the show, you and I will enter their lair and rescue Damalis and the sword, if it is there. How does that sound to you?" The great bird looked down his beak at me with one eye.

"That's an excellent idea. We're going to need a lot of birds, though. Can we gather them together quickly?"

"Don't worry about that. The Knight will arrange everything. She knows all the birds, for she is the twice-born airy one. Your job will be to print some posters advertising the Air Show for next Saturday, and distribute them around the village. We will do the rest and assemble the birds. Now, go to sleep and I will rock you until the morning comes, when I must leave." The albatross settled himself more firmly on the sill and, as the bird gently rocked me, I felt my eyelids closing and dozed off.

The next morning I awoke, feeling wonderfully rested, and said goodbye to the albatross. I found the monastery printing press and soon had posters ready in a pile for distribution. Before I left in the rowing boat, I put on a wig and sunglasses, for I didn't want the Shades to recognize me in the village. The posters I put up in all the most public places, and soon people were gathering in excitement.

"An Air Show! We must come and see that. It's next Saturday. Let's bring a picnic."

"The birds are putting on a show! They haven't done that for a while and it should be fun. We must watch it."

By the following Saturday, dozens upon dozens of birds were

congregating around the village. Every tree, fence, chimney and roof was covered with different birds, while many diving birds and seagulls floated in the harbor, and pipits of every size ran along the beach. The albatross was in charge and the show was scheduled to begin at six in the morning.

This was much earlier than the Seven Shades normally got up – since they were most active at night – but the noise of twittering and crowing and the general clamor excited them, and soon the green door opened and they came scurrying out, holding their binoculars and searching the sky, each one carrying a brown bag lunch. I was watching, expecting only six figures, since I assumed one of them had died in our previous encounter. But there were – seven! How was that possible? I didn't have time to consider this as the albatross and I were hidden in a bush beside their lair, ready to break into the house.

The Shades had locked their door, but it was easy to jimmy it with the albatrosses' beak. We crept inside the filthy room and heard a faint groan coming from a corner cupboard, which we hurried to open. There we found Damalis bound to a small chair that had been forced into the cupboard, her arms and legs lashed to the sides. I picked up the chair with inhuman strength and carried it outside, where the bird quickly slashed through her bonds and we laid her, fainting, on his back. He ran up the street to gain momentum, taking off and circling around to show me that he had Damalis safely in his feathers and out of the way.

My job was to return inside to look for the missing sword. Damalis was too faint to tell me where it was. I could hear cheers coming from the crowd as the Air Show continued and I hoped that the Shades were still watching the fun. I searched every corner of their disgusting place, which hadn't been cleaned in years, with fleas jumping up onto my legs and cockroaches crawling everywhere, but I found no sign of the little sword.

What I did see, to my consternation, was a brown bag lunch sitting on the greasy table. One of the Shades must have forgotten its sandwiches, and was sure to come back. Now my time was limited indeed! There must be another room, another corner, where the missing weapon might be.

My search was interrupted by the sound of shuffling footsteps approaching in the cobbled street, and a rasping cough. It must be the Shade, come for its lunch. I ran to the door and bolted it, looking around frantically and racking my brains for another exit.

Of course! The Shades belonged in the underworld. There had to be a trapdoor in the floor somewhere leading down. I soon found it – a small door matching the grubby floorboards, with dirty fingerprints smeared around it, lay in a corner. I hastily opened it and looked down. The mouth of a tunnel was below, and I didn't know where it led. I had no choice but to go in, even though I risked being trapped below. I slid quickly over the edge of the opening and closed the trapdoor over my head, then bent down and began crawling along in pitch blackness, feeling my way. I could hear the door of the house rattling above and then swing open with a groan as the bolt came loose.

The tunnel turned left, then left again, and then a third time left. A fourth turn would bring me back to the original tunnel, but instead, it started to dip downwards at such a steep angle that I found myself sliding out of control down the muddy slope. I grabbed for a handhold on the slimy walls, but there was none. I was going down faster and faster, and I didn't know where it would end. Behind me I heard the faint slam of the trapdoor and heavy panting as a large body slithered down the tunnel behind me. I gave up trying to control my rapid descent and tried to relax in order to fall faster and keep ahead of my pursuer.

A gleam of light gradually entered the tunnel and I dropped out of it abruptly onto the baked earthen floor of an underground chamber. I felt some pain in my left ankle, and as I was struggling to stand up, I saw the Knight of Swords and the albatross in the shadows by the far wall standing silently and stiffly. They didn't acknowledge me, and I didn't have time to address them, as a loud thud behind me made me swing round quickly. A filthy masked shape lay on the ground under the tunnel for a moment, then quickly jumped up and took the form of a Shade, and in the folds of his garments I saw the glitter of a short sword.

The figure lunged towards me, pulling the glinting blade from its garments, and I twisted and jumped back to avoid the strike. I had no weapon, and glanced around me to see if anything was to hand. The Shade coughed horribly, spat, then attacked again, jabbing with the sword, in which a great emerald gleamed fitfully. My fur cloak swung around me as I avoided the blade, and I quickly unbuckled it from my shoulders and brandished it in front of me. The Shade jumped aside to get a better view. I crouched, wielding the cloak, and as he lunged forward, threw the heavy garment over his head, smothering him and wrestling him to the ground. Setting my knee on his right arm, I wrenched the sword from his hand, and held it up for the Knight Typhona to see.

Typhona leapt forward, followed by the albatross, and took the weapon from my hand with a whoop of joy. They soon produced a rope and the Shade was securely tied up and bundled onto Swirls' saddle.

At that moment, a small figure came out of the shadows, and I recognized Damalis, who ran to me with joy and embraced me.

"You have saved me again, and I am eternally grateful. Thank you, thank you. I know I shouldn't have listened to the Shades' alluring words. I'll be stronger now."

"I'm glad that you're all right." I responded. "You must listen to your Higher Self, the monk, and stay away from the evil ones in future. Now, we should get out of here – the other six Shades may return and look for their missing ally. Where is the entrance to this cavern?"

Typhona, leading Swirl, led the way in a gradual ascent up a maze of narrow tunnels in the rocks, and after climbing for a while, we emerged through a gap in the rocks above the town, onto a grassy hillside. The Air Show was still going on as a flock of geese flew high above us in a tight formation, somersaulting and twirling as the crowd below gasped. We were able to sneak quietly down to the dock with our smelly bundle and load the pinioned Shade onto the rowboat, where the monk waited, without anyone noticing. Damalis and I got into the boat, and we rowed smoothly out towards the monastery.

Silence enveloped the boat as the three of us each contemplated our own thoughts. I had a pressing need to ask the Knight a question, but she wasn't with us. The monk answered my reflections.

'Typhona will meet us at the monastery. You have a question to ask her. I can answer it for you, to save her embarrassment." The monk glanced at me as he rowed, and I nodded.

"You can't understand why Typhona didn't come forward to help you when you were attacked by the Shade, isn't that it? You see, Typhona couldn't grasp her sword yet, for she is not a fully-fledged Knight, but an initiate. She has great intellectual depth and is a fine scholar, and she is working on her ability to take on these challenges. But there is another more important reason for her withdrawal. Believe me, her heart was with you and she was rooting for you, but she also knew that you had to face the Shade alone to pass your test. That was "to learn to avoid becoming the victim of evil powers" wasn't it? Now, you may understand why Typhona did not help you." The monk smiled slightly as we drew up at the dock.

"Oh! I do understand now. Thank you for explaining that I had to take the test alone. Have I passed it now?" I was anxious to find out.

"Typhona will tell you the answer. She should have landed on the roof by now."

We carried the unconscious Shade along the dock and thrust him into a small prison that was cut out of the rock wall. "He can stay there for now and await the other six." The monk announced cheerfully. "However long that takes…"

We all climbed the narrow staircase to the monastery and continued up to the roof. There, the Knight and her albatross had just landed. "We'll take Damalis back to the Castle of Air with us. The King needs a lapidary, a stone-cutter, for he has many fine uncut precious stones. And the sword will go with her, and remain in the Castles' armory for safe keeping." Typhona looked deeply at me. "You have passed the test that was set for you. We'll celebrate at the Castle, and then you may continue on your next mission."

The monk remained at the monastery to guard the imprisoned Shade, while Typhona hoisted Damalis onto the albatrosses' downy back, and I jumped up on the pillion behind her. With a wild jerk, Swirl leapt into the air and we were off, the bird gliding beside us, skimming over the wild waves of the Lagoon, on our way back to the Castle of Air.

Queen of Swords - Rules Five and Three of Swords.

We arrived back at the Castle of Air exhausted after our flight. We were to present Damalis to King Atmos, who was busy at his desk in the large lecture hall preparing for a group of students. The King always kept the windows open, and a chill wind blew through the hall, setting the chandeliers tinkling and ruffling the gauze curtains around the stage.

I shivered as Typhona whispered to me. "King Atmos is a bit of a blue-stocking, you know, always absorbed in his books. He is one of our best philosophers, though. Absent minded, you understand. He has to work in a breezy atmosphere. Above all, don't disturb him suddenly, he will freak out and begin to spin around." The King was a lean and handsome man whose face was austere and crowned with black hair. His green rather dreamy eyes gazed at me vacantly. He was pale and obviously not an outdoor type.

"How should I approach him, then?" I murmured.

"Blow in his ear. When he becomes aware of your presence, then you can introduce Damalis to him and suggest the lapidary work."

I crept up to the King quietly and leant forward, directing my breath towards his left ear and blowing softly. He turned and gave me a brief look.

"Mi Lawd. May I introduce the Lady Damalis, who would be honored to serve in your employ as a stone cutter. For many years you have sought a skilled person to handle your jewels. She could be the one you are looking for." I stepped back and handed Damalis forward, and she curtsied.

"Ahhhh!" The King let out a gusty breath, which whistled past my ears. "That is true. I shall be happy to find a stone cutter. I have a large uncut emerald that I want to make into a diadem. Let me see, now, whoever it is – Dam – whatever - please consider yourself hired. Now I must continue with my lecture preparations. You'll find Queen Phere up on the mountain in her eyrie. I suggest you go up there and ask her about your next test."

We politely backed away, leaving Damalis in the lapidary room, where she set about organizing the cases of jewels. We descended to the courtyard, where a constant wind stirred the willow trees and ruffled the surface of the ducks' pond. The albatross swooped down and greeted us. Typhona was to escort me to the eyrie of the Queen, so I climbed onto Swirls' pillion and we set out across a windswept plain for the distant peaks at a gallop, which gave Swirl the momentum to rise into the air.

We then made swift progress to the foothills, where we decided to take a rest. I sat down on a boulder and looked out over the view of the Lagoon with the Castle of Air below me. In the distance, I could see the pivotal Isle with its great White Pyramid shimmering like a pearl in the center, and I wondered what went on there with the four Aces. Speculation about their secrets was useless, however, and my thoughts returned to the present.

"What is Queen Phere like?" I asked Typhona.

"Queen Phere is a tough customer and not very approachable. She specializes in overthrowing existing regimes, particularly if they are evil ones. She doesn't pay attention to people unless they have a serious cause. You'll need me, in any case, to talk to her, for she knows me well."

"H'mm. Then, how would we get her interest?" I wondered, as we remounted and continued our flight ever upwards towards the isolated peak of the mountain, which was shrouded in fog.

"Well, she has to give the next test to you. That will be enough to get her to pay attention, I think." Typhona smiled. "We can ask her advice. She likes to lecture people and everyone at the Castle is glad when she is in retreat at her eyrie, because they get some peace."

"Do the King and Queen have a family?" I asked. "Queen Soyla has ten children and is always busy in the Castle kitchens."

"No, they didn't have any children, and she doesn't interfere with the cooks. Instead, the King and Queen have built and financed many universities and institutes of learning near the Lagoon, and they have close relationships with some of their more outstanding students."

While I digested this information, we continued up the mountain, with Swirl swooping low over boulders and skimming thick underbrush. We emerged on a bare plateau split down the center by a narrow fissure. On the left side of this ravine Queen Phere sat coldly on a magnificent throne of black obsidian, which glittered with moisture from the surrounding fog. A large golden eagle perched behind her.

The Queen was beautiful in a cool fashion and of slim build. She had a serious face with black hair and blue eyes, a sculptured mouth and aquiline nose. She held in her left hand an egg and with her right arm pointed a sword towards a tall and distant peak, barely visible through the clouds. Phere barely glanced at us, but called out in a sibilant voice, like the rushing of a sudden gust of wind.

"Ssh, Arbil, Arbil, come hither, my pet."

Instantly, from the other side of the fissure, a small mongoose jumped over and landed at her side, then slid up into her lap and regarded us with bright inquiring eyes. Phere then turned to us and, without rising, formally acknowledged our presence by lowering her sword and raising her hand in a vague gesture.

Typhona addressed her. "Ma Dame, I am happy to present the Navigator, come to receive information regarding the next trial."

I genuflected briefly and assured the Queen. "I am honored to make your acquaintance, and look forward with eagerness to the test which you will set me."

"Behold the egg of the eagle, in which is hidden your potential." Queen Phere said in a gusty voice. "You must break through the shell which surrounds you, just as Typhona had to disperse with some of her psychological armor, as you recall. For I tell you each one of us is surrounded by an invisible egg, an aura, and within it we incubate untold possibilities. Your test is to "**crack the code behind the creed**" and you will find your adventures will be both intellectually fascinating and philosophically valuable."

Thanking the Queen, I asked her if she would be accompanying us.

"No, I'm afraid not. I don't enjoy traveling, because it interrupts my research. You will not need me. Besides, at this moment I am very much occupied in unseating an African tyrant, and I cannot leave, but I will send my mongoose Arbil with you. He will confront the foe that awaits you with courage." Phere stroked the little creature and then placed him in a feather pouch, which she hung over my shoulder. "Go now, for you still have many tasks before you and this one will be very difficult. I will be able to observe how you are doing from here, for I can oversee much of this land and I am extremely watchful."

The mongoose in his bag felt warm against my body, but all around us was bitter cold. "We will go, then, Ma Dame." I told the Queen. "When my test is complete, I hope to meet you again. Thank you for loaning Arbil to me. I'll take good care of him."

We rode back to the castle as swiftly as we had swept up the mountain. Parting from Typhona and thanking her, I asked her to keep Arbil for a short while until I needed him and then made my way down to the lagoon, where I expected to find my boat. To my surprise, the punt, which I hadn't seen since we abandoned the crusader castle with Ganieda and the jackal, was not in its place. Instead of the punt, the same little rowing boat that the monk had used to escape from the Seven Shades floated amongst the rushes, with my dwindling collection of waterproof bags hanging around the thwarts. I was very surprised. I had never been in a rowboat before and I didn't know how to use the oars, as I had previously used paddles. They looked much too long for the boat. My heart sank. This was completely different. I heard a small chuckle behind me and turned to see the old man, my Guide. So, he had turned up again.

"Where's my punt gone?" I was peeved. "What's happened to the rattlesnake? I really like him."

This exchange of boats had happened several times before on my river journey, and I always resented the moment when my Guide altered my vessel, as each time I had become used to the previous boat and didn't want to give it up. It was irritating to have to adapt myself to something new all the time. Now I couldn't use the snake as a pole and I would miss him. I would have to row, and that would be hard, because I wouldn't be able to see behind me.

"It was time," said the old man. "You need to be able to go faster. Don't worry about visibility, there is more than one way to row a boat. You will find out for yourself. The rattlesnake is on vacation, sunning himself in the Mojave Desert, but he will return in due course. You are to travel astrally to the shore of the hedonistic ones, and you will there learn about false creeds and their effects. This will be useful when you reach the Mystic SEA, where there are many paradoxical implications. Climb aboard and I'll push you off." He leant down and took hold of the stern.

"Wait!" I called. "Let me make sure I have two oars. Last time you let me go without a pole."

The old fellow laughed. "Yes, that's right. Well, you do have oars but they are more difficult to handle than a paddle. Just take your time learning, and have a safe trip."

He pushed the rowboat off and I sat in the center facing the stern and placed the oars in the rowlocks, then dug into the water. The boat shot forward and I fell off the seat and landed on my back in the bilges. I dropped one of the oars overboard and I had to maneuver the boat and lean over the side to retrieve it, nearly capsizing the unstable craft. Annoyed, I got up, again sat down, and spent the next two hours catching crabs with the oars, spinning around in circles, and ending up soaking wet before I finally got the rhythmic feeling of rowing. I still had to crane my neck to see behind me, though. I thought for a moment. How could I face forward so that I could see and be able to row? I finally assumed a standing position facing the bow and, pressing the oars forward, I managed to make good headway as long as it was not too rough.

I had been so busy correcting my oarsmanship that I hadn't noticed I was rowing close by a large town, fronted by expensive hotels, with a crowded, sunny beach on which topless girls were lying. I was about to turn in towards the beach when a voice hailed me from a large yacht anchored nearby.

"Hey! It's you, isn't it? I know I've met you before." A young and beautiful woman, dressed in black, was waving to me from the deck. "Come over here for a moment."

Turning the rowboat towards her, I immediately recognized the Princess Maali, whom I had rescued from a ledge in the Carpathians. So she had come to live the good life, which is what she always wanted, I thought. She tied up my little boat and invited me on board the yacht, which was 300 feet long and of Italian design, very beautiful and ornate. She showed me around, taking her time. There were staterooms with satin bed sheets, thickly carpeted saloons and bathrooms with gold fittings, a large tropical aquarium and three different speedboats.

It was soon clear, to my amazement, that Maali was the captain of this luxurious boat. Since the owner was in America for a few weeks, the yacht was lying off the French Riviera awaiting his return. We settled down for a drink in the wet bar. Over a White Russian, Maali told me her story. Of course, we were soon joined by my old entity Pompeybou, for he could never resist a drink and a yarn or two. The old phony looked in much better shape than I had last seen him, having rid himself of his ragged clothes, and Maali didn't seem to mind having an extra guest.

I recalled that I had left Maali in the care of a kindly matron, for she was pregnant by her fathers' architect and the king had banished her from his court. Her lover had disowned her, and instead, made advances to me under cover of the forest. She told us what had happened to her since we parted.

"My time came, and I was delivered of a fine son, who looked just like his father. The only problem was that he had two small bumps on his head, which started to grow. We tried surgery to remove them and swabbing them with tea tree oil, but they kept on getting bigger and bigger, and the only way we could hide them was under a top hat.

"Finally, I felt I had to leave and move away. I couldn't handle the embarrassment of taking him out in public. Just think - a baby in a top hat! Before I went away, I made a pilgrimage to the ledge where you found me. There I picked up the pearl necklace we had left and returned to the matrons' house, where I arranged it around the neck of my child as a keepsake.

"I left him – his name is Reficul – with the matron and got a job as cook on a large boat. It has been three years, and I soon found I wasn't cut out to serve people. After all, I had been a princess. Well, you won't guess, but this fellow here…" She indicated Pompeybou… "Showed up one day in a local bar and persuaded me to study for my skippers' license." Here Pompeybou stuck out his chest and grinned.

Maali continued. "The examination was hard, but I did pass. It helped to have the most recent electronic navigating aids. After that, I was in great demand in this area, for I have both looks and abilities. I caught the eye of Prince Amgodovich, a wealthy Russian exile who is one of the leading Christian preachers in America, and has made millions of dollars from his huge following. He invited me to skipper this yacht, and we got married a few weeks ago. I'm so happy."

Maali finished her interesting story. Her eyes were starry, and she had the air of a new and hopeful bride, yet a quiver of fear shot through me and I shivered involuntarily. What could be wrong? It was a real success story, wasn't it? Yet, I remembered Bardogians' words when he spoke about religious zealots. They all seemed to make lots of money. Now, Christ hadn't been very successful financially, had he? I looked forward with trepidation to meeting the Prince.

After a wonderful dinner together, serve by two very smart stewards dressed in feathered robes with ostrich head dresses, Pompeybou and I rowed ashore and spent the night carousing in a local bar with some rowdy yachtsmen. In the morning, I saw the American newspapers.The headlines read. "Russian Prince Amgodovich caught in fraud scandal. The Prince has been arrested in Miami for disseminating false doctrines. His word is no longer valid."

Well, what a strange kettle of fish! Apparently, the Prince had become fraudulently dogmatic during his sermons. A small boy in the crowd had called him on it, wanting proof of what he said. The boy, a child genius, was only three years old and wore a pearl necklace and a strange top hat, which he refused to take off in spite of requests from the press. It went on to say the boy was a visitor from the Caucasus and a descendant of an obscure Gnostic hierarchy.

I had no doubt that the Princess must have heard the news. I hastened to my boat and rowed quickly out towards the yacht. When I was half-way there, the noise of an anchor chain rattling in the winch confirmed the fact that the yacht was making a hurried departure. I shipped my oars and watched her steam away. What happened to Maali, I never learned, but I felt sure she would find many future opportunities to serve her self-aggrandizing purposes. As for her 3 year-old son Reficul, he sounded a most intriguing person, and I hoped that one day I would meet him.

After this digression, Pompeybou and I took ship on a freighter together and returned to the Lagoon with the rowboat safely lashed down on the deck. The ship called at a coastal port near the Lagoon, and the plan was to lower the rowboat and simply make our way by sea back to the Lagoon over the Bar. Strangely enough, the freighter was unable to lower the little boat. The davits became jammed, and each time they repaired them, they would stop again, and the cables would twist. There was no way to get the rowboat into the water of the Mystic SEA. It was very peculiar. The crew eventually arranged for a truck to come and take the rowboat to the Lagoon overland. When we arrived there, Pompeybou went on his way, with much backslapping from me. I was glad to see that he had recovered some of his former bravado, as he had suffered a humiliating blow during his previous travels in the Indian Ocean.

I had to row for a couple of days along the Lagoon to reach the Castle of Air again. Once there, I tied up the boat and made my way back to Typhonas' quarters. I took with me the pearl bracelet that Maali had given me on my river journey, thinking that it would just fit the little mongoose Arbil's neck. I held him and petted him fondly.

"Arbil, you're coming with me this time," I crooned, fingering the pearl bracelet as I put it around his neck.

Then something struck me forcibly. The bracelet must be identical to the pearl necklace that Maali had placed around the neck of her son Reficul! There was no way to mistake the tiny, unique pink pearls that formed the two pieces. There was evidently a strong connection between the two. Maybe in some future time the matched jewelry would be together again, and maybe that would happen when I and Reficul finally met.

My Guide, who had not been much in evidence so far, met me as I walked down to the shore. He looked serious.

"The Castle of Air demands much of its initiates. Swords is not only a difficult and cruel suit, but the rational mind is calculating and underhand, and relies greatly on the direction of your ego Belvedere, whom you met at the amethyst tower recently." The old fraud smiled. "You will be on your own - crossing to the plains below the mountain range in the south, but there you will be met by a manipulative entity you will not like, and who will try to benefit from you. Keep your wits about you, for you must succeed in the test set for you by Queen Phere."

"Haven't I met this entity before?" I inquired.

"No, not this one. There is also another that you have met, and he is dangerous. The mongoose Arbil will protect you from him. Now, go on your way." The old man pushed off the rowboat as I hung Arbil's feather bag from the thwart.

I rowed for many days over an expanse of ocean, eventually reaching a long inlet that led up to a river winding its way through flat and dusty plains. In the distance, several herds of cattle grazed, tended by vacqueros on horseback. I hid the dinghy in the reeds and headed for the foothills where the live oaks grew, which was the land of the warring Kings. As I walked, I formulated a plan to deal with them.

The old King Delsin, who had been gravely wounded by his younger upstart Jolon, must have recovered by now. I would go to the church where we had left him, and speak with the priest. I needed to have Delsin released, so that I could place him on his throne once more. Then I would feel a lot safer. I wanted Delsin, who represented my old habits, securely in my life, in order to move forward. I arrived at the church and stepped inside. A gnarled figure was plying a broom in the corner, sweeping out dead leaves. I asked him if I might speak to the priest, and as he raised his head to reply, I recognized King Delsin.

"Why! It's you, Delsin. What are you doing sweeping the floor?"

Delsin obviously knew me, for he rolled his eyes nervously.

"Hello. I remember you. You saved my life, when the young King Jolon would have run me through with his sword. I am much better now, and I'm happy here working as the janitor for this parish. The priest is a good man and nursed me back to health. My wounds are completely healed."

"Delsin! I need to put you back on my throne. You must return to rule, for there is no other I can trust. Please come with me, and we will have a new coronation." I took the broom from his hand and leaned it against the wall. "Come, now."

The gnarled old King protested. "I don't want my throne back. I'm satisfied to stay here. You can't bring back the past, even though I'm still alive. You must prepare for a fresh attitude in the future."

My heart sank. He was the only ruler I knew in my life. How could I handle the future without relying on the habits I had learned from him? I remained persuasive, taking him by the arm and moving towards the door, with a pleading gaze into his bleary and reddened eyes. He looked guilty, but reluctantly agreed to accompany me.

"The priest will not like it, but he is away tending to a dying man. I will come with you, for I too would be dead if you had not stayed the hand of the young King. But I confess I am disinclined to become the monarch that I was." Delsin sighed.

"Your reign will be crowned with success." I assured him with some trepidation. I didn't really believe what I said. "We'll go back to the foothills and crown you there."

Delsin and I began walking, and it wasn't long before I felt the footsteps of a third person walking beside me. I looked over my left shoulder, and there was a tall, thin woman with a cunning look on her long face. She pursed her narrow lips.

"I am Ploitinda, your manipulative self. You asked me to come with you and solve this problem by lying to Delsin about the success of his reign. Nevertheless, I can put him back on your throne, do not fear, and together we will devise a plan to do it."

The three of us walked uncomfortably for some hours until we reached the oak trees. Arbil was still in the feather bag over my shoulder, so I let him out for a run. Ploitinda took a jesters' costume out of her bag and put it on, then skipped over to Delsin, who was sitting plaintively on a rock, his head in his hands.

"Come along, come along, come, now," she sang in a low voice that had a sibilant ring to it. "I will dance for you, and we will tell some jokes. How do you like feet-a cheese?"

Delsin looked up and couldn't resist a little grin, but when she tried to crown him with a wreath of oak leaves, he pushed her away, got up, and began to run awkwardly towards a cave in the rocks some distance away. We followed him at a discreet distance, not wanting to upset him further.

The entrance to the cave was narrow, and as our eyes adjusted to the darkness within, a vile smell assailed our nostrils, and suddenly the flapping of hundreds of leathery wings filled the air as dozens of small vampire bats skittered past our heads. Meanwhile, I had kept an eye on Arbil, who was nosing around some rocks. Suddenly the little mongoose jumped back, arching his spine and hissing furiously. Out of a crack came a lithe, slinky reptile with a red frill around its neck that rose up and shuddered in the wind. To my horror, I recognized the basilisk that had controlled me during our wild ride from Merry Birdland. I thought he had gone for good, but here he was, back again!

Arbil backed away and feinted as the reptile moved forward threateningly towards me. He then ran in from the side and swiftly nipped the basilisk in the neck, withdrawing equally quickly. The reptile snarled, a terrible sound, and then it ran forward with its mouth agape and its intentions clear. I was the target, and Arbil merely a temporary obstacle in its path. In a flash, Arbil jumped in front of me and ran to one side, slashing again with his sharp teeth as his slower opponent turned, too late. A spurt of blood showed on the reptiles' left flank.

With a hissing growl, the basilisk leapt for my throat, clutching at my neck with its sharp claws. I started back, tearing at the horny thing and gasping for breath. I knew it was going for the jugular, so I kept my hand over the artery and tried to grab the body of the basilisk with my other hand as it flailed and scratched at my throat. The little devil never reached its objective by taking my life. The mongoose came at it from the rear in mid air, grasping it by the back of the neck, and they fell to the ground in a tight and furious ball of flying fur and scales. I watched the struggle, wringing my hands and silently cheering Arbil on as he fought one of my greatest enemies. Arbils' attack was fatal. The basilisk tried to strike, but its movements became weaker and weaker, and it sank down in a pool of blood, dying at my feet.

Ploitinda skipped over to me from the rock where Delsin sat, looking upset, her jesters' hat flopping over one eye. "That's a shame. We needed the basilisk to complete Delsins' coronation." She complained callously. "He wanted it to stay with him and share the throne."

"Well, it's too late now," I pointed out, dabbing at the wounds in my neck. "Arbil has killed it. That must have been why Queen Phere loaned him to me. I didn't think Delsin was allied with it, but now I'm wondering what the deal is."

Ploitindas' eyes narrowed. "Delsin is reluctant enough as it is. This is a setback. We must make promises to him. It doesn't matter whether they are kept, or not. The point is, to get the coronation over with before the young King Jolon puts in an appearance, for I can already hear the trumpets of his followers coming up from the south."

It was true, for on the air came a faint sally of trumpeting and the march of many feet. Ploitinda did a quick handstand and somersaulted back to the old King.

"Come, Sire. We have reached an agreement. A cruise on the yacht of the Princess Maali on the Cote d'Azur and invitations to all the most important events, including the Cannes Film Festival, will be yours. You will meet the cream of European society. You will have all that for a simple five-minute coronation."

Delsin looked pleased. "I have always dreamed of mixing in society. I never thought it would be possible, as I am a minor King. That would please me greatly." He got up.

"Please step up here and sit down. Never mind about the basilisk. I will arrange for another one to be sent from the zoo." Ploitinda indicated a large flat rock on which she had placed a bouquet of rue. Delsin sat down and I stepped forward with a crown of deadly nightshade. I was about to set it on my Kings' brow when the mongoose leapt up and bit me on my hand with his sharp teeth.

I stepped back, astonished. Why would Arbil turn on me? He was supposed to be my ally, wasn't he? Blood was flowing from the bite, so I had to find some leaves to wrap around my hand. This took several minutes. By the time I again picked up the crown, King Jolon and his cohorts were upon us and surrounded the rock on which Delsin sat.

Jolon glared angrily at me. "When are you going to learn? Last time, when I should have taken over the throne, you stayed my hand. Don't you understand, it is time for old King Delsin to be detached I will bring new thoughts and behavior to you in my reign. I insist on taking his place."

"I don't want Delsin to die." I was upset. "He has been with me for a long time, and I'm used to his ways. I don't want any changes now. Please go away." I could see Ploitinda sneaking deceitfully away out of the corner of my eye, like the coward she was.

"Get that woman!" King Jolon ordered. "Put her in chains, for her ways are immoral. She shall not show her face again."

He turned to me. "Do not be afraid, for a new beginning awaits you. You will not regret this change. You no longer need to manipulate people to get your way. We must silence Ploitinda for good. Allow me, now, to fight the last battle with King Delsin, and let it be ended. Do not stop me, for this battle is fought for your life and happiness."

Jolon unsheathed his sword and moved towards Delsin. "To arms! Today will mark the end of your reign, old King."

King Delsin pulled a rusty sword from its sheath and stood up. The battle was long, and for a while I felt sure that Delsin had the upper hand, but in the end a slanting blow from Jolon removed his head, which fell to the ground at my feet with a horrible thump. With great sadness, I walked over and shook Jolons' hand.

As my palm met his, an upswelling of unbelievable joy swept through me. I was free! I saw, with awful clarity, the outmoded reign of Delsin in my life that swept before my eyes. What a fool I had been! His point of view was rigid and negative, and I hadn't recognized it. The happiness I now felt was part of a new self-confidence, an integration of my personality and a centering I had never known possible. I would immediately crown Jolon so that he might stay with me forever. I had cracked the code behind the creed of false beliefs and habits and the reign of the basilisk was over.

I left my young King Jolon seated firmly on his new throne by the forest of oak trees. He would have many years ahead of him to reign. I now understood the meaning of the test "crack the code behind the creed." The creed must have been the habits of my old King Delsin, because the word "creed" meant an authoritative formula that one was obliged to believe in without further question. The "code," once cracked, led to new thoughts and ideas – the realization that life held far more under its surface than mere rote, and the idea of deciphering this code in the future flared briefly in my mind, accompanied by a strange longing.

With Arbil in his feather bag, I rowed swiftly and silently back from my trip to the Castle of Air. I knew that King Atmos would be giving me my next test, and I hoped that it wouldn't be too challenging intellectually. With much petting and a touch of sadness, I gave brave Arbil, the little mongoose who had saved my life, to the Page of Swords, Breata, who was on her way to see Queen Phere up the mountain, hoping that the Queen would be well satisfied with my answer.

King of Swords - Rules Four
and Two of Swords.

A light breeze fanned my face as I stood in the courtyard of the Castle, gazing at the battlements. Abruptly the wind increased, whipping at my tunic and sending strands of hair into my eyes. The gusts of wind grew stronger and stronger, and soon I was unable to stand against their force and I found myself lifted off my feet and whirled up to a tall tower that jutted out from the Castle battlements over the Lagoon. I hovered over the top of the tower and saw below me the King looking upwards, then, as the wind slowly calmed, I floated down and was soon standing beside him. King Atmos gazed at me coolly, motioning me to follow him down some steps into a small chamber at the top of the tower.

Many scientific instruments, including wind measuring gauges, screens with videos of active tornadoes, and a chart of the latest hurricanes filled the room. I sat down and Atmos spoke to me gravely.

"You are my special guest, for alone you are facing the tests of the four

Castles at the Lagoon. Before you leave the Castle of Air, your mission is to **purify recognition in order to allay suspicion.** You did well on your previous trial, by recognizing the need to change your ruling habits and discard them for new reasoning by getting rid of your old King. Here we always respect people who deliberate carefully, for the element of Swords symbolizes rational thought."

The King sounded breathless, and gasped as he took in great gulps of air, as if the very act of talking was too much for him. Then he continued.

"Excuse me. The air at this material level of existence is too polluted for me." He coughed politely. "You will remember the twin towns in different countries that you visited on your river trip. A bridge joins them across the river, yet the people in both towns were at war recently. Your friends Chance and Chad succeeded in negotiating an end to the conflict by supporting the poor people in the southern town with financial contributions. One would suppose that would be the end of it. Alas! In this world one solution always leads to another problem. We must fight this battle rationally on all fronts. Suspicion and distrust are at the root of all disagreements. It's hard for people to distinguish the real truth. You must return to the two towns, for a new and dangerous situation has now arisen. Your test will be there." King Atmos sighed heavily. "Breathe deeply and go with the wind."

The open window rattled, and a cold finger of air plucked me from the Kings' chamber and dropped me off at the shore by my rowboat. I knew where to go, and was soon on my way down the great river which divided the two countries.

Arriving at the house of Chances' sister Cheryl in the northern town, I was warmly welcomed, but felt an atmosphere of tension and despair amongst the family. I observed, in the streets of the town, many stalls that had been set up, displaying peppers, beans and fish tacos for sale, and on every corner stood groups of laborers, their hands thrust into their pockets, staring down the road. The town had become disheveled, plastic bags and torn paper chased across the street and garbage piled up in the gutters, while the carcass of a dead dog draped itself across the nearby curb. What had happened to the neat, prosperous town that I had left?

I asked the family about this problem.

Her brother Chance responded. "When you left us, we put into practice your suggestion of a truce, which was completed in the sanctuary of the blue goddess on the south bank of the river. Our town agreed to finance development amongst those who were in poverty to the south, to try and equalize our basic human rights." He paused and muttered to himself, then went on. "All went well at first. The people on the south side were delighted and grateful for our help and they began to prosper. Instead of cardboard shacks, they built small sturdy houses of concrete blocks, bought cell phones and televisions, and began crossing the river to buy luxuries over here."

Breaking in, I interjected. "They must have benefited from that!"

"You would have thought so, but the desire for more material goods fiendishly possessed them. They wanted cars, then big trucks, then plasma TV's and the Internet. They came pouring over the bridge, more and more of them, until they inundated our town with too many people seeking work. Now the town has gone into an economic decline and relations between the northerners and southerners are fraught with suspicion. I'm afraid that riots will break out soon." Chance looked grim as he raised his hands in desperation.

"Where is your brother Chad?" I asked him.

"Chad is here. He and his family moved over to this side of the river. When he left the south, many of his followers also came with him. He tried to send them back, but they felt they had every right to be here, since he was living here himself."

"That seems reasonable." I agreed. "I wonder why the southerners weren't satisfied with their improved living, though. Why did they think things were better over here?"

"Well, as I said, although their standard of living had improved a lot, they began to want more, and they became greedy. We are the Jones's, and they think they deserve everything that we can afford to buy."

"Why shouldn't they? Do the people here look down on them because they came from poverty?" I was puzzled. It made sense that if people were willing to work, then they should be able to spend their money on whatever they wanted.

Chance responded. "Well, they don't belong here. They aren't part of this country and they don't speak our language. The bridge is the division between us. People here have become angry and resentful at these invaders, and will not mix with them. I suppose, ideally, that Chad should return to the other town and make good there. Then he would set an example that people might follow. But that is not a practical solution at the moment."

I thought for a moment. "You reached a solution before. As King Atmos told me, every solution leads to a new problem. It's an endless succession of problems that have to be solved. The townsfolk here are dealing with lack of familiarity with the southerners, whom they do not trust and regard as intruders. Maybe if they were to intermingle more freely with them, they would realize that these people are human beings with needs exactly like theirs. How could we encourage that?"

"There has been a system in Europe and America for years which provides exchange students a place with the family of a different country. The students learn the customs of that country and make friends with their contemporaries." Chance was thinking deeply. "That could be tried here. Families in this town would exchange their teenage children with each other, and each child would spend six months with another family from the opposing faction."

"I think that is a good idea. Can we arrange a meeting in the sanctuary to discuss this possibility?"

"Let's do that. I'll go ahead and get hold of Chad, and we'll set it up." Chance was encouraged. "In the meantime, please stay with us and help to mediate at the meeting, if you would."

"I'd be happy to help." I said, as Cheryl led me into a large guest room. I spent the next few days enjoying my stay at their house and discussing ways of avoiding the explosive state of affairs they were facing.

A few days later, four leaders from each side of the river met in the sanctuary for talks. Chance and Chad were there, along with three deputies from each town.

Sad to say, I felt that the discussions were an unqualified failure. As an observer, I was frustrated with the attitude of the deputies, since each one was suspicious of the others' motives and stuck firmly to his own agenda, refusing to compromise.

When we broached the subject of family exchange, it was turned down without further debate, and a fist fight between the deputies erupted. Battling each other, their elbows, knees and knuckles punching, kicking and bruising, the combatants stumbled close to the pedestal on which the blue goddess stood. Seeing that it was wobbling on its base, I grabbed the little statue tightly in my hand, before it could be knocked down and broken. A massive tremor immediately shook the ground. I ran swiftly out of the sanctuary, dodging the rumbling stones that fell from the walls The sides of the building were collapsing, and from inside came screams and moans as the weight of falling stones crushed the combatants. I stopped for a moment and looked back, searching frantically for Chance and Chad, but could see them nowhere.

A swelling roar assailed my ears, and up the hill and over the bridge from both towns poured a vast crowd of angry people, shaking their fists and hastening towards the ruins of the sanctuary. I didn't hesitate, but ran for the river and dove into the current, which swept me underwater until I had covered some distance from the bank. When I surfaced for a breath of air, I could see the crowd surrounding the sanctuary, scrabbling in the broken building to rescue their leaders as they searched, sobbing and swearing vengeance on each other.

Swimming with one arm, I allowed the river to edge me gently towards shore as I held the statue of the goddess in the other hand. I reached my rowboat and climbed in, leaving the vessel to drift rapidly downriver with the current. Then, overcome with guilt and shame, I steered into a little inlet where the river had left a small sandy beach, and sat down on the ground, still holding the goddess. In my haste to rescue the statue, I had not thought about my friends in the sanctuary, and now I assumed they had been buried beneath the fallen building. The crowd, rushing up so suddenly, had scared me and I had instinctively fled to protect the statue. I opened my hand and looked at her. Had the sanctuary fallen because of her removal from the pedestal? If so, that made the situation worse, for that meant I had killed all the deputies by my action. I sank into depression and soon found Globdinig sitting down beside me with a squelch.

"Oh dear! I'm feeling your shame. You know, there's no cause for it. The fighting started before you took the statue, remember, and the goddess is much more important than your two friends Chance and Chad. They actually contributed to the problem in the town, as Chad left his town initially and then switched back, removing his family from the poor town. People there felt resentful. They had regarded him as a strong leader, and he chickened out on them."

Here she sniffed and mopped her eyes with a crocodile bandanna. "No. I wouldn't waste time worrying about them. If they made it, they made it, and if not, too bad. Such is life. You have the goddess. When I leave, which is after you cheer up, you might want to ask her whether you did the right thing."

"How can a little statue be more important then two people?" I disagreed, nevertheless perking up at her hint about the statue having the answer.

"That depends on the power of the goddess. However, I'm wasting my time here advising you, because I can now see that you aren't depressed anymore. So, goodbye, I'm not staying around to be insulted by your cheerfulness." Globdinig looked annoyed and soon slid back into a small cave at the end of the beach.

I didn't care about her disappearance, for she always aggravated me. I looked at the statue. The goddess was of pure blue lapis lazuli and held her hand in a gesture of forgiveness. The piece was about 9 inches tall and quite heavy. Should I replace it? That could not be, for the sanctuary was ruined now. I would have to take her with me. I was just about to put the statue in one of my pouches when a muffled croak sounded from Oojo's bag.

"Stop! Don't bring her! She is evil. She has usurped the rightful place of the risen hierophant, and taken over his philosophy. She claims to be the lawful heir to his throne." Oojo punched the side of his bag. "Get rid of her!"

"You're always so adamant, Oojo. Why can't you be calmer?" I admonished the toad. "How do you know anything about the goddess? You can't even see her unless I let you out of your bag."

"I know her because I met her in the Dark Ground. She is a fraud. You will see. But – go ahead and keep her for all I care. I'm just warning you." Oojo subsided with a disgusted croak.

Well, I didn't trust him. He had pulled the wool over my eyes before and was pretty tricky himself. Therefore, I put the blue statue in a pouch until I had time to reassess her status, and rowed down the swift river until I reached the great gulf, where I set a course for the north of the cultured lands.

After many days of rowing northwards across the great ocean, which was extremely rough, I navigated around the peninsula and turned south to make my way down the strait between the mainland and the island I was seeking. I struggled to dip my oars in the water between the wave troughs, spray blinding me. At last, I saw land arising from the misty sea and recognized the ruined building on the north end of the island that I had visited with Bardogian, my poetic entity. I pulled the boat into a tiny creek where a few small fishing boats lay, made fast the lines, then walked up the gravel road to a small café, where I ordered a large coffee and two cinnamon buns.

The waitress who served me looked familiar, and wore her hair in a curious upswept style topped off by a sticky-looking cinnamon bun. I wonder why she didn't eat the bun and be done with it, but maybe it was for reserve rations. As I sipped my coffee, I shaped a poem, absent mindedly, about the conflict in the two towns. It went like this:

"Why can they not agree? It seems simple to me.
"Who is at fault here? The answer is not clear.
"What can be done to help? I sense the black dog's yelp.
"When will the conflict cease? At the goddess' caprice?"

A chair scraped back, and I looked up to see Bardogian, as scruffy as ever, sitting down opposite me.

"That's a rotten poem. Can't you do better than that?" He scoffed, and went on. "Did you notice that Fontanova is working here as a waitress?"

So that was why I had recognized her. Fontanova was my creative self, and had to work because my journey meant that I was not able to complete any artwork to sell. Too busy, I thought regretfully. Anyway, it was extremely difficult to handle a big canvas in a rowboat.

"Did you get her the job? I know you often come to this island to get away from the cathedrals. There aren't any cathedrals here, are there?"

"That's right." Bardogian replied. "I get tired of waiting for the archbishop to return, and listening for his footsteps is very stressful. I'm here to conduct an experiment up at the northern building, and Fontanova will help me, for the ritual demands the presence of a man and a woman."

"What are you planning to do?" I asked, curious.

"It is a Tantric Mass. It is described as the spiritual joining of male and female energies. Fontanova and I love each other, and although we don't always agree, we want to be closer. You will be there too, to officiate and bless us. Now that you have arrived, we can start for the place straight away."

It was agreed and, taking a few provisions, we set out for the battered shack I had visited before, where the signs of an old Satanic ritual lay scattered on the dirt floor. We were passing a small cove when a woman ran up, waving her arms and shouting.

"Hey! Stop a minute. I met you last year on your river journey." She arrived, breathless, and continued after a moment. "My name is Nissa. I'm a mediator. I help people who are going through conflict. You came by and assisted me last year when I was trying to mediate between a divorced couple with three children. You suggested I withdrew from the mediation. That was the right thing to do, for the children told me they didn't want to see their father ever again, because he was always shouting at them."

"I remember you. What happened, then?"

"The husband left the country after his children repudiated him. He was very sad, but he was in denial about his part in the divorce. There was nothing I could do for he refused to change and wouldn't admit that his abusive attitude caused the conflict."

"Verbal abuse is just as bad as physical abuse." I agreed. "It strikes at a persons' psyche, and can be very destructive, for it brings down their self-confidence. Sometimes that's the best thing – separation with many miles between them, for the time being. Has anything been resolved since then?"

"Yes, they have finally settled their divorce, and he is permitted to spend time with the children. Everything is much calmer now, I'm glad to say."

"That's good. What are you doing now, Nissa?"

"I'm between jobs – any suggestions?"

"Why don't you come along with us? We're trying an experiment and I'm the observer. We might need you if the parties get confused."

"Well, I don't know what it is, but I'm up for it." Nissa fell into step alongside me as Bardogian and Fontanova dropped behind. They were holding hands and whispering together.

"Who are those two? They have a strange look about them, as if they weren't real." Nissa asked.

"Well, in a way they aren't. They are part of my personality and come along with me when I'm feeling poetic and creative. They have a relationship with each other, too. It's not easy for them or for me, because they argue inside me and each tries to push their agenda and get my attention. Now we're all going to try a Tantric Mass. We're going to the old shack at the north of the island. Do you know it?"

Nissa shivered a little. "Yes, I do. They used to celebrate the Black Mass there. That was before my time. It hasn't been used for years."

We bought some candles on our way and stole a fine looking rooster from a local farmyard. I also carried Oojo, the toad, in his little bag, in case his presence might be appropriate at the ceremony. We arrived at the shack after walking for several hours, and made camp inside with a small fire to cook supper. Night was falling, so we rolled up in our cloaks and lay down to sleep on the ground.

I had scarcely closed my eyes when a low moaning awakened me. The wind had risen, and the shack door was battering to-and-fro. A frisson went through me and I felt the hair rise on the back of my head. Was that a shape moving in the dark? I was sure something had brushed past me. I looked over to the others and saw the form of Nissa as she lay curled up, but there was no sign of the other two. Bardogian and Fontanova had disappeared, and I heard Oojo croaking in a strange rhythm as his bag shook violently with some unseen energy.

Of course! I had stopped thinking creatively when I went to sleep, so my entities couldn't stay around, since they were a part of my thoughts. I decided not to arouse them until morning, when we would commence the mass, and went back to sleep.

I was soon disturbed again. Something tapped me on the shoulder and I awoke. A voice hissed in my ear. "You must leave here immediately. Do not allow Bardogian and Fontanova to complete their operation. On no account bring them back, for you will put them in danger. Keep your thoughts focused on logical issues until you get clear of this place, and take Nissa with you."

Staring up at the speaker, I caught sight of the dim figure of the old man that I knew so well, my Guide. "What's wrong? It's just a game. I want to find out what they're going to do."

"They are not ready to amalgamate yet. It could be fatal to that part of you. You would lose all creative ability, for they might burn up during their efforts. The time is not yet ripe for their union. Believe me, and leave here without delay." The old man patted my shoulder, and left.

I went back to sleep, and in the morning I thought that the visit from the old man was a dream, and unimportant. I went ahead and lit seven black candles, fed the rooster, and created in my mind a stage setting with a canvas background and a painting/poetry reading that was set to music. Bardogian and Fontanova liked it very much, as soon as they reappeared, looking somewhat flushed and disheveled. I was keenly interested in the idea of the Mass, and I watched while Bardogian took the stage, reading some of his wonderful poetry while Fontanova got out her oil paints and brushes, and worked on an inspiring colored background in rhythm with the words and music.

The harmony, played by the invisible orchestra I had envisioned, wandered amongst some of my favorite tunes, lilting gently at first and gradually swelling to a crescendo that almost drowned out Bardogians words. I saw his face begin to change and take on a dark glow as he suddenly moved from his own poetry into the medieval poems of Carmina Burana, and the music followed suit, the singers shouting out the words in time with the poetry reading. The deafening noise, accompanied now by hysterical croaks from Oojo, went from operatic to frenetic, and Fontanova threw down her paintbrush and began to reel around the stage in a most lascivious dance, tearing off her clothes to reveal an immaculate bosom and astounding legs. Bardogians' face grew black, and he rushed towards her, shedding garments as he leapt into the air like a ballet dancer, his lithe, tight buttocks gleaming in the moonlight. Their bodies united in mid air and they fell to the floor, undulating without cease, and I turned away in confusion.

Fascinated by the scene unfolding in front of me, I had forgotten about Nissa, who was also watching the stage, her face now a mask of horror. She jumped to her feet and struck me on the back of my neck, nearly knocking me to the ground.

"Stop! Before it is too late. I feel the malice you have created. It is everywhere!" Nissa strode forward to the stage, which vanished as the music ceased, leaving the naked couple lying bemused on the ground, twigs in their hair and dirt smeared over their bodies. She ordered them to their feet and told them to get dressed, while she extinguished the candles and released the rooster from his shackles.

"You are under arrest, by order of the government! I am a police mediator, fifteen years in the force here, and this is intolerable."

As they shuffled on their clothes, she handcuffed them to each other and promptly led them outside the shack, where a police wagon drawn by two black horses waited with barred doors. She bundled Bardogian and Fontanova inside, along with the candles, the toad Oojo and the rooster, who cackled in protest as his tail feathers were torn out. Then Nissa leapt into the wagon and drove off at a furious pace into the night, I knew not where.

The sun rose, but I had not slept. My creative selves – my poet and my artist – were gone, arrested! I had to get them back. Life would be intolerable without their juicy participation. I set out on foot back to the town where the cafe was, hoping that it was all a bad dream, and that Fontanova would be there, serving cinnamon buns.

She was not waiting at my table when I sat down and ordered breakfast. I could not think of a poem, nor could I visualize the pencil sketches for a new painting. All was blank, and I began to sob bitterly. Globdinig sat down beside me.

"You are very miserable and I don't know why." My depressed, sad entity did not know of my creative entities. "Things have turned out badly for you. Do you think the goddess might be able to help?"

Ah, yes! The statue of the goddess was in one of my pouches! I rose without drinking my coffee and ran down to the rowboat, where I hurriedly brought out the blue goddess, turning the statue over and over in my hands as I sought an answer. I began rubbing the folds of her gown, and an opalescent blush slowly grew before my eyes. Soon the entire statue rippled with this strange glow, and I set it down on a rock. The lips of the goddess moved, and she spoke softly.

"You did wrong to take me from my sanctuary. You thought to save me, but instead the sanctuary collapsed without me. You are the only one responsible for the deaths of many of the deputies, for you must understand, although they were arguing, that is the method they use to reach agreement." The goddess paused. "Now, because of your interference, you have attracted harm to yourself, and Nissa has, in turn, interfered with your creative processes, as any authority will, alas!" She nodded sadly. "Now, listen carefully. You must return me to the place where the sanctuary was, as soon as possible. Beyond that, I cannot say what will happen. Do as I tell you, and have faith that you can undo the damage you have caused."

The little statues' fire grew dim, and she became silent. I replaced her in the pouch, launched my rowboat and dug the oars into the water, pulling as hard as I could to make speed back to the twin towns on the great river.

I arrived exhausted after a most strenuous trip, and pulled the dinghy up on the shore by the sanctuary ruins. I took the statue of the blue goddess in my hand and slowly walked up to the jumbled bricks of the building. The townspeople had evidently dug up all the bodies of those that were crushed and removed them. I wandered amongst the rubble and soon came across the pedestal where the statue previously stood. It was unbroken, so I raised it up and set it close to its original spot, clearing some bricks to make a space. I carefully placed the goddess on her pedestal and stood back, outside the ruins.

To my amazement, the bricks on the floor began rising up, one by one, and rebuilding the sanctuary. The door jambs went back into place, the roof supports flew to their niches and the tiles quickly rearranged themselves on the roof, even mending themselves where they had been broken. As soon as the building was complete, the sound of voices arguing inside could be heard, and I ran back and looked through the door. The sanctuary was filled with people, the deputies arguing fiercely amongst themselves as before. This time, I waited and listened as the disagreements gradually died down and people began nodding their heads and shaking hands. After a while, they all moved in unison out of the door, and divided into two columns, one heading towards the southern town, and the other across the bridge to the north.

A vision came to me of the ultimate settlement between the two towns, as peace reigned and their problems were resolved. Bardogian and Fontanova stood beside me and spoke as one, for their prison bonds had dissolved as the sanctuary rose again, and they had escaped Nissas' clutches.

"Arguments leading to war are often the only way to resolve differences." They spoke gravely. "Do not be afraid of confrontation, which often reveals the truth. That is why we two cannot cease from disagreeing, for conflict leads us on to further developments and knowledge. Those who give their lives in battle are truly heroes, for they die to advance the understanding of man and his progress towards spiritual growth."

Embracing my two entities, who dissolved into mist in my arms, I fell on my knees and thanked the goddess for her wise counseling. I would be careful not to interfere in other peoples' differences again, for recognition of their case would allay suspicion of their intentions.

Page of Cups - Rules Ten and Nine of Cups.

My small boat was waiting for me and, leaving the two towns on the river to sort out their own problems, I rowed swiftly back along the eastern shores of the Lagoon. I did not want to disturb King Atmos, so I pressed onwards, thinking about my adventures with the Court Cards of the Castle of Earth and the Castle of Air. I was wondering what tasks awaited me at the next Castle, when I saw slowly arise before me a shimmering, dripping flow of everlasting streams which descended into a glistening moat in delicate falls of silken lace. This must be the Castle of Water, although it remained hidden behind its curtain of secrets.

I approached the Castle, making out the soft lines of battlemented towers, under the edges of a structure that seemed to appear and disappear as the water flowed over the building into the surrounding moat. Reaching out from the walls that contained the moat were mud flats that slid into the shallow waters of the lagoon. I pulled into the basin of a large fountain on the edge of the lagoon, where I had no recourse but to row under the tumbling water. I suspected I was going to get very wet, but as I pulled into the falling spray I couldn't feel the water touching me at all, and soon I was on the other side, still dry, and mooring the boat by some slippery weed-covered steps.

Mounting the steps, I walked up to the edge of the moat next to the Castle wall, which was a flowing sheet of glassy water. There I saw a young and nubile woman, clad in the garments of a Page – a blue cape and breeches and an orange tunic, leaping up from a picnic that she had set on the mud flats near the Castle. She ran forward, gazing up at a large cloud that was passing, and, following her gaze, I saw the shape of a large Cup slowly forming in the cloud as she gestured towards it. Then the vision faded away and as she turned away sadly, shaking her head, I saw only a group of seals basking on the distant rocks.

I went towards the young girl, who smiled vaguely in greeting. She had the bluest eyes and sleek blonde hair in a bob that fell about her round and even features. She held out her hand.

"Oh! I just glimpsed the Cup I'm looking for, but the vision is gone again." She sighed, then held out her hand in greeting. "My name is Rivula. You've come to take a test here, haven't you?"

"That's true." I rejoined. "Do you know what the sentence is?"

"Yes. It is **"to take from the cup and give to the platter."** Does that make sense to you?"

I ruminated for a moment. "Well, I know that the Cup represents emotions, and also in some convictions it is the Grail. However, there are distinct alchemical ideas that insist the Platter is the Grail, not the Cup. This test seems to indicate that belief." I shrugged my shoulders hesitantly. "What do you think?"

Rivula put her head in her hand as she gazed down at several shells lying on the mud. "Let me see. One shell is long and pointed – that is the male shell. The other is big and rounded, more open. That must be the female element. The Cup is receptive, very feminine, and the Platter – well, it is also a receptacle, but open to influence from all sides. Wasn't John the Baptists' head presented on a platter?"

"Yes, Salome asked for his head and brought it before the King after he had been beheaded. If you take it literally, "be" – that means being, and "headed". That seems as if he existed in his head only and didn't need his body, doesn't it?"

"So, what you are saying is that the platter is the container of the head – that, in a sense, it cuts the head off from the body, right?" Rivula went on.

I nodded. "In that case, the Cup, which contains emotions, may need flattening like a plate, so that it can support the head. Emotions are like waves, they are like a rough sea in a gale sometimes. We have to look beyond those ups and downs, and learn to be more detached and temperate in our lives. If we smooth out our path, we are not so concerned with the body and its functions in the material world."

"Wonderful!" Rivula clapped her hands in glee. "You have already passed the trial that was set for you. I am amazed! You have taken from the Cup and given to the Platter. Now we can go on our adventures together and see what happens." She took my hand excitedly, and we ran together up to the Castle of Water, over the moat on a bridge of sighs and through a liquid portcullis that spouted water from above and both sides in a wavy diagonal pattern.

"Tell me about yourself." I begged her as we sat in the servants' quarters and ate some soused herring and rye bread. "What is your story?"

Rivula looked serious and her lip quivered. "Do you remember Omo and Yami, the couple who were fighting with each other in the Ten of Cups? They are my parents. For many years, they have had a drinking problem that you tried to solve while you were traveling on the river. For a while, they followed your advice, but it didn't last. Now they have drunk themselves into a state of total indolence. They have no vocation, no motivation and no hope for the future. I would dearly like to see them shaken out of their present state of apathy. Could we do something to help them?"

"That sounds like a plan. Where are they now?"

"They are lying in a mud bath not far from the Castle. I can take you there now if you like." Rivula rose from the table and washed her plate. I sensed her wipe a secret tear from her eyes.

'Let's go." I said as we left the servants' quarters and strolled out along the sludge towards an area where volumes of steam rose into the air. We found Omo and Yami up to their necks in a hot mud bath and in danger of sinking below the surface. As I leaned over them, inhaling the steam, it produced in me an astonishing lassitude, and before I could address them, I found myself removing my clothes and sinking into the warm mud beside them, heaving a sigh and relaxing completely. Rivula tried to arouse me, but to no avail. She began to sob and streams of tears ran down her pretty face as she begged me to pay attention to her.

I stretched out in a misty trance until I heard a loud snore beside me on the left, and there lay, covered in mud, a strange figure that rumbled and bubbled disgustingly. Its large and bloated body undulated beneath the mud as the face, encased in fat, rose up and down with heavy snorts. The puffy, pale lips oozed glistening bubbles of spit and it clasped two fat hands over its stomach, while the slit eyes gleamed venomously at me.

With an effort that seemed scarcely possible, I asked the creature who it was.

"I am your personal sloth bear...." It enunciated with slow precision. "My name is Spredaloth, and I am always with you when you become lazy and can't make the effort to do anything."

"I'm not like that." I protested. "I'm very invigorated most of the time. I can't understand what has happened to me!"

"A-hah! You inhaled the steam. The mud baths are like that. They can suck you in. That's what has happened to Omo and Yami. They lost their motivation and focus through the fumes of alcohol. They began to sit about and finally they were attracted to the mud. Once you get into this space, it's very hard to get out, it's comfortable, you understand." Spredaloth gave a snort. "I know I intend to stay here as long as you do. In fact, I can't leave without you as I am your lazy self."

"But I can't stay here! I have to leave. I only came down to try to get Omo and Yami back on their feet. Now I'm stuck. It's not fair."

Glancing up at the bank, I saw Rivula hunched over just beyond the cloud of steam, sobbing into a bandanna decorated with crocodiles that I recognized all too well. "Hey! Rivula! Stop crying and get me out of here. We'll never be able to help your parents if you don't get it together. And whatever you do, don't inhale any steam – cover your nose and mouth with that bandanna."

Rivula looked up and gulped slowly. "What can I do? You're trapped. I'm afraid if I come down I might slide in as well. I can't help you. Ohhhh!" She ended with a further burst of sniveling.

"Pull yourself together!" I ordered sharply. "It's sobriety we need here, not sobbing. You must go to the nearest oasis and find Tabansi the purple camel driver. He is sober now and will know what to do. Now, hurry."

"Where is the oasis? I can't find the oasis. Which way could it be?"

"It's in the direction of the Castle of Fire, of course. It's hot there and they all live in a desert where there are a few oasis, and it isn't that far from here if you take my boat and row over there." I was finding it an effort to give her directions. My whole body seemed to resist any sort of planning. "Will you do that for us?"

"All right, I will. I will go and find Tabansi, whoever he is." Rivula rose falteringly to her feet and disappeared towards the fountain to get the boat. I made a huge effort to rise from the mud, but could not, for my limbs were like wet dishrags. Knowing I would have to wait until she returned, I slumped back into the stupifying mire.

Struggling not to fall asleep in my torpor, it seemed hours before I heard, through a haze that seemed to deaden my brain, the sound of voices and the pad, pad of footsteps. With an effort, I turned around, the mud sucking at my body, and saw Rivula with Tabansi on the bank. And, oh! Joy. He was leading Lemig, my beloved camel, whom I had not seen since our adventure in the desert.

"We brought Lemig to help pull you out." Tabansi explained. He looked fit and well, and seemed very happy. Lemig licked him and I felt a pang of jealousy. "Here, take this rope. It's attached to his saddle. Hang on tight."

A rope landed in the mud beside me, but I couldn't summon up the energy to grab it. "It's no good. I'll have to get rid of Spredaloth first. She is holding me back." With an effort of will, I wrestled with the overpowering torpor that assailed me, seeking in my brain the motivational spark that had vanished. I shut my eyes, focusing deeply on the spot between my eyes. A dim glow soon appeared and gradually grew brighter, although it was not as brilliant as usual, and Spredaloth sank slowly beneath the mud. I was a little concerned about her welfare, but my priority was to save myself, so I reached out for the rope and got a grip on it. Tabansi made Lemig back up, and with a loud sucking noise, I was out of the mud and on the bank, gasping. Lemig put his head down and nuzzled my face, and I reached up to pet him and immediately felt better.

"Now we can pull Omo and Yami out," said Rivula as she hurried towards them. "Give me the rope, quick."

We struggled to pass the rope around each one and tie a bowline, as they were unable to help themselves, and one by one, we dragged them from the encasing sludge and laid them side by side on the bank. They were in terrible shape, thin and undernourished, their faces lined with exhaustion and apathy so that I barely recognized the vibrant couple I had met previously.

I bent over them as they opened their reddened eyes. "Do you remember me? You ferried me across the river when I lost my coracle, and saved me. Now it is my turn to help you. If you go back in the mud, you will never get out again. You were almost under the surface when we arrived. Rivula has been very upset, because she loves you both. Will you come with us to seek support?"

Omo groaned and passed his hand over his eyes, shaking off the mud. "I don't think we need help. We have always had each other, and that has been sufficient. It's true we've argued and fought, but what couple doesn't? I don't have a problem with alcohol – I can manage my life perfectly well and I don't need rehab, I tell you." Here he began to look increasingly annoyed. "Dammit! Why didn't you leave us where we were. Life was easy in the mud and I didn't have to think. Why don't you leave us alone?"

Yami looked doubtful. "My dear, maybe they're right. We haven't done much with our lives lately. Why don't we give it a try? You never did finish building that new raft you wanted, and our house was in quite a mess when we left it to come here. Besides, there is our daughter Rivula. We're setting her a bad example and she is obviously extremely upset about our drinking and slothfulness. Personally, I'm willing to go along with them. You can stay here if you want......" Her voice trailed off doubtfully, yet she had made her point.

The upshot was that they both decided to throw in their luck with us. Lemig could only carry two passengers, so we borrowed two large dolphins from the Castle Aquarium and set off on our journey up the river of remembrance to the source of all troubles. Lemig, led by Tabansi, loped along on the bank with Omo and Yami clinging perilously to his saddle while Rivula and I rode the dolphins, which were part of Queen Fluvias' retinue. A drenching rain that seemed never to stop soaked us through, yet we pressed on, sleeping at night close to Lemigs' steaming flank under the leaves of a tropical palm tree.

After two days' travel, I began to notice Lemigs' increasing exhaustion, brought on by the humid environment we were traveling through, caused by the elements of the two Castles of Water and Fire intermingling. The camel was familiar with hot, dry desert weather, and I was worried. Soon, because of the constant soaking, I too became depressed, and my sad entity Globdinig reappeared and was forced to accompany us. I could hear her complaining and stomping along behind Lemig, snuffling into her bandanna, which she had taken back from Rivula. I thought I had rid myself of her before now, and, in fact, she had nearly drowned, but for some reason she seemed to survive repeated dunkings. It must be her phlegmatic attitude, I decided.

As we wound our way up the river, it gradually became smaller and shallower, and the time came when we had to say goodbye to the two dolphins, who returned to Queen Fluvia with regret. Lemig had also developed severe bronchitis, and after a discussion with Tabansi, we felt it was imperative for the camel to return to the desert around the Castle of Fire, before his cough grew worse and turned to pneumonia. Tabansi told me in private that he had several long conversations with Omo and Yami on the trip, telling them about his own addiction and how he overcame it, which he felt encouraged them to continue on their way even though he had to leave to care for Lemig.

The five of us struggled on without them, Omo making slow progress by himself while Rivula supported her mother Yami as she hobbled along beside Globdinig, who refused to leave as she was enjoying the heavy rainfall. I hated the soaking we were getting but we had to squish on for another three days before we reached the source of the river, which bubbled forth from a spring under a rocky spur and formed a delightful pool. Far back under the overhanging rocks we could make out the blue shimmering form of a cave that disappeared underwater, and in the pool at the entrance to the cavern a beautiful Cup floated that I fished at with a willow stick, but failed to capture. Amidst dreadful complaining, we then made a damp bivouac for the night slightly above the pool's edge.

It was still dark when I woke suddenly to the sound of rushing water to find that the level of the pool had risen and it was overflowing, with huge bubbles bursting from below the surface as if someone was exhaling deep breaths underwater. I sat nervously watching the water, which gradually formed itself into a slim, beautiful body that rose up before me, fixing me with a liquid gaze. I was transfixed by the sight and even more surprised when the opalescent figure spoke.

"I am Anahita, Goddess of Spring Waters. It is time to get rid of Globdinig now, for there has been enough misery over the last few days. You must banish her until you meet her on your journey in the Islands of the Mystic SEA. It is only then that she can be of further use as a crew member, because her naturally cautious and gloomy character will help you to avoid the rough weather which you would take on unthinkingly. You are inclined to be rash, you know." Anahita laughed softly. "Here, take this Cup…" At that instant the shining Cup seemed to float towards me of its own volition as she continued. "…and squeeze Globdinig into it. You must fit her whole body into the Cup and she must not slop over the edges, otherwise the spell will not work. At the same time, you must take on the Optimistic Attitude."

"What is the Optimistic Attitude? How can I fit that huge lump of jelly into this little Cup?" I said rudely as I questioned the Goddess in perplexity.

"The Optimistic Attitude is as follows. Instead of considering your Cup to be half empty, remember it is half full. Every event in your life has a positive side to it – for example, you might be delayed during a journey that you want to complete as soon as you can. Supposing that delay means that you will not be on a particular path when a boulder crashes down. If the delay had not happened, you would surely have been crushed by that boulder. Instead, you will find the boulder already on the path, and you will be able to walk around it. However, you will not realize that your delay has saved you from instant death. You will not even consider it! Such are the workings of the Universe. Do not try to wonder how many times death has averted itself from you, but only be always optimistic and positive about your future. Now, if you remember while you are pushing Globdinig into the Cup that it is always, paradoxically, at least half empty, you'll be able to fit her whole body in and fill it. Try it and see what happens."

This idea made me feel even more miserable, and I glanced sideways at Globdinig, who didn't appear to have heard the Goddess' instructions. Maybe she wasn't aware of her and only I could see her, I thought, as I sidled towards my sad counterpart cautiously. Retaining my gloomy mood, I took her by one of her body folds and motioned towards the Cup, which I now held in my left hand.

"Lean forward, and drink from this Cup. The water is good up here." Globdinig shuffled slowly up and bent her vast head to drink from the rim. As she did so, I forcefully changed my mood to one of boundless optimism, and the vessel immediately began to suck in her head with a horrible gurgling noise. Since I had changed my mood, she could no longer stay, and the Cup slowly swallowed her like a giant python engorging its prey. With a final squeak like a flat balloon, she was gone. I felt a little guilty but saw that Anahita, who had been watching, was giggling.

"That Cup is so useful. I keep it for all the people that annoy me by their emotional attitude, and after I have sucked them in, I empty them into the bottom of the cave, where they must stay underwater until I decide to release them. Now, to business. You have brought Omo and Yami here for help. They can be rehabilitated, but one person must offer themselves as a hostage during the time they are undergoing treatment, to remind them not to escape. After all, everyone who drinks too much holds their friends and family hostage, don't they?"

I had to agree. "So - the hostage. I would be willing to volunteer for that. What does it involve?"

"Yes, I thought you would step forward and offer, but because these people are Rivulas' parents, they will be more likely to get through the drying-out process if they know that she is the hostage. You are a comparative stranger and don't mean anything to them, you see."

"So Rivula must be the hostage? What shall I do to help?"

At this point Rivula burst into tears and sobbed convulsively. "I don't want to be their hostage. They have treated me badly and abused me all the time when they got into their drunken rages. I don't owe them a thing!"

"You're wrong, of course," pointed out Anahita. "You chose them as your parents, and therefore you are responsible for them. In return for giving you life, you must now help them get their lives back together. Dry your tears, now, for your position as hostage will be far more pleasant than the task of drying them out, you will see."

Rivula threw back her head and sniffed bleakly. "What shall I do, then?"

"Come with me now, and we will go down to my temple under the waters." The Goddess held out her hand as she hovered over the pool. "Do not be afraid – it's beautiful down there."

"I'll drown!" Burst out Rivula. "I don't want to go under the water. Riding the dolphin was scary enough, and that was on the surface. I can't do it."

The voice of the hovering Goddess became stern. "I am sorry, but you made this choice before you were born. There is no way out, for this is your Destiny. Come now." With that, she suddenly swept across the pool in an explosion of fine mist, and Rivula found herself lifted high in her arms in a gush of spray. In a moment, they had sunk beneath the surface, leaving a trail of glistening bubbles, which spread across the pool in ever-widening circles.

I was very concerned, for I had grown to like Rivula, although she was rather a cry-baby. I sat down on the edge of the pool and waited. For an hour, there was no movement, and then the surface of the pool bubbled as before and the Goddess reappeared. She signaled to Omo and Yami, who had been sitting silently watching the events from their bivouac. They slowly rose to their feet and ambled towards us.

Anahita spoke to them in a serious tone. "You are here to be rehabilitated, and that means drying out. In order to dehydrate you completely, you must be flayed and your skins hung up in the sun, if it ever stops raining, and a fire lit underneath. Your skinless bodies will be preserved in a vat of olive oil, which will keep them supple, and when your skins are scraped free of toxins, you may put them on again."

Her words were greeted with a shriek of horror from the couple, as they shrank back and turned to run. I was dismayed and revolted. Surely, this was not necessary? I glared at Anahita, and she threw back her head and laughed at them.

"You agreed to the process and you have come all the way here to clean up your act. Trust in me and do not be afraid, like your daughter was. She has agreed to be hostage, and understands now that there is nothing to fear. It is simply a cleansing process. Get your things in order, for we start early tomorrow morning. And don't try to escape – for if you look around, you will see that you are now isolated on an island in a lake infested with crocodiles."

It was true. As the Goddess spoke, the ground on which we stood separated itself from the bank and the waters of the pool flooded around us, expanding as far as we could see in all directions. The surrounding land had disappeared, and the only dry ground was now the small island with the cave underneath the rock. On the surface of this vast lake, I saw the snouts of several crocodiles as they pushed through the water towards us, leaving a v-shaped ripple behind them. We were trapped!

The following morning Anahita emerged from the water carrying a Cup that held a pink liquid. She gave it to Omo and Yami and told them to drink two deep gulps each.

"This is a specially brewed liquor that is made to calm your nerves. Taste it, you will find it is delicious."

They each took two swallows from the Cup and then she handed it to me. "The rest is for you, to give you courage."

I took the Cup and drank. The liquor had a flavor of citrus to it, and yet it seemed smooth and mellow. I felt strangely calm. It must have some kind of drug in it, for Omo and Yami were already lying stretched out on the ground and quietly laughing together, while I felt myself lurching towards them. I forced myself to think clearly, so that I could hear the Goddess' instructions.

They were quite relaxed and not at all fearful as we tied them down to pegs in the ground and she brought out a short curved knife which glistened as she swung it through the air, then knelt down and drew it over them evenly, first their arms and legs, then their torsos, and finally their heads. The flaying knife did not seem to touch them, and I heard no cry as they lay still, yet when the Goddess rose, in her hand were the two skins, complete and undamaged. She handed them to me, and as I took them they seemed heavy, and sodden with a vile smell of alcohol.

"Take them to the lake and rinse them." She instructed. "Now, as soon as you return, you can fetch those two large jars leaning against the rock and fill them with olive oil from my underground supply." She pointed to a large pump that I had not noticed before with a hose attached to it.

I was glad to dump their filthy skins in the water and weigh them down with some rocks to soak. The crocodiles began to swim in, so I hastened with my task. I then rolled the jars over to the two flayed bodies and pumped them three-quarters full of oil. We gently lifted the bodies, first Yami, and then Omo, who were almost unrecognizable without their skins, and slid them into the jars, where they fitted very comfortably with only their noses poking out. At this stage I could see they were completely out of it, which was probably a good thing, as we set the jars upright.

"There," announced Anahita with satisfaction. "The oil will leach the remaining alcohol from their bodies and they will detoxify nicely."

"How long will they have to stay in the jars?" I asked her.

"It depends how long the skins take to be purified. Some people are not heavy drinkers, so their skins are easier to detoxify. But these two – they've been at the bottle for years and the process will take longer. Now, take this soap and deck brush, and scrub the skins and rinse them until they smell better. Then we can peg them out and begin scraping the filth off the inside and drying them out."

I went down to the shore of the lake and scrubbed at the disgusting, floppy skins for several hours, exhausting myself and nervously watching the waiting crocodiles. I wondered what Rivula was doing and hoped her task wasn't as hard as mine. Finally the skins looked and smelt better, and we hung them over the rock to air for the night.

The following day there was a drying frame set up. We laid the skins out on the ground and scraped the insides thoroughly with a sharp flint knife, then rinsed them again and lashed them to the drying frame. From time to time I went over to the jars to see if Omo and Yami had woken up. Fortunately the liquor had done its work well and they remained asleep, their nostrils bubbling gently at the surface of the oil.

Several days would pass before the lustrous skins were dry enough to insert the bodies of Omo and Yami, and so, to pass the time, Anahita clasped me to her damp breast and descended into the pool with me. As we sank below the limpid surface, I automatically held my breath for as long as I could, but when we slipped down deeper and deeper under the rock, I remember having to exhale my remaining air. To my surprise and relief, I found I was able to inhale underwater, and she set me down on a white sandy floor and led me forward into the cave, holding me by the hand.

We walked, or rather floated, along a narrow passage lined with beautiful rock formations - draperies, stalactites, soda straws, columns, they were all there- and amongst these marvels danced thousands of tiny bubbles, forming a multicolored pattern that was quite entrancing. A short while later the passage opened up into a stunning underwater palace, displaying hundreds of different and fascinating rock formations, in the center of which stood a throne with a smaller seat beside it, on which my friend Rivula was sitting.

"Oh! I'm so glad you're here." Rivula gasped and held out her hand as Anahita handed me over to her. I let go of one hand and grasped the other to control my tendency to float away, as I was not used to being submerged. Rivula laughed prettily. "You'll soon get used to being underwater. It's like being weightless and so free! You can move in any direction without gravity. Here, try it."

She rose from her seat and we floated off together, holding hands at first until I got the idea of using my arms to control lateral movements. An exploration of the cavern palace was in order. Rivula explained that the cave had once been above water level until a massive earthquake had caused it to sink. At the back of the large cavern a narrow crack appeared in the rock wall, and Rivula pulled me away hastily.

"You may not go in there." She warned. "The Goddess told me there is another subterranean cave where those she catches are kept until they understand certain mysteries. It is like a tough school for ignorant people, I think. I'm glad I didn't have to go in there too. In fact, I've been treated very well as a hostage. The fish banquets are very tasty and all kinds of sea food is available here. There are also water melons, water chestnuts and other watery dishes. I'm not sure why I've deserved such courtesy....."

Here we heard the liquid sounds of the Goddess' voice. "Rivula deserves the best. She is a Page at the Court of the King, at the Castle of Water. She will soon be elevated to a Squire, and will serve the Knight at the Castle. This is her final test. I expect her to pass and then I will gladly recommend her to the Court."

Rivula clapped her hands in delight and burst into tears, but because she was underwater, this had no effect, and no bandanna was available to mop them up. That reminded me of Globdinig, and I wondered if she was also down in the other cave, but I was determined not to be depressed any longer. I had made that decision for good, and so I switched off those thoughts and merrily agreed to a game of underwater polo with Rivula.

Several days passed happily, and then the morning came when all three of us rose up to the surface of the pool once more and tested the skins to see if they were dry. Anahita announced that the process of fitting the skins on Omo and Yami could commence, so we went over to the jars of oil.

"The oil in the jars is now contaminated, and must be thrown away. I have a special storage area for it over here." The Goddess walked over to a crevice in the rock. "Pour it down here. In a million years it will be useful, for people will pump it up and use it for abominable purposes. I know not of that era, for it is far into the future, and I dread the outcome when the toxins in the oil are released. It will be very unfortunate for humanity."

We dragged the heavy jars to the crevice and tipped them over, holding onto Omo and Yami while the oil drained away. We then gently carried the two bodies to a small altar, where the Goddess laid them side by side and drew a circle around them, which she blessed with strange vibrating words. We remained outside the circle as she carefully placed the dry skins correctly over the bodies and then suddenly struck the ground with a willow wand. A fountain of pure sparkling liquid surged up between the two and sprinkled them with healing water, and I could see their skins carefully folding themselves around their bodies. When the skins were in place, Omo and Yami sat up and clapped their hands as the spray gently floated down on them.

Anahita took their hands and raised them to their feet. They stepped outside the sacred circle, smiling and looking twenty years younger, and greeted Rivula with cries of joy as she ran forward to hug them.

I turned to the Goddess. "There is one thing I don't understand. May I ask you about that?"

"I know your question." Anahita said quietly. "You are wondering why I gave Omo and Yami a drugged liquid to drink when they were here to get rid of their craving for alcohol. My answer is, the alcohol that is made by man is toxic and considerably inferior to the elevated processes we use for fermentation here. The drink they took from me is the veritable nectar of the spirit, and can do them no harm. In fact, it is invigorating and has rebuilt their natural energy, which will last for many years, so that they may be joyful and live a life of fulfillment from now on."

With Rivulas' parents fully restored to her, we bade farewell to Anahita and slowly wound our way back to the Castle of Water, where Omo and Yami mounted the two dolphins, who whisked them homewards. It remained only to say that the Page, Rivula, was received with great honors, and elevated to the position of Squire to the Knight Surgey, who was to give me my next test in the Water element.

Knight of Cups – Rules Eight and Seven of Cups.

The King granted Rivula her promotion and, after seeing her settled in her new position as Squire to the Knight of Cups, I was about to talk to the Knight himself, whose name was Surgey, to enquire about my new task. Just then, an equerry ran up to Surgey to inform him that the King had received an urgent message. Compos, the King of Pentacles, had flown into a terrible rage, stamped his feet, and caused a great earthquake west of the Mystic SEA. A tsunami warning had come over the King of Cups meteorological equipment, which he kept in the west tower of the Castle of Water. The tsunami had been measured at about 80 feet by the nautical instruments dotted about the Mystic SEA, and was due to arrive in six hours.

They decided to send Surgey to hover over the Lagoon, as he was the only one likely to save the castle by blocking the great wave with his Magical Weapon, the Cup. The task was urgent and the Knight leapt to horse and galloped out of the compound down to the shore of the Lagoon, where I saw him make a great jump over the water and, flying low over the waves, he soon vanished from sight. The groom explained that it was not the water itself that caused the damage, as the Castle was always wet, but the force of the great wave when it hit the structure.

"That is bad news for the Court. I hope Surgey will be able to hold the wave back. How can I find out what my next trial is, then, if he is busy?" I was selfishly crestfallen.

"He left a message for you. Take your rowboat and start for the island in the center of the Lagoon. He will meet you there."

"But if a storm is coming, I shouldn't be out in the boat," I remonstrated.

"Those are your instructions. I have no further information to give you." The groom shrugged and turned away.

This test was important and I was scared, but I reluctantly walked down towards the boat, and then remembered that Rivula had taken it to go and find Tabansi. How annoying! I went to find Rivula, but could not locate her, so I set out along the shore towards the Castle of Fire, which I could see burning far in the distance. About halfway there the land changed to desert, and I soon found the boat tied to a stake nearby. With a sinking heart, for the wind was piping up and sending spray off the Lagoon high in the air, I launched it and began to row towards the White Pyramid in the center of the Lagoon, which was just visible through the deteriorating weather. A line of breaking foam some miles away showed where the storm was crashing into the seaward side of the Bar.

It was rough enough even in the sheltered waters of the Lagoon, and hard to row standing up against the increasing swell. Spray blinded me, and I didn't notice a bigger wave than most hit the side of the boat. I staggered and grabbed the thwart to steady myself, but I lost an oar, which the surf caught and hurled from me. Kneeling at the transom, I continued to scull with the remaining oar until it, too, was ripped from my grasp. Then I could do nothing but hold onto the sides of the wildly gyrating boat and hope for rescue. I begged the Knight to search for me without delay if I didn't arrive at the Island.

Surgey must be busy, I reasoned as, soaking wet and shivering at the mercy of the increasing storm, I remained clinging to the boat for six hours. As the size of the waves grew bigger, I was thankful for the protection of the Bar, but as night began to fall, I saw a huge wave cresting over the Bar and realized the tsunami had arrived!

Powerless as the wall of water bore down on me, the crest foaming high above me and breaking with violent froth, I watched as it roared, spreading, over the Lagoon. Another moment and the great wave hit my boat, throwing it forward with full force, bow down, and leaving me thrashing in the churning water overboard, gasping for breath. I went down, came back up madly flailing my arms, was flipped over, took a large gulp of water, and blackness began to descend as I fought for air. At that moment, I heard a whinny, and the Knight of Cups reached down and plucked me from the wave as it bore me towards the Castle of Water at great speed.

"Hurry, we have no time to lose." He instructed me breathlessly, and threw me up on the pillion as I coughed and spluttered. "We must turn the wave before it hits the Castle." He put spurs to his horse Catarack and swung in front of the tsunami, raising in his hand a great Cup that he held out in front of the wave. Then there was a sudden jerk as Catarack caught a foot in the rough water and the Cup fell from the Knights' hand. The wave failed to stop, and roared on catching all of us and tossing us up and over, as its crest finally broke on the Castle walls. We clung to the swimming horses' bridle in churning foam as I saw the peasants and members of the court on shore running for their lives, and the wave hunting them and plucking them off the ground, to be lost in a welter of water and debris.

We washed up on the beach to find utter devastation, and Surgey groaned aloud as he floundered by my side.

"If only I had been taken and dashed to pieces by the wave! Now I am alive and must stand and be judged for my failure to grasp the Cup. The Castle and its buildings are badly damaged and if the King has survived, I might face death for this, yet I must go ashore and help in their rescue."

The next few hours were a nightmare as we attempted to save those who were still alive, pulling them from the rubble left by the huge wave and tending to their wounds. The dead were tenderly placed on the beach to await transportation to the Island of the White Pyramid, where the physical bodies of all those who lived in the four Castles, and had passed from life, were embalmed and preserved in the vaults. I found the entire royal family huddled at the top of the Castle tower, and I was relieved to see that they had all survived, yet with cuts, bruises and a broken bone or two.

The King of Cups was furious and extremely shaken, which was unusual for him, since he normally had a mild and kindly disposition. "Where is that Knight?" He yelled. "Bring him to me this instant."

A valet scurried out to find Surgey. I felt sorry for him. He had let go of the Cup, and that was obviously the problem. I remembered that the other two Knights, Terramud and Typhona, had not been able to grasp their Magical Weapons, either. What was wrong with the Knights? Maybe I would find out soon.

The door banged open, interrupting my thoughts as two guards came in with the Knight, soaking wet, his hair plastered to his face and drops of water oozing from his nose. He had the courage to stand in front of the King, his shoulders thrown back, and hear the worst.

"You let the Cup drop! After all the training you have had, the hours of practice in grasping the Cup.... What is going on with you – idiot!"

"You are right, Mi Lawd. I dropped the Cup when Catarack stumbled. It was slippery and I couldn't hang onto it. Now I beg for your mercy, for you will need me to help clean up and rebuild. Spare my life, I implore you." Surgey dropped to his knees, his head bent down in abject misery and a sob catching in his throat.

"You will not die, for that would be a waste. All hands here are needed to clear the rubble and rebuild the Castle. No, I will think of a suitable punishment for a while, to keep you in suspense. Now, go to your quarters, put on a tunic of sackcloth, and spread ashes from the kitchen fire on your head. Then get to work with the repair crews. Why am I cursed with these space cadets? We're all just too emotional at this Court and take things too sentimentally, and that stops us from focusing on the job at hand. If only the Cups were more rational - I need the King of Swords here to enforce some discipline! Dammit! I can't even control my own emotions." The King began to weep copiously and sniffed into his ermine sleeve.

I stepped forward quietly. "Mi Lawd, I am still awaiting the Knights' instructions as to my next test, and in the meantime I have had an idea. I recently met a group of people, the Hodians, who are from the rational sphere of Hod, and they have no emotions at all. Would you allow me to take Surgey to the Hodians Center, where he might be trained to hold the Cup properly, while he could interact with them and teach them, in return, how to understand their feelings and be kinder and more warm-hearted like yourself?"

The King brightened up a little and wiped his nose on his robe. "Hmn! That's a good idea of yours. Valet, bring Surgey back again. He can keep the sackcloth on, but brush off the ashes. Tell him he is going on a journey to atone for his horrible mistake." Here the King burst into tears again. "Oh! Dear. We will have to start rebuilding without him, I suppose. What a life!"

Hastening to meet Surgey, I helped him into the rowboat, which had washed up on shore. We searched for the oars and found one of them on top of the pigsty and the other slung up as a flagpole over by the serfs' shacks, which they were reluctant to part with. The boat had suffered minor damage but not enough to stop us, and the little bags with my items in them were still attached to the thwarts. I checked Joanas' pulse, which was racing, but she chirped up as we set out for the river that led to the Land of the Dreamers where the Hodians had built their Center, leaving those who had survived the tsunami to begin the long task of rebuilding.

Some time later we were passing through a mangrove swamp and, paddling up river one on each side of the boat, we found the tributary that led us towards the Hodians' Center. I spied movement on the huge dunes that led down to the river, and soon made out a large sand sled pulled by eight jackals with orange collars, which pulled up sharply as four robed figures jumped out and made their way to the riverbank.

We stepped ashore and I introduced their leader, whom I had met previously, to Surgey. "This is the Knight of Cups, a worthy Goodman, who needs to learn some discipline. He is very softhearted and too generous a soul."

Their leader answered in a metallic voice. "We have little time for emotional matters here. You know what happened to Koorong – he was such a Dreamer. We had to blow him apart to get at his brain. It was definitely worth obtaining for the eight-year survey we are conducting into dreaming and how it affects the rational mind. You'll be happy to hear that Koorong has fully recovered, since we mounted his mental function on the wall with a beautiful inscribed teak shield around it. His body was worthless, so we threw it away."

With an abrupt movement, the leader motioned us into the sled, and the jackals whirled us away over the dunes, up and down, passing a line of radio masts at the top of each dune, until we reached their quicksilver building, which shimmered in the desert sun like liquid metal.

After we entered the strange building, which was kept cool inside by the wings of thousands of birds flying near the ceiling overhead, I didn't realize that my presence was no longer required until the Hodians headed towards the swing doors with the jackals' head emblazoned on them, holding Surgey firmly by the elbow.

"Stop!" I shouted. "Just a moment. Surgey, you need to tell me what my next task is. I must return to the Castle immediately."

"Oh! My goodness. I completely forgot. The phrase is "**to retrieve the creative act from the pit of destruction,**" whatever that means. Good luck, and I will see you back at the Castle, I hope."

Surgey disappeared through the swing doors with the encircling Hodians, and I hastened to summon the outgoing sled with the wildcat driver, to return to the boat before I saw something disastrous happening to him. Had I done the right thing? I hoped that the group would not have to blow the Knight up to get at his kind nature. Certainly, if Surgey succeeded in learning to grasp his Magical Cup, it would benefit the Castle of Water immensely. If he failed there would be no question as to his fate, were he ever to return, for the King awaited him in great doubt, and would collapse with a nervous breakdown if his Knight failed to become more rational.

My journey back in the rowboat alone was long, and I amused myself by creating little theatrical scenes, plays with backdrops and actors promenading across the stage. It was not long before I smelt the odor of a cigarette, and there was my creative entity, Fontanova, sitting on the thwart beside me. Recoiling slightly from the unpleasant smell of the cigarette, I asked her how the artist Julian had been getting along. She suggested that we stop in the city built on seven hills on our way back. The Father was hosting a huge party in his Palace on the hill the following week, to select a new artist for a mural he wanted, depicting "The Battle of the Haves and Have Nots." Many artists had submitted cartoons, and Julian was one of them. I was excited to see how his work was progressing, as I had great faith in him. Fontanova had acted as a mentor and pulled him out of the slump he had been in, and he had stopped drinking, she assured me.

We therefore rowed up the main river into the city and moored the boat by some decrepit steps, up which we ascended to the huge doors of the Fathers' Palace. People were pouring in from all directions and passing through the doors, handing the doorman some sort of rolled parchment as they went by. We approached the entrance and he stepped in front of us belligerently, holding up his hand.

"Where is your scroll of entry?" He demanded. "Nobody is allowed into the festivities without donating a valuable parchment, the like of which is unique and not to be found anywhere else."

Fontanova took him aside and whispered something in his ear, and immediately his face relaxed. "Oh! I see. You are envoys from the esteemed Society of Enochian Anchorites. You say your protégée is one of the artists here. And who is this?" He asked, pointing at me as I stood there.

"This is the Navigator who is a world traveler and student of the Cabala. I am firmly attached to this personage and form a part of the character of this individual." She smiled charmingly at the door-keeper, as he allowed us to pass without a scroll.

"That was lucky," I said. "I wonder why everyone has to donate a scroll to the Father? He must have hundreds of parchments."

"It is for his library. He is determined to collect every book that was ever written about the Hermetic Arts and hide them away from the world. He would then possess all knowledge and be able to promulgate only his own doctrines, since there would be no-one out there who could question his dogma." Fontanova laughed. "The Father does not know that your entity Einerline has already stolen some very valuable books, which he is studying at this very moment. From his enquiries, the word will spread of a new approach to theology, one that will gravely challenge the precepts held dear by the church for many centuries."

"I remember the theft well. Einerline and I were together, and we nearly got trapped in the library. But we managed to exit through the four hidden rooms with Zolas' help, while the henchmen of the Father foolishly set an ambush by the elevator, which they thought was the only way out for us, and they were disappointed. Now, let us go and join the others at the party, and we will find Julian."

We began to climb a vast marble staircase as we spoke, at the top of which an opening between two pillars led into a grand ballroom filled with people of every different race and nationality, so that a babble of voices rent the air with languages of every kind. The atmosphere was heavy with sweet smoke originating from censers that hung at intervals along the ceiling. We elbowed our way through the crowd and finally spotted Julian, surrounded by a group of admirers. His cartoon hung on the wall along with the other entries, ready to be judged by the Father.

The sound of rock music filtered through the windows of the Palace as many guests gathered at the door with their greetings. We joined in the conversation, and took drinks from a bald headed butler who came round holding glasses of a strange coal black liquid on a bronze platter. I sipped the drink and found it absolutely delicious - a mixture of coconut, Devonshire cream and what I imagined essence of lotus would taste like. I felt a burst of energy, and realized that all the people in the room were experiencing the same excitement, in fact, the crowd was beginning to sway to-and-fro in the manner of a mob, and a wave of party spirit overcame me.

"What sort of drink is this?" Fontanova asked, as she took a glass from the butler. "It doesn't look like my usual glass of wine."

"These are drinks that rich people serve." I explained, as I took two glasses from the tray and glared at the butler who, after raising his eyebrows at a filthy looking fellow in ragged clothes that was elbowing his way towards us, hastily departed. "Be careful, they're martinis – pretty strong – and you can eat the olive."

The scruffy bum sidled up, snatched the drink from Fontanovas' hand

and downed it in one gulp, including the olive, wiping his mouth on his sleeve. "Gadzooks! That was good. Where did that dressed-up geezer go? Let's find some more drinks."

I quickly realized who the fellow was, as I polished off another drink. My heart sank as my efforts to warn him about the use of strong alcohol went unheeded. We were soon both quite drunk. The wild-looking young man, his blond hair spiking in every direction, was soon laughing and joking, gesticulating and spinning on his heels with abandon. I turned to him and slapped him on the shoulder.

"Welllll – come, my frien'. Havin' a good time? Here, have another drin'." I was slurring my words. "Wa'sh your name agin?"

"I'm Fes'erbas', I am. Yer party man, I am. Yer hedonish'ishtic shelf, thatsh me." He replied with some difficulty, hiccuping the while and reeling back and forth on his heels. "I love ter party, partyyy all th' time – if poshible."

Here he burst into a fit of giggles and tottered off to collect some more drinks for us, as we made our way, shoving through the crowd, toward our hosts. I did not complete my intentions for, halfway across the ballroom, things started to whirl around me, and I staggered to a couch in one of the waiting rooms and fell onto it, passing out instantly in a dead stupor. But a dream intruded.......

It seemed that my parents Lance and Gwen had joined us at the Father's Palace with their own party, were making the rounds, chatting to everyone and introducing people who then sometimes stood awkwardly eyeing each other. It appeared that their party was in aid of starving Ethiopian Coptic priests, who were volunteering as anchorites in the desert. Neither of us had any money and Gwen pulled me aside and asked me where I had found that dirty peasant, so I told her that my friend was wearing fancy dress because he had mistaken the party for a masquerade. She seemed satisfied and invited us outside to see the source of their wealth, gesturing widely in the direction of a greenish lake into which cascaded a blue waterfall.

We teetered carefully through a magnificent garden, Festerbash staggering at our heels as Gwen showed us the great falls that plunged into their natural lake. The foaming water was filled with gold coins glittering and bouncing as they fell showering into the lake, and a gardener in a boat busied himself fishing net loads of coins out of the water. I thought I recognized him, as he was quite tall, about seven feet, and had an extraordinarily long nose, but I wasn't sure.

"Where is the source of this wealth?" I asked, looking up at the top of the falls. "It must come from up there."

"We don't know and we don't ask," replied Gwen. "Ever since we started to give money away, the gold coins have been falling faster and faster. Now we can afford to give much more than before, and yet maintain a comfortable style of living."

"That's wonderful," I heard myself saying. "You have learned to temper acquisition with cautious moderation." Where had I heard that before? I slid a glance at Fontanova, but she had fallen to the ground drunk and was snoring heavily, while Festerbash was making an utter fool of himself, throwing plates of food at everyone when they approached the buffet. "I would like - just out of curiosity, of course - to climb the waterfall and see what lies at the top."

Gwen did not seem interested. "Go ahead, and see for yourself if you want. There seems to be some disturbance over at the buffet. I must return to my guests and we'll have more time to talk later." She turned and went back towards the buffet, where the egg-headed butler, covered with pie, salsa and blancmange, was battling with a greasy Festerbash on the ground. A crowd began to gather around the thrashing pair as the fight grew fiercer. I walked unsteadily over to the buffet, as a dull clang accompanied by a shocked gasp from the onlookers told me there was trouble – big trouble! I broke through the crowd and knelt down beside Festerbash, who was crouched over his opponent. The butler lay on the ground motionless, a large wound spilling blood from his skull onto the freshly cropped grass.

"Call 911!" I yelled to someone. "Get some help! Is there a doctor here?"

A small man stepped forward and pressed a burlap tea towel to the butlers' wound. "This could be serious." He said. "Its possibly a skull fracture and certainly at least a concussion."

Festerbash was standing awkwardly, twisting his fingers together and squinting carefully at the fallen butler. A large bronze platter lay nearby. It wasn't more than a few minutes before we heard the sirens and several EMT's along with police officers ran onto the scene. A furious debate ensued, and as there were many witnesses, it was inevitable that Festerbash was soon handcuffed and led off to the murmurs of "attempted murder" "butler basher" "crazy loon drunk" and at which I immediately sobered up. Since Festerbash was my entity, I knew I didn't dare take another drink or I would end up in the slammer with him..........

At this moment. I woke up and got back on my feet, remembering that I was at the Fathers' party. I hazily remarked that Fontanova had recovered her balance and slipped away, and a stranger had joined the group near Julian and was arguing with him fiercely. I shook my head and rubbed my eyes. I leaned closer to listen. The stranger, who was extremely eccentric, had wild blonde hair in peaks all over his head and a large hooked nose, full lips and a frenetic expression in his eyes. This was deja vue, for sure. He was verbally attacking Julian, accusing him of sucking up to the Father to influence his choice of cartoons, and Julian was getting very mad. I accosted the fellow, not realizing it was Festerbash,

"Who are you, anyway, to make accusations like that?" I asked, frowning at him, but at the back of my throat a bubble of laughter welled up and the wild stranger noticed it, threw back his head, and guffawed in a most discourteous manner.

"I'm Festerbash, you f'in idiot! I'm your 'edonistic self – th' one you party with – when tha' Pompeybou isn' aroun' with his'ndless sea stories – wha' a-bore that ole halfwit is….. "S,anyway…" Here he took a swig of his drink at the same moment I raised my glass… "I'm here ter 'njoy meself an' if tha' include th'baiting off'n yer mis'rable artist frien', I'll go rahht a-head." He snorted and regarded me fiercely, then went into a crouching position and, to my horror, raised his fists in the air and challenged Julian to a fight.

At this juncture, there was the sound of trumpets and a herald announced the arrival of the Father, who was to judge the cartoons. Everybody craned their necks to see what was going on. In order to be visible above the crowd, the Father had arranged to be brought into the ballroom in a tumbrel, drawn by two mules, which caused a great deal of merriment. He didn't seem to notice the suppressed giggles as he was driven slowly down the row of cartoons hanging on the wall, until one of the mules raised its tail and gave off a large and odorous fart, followed by a fat pile of turds. At this, the entire company exploded with laughter and the Father glared around at everybody in a rage.

"You dare to laugh at the head of your church!" He yelled, beside himself. "To perdition with your cartoons! Take them all down and burn them. Dismiss the guests! The contest for the mural is cancelled – get out of here, all of you!"

A shocked hush spread over the crowd. The only sound to be heard was the raucous cry of Festerbash as he challenged Julian to battle. I seized Julian by the arm and hurried him out of a side door and, as I was returning, the butler came forward and made an attempt to grab Festerbash, who appeared to have gone completely mad. He slipped from the butlers' grasp and, grabbing the bronze tray, brought it down heavily onto the bald head in front of him. The butler groaned and fell to the ground, and several people rushed forward to put Festerbash in an arm lock, when they threw him down and sat on him amidst a welter of broken glasses. There was a frantic struggle, for Festerbash had the strength of ten and he quickly broke free. To my horror I found myself joining in the fight, as Festerbash and I fought side by side against the authorities.

The battle spread to those on either side of us, and people, crazed by the black drink, began punching each other indiscriminately. Each person pounced on the one next to him, and so it went until the entire ballroom was a mass of struggling, heaving forms, one on top of another, with the cries of the wounded and the shrieks of the maddened adversaries creating an enormous melee over which the Father, still ensconced in his tumbrel, stood in dumb shock.

His faint admonitions faded into thin air. "Stop! This is most unseemly. You are in the Presence of the Father. How dare you behave in this fashion?"

Festerbash and I were drunk with excitement and loved the challenge of the fight. We punched, slapped and kicked our way towards the tumbrel until we were right in front of the plump and sloping robes of the Father, who looked down on us with utmost distaste. Festerbash gave a terrifying cackle, and as he did so, his long arms reached out and grabbed the robes in front of him and he began to climb up the side of the cart. Without thinking, and in the flush of the moment, I followed, and we manhandled the pompous old phoney up and out of the tumbrel and down onto the ground, where we tore off his white pontifical robes and, to our surprise, saw that the old man was dressed entirely in green feathers underneath his ecclesiastical outfit.

Well, those nearest to us surged forward, screaming with delight, and picked up the heavy feathered object, tossing it to the next group, and so on and on, across the entire ballroom, with the Father yelling out in fear as his feathers were torn and crumpled and he suffered many bruises and scratches. Finally, with an awful screech, he must have reached a decision, for he tore away the battered verdure to reveal a red scaly monkey-like creature with baglike fleshy wings that flapped ponderously away and sat up in the main chandelier, where it chattered and squawked at us harshly as it swung to and fro.

By now the whole crowd was staring, stupefied, at the creature on the chandelier. Being still under the grip of the black drink, Festerbash and I were shoving our way through the crowd, pretending that we had nothing to do with the defrocking of the Father, but I could see that the creature had its malevolent eye on us. Suddenly we tripped over the prone body of the butler, who, it appeared, had come to after the bashing with the bronze platter, and created a diversion by screaming at the top of his voice and pointing to Festerbash with a shaking finger.

"That's him! That's the feller who whacked me. Capture him! Don't let him get away!" This as Festerbash attempted to slide under the nearest group of people, who grabbed him and held him until a squad of the Father's police arrived. As the police locked the handcuffs on my entity, I immediately sobered up. After all, they were arresting my hedonistic self! The moment my pleasure-seeking feelings disappeared, Festerbash vanished and the handcuffs fell to the floor with a clink, leaving the police staring at an empty space. Festerbash had escaped their net once again.

Quickly I turned to the police and pointed up to the swaying chandelier, where the metamorphosed Father clung. "There he is, the trickster! He escaped from you very cleverly, and now, see how he mocks you."

With one accord, the cops rushed forward and were soon climbing on each others' shoulders to reach the chandelier. Just as the topmost officer grabbed for the creature, it took off and glided on flap-like wings across the ballroom and out of the door. The police gave chase and the whole crowd swarmed after them, down the stairs and out of the palace onto the great courtyard in front, where they ran to-and-fro aimlessly, for the red creature had completely disappeared from view.

After all this excitement, I left those who ruled in the Palace to sort the populace into Haves and Have Nots, which was quite easy merely by looking at their clothing. As I walked back to my rowboat, I could hear angry protests echoing behind me.

"Hey! I don't have any money."

"You can't tax me, I'm poor."

"How dreadful, they have accused me of mercenary tendencies, for I am a Have." "You've got the wrong person – I am the captain of the Fathers fleet of galleys. I am, of course, well recompensed for that, so take your hand off my sleeve."

I rowed silently down the muddy river alone and out to sea, and after several days, I reached the Lagoon and attempted to cross the Bar with the boat, but try as I would to pull the dinghy over the sand, something prevented me, for the boat became impossibly heavy, and would not move. I finally had to row south for some miles and enter the Lagoon through the mouth of a hidden river. This gave me some thought, for I remembered that some time earlier we hadn't been able to unload our vessel from the freighter into the SEA, and had finally transported it overland. There was some sort of barrier that I could not cross between the Lagoon and the Mystic SEA, and I was curious to find out how I could breach it.

I arrived back at the Castle of Water to find that virtually nothing had been accomplished since the tsunami. Of course, it was hard to know how long I had been away. Was it a month, a week, or merely a day? I remembered the task I had been set, "**to retrieve the creative act from the pit of destruction**". Well, there was certainly a pit of destruction here, so I set about organizing gangs of shepherds, kitchen staff, grooms and gardeners to begin clearing the rubble and sorting it into usable piles of materials for rebuilding. They were slow to start and complained a lot, for they were, as usual, overwhelmed by uncontrolled emotions, but eventually I encouraged them by promising a special banquet for all when the work was completed.

Realizing that I was beginning to retrieve the creative act from the pit of destruction, I pondered on its exact meaning. At the moment, there was nothing for it but to complete the reconstruction of the Castle of Water, settle the Court back in a safe environment, and then I might find out.

The labor of rebuilding went on for six months, under my direction and insistence. At the end of that time, I received a message from the Hodians. Their message was delivered by a strange bird that strutted forward on lanky legs and had a burst of small black quills adorning its head. The bird approached me and regarded me with a reddish twinkling eye as it spoke.

"You may remember me, for I am a secretary bird. I gave you the round piece of parchment with the sigil on it. My name is Isa Real Gardy, late assistant to the Crow, who at present awaits you on the Island of Malkuth. I have a message from the Hodians. They tell me that the Knight of Cups has completed his rational tests and is now able to grasp the Cup firmly. He is ready to return to the castle, but doesn't know the way. He needs a Navigator to help him. You are the one, and you must journey immediately to the Land of the Dreamers to get him."

I was not overjoyed. The journey by rowboat would be long and arduous. Isa Real Gardy must have read my mind, as most really good secretaries do, and he made a suggestion. "There is another way to reach the Land of the Dreamers, and that is by dreaming. It is sufficient to send your astral body to fetch the Knight. Because he has now grasped his Magical Weapon, he is able to travel telepathically. Now, you will go to sleep and dream Surgey home."

With that, the bird sprinkled some dew off an early morning leaf onto my eyes, and I lay down and instantly fell asleep.

I'm dreaming that I am flying over vast oceans towards the south. Beside me, a dim figure with a crest on its head is beside me, holding my hand.

Now, through the gloom, I see its head is the head of a great hawk – there is the curved beak, the smooth feathers, the glittering eye...... I allow myself to relax in the presence of this wonderful being, who seems a part of me, but is not quite so, as yet. We circle down towards the great dunes and see in front of us a group of five people, standing by a sand sled driven by a wildcat in dark goggles, so that its eyes can't be seen. One of the group is Surgey, but he looks different somehow – he seems metallic and he's quivering in incredibly rapid vibrations. I swoop down, letting go of the hand of my companion, and reach out for Surgey. My hand goes right through him! I can see him as a definite object as I circle around his head, but I can't grasp any part of him.

A thought comes into my head. Don't try to touch the Knight. You see his astral body. Merely think of him flying beside you, and he will be there. I know the message comes from the hawk-headed entity, so I obey, visualizing Surgey flying beside me. He immediately takes off and, circling round a little clumsily at first, joins me. He is carrying the large Cup very carefully. I think about being back at the Castle of Water, and ....

I stirred and woke suddenly. Turning over, I saw that the Knight was lying on the ground asleep beside me, holding the Cup, so I shook him lightly and he woke.

"How did I get here?" Surgey asked. "I feel really strange, as if my whole body is vibrating at an incredible speed. I don't feel the same as I used to." He felt himself all over gingerly.

"You have absorbed a different vibratory rate at the Hodian Center, and you can now control your emotions more firmly. The Cup is yours to hold. Although emotions are more primitive than logic, one must combine the two in order to stay successfully on the Middle Path." I advised him. "We should go up to the Castle now and present you to the King. He will be delighted."

Surgey was amazed at the reconstruction of the damaged castle as we walked up to the walls. He could see that we had achieved a great deal of work in his absence, although much remained to be done. He turned to me as we stood at the entrance to the Kings' audience room. "You have passed the test set for you. By helping me to balance the two spheres of Hod, which is logic, and Netzach, which is emotion, within myself, you have created an act of wonder, and now I travel the Path of Art and will meet you in the Mystic SEA. Adieu, for now I must speak with the King."

Surgey disappeared through the doors and I heard the Kings' voice strike a sentimental note as he wept with joy for the return of his best-loved Knight. He immediately ordered a great banquet for all the workers, and we sat down to a table loaded with every kind of fish and seafood one could imagine, mussels, crab, turbot, shrimp, all served with oysters, seaweed and delicately flavored urchins. We finished off large quantities of kelp wine and krill beer, and thoroughly enjoyed ourselves.

The following day, I went to the Queens' quarters to receive my next orders.

Queen of Cups - Rules Five and Three of Cups.

My search for the Queen of Cups around the Castle proved fruitless, until I came upon her empty chamber, where a lady-in-waiting was making up a large water-bed. Upon my approach and question as to Queen Fluvias' whereabouts, she told me that the Queen spent a great deal of her time out on the waters of the Lagoon, especially at the full moon. It was at present the dark of the moon, so Fluvia was in a quiet mood and might have some time to spare. It all sounded rather odd, floating around in a boat, but I decided to row out to the center of the Lagoon to find her.

I didn't get as far as the Isle of the White Pyramid, although it fascinated me, for I spotted a small red funerary vessel drifting in the center of the current which ran gently through the Lagoon. The boat was of an ancient Egyptian type and carried a throne of black granite upon which the Queen sat, dangling her foot in the water and idly watching two dolphins who cavorted before her. I recognized the amiable creatures that had carried us up the river to Anahitas' cavern.

Fluvia was a delicate white-blonde beauty with dark blue eyes and a creamy skin. Her look was soft and her mouth, which was full, rested in a gently mocking curve. She looked up as I approached and her two dolphins frolicked beside my boat as I shipped my oars.

"Good evening, Ma Dame." I lowered my glance politely. "I have come to receive the test message for my next trial. Do you have time to give it to me?"

"I rarely have time, but for you I can make time at this time, for it is the dark of the moon." She said gently. "It is always the tides that will not wait. It is easier when the moon is dark, for the neap tides are not so difficult to control. When the moon is full, I must focus my energy to make sure that the tides are ebbing and flowing properly, and I spend a great deal of time reflecting on the lunar situation."

"That is true. Time and tide wait for no man." I reminded her, glancing at the slowly moving tide, in which a stream of bright tiny lights flashed and seemed to envelop the bodies of the dancing dolphins and the drifting vessels. "It is beautiful out here on a moonless night, with the phosphorescence gleaming in the water all around your boat."

"That is partly why I stay out here so much. Sometimes I get very moody, and because the King is also subject to dejection, we try to stay away from each other except on the night of the darkest moon, when I have conceived all my children. Did you meet them yet?" The Queen looked towards the Castle fondly.

"No, I haven't. Do they have a big nursery like the Queen of Pentacles?"

"Good heavens, no! They live in the swimming pool, of course. They were born underwater and don't feel comfortable coming onto dry land. In fact, they still have their gills, so that they can breathe without surfacing at all."

"Then, who looks after them?" I was puzzled. "Is it a fish? Or maybe it's a shark?"

Fluvia sighed. "You jest, naturally. Since there are seven of them, the nurse has to be an octopus, of course. She has an arm to hold each of them and one left over to spank them with."

"So you believe in chastising your children?" I was taken aback by this pronouncement. "In the world I come from, no-one is allowed to smack their children and they are permitted to run wild, for the idea of discipline no longer exists."

"That is a grave problem which will eventually destroy your world." A slow tear welled in Fluvias' beautiful eyes and reflected the sparkles in the water around her. "When discipline is not considered important, commitment, honesty, reliability and responsibility for ones' actions disappear. When I look into the water and reflect, the moons' ray shows me pictures. I see the disintegration of a nation that, once so proud, became over-confident and power crazy. Rome was like that. The ruin of Rome happened for many reasons – greed, decadence and over extension of forces were included. It is part of the flow of time. What expands must eventually contract, just as the tides do. This is the eternal flux of time that cannot be altered." The Queen sighed and threw two fishes to the dolphins. "We must not dwell on the physical death of a nation that might have become great in spirit. Now I will give you your next test. It is **"to divert reflection from illusion into connection"**. Think about it as you return to the Castle of Water and I know that you will find the answer."

Fluvia motioned me back towards the shore with a wave of her hand. The dolphins accompanied me most of the way. We chatted and they reminded me of a time in the past when they had guided a small kayak through a fierce storm to safety on a beach of black sand. I understood that they had always been there, and would be by my side when the time came to enter the Mystic SEA.

Rowing back to shore, I felt very poetic, and when I landed I saw a familiar figure sitting on the muddy bank gazing out to sea, his chin in his hand. It was Bardogian, my lyrical entity. He looked very reflective, and I sat down beside him and remained very quiet. Finally he spoke.

"We are together again after that dangerous Tantric Mass. It was an awful mistake, but Fontanova and I were caught up in the moment, and we learned a serious lesson." He paused and frowned. "Now we must rescue Jafar, who we left at the Viceroys' mansion. He is under the illusion that he is a cuscus, as a result of the deadly spell cast by the dark liquid that he took from the Viceroy of Muckabad. The deception has been so powerful that it has caused his body to metamorphose into that very animal, while his soul and his spirit remain human still. He has become a chimera, half man, half beast – a cruel, cruel fate. We need to leave for the Viceroys' domain immediately, and we must stop at the dark bazaar to find your trickster friend, for he is sure to be lurking there with his golden cushion of velvet."

"How do you know of him?" I asked. I knew that some of my entities were beginning to suspect that they were not alone, and were becoming aware of each other on a limited basis. I shrank from the thought of any chance meeting between Bazoom, my angry entity and, for example, Ploitinda, who represented cunning and manipulative me.

Fortunately my new King, Jolon, had put Ploitinda in chains and I hoped she would never be set free. The mix would be even worse if the trickster were to gang up with those two.

However, since Bardogian had rather a calming effect on other parts of me, I reckoned he could probably handle Kracklewergen, for I knew that was the entity he referred to. When we got into the boat and I took up the oars, Bardogian told me that they had met during the time he had destroyed the tin cathedral. He needed Kracklewergens' help to trick the directors of that religion to let him into the cathedral, even though they were not using it anymore. They had become bloated bureaucrats who ran some of the biggest companies in the world.

I knew that I had abandoned the unfortunate Jafar. I had been too intoxicated by the black liquid at the time to attend to his problems at the Viceroys' party during my river journey. Now we were returning in the hope of finding him and releasing him from the Viceroys' spell. We traveled for several days and finally arrived at the mouth of the sacred river where the Hindus have their burning ghats. The Viceroys' mansion stood, its marble stairway stretching down into the water, as it had before, but this time there was no celebration and all was deserted. Bardogian and I disembarked and tied up the boat. I had to remain in an elegiac frame of mind in order to keep him with me as we mounted the steps and knocked at the large door.

A footman answered the door and when we asked whether the Viceroy was keeping a pet cuscus, he nodded and said it was in a cage behind the mansion where the Viceroys' private zoo was. He couldn't understand why we should take such an interest in the animal, but we explained that we were doing research into the DNA of rare animals and we wanted to take a sample, which seemed to satisfy him. The Viceroy was away and we were able to arrange a visit for the following day when we would bring our "medical equipment" - and Krackenwergle – to the zoo. Thereupon I decided to make an earlier surreptitious visit in the small hours while the footman was asleep, to avoid complications.

We took the boat and rowed upstream to the street that led to the dark bazaar. It didn't seem safe to leave the boat unattended, so I picked a reasonably honest looking boatman, making sure I was nowhere near the mango-seller that I had cheated, and promised to give him a tip. Before we left, I had a feeling we might need Oojo, the toad, who was under a spell himself, so I took along his little bag which had been hanging on the thwart. We walked up an alley with many stalls set up each side and the smell of curry drifting through the air, and came to a stall that I recognized. It was selling Turkish delight, a sweetmeat that I loved. I wondered how I could trick the vendor into giving me some of his sweeties, as I had no money to offer him.

As my mouth began to water and I bent over to see the object of my desire, I began to compose a poem. "Oh! Sweet sweetmeat, How I want this treat. Life will not be complete, Until I get…."

Here Bardogian rudely interrupted by prodding my arm and pointing into the darkness behind the stall. I spotted a tall, gangly fellow hiding behind the awning of the booth. He grinned at me with a toothy mouth over which was the longest nose I had ever seen. It was Krackenwergle, my trickster self, and as I waved to him, he replied.

"Hey, twit! Er-hem. How come you're here again?" He laughed. "I see that your buddy Bardogian has been er-forced to leave all of a sudden, hem. Can't handle being around with me, eh? Too bad, he needs to lighten up, hmmm, and not take life so seriously."

It was true, Bardogian had vanished. It was, as yet, impossible for me to compose tricky poems that would keep them both in attendance together. I did want them to meet if I could think of a way – limericks, maybe? Never mind, the trickster would be the more useful of the two during my visit to the Viceroys' zoo.

"What's that in your little er-bag?" Asked Kracklewergen. "It's jumping about a bit. Alive, I suppose? Hmmmm. Smells of a spell, I swear it! Let's have a look." He bent forward and I opened the top of the bag a little crack. "Ouch! It spat at me. Hmmm…. Tricky little er-devil, I acknowledge. What's his name?"

"This is Oojo, the toad. It's true, I don't know whether to trust him or not. Sometimes it seems he is on my side, and then he does something unexpected and dreadful. He attacked Fola and nearly killed her, and he has tried to digest my favorite cricket, Joana, who lives in a cricket cage on the boat. Fortunately she was too hard-shelled to be digestible." Here I looked shamefaced and Krackenwergle begin to guffaw loudly. "I disobeyed my better self, who advised me to leave the toad at the zoo. But Oojo can be very charming and he talked me into taking him along."

I could see Oojo poking his head through the crack in the bag. "Let me out!" He croaked. "I promise I'll be good."

"No. You must wait until we get to the Viceroys' zoo. There is a task for you there. You had better get it right, or there'll be trouble – it'll be extra bag-time and no excuses for staying out late." I pushed his nose back firmly and closed the bag. "Will you help us with a tricky problem tomorrow morning, Krack? Jafar is trapped in the zoo. He is still a cuscus. You know about that unfortunate event, don't you? He can't remain a half-and-half. Will you come with us? We have to lift the curse of the cuscus."

"Er-hem. OK. I er-suppose I will. What sort of time?"

"Three o'clock. In the morning, not in the afternoon. Oojo is at his best then."

"Oh! No. That's much too early. Hmmmm…. I sleep until ten. I'm an evening person, you know. Please er-make it later."

"That's not possible. We are working with the Three of Cups. That is the only time the spell can be lifted."

"Hmmmm…. All right, then. Er- I'll meet you here at two-thirty. Here, take this cushion, you can er-use it for a pillow tonight in the boat. Goodbyeee." He threw me the gold velvet cushion with red tassels and disappeared.

I went to bed early in the boat after persuading the boatman that I needed to leave it there for another day, at which he grunted disbelievingly. Two thirty came far too soon. I slumped up the dirty alley and met Krack, and we set off on foot for the mansion, so as not to appear too obvious at that early hour. Fortunately, the footman had been slack and the gate to the zoo was open. We wandered around the cages, which, although dark, Kracklewergen could see into fairly easily, as he had excellent night vision.

"Ah! Hmmmm. There he is." He pointed to a little furry animal crouched in the corner of a small cage, its huge liquid eyes turned beseechingly upon us. "What do we do now?"

"Keep your voice down." I whispered. "It's easier to lift the spell here and then he can walk out himself." I opened the bag and took out Oojo. "Now, Oojo, do your thing. Release him!" I pushed the toad through the bars and waited, holding my breath.

Oojo hopped forward slowly, approaching the furry creature cautiously. Some sort of communication seemed to pass between them, and their noses touched. Oojo looked at me, his heavy eyes blinking.

"He needs the black drink. The hair of the god that bit him, as it were. We have to get the drink somehow, otherwise the curse can't be lifted. I'm sorry." The toad turned away, and as he did so, I spotted a faint gleam in his eyes.

My heart sank. That meant going into the mansion in the middle of the night to search for the Viceroys' liquor cabinet. Jafar had to be set free, there was no doubt of that, so Kracklewergen and I nodded, leaving Oojo in the cage with Jafar, and crept towards the kitchen door of the building.

To our surprise, the kitchen door was unlocked. Evidently the servants were at play while their master was away and we soon found them, sprawled on the floor of the smoking room by the liquor cabinet, on which stood a large half-empty flagon of the black drink. There had been some sort of orgy, at which Kracklewergen showed interest, as usual, but what intrigued me more was the leftover booze. I steeled myself against it – neither Pompeybou nor Festerbash, my drunken entities, would be any use in these circumstances – but then Krack was quite a party-goer too. He leaned towards me, his toothy grin wide, and pointed to the flagon with a knotty finger.

"Let's have a snifter, eh. Hmmmm…… It won't do any harm. Give us er-courage, don't you know." Without further ado, he picked up the flagon and took an enormous gulp, tossing it down his stringy throat without swallowing, as if drinking from a bota bag.

"Don't! Krack – put that down." I grabbed at the flagon and some liquid splashed out onto my face and trickled down. I licked at the drip and that was it – I upended the flagon and took a huge swig of the drink myself.

Well, that did it. We barely crawled out of there holding what was left of the black drink unsteadily, and tottered towards the cuscus' cage. It was darker than ever. I could see no sign of the two creatures.

"Can you see them?" I asked Krack.

"No, I can't, er-hem. They must have er-escaped! Hmmmm… that's a terrible thing to happen." In the dark, I thought I could make out the ghost of a grin on his face, but I felt sure I was imagining it.

The cage was empty, although I ran my frantic gaze over every corner. Jafar was not there, and nor was Oojo. The toad had somehow opened the cage door and fled with our cuscus, and they were probably now both roaming the streets of the town, nowhere to be found.

"Damn! I should have realized. Oojo played a trick on us. He never meant to lift the curse, but wanted us out of the way so that he could run off with his cursed friend. The two of them are together now, but under different spells. That is going to be a doubly difficult problem to resolve." I was interrupted by a coarse laugh, and I whipped around in a flash, my heart pounding.

"My God!" I exclaimed, for the figure that stood before me was not Kracklewergen – or was it? No! Impossible! The person I now saw was the Viceroy of Muckabad himself, laughing hysterically.

"What are you doing here?" I was flabbergasted. "Wheres' Kracklewergen?"

"My dear comrade, when you try to trick someone and come creeping around in the middle of the night, remember that the trickster is smarter at tricking than you are. In fact, you are merely an amateur! I wanted to keep Jafar under my spell for a while – I'm observing the problems he is having, being a half-and-half. You entered my premises in the dead of night, unannounced and uninvited, and tried to steal the cuscus and spoil my experiment. Now he has escaped, along with that damned toad. I won't have that! Since you seem to enjoy partying around here, here you will stay for a while, and party on in my dungeon. Footmen, seize the Navigator!"

Instantly two very alert footmen stepped forward and clamped their huge hands around my arms, dragging me into the mansion and down a set of stone steps to a cellar underneath the building. There they threw me into a corner and abruptly left. To the sound of the river damp dripping through the walls of my prison, I sobbed myself to sleep, and Globdinig did not come to comfort me, for she had been sucked into Anahitas' Cup, and remained in prison underwater.

A dim light showed that it was morning at last. Through the day I waited, but no-one came. Thirst assailed me, and I forced myself to lap the slimy trickle that oozed down the damp walls behind me. Another night fell and I found myself dealing with hunger cramps that knotted my stomach. I chewed on a loose piece of leather from my sandal to ease the pain. The day passed agonizingly slowly and the next night and day dragged by. As the fourth night approached, I could only be thankful that I at least had some liquid available, however foul it tasted.

I fell asleep uneasily, tormented by the thought that I had been forgotten and would eventually die a painful death from starvation. As I slept, a dream came to me.

I'm languishing in a deep cavern, where I have been left by a person with the head of a hawk. I can see him walking away, the crest of feathers visible on his head. "Don't go!" I yell soundlessly. "Help me, please!" The sound of distant laughter echoes through my head and a voice says "You are a Fool. Three times tricked! Once by the toad, once by Kracklewergen, and, worst of all, once by yourself, for you thought to trick them. Yet I will have pity on you. At the dead of night I will return and wake you, and we will divert the reflection from illusion into connection…." The voice faded and a thousand bats were suddenly all around me, squeaking and flapping their leathery wings in my face. Frantically

I brushed them away and found myself on a stone jetty reaching out into a large
bay. Beside the jetty lay a rowboat. I descended a rusty iron ladder and untied
the boat. I was drifting into the bay when I saw that the oars were missing...

A soft tap on my shoulder woke me and a voice whispered close to my
ear. It gave directions that I must follow, and I rose to my feet shakily, my
legs feeling like jelly, and staggered to the door of the prison. There I noted
the directions I had been given, staring fixedly with all my might at the
lock on the door until a faint glow grew from it. I could feel the touch of
a hand on my shoulder from which energy flowed, but couldn't see who it
was. Gradually the lock brightened, and after a few moments it burst into
flame, the metal shining red hot and eating away the surrounding wood
of the door, until the melting lock fell to the floor and the burning door
swung open. I felt a little push from behind as I stepped out, and made my
way as fast as I could up the stone steps to the kitchen, first making sure
the room was empty, then out of the back door, down the garden and out
into the street with a gasp of relief. I looked behind me as flames began
shooting out of the basement and the fire alarms' strident sound mingled
with the clattering of horses' hooves as the engines galloped towards the
Viceroys' mansion in great haste.

Hurrying back to my boat, where the gold cushion still lay, I rowed out
into the river before the boatman woke up, as I had nothing with which to
pay him. Flames from the burning mansion lit up the sky and reflected in
the muddy river waters. I could see the fire trucks, their horses stamping
nervously, as the firemen set up a pump to draw water from the river. I felt
bad, but my main intent was to find the cuscus and free him from the curse.
As far as Oojo went, I hoped that he had disappeared for good. I hated him
with a passion. He had humiliated me! As for the problem with the fire at
the Viceroys mansion, I felt no guilt whatsoever.

I was starving hungry, so I looked for food in the gutter and found
some discarded vegetables, which I greedily consumed raw. I now had time
to wonder who my rescuer was and why he had not shown himself to me
except in my dream, and where to find the missing toad and Jafar.

I rowed fast and furiously and the dawn broke misty and uncertain.
Where was I? Soon a vague coast appeared and I made towards it. As I got
close, I recognized the island where the archaeologist Donald was digging
for early man, and where the members of the strange cult concealed
themselves on the far side of the island, away from spying eyes. I landed
on the beach and pulled the rowboat up on the sand, attaching the painter

to a log. Then, walking towards the sound of voices, I came upon the dig and found the workers gathered around an early cup of coffee.

"Hello," I volunteered, as Donald and Namrata recognized me and leapt to their feet in welcome. "Thank goodness I've found you. I have to complete a test that is about illusion. I think it has something to do with the cult over the hill, you know, the one we saw last time I was here."

"We've been expecting you." Donald said in a serious way, handing me a mug of coffee. "We have to do something about that cult. It has grown huge. In fact, if you listen, you can hear the rustle of their leaves underfoot from here, as they walk around their leader in chains. They are about to overwhelm the entire island, and then our researches into the past will be ruined, for they care nothing about learning from the past, but only have an insidious fantasy about the future that their leader promulgates."

"I expected the cult would grow." I mused as I sipped the good coffee. "We were fortunate to rescue Namrata from them last time. Now, we must somehow destroy the cult. How can we do that? Let's have a brainstorming session this morning. Can you suspend operations for a couple of hours?"

"Yes, of course. This problem is critical for us. There are, basically, four ways to get rid of the group. They are by burying alive; raking the island with a hurricane; drowning them; or setting fire to the dry brush."

"Well, we have to remember that we are working in connection with the Queen of Cups. She lives in the Castle of Water and controls the tides, and she would never approve of methods using the other three elements. Maybe we can raise the tidal flow gradually, until that part of the island is under water. Then they would have to leave or be drowned."

"That won't work." Namrata disagreed. "They will simply have time to move to the high ground, and that will put them right next to us."

"True. Then it must be done quickly, at the risk of the dig itself, for if we raise the water level, the dig will be flooded too."

Donald thought a moment. "We have a type of plaster that we can mix to preserve the impression of a valuable find. We can pour this plaster into the section where we are digging. It will harden, but be easy to chip out after the water has gone. We must also evacuate and take all our tools and found objects with us until the water has subsided."

"Right! The next question is how to raise the water level quickly enough, so that they have no time to escape drowning." I thought for a few minutes. "Ah! I know of someone who may be able to do that. He is the Knight of Cups, who has learned how to grasp his magical weapon, and therefore can control the waters of the sea. Let's call on the Knight."

Surgey was on a mission preventing a flood that threatened the delta lands where many poor people lived in simple houses on stilts. He promised to be with us as soon as he could. In the meantime, while Donald and Namrata packed up their tools and valuable objects and took them down to their boat, I crept over the hill to take a look at the center of the cult. As I got nearer, I could hear the loud chanting of thousands of voices accompanied by a weird kind of rustling noise, which crackled in my ears like static electricity, so loud was it. I wriggled up the low, sandy bluff and peered over.

Astonished at the changes wrought on the site since I had been there, I glanced down to the waters' edge, where dozens upon dozens of fishing boats were drawn up on the sand. A large fish cannery was churning, as crates of cans were loaded onto a small freighter that lay at a newly-built dock. Nearer to me, a vast circle of moving people shuffled waist-deep through vast heaps of dead leaves, and in their center rose up a figure in brilliant red robes slashed with purple, who sat upon a makeshift throne of rusty iron. This throne had been raised up since I was here last, and now stood atop an inverted pyramid, its apex buried deep in the sand below. From each person there extended a thin silver chain leading from their solar plexus to the lower regions of the monarchs' garments, where it disappeared. As they walked, they chanted, yet the chant held a desperate note, and their faces were clouded and wary.

I saw that any high seas would instantly swamp the place and swill over the entire island, which was only about fifteen feet above sea level. It was no good worrying about the people ensnared by the cult, but I felt a twinge of guilt. How could I warn them? If I showed myself and warned of a tsunami, they might not believe me. But I felt a great need to save those who had lent themselves to the monarch, thereby dropping their energy as leaves fell off a tree, while they nourished the evil entity in their midst. I wondered if there was some way I could bring the monarch down before we resorted to such desperate methods. I decided to return that night and investigate further.

Donald and Namrata were ready to evacuate their crew when I returned to the dig, and were busy pouring the plaster around the delicate areas of the foundations. At that moment, I heard a whistling noise in the air above, and the Knight of Cups arrived on his horse Catarack, landing on the ground with a soft thud, his hooves spattering sand. I greeted him instantly.

"Welcome, Surgey! How was the delta rescue? Successful, I hope." I glanced at his face. "We need your help here now."

"My grasp of the Cup worked! I was able to hold back a monsoon flood, and saved 30,000 people. What rewarding work this is! It is wonderful to have control of one's Magical Weapon." Here Surgey brandished the great Cup. "Now, what can I do for you?"

"Leave Catarack here and come with me and I'll show you. But first, let's say goodbye to Donald and his crew, for they must leave now for the bigger island." I introduced the Knight to the archaeologists, and we watched them board their vessel and cast off, motoring across the strait that separated the island from the larger group.

We turned then and quietly crept back to the bluff, and I showed Surgey what was happening down on the hidden side of the island. He obviously had the same doubts as I had. Was it right to sacrifice thousands of people just because one person had raised himself up as their savior? In spite of doubts, I was still in favor of guilt by association, and Surgey pointed out that they had been free to choose their course initially, so they were responsible for their ultimate fate. Further, he felt sure that those whose character retained some willpower might yet be able to escape the wave and save themselves – the responsibility for their fate resting with them.

Priming our motivation with these decisions, we decided not to risk a closer inspection of the monarch that night, but to set the wave in motion as quickly as possible. We mounted Catarack, I riding pillion as before, and took off into the sky, skimming low over the waves to avoid being seen by the cult. Approximately 300 miles off shore, the Knight aimed his horse at a point above the ocean bed, and before I knew it, we were entering the water and descending in a rapid dive towards one of the volcanic vents below us.

Again, I found no difficulty in breathing underwater, as I had ascertained on my journey with the Page of Cups. The vent below us was sending forth large bubbles of steam and the sea floor heaved and cracked, moving back and forth. Surgey leaned forward and placed his Cup upside down over the vent, then drew it back and up sharply, as one would a plunger. At the same time, he rapidly reined in Catarack and threw him backwards in a somersault. This happened so fast that I was able to hang on and watch as, in front of us, the vent ripped open with a loud fizzing and the crack in the sea floor opened up, splitting and heaving away from us in a long zigzag pattern as far as we could see. We rose quickly to the surface, taking off and flying low over the sea as a huge mound of water rose beneath us and formed into a giant wave that rolled at great speed towards the island. We flew above this wave and I knew I was about to witness what followed when it hit the island.

The people in the cult were smart enough to realize that a big wave was coming, as they saw the tide run out along the shore, leaving the freighter high and dry, and they attempted to scatter and make for the trees. Unfortunately, by running to-and-fro they entangled the silver chains that attached each person to the monarch, and the combined weight of the knot of chains pulled him from his perch. He fell, his robes ripping to shreds as they caught in the rusty iron, shrieking as he bounced off the base of the upturned pyramid and fell the remaining fifteen feet, hitting the ground hard and splitting his head, from which the blood began to gush. The terrified crowd struggled over the mounds of leaves towards higher ground, dragging him behind them and ignoring his screams. His mouth soon filled with leaves, blocking his breathing, and he quickly suffocated and became silent in death. As this happened, the silver cords melted and the people in the cult suddenly found they were free. A great sigh went up, they dispersed to all points of the compass, some climbing the trees on the bluff, others putting ladders up to the roof of the cannery, and more taking to the fishing boats, which were aground, but which held some hope. The body of their leader lay abandoned in a pile of disheveled leaves heaped in the compound.

"Quick! Surgey. We must stop the wave!" I tugged at his shirt wildly. "The monarch is dead. The spell is broken and they now have a chance. We can't let them die. For Gods' sake, stop the tsunami!"

The Knight heard me and nodded his head. He wheeled his horse and rode towards the wave as it rose up the beach. Holding up the Cup, Surgey ordered the wave to retreat in a commanding voice. The wave broke early, and the waters dissipated with a hissing motion as a fierce riptide set up and pulled its force back to the ocean.

All the people were amazed. They kept looking each other over, as if they had met for the first time, shaking hands, clapping each other on the back, and hugging. They trampled over, kicked and stoned the body of their monarch, uttering shouts of glee, until it was completely unrecognizable. Surgey and I landed on the beach, and the people swarmed around us, congratulating us on their rescue, and chattering excitedly about being free to leave the island. He turned to me.

"You have passed the test the Queen gave you, to divert the reflection from illusion into connection. The reflection was your thoughts followed by action; the illusion came from the brainwashing of the cult, and the connection between them will now last for all of their lives, since they have had a very vital shared experience. Well done, my friend, I congratulate you. I will now have to leave, for the Queen has ordered me to my next task – to prevent the collapse of a dam in the Rocky Mountains, before the reservoir inundates a nearby valley and drowns the inhabitants. Farewell, we will meet again, for your next task is the one the King will set you."

With that, the Knight was off on Catarack, soaring over the ocean. I watched him until he was a speck in the sky, and then bent to the task of arranging a ferry service to get all the people back to their original communities.

Once all the misguided cultists had been ferried off the island, I returned to their center, now lying in chaos. I went to the body of their monarch and turned it over. As the badly disfigured corpse flopped onto its back, I stared at what was left of the face in horror. It was still clear to see that the monarch had no facial features whatever, but presented a blank look to the world that I had not noticed from further away. I then saw, looking closer, and wiping the dirt from the flaccid countenance, that there were faint scar marks where the eyes, nose and mouth should have been, as if someone had surgically removed them and then sewed up the holes, leaving a small blowhole in the leaders' throat for him to breathe. The ears were still there, pointed and furry as they thrust forward in a listening attitude from beneath a thatch of black hair.

The monarch was blind and could neither smell, taste nor speak! However, he had still retained a keen ability to hear. I wondered whether his sense of touch remained, and searched under the draggled robes for his hands. I ran my hand along the limp arm, and came up with a stump. His hands had been cut off at the wrists, and, as I soon discovered, so had his feet. All that remained was a featureless head, attached to a torso with no means of propulsion or sensitivity of feeling. Where did the tangled silver chains lead? I had to find out. I pulled aside the robes and saw that the chains, which seemed to be melting as I worked, disappeared up his anus, which was torn and bleeding.

How disgusting, I thought. All his followers were chained to his backside! How low could they go? I wondered if any of them had investigated as I had, and decided that they had not had the great opportunity presented to me. I gave the corpse a kick, and left the area, rowing back to the dock near the hotel of the larger island, where, during a hearty meal, I reassured Donald and Namrata that they could resume their archaeological work without further interruption. I then bade them goodbye and turned my boat towards the Lagoon once more.

King of Cups - Rules Four and Two of Cups.

Relieved to see the Castle of Water after a long trip back from the island where we had destroyed the cult, I moored the boat and walked up towards the rebuilt fortifications. The servants and residents of the Castle had done a magnificent job of repair after the tsunami hit them, and they had ferried their dead over to the Isle of the White Pyramid with great solemnity. I asked an equerry about the ceremony for the dead, but to my surprise he looked at me as if he had seen a ghost, and refused to answer. I mentioned the matter to several other people, who looked equally scared, but would reveal nothing of the burial arrangements at the Pyramid.

The King of Cups was not in his quarters, his valet explaining that he was "occupied with the gusher." Did that mean he was discussing something with an obsequious and annoying old woman, I wondered? The valet, however, pointed out of the turret window towards a desert area that spread out beyond the tropical, watery surroundings of the castle. Between the distant dry ground and the humid surroundings of the Castle of Water a large section of many colored hills stretched, their shades varying from yellow sulfuric hues of ochre through burnt sienna to a warm grey. Adjusting my focus, I saw a figure in blue robes standing on top of one of the gushers, surrounded by steaming geysers that shot up and fell back at regular intervals. It was the King, and his body seemed to sway to-and-fro as he held an enormous Cup over his head from which a fountain of water issued.

I decided to investigate this phenomenon and, after a short trek dodging small geysers that erupted under my feet, and avoiding several pots of boiling mud, I reached King Jetspur. The King looked down at me gently. He was balancing skillfully on a large jet of water that burst forth from a sinkhole under his feet, and directing the water into the Cup, where it sallied forth clear and sparkling. It was a beautiful sight, for Jetspur was tall and fair, with waving white-blonde hair and huge blue eyes of an intensity I had never encountered before. His lips were full and curved in a slight smile as he flexed his muscular biceps to hold up the Cup.

"I have come to ask your favor, Mi Lawd. Will you give me the essence of my next task?"

Jetspur spoke slowly and with a melting tone to his voice. "I am so relieved that you were able to inform me of the Hodians, for they have retrained Knight Surgey well. I hear that he has recently not only stopped a great tsunami, but managed to start one as well. That shows great skill, for he had previously honed his underwater practice at the volcanic vents to a fine art, and it only remained for him to handle his Cup correctly." The King smiled modestly. "Now, for your next test, you have **to investigate and filter the emergence of seduction and devious treachery.**" I believe it concerns the missing toad and his friend Jafar, the cuscus, but before you resume your search for them, there are two more important problems you must confront, and you will find out what these are shortly."

I wanted to ask if the King would be coming along on my next adventure, but I didn't dare. He looked so preoccupied with the water filtration, I assumed that he couldn't leave at a moments' notice, so I thanked him and wandered back to the Castle. On the way, I came upon a wide river that I hadn't noticed before, and on it were three sailboats. One boat was running free before the wind, the second was close-hauled and making short tacks up the river, and in the distance I could see a boat high aground on the shore. At the top of a cliff overlooking the river I came upon two weird unclothed figures wearing platinum jewelry, who were arguing fiercely. The smaller fat man gave his companion a vicious push with his hand.

"That is absolutely impossible, Fayza! You know perfectly well that the two billion dollars we distributed amongst the farmers of that poor continent for agricultural improvements went into the pockets of the overseers, and we achieved nothing. There is no point in giving more until we can root out the corruption over there."

"How do you expect to reduce corruption when the reason for it is poverty in the first place?" The lanky woman shot back angrily. "The whole point of aid is to try and boost the economy from the bottom up, and until the peasants are solvent, they have no power and can be manipulated by those above them."

"Then how do you propose to stop their government officials from filching supplies, since we aren't occupying the country? The goods never get to those they are intended for. It would take dozens more administrators that we don't have."

"Then let's hire more! We have the funds to do it, Yukio. I just feel committed to the people over there. I've seen their circumstances many times during my visits. We need more help with the distribution of our funds, that's all."

"It's a waste of time! We've tried that before – in fact, you yourself have been in that country seventeen times, and they still laugh at you behind your back, those thieving bureaucrats." The little man was quite irate. "I propose that we cut off funds over there and send three billion dollars to open up the far north, so that underground villages may be built for the huge rise in population that we know is coming."

"The population has grown enormously because we have succeeded in eradicating most epidemics worldwide. We made a big mistake there, incidentally, distributing medication throughout the third world. Fewer people died, and now there are many more to feed, and they are reproducing frenetically. I propose, rather than throwing money at underground bunkers, that we boost the level of hydroponic gardening in that area, since the available land is exhausted and produces nothing without tons of fertilizer – which the environmental officials have refused to distribute because they say it pollutes the rivers. We need food first, then we can worry about housing the poor." The tall woman turned angrily and stared out across the wide river, trying to regain her composure.

Approaching them, I held out my hand. "Can I help you with anything? It seems you are having a disagreement. Maybe I can arbitrate for you both." As I spoke, they reluctantly broke off their argument and we all shook hands.

"It's true that we don't agree, and never have, really," explained the shorter of the two, an annoyed look on his round face. "I am Yukio, and this is my business partner Fayza. We each took over half the worlds' business and then decided to amalgamate, so that we could form a vast philanthropic organization to benefit the worlds' destitute nations. Now, our problem is that we can't agree as to where the money should go, as there are so many undeveloped areas of wasteland which are flooded by overpopulation."

I had to remind them. "Part of your problem may be that, in order to build up your businesses, you exploited the resources in many places, draining the oil reserves, logging the forests, damming rivers for hydroelectricity to run mills, and overbuilding in unsuitable territory where much of the population has been forced to leave because of violent weather." I could see that both of them were not too pleased with my statement, but it was the truth.

Yukio passed a hand over his sweaty forehead, glaring at me. He looked extremely upset. "You are wrong. As we expanded our enterprises, we created factories and mills to serve the areas with low employment. We built cheap housing. OK - so we offered low wages, but they had no work at all before we took over. Money in their hands has enabled them to spend money, and thus our other businesses boomed, because they bought goods from us. But the poor were still there – a fact I don't understand." He finished lamely.

"The poor will always be there, no matter what you do to help them." I said with regret. "The current situation is that you created a false economy by tempting the people to buy things that were not necessary for their livelihood. The trade in luxury items has reached such a pitch that once they have their survival needs satisfied, people can think of nothing else, and the world is becoming cold towards those who have not succeeded. The fault lies with you both, for you now virtually own every working man and woman on the globe and hold their fate in your hands, since your company is the only remaining employer. Now you are in a serious conflict yourselves, which does not bode well for those who are powerless without your help."

I looked at the tall skinny woman Fayza, whose dry, bony face twisted into a hideous scowl. "How dare you come here out of the blue and tell us these things!" She shouted, brandishing her fist in my face. "What do you know of success – you miserable ragged rat!"

Shocked, I took a step back, but continued. "The greatest evil is closest to the greatest good. Beware that you do not fall into that pit – for if you lose control of your empire, anarchy will result. The rule of the tyrant, once toppled, creates a vacuum that allows the forces of chaos to pour in and infest the space that has been created. Ask yourselves, with all that you control, are you now on the verge of megalomania?"

Yukio was now also furious and, stuttering, defended himself poorly, falling further and further into the web of lies that he had constructed to achieve his fortune. Fayza tried to shut him up, denying the truth behind their prosperity. In another minute, they were at each others' throats, struggling and yelling as they kicked and punched. Fayza managed to trip Yukio, and he overbalanced and tottered at the edge of the cliff. I wanted to pull him back, to save him, but it was written in their Destiny, so instead I stood still and watched as he grabbed Fayzas' ankles and the shale slid from under them both. Screaming, they fell over the cliff and I heard a loud splash in the river below. I rushed to the edge. They had already disappeared under the fast flowing water.

Bracing myself, I took off in a swallow dive over the cliff face and hit the water hard. The cliff was higher than I had thought, but I recovered after a moment and set off downriver, swimming rapidly with the current, in the foolish hope of saving the capitalists. In the fast flowing stream it was hard to see anything, although I scanned the surface for bobbing heads and waving arms. Occasionally I dove deep under the water and searched amongst the weeds and silt, disturbing the mud so that it rose up in little clouds, yet saw no bodies.

The river swept me along, and I found it was easier to ride the wavelets by lying on my back, feet first, and sculling gently with my arms to slow myself down. The waves became bigger and the water more disturbed as I rounded a bend and saw in front of me a section of rapids in the river, where the water tossed and foamed amongst large boulders and boiled over sinkholes that might hold me down. I didn't want to get caught in one of those, so I pretended I was a kayak, and used my arms as paddles to steer through the rapids.

Avoiding the boulders, and the undertow that pulled me towards them, made shooting the rapids without a vessel extremely perilous and I began to tire. As far as I could see ahead, the foaming water continued, while above the chattering river I heard a sound that sent chills down my spine – the ominous roar of a waterfall! It was time to edge to the side somehow and reach dry land, which I managed to do, dodging a number of large boulders, and teetering wearily out across some slippery pebbles.

There was still no sign of the capitalists, so I covered the distance to the edge of the waterfall and looked over. I was astonished to see two bedraggled figures clinging to a large, jutting rock halfway down the waterfall.

I waved at them and shouted.

"Are you OK? I've been looking for you everywhere. I felt sure you had drowned. I'm so glad you're alive!"

Calculating my chances of reaching them as zero, for the massive quantity of water rushing past them into the basin below was far too powerful, I decided they had to be reached by water – but how?

Fayza gave a desperate call. "Oh! Thank heavens you found us. We're stuck, as you can see, and my hands are so cold I can't hold on much longer. Please help us, quickly, please!"

The rescue had to come from below, since the invention of the helicopter was far into the future, and a strong swimmer would be needed. I thought of the two dolphins that belonged to the Queen of Cups. Dolphins often helped humans, and two dolphins had saved me from a gale at sea by steadying my kayak, so I called out to Fayza.

"I'll run back to the Castle and ask Fluvia if the dolphins can come up river. They can bring a net with them. You will have to let go and jump into the net, and you must not be afraid of the confusion and splashing below the falls, for they will stabilize you and bring you to the bank. I'll be back! Hold on!"

Turning, I ran swiftly back to the Castle, where I was able to get the two dolphins and ride upriver on one dolphin, until we were in the welter of churning water under the falls. I looked up and saw, about 100 feet up, the rock jutting out and the two capitalists clinging to it.

"Jump!" I yelled as loud as I could above the roar of falling water. "We will catch you in our net."

A faint voice came down to us. "I can't. It's too far. We'll be drowned. I'm afraid to try it. Please think of something else. We can subsidize a company to invent helicopters…."

The voice trailed away.

"You have no choice." I shouted back. "You will fall anyway, when your grip loosens. Don't be afraid to take the chance – you've taken enough financial gambles, now you have a physical risk in front of you. We are waiting here to save you."

I saw Yukios' fat legs dangling over the side of the rock, and suddenly he was plummeting towards us. The dolphins knew exactly where he would hit the water, and we were there to support him in the net as he climbed onto the other dolphins' back. The animals swam to-and-fro under the rock, and I called up once more.

"Fayza! Fayza! Let go and jump. Yukio is OK. We caught him in the net." I could see Fayzas' face peering over the side of the rock as her hands clutched the slippery surface, and in an instant she let go and fell, turning over and over, her long, skinny legs and arms flailing the air. We were in position to catch her as she plummeted down, and I gave up my dolphin ride and swam between the two dolphins, as we turned downriver towards the Castle.

Fayza dashed the streaming water from her eyes. "Yukio, you saved me back there. I'll never argue with you again. I owe my life to you and I'm eternally grateful."

She turned to me. "Yukio is so fat, he floated just like a life raft, and he supported me in the water until we were sucked over the waterfall. Now that I have my life back, I understand the meaning of my existence much better. Making money is not what lifes' about. Having friends and people who help you when a crisis comes is very important. Thank you, thank you, for saving us! We will never forget you."

We deposited them at the Castle, where the servants gave them a hot bath and put salve on their bumps and bruises, and then we sat down to a dinner of several different fish platters.

My sojurn at the Castle of Water had been neither successful nor enjoyable so far. Emotions ran high there and were often out of control. I compared this warm but uncontrolled Court with the cool dispassionate atmosphere at the Castle of Air, and the practical, earthy surroundings at the Castle of Earth. I had one more task to perform here, then I would move to the Castle of Fire, and I wondered what lay in store for me there.

Now I found myself floating in my rowboat on a large lake close to a field of bright poppies where a number of people were working furtively, shrouded in the darkness that was approaching and would soon mask their labors. It seemed strange that they would choose to work at night. I tied up the boat and moved stealthily towards them, keeping my head below the level of the poppies. Closer inspection revealed that they were extracting opium from the seed pods of the flowers by scraping the black sap into containers, which were then placed on little radio flyers and wheeled over to a large truck. Up the ramp they went, and disappeared inside the truck.

Knowing that this was an illicit practice, I rowed silently over to the other side of the lake and looked around for the tall woman that I had met before, Freya, who owned the poppy field. I found her in a dilapidated trailer by the waters' edge, and when she opened the door, I saw that opium still had its hold on her, and that she was near death. Her face bore the marks of her struggle with the drug, and her body was weak and emaciated.

I was saddened. "Whatever happened, Freya? Last time I was here you were with Fontanova, and she was taking you to rehab. Where is Fontanova now?" I was worried.

"Fontanova could only stay while you were in a creative frame of mind. She is your artistic entity, after all. She faded away, leaving me outside the door of the center, and I have since heard that you have called her to be active in other endeavors. She can't be everywhere, you know." Freya sighed deeply. "I was too frightened to go into the rehab center. I came back here, where I still had a stock of opium......." Her voice trailed away and she looked desperate.

"We must do something about that. But first, I have some bad news. You know that fellow Ramiro, who worked for you and who you tried to poison. He is taking his revenge at this moment, deceiving you again. There are many workers over in your poppy field, harvesting the opium under cover of darkness and loading it into a large truck. They have to be stopped somehow, but of course we don't want to call the cops, since the field belongs to you, and there would be unnecessary enquiries." I scratched my head.

"Maybe that is the very best thing to do, you know." Freya said slowly. "Bringing the whole operation out into the open would rid me of Ramiro and his gang, and although the authorities would then implicate me, they might be able to help me before it's too late. I know I am dying, and I don't have the willpower to kick my habit without discipline. I think we should go to the police." Freya slumped onto an overstuffed couch with greasy arms and the ripped marks of constantly clawing cats on the sides.

I agreed. It might save her, after all. She would be forced into rehab then, and that was the best thing for her at this stage. Otherwise it would be all over for her, too soon. I got up and, taking a bicycle from outside the trailer, rode off around the lake to where Ramiros' men had parked the truck. As I cautiously hid behind a bush, the vehicle started up and rumbled slowly away with its' cargo. By pedaling furiously at a distance, I was able to keep up and saw the truck stop outside a large warehouse on the outskirts of town. It backed up to the loading platform and the doors opened.

Quickly I made my way to the police station. I told them of the opium load, but they had a suspicious gleam in their eyes as they looked me over. Of course, my strange attire - the hemp tunic, sandals and fur cloak did not help. It seemed clear they did not believe me. I remonstrated with them for some time, and eventually one policeman reluctantly followed me back to the warehouse, where he observed that I was speaking the truth and quickly called for reinforcements. They were able to catch the thieves in the act.

When the turmoil was over, inevitably they began asking questions about the source of the drug. I told the cops that I would introduce them to the owner of the field, and we all drove to where I had left Freyas' trailer.

To my horror, all that remained of the trailer was a burning pile of metal shards and ashes, with the flames still licking along the rubble, and no sign of Freya. I hoped she hadn't perished in the fire. Had she escaped, and if so, where was she? Did she deliberately set the fire? Was this the sign that she had backed out of our agreement? I was extremely concerned.

"There will have to be an investigation." The sheriff announced. "How do we know who set this fire? Was it you?" He turned towards me accusingly.

I didn't know what to say, as a stab of fear shot through me and some small arms gripped my waist. I knew Paragutt was behind me with the yellow streak down his back. I had an alibi, didn't I? I reminded the cops that I had spent several hours persuading them of the drug operation and leading them to the warehouse where they discovered the opium, and then waiting while they arrested the thieves and made their report, and that included driving back to the trailer with them to find Freya.

They said it depended at what time the fire was set, and that couldn't be decided until they concluded their investigation. A fire truck had arrived and was squirting water on the burning trailer as several officers searched the rubble for any sign of a body. They found none. So Freya might still be alive somewhere, if she hadn't walked into the lake. I was frustrated. Where could she be? Was there a black hole somewhere containing all the missing people?

The police established my alibi, fortunately, when they found out the fire was very recently set and I had been in the police station at that time. Paragutt left abruptly as soon as I was out of danger. I realized that Freya must have set the fire herself. I had to find the missing people in this puzzle. The one thing all of them had in common was their ability to deceive others as to their real intentions, with the result that they brought karmic justice upon themselves.

Remembering the test that the King had set me, I resolved to return to the hot springs where his geyser was in order to request his help, which I had not dared to do before. He must know all about things and people who were hiding underwater, since his emotions connected him to the submarine world.

Finding myself again in front of Jetspur, I bowed and told him of Freyas' disappearance, and how she departed without leaving a clue as to her whereabouts. He smiled mysteriously and silently stepped off the geyser that was supporting him, taking my hand. A huge jet of hot steam swept us up and enveloped us in a warm fog, and I felt myself sliding downwards, holding onto the blue robe of the King as he rode the center of the rushing plume of water. For a moment, I couldn't work out why we weren't blown into the air, until I understood that there was a small hole in the center of the gusher which was clear of water, rather like the centrifugal force around a drain. We fell together, spiraling down, Jetspurs' face mirroring a thousand different emotions as we plummeted downwards.

All was pitch black around us as we landed at the bottom of the gusher, but I could hear a faint voice whispering in the darkness. It sounded like the Water Goddess Anahita, she of the Spring Waters, and I felt comforted knowing that I was with the Goddess and the King. I was used to being underwater by now, as we found ourselves in the cavern where Anahita lived under the spring. I remembered playing at underwater polo with Rivula, and the dark fissure at the back of the cave where the Goddess told me she put all the people that annoyed her. I wanted to peek inside the fissure and see who was there, but a most intriguing scene swiftly distracted my attention.

Anahita was clearly flirting with the King and I could see very well that he was responding to her advances. I made myself small behind a rock and watched them as they exchanged heated glances and then touched hands. Before a moment had passed, they were in a tender embrace, from which they fell to the floor of the cave in a squirming heap of passion, emitting heated moans. A swarm of tiny bubbles frothed around them and rose up through the water, gradually expanding until they burst at the surface of the pool. Feeling embarrassed, but taking my chance at their conjugation, I scurried – as best I could underwater – over to the fissure and squinted my eyes to make out the forms in the darkness beyond.

There were probably five dozen creatures in the smaller cave beyond the fissure. I won't call them all people, for they were of all shapes and sizes, from small chickens who had tried to cross the road; to frogs that ventured too close to sewer outlets; cows that had refused to let down their milk; alligators that had eaten styrofoam boxes; and many others. Of course, there were lots of people, too. They ranged from astronauts whose rocket had misfired to surfers who had been mistaken for seals by sharks; half-wits who did not use pedestrian crossings; sailors who set out before checking the approach of a hurricane; and many more whose decisions had been foolish in the extreme.

Running my eyes across the crowd, I spotted a small furry hump in the corner whose liquid eyes were turned beseechingly upon me, and hiding behind the creature, a little wide snout with gleaming eyes took me in, as the toad Oojo - for it was he - tried to squeeze out of sight behind the cuscus. Next to them was a tall, emaciated figure that I recognized as Freya, and so I waved to her.

All the missing persons in the whole world were here. The Goddess had sucked them into her Cup because she was annoyed with their foolish behavior. I listened as they told me how she had caught them.

Freya admitted that she had set fire to her trailer and had then swum out into the middle of the lake, hoping to drown. As she went under, she felt the suction of a large container, and remembered nothing further. As for Oojo and Jafar, they told me that they had to escape through the sewers under the dark bazaar, but had been suffocated by the smell and swept out to sea.

All three had gone underwater, and Anahita had saved them from drowning. They were alive and deeply sorry for their antics. I promised I would try to get them out. Of course, there was still the curse on Jafar to be lifted, too.

I backed out of the fissure and politely waited until the groaning couple on the floor had completed their tryst and arose. I realized that the situation was in my favor, as I could use blackmail to pressure Anahita to give up her three captives. At first I pretended I had seen nothing, as I strolled up to the Goddess, keeping my balance in the water by swishing my arms to and fro, and begged her to give up the prisoners. When she refused, I winked at her and then pointed to Jetspur and made a somewhat rude gesture, indicating that I had observed what was going on. I also pointed out that I was a close friend of Queen Fluvia, who might be upset if she heard about their little tryst.

This did the trick. Anahita soon released the three captives and we all floated up to the surface. The King came with us humbly, and I had a word with him before we returned to the Castle. I promised to say nothing of his seduction, provided he gave a great banquet to celebrate the rebuilding of the Castle and Jafars' escape. He swiftly agreed and gave me a sly wink. I was able to catch the penitent Oojo and return him to his little bag in disgrace, and we carried the cuscus back to the Castle with us. When we got there, Freya was put under the care of a young equerry in a clean white coat, who whisked her off to his sanitarium. Meanwhile, Yukio and Fayza, who had taken a terrific dunking under the waterfall and had a narrow escape, decided to split up their world-wide business into a trillion little businesses and distribute them to all the poverty stricken peasants around the globe, while they got married and went off on a charter yacht to the Riviera.

The lifting of the spell on Jafar was the only thing left to do. There was no baptismal font at the Castle, for all the Royal Courts were agnostic, but I thought Fontanova might be able to do the trick. She had let me down by leaving Freya outside the rehab center when she should have made sure the addict was signed in, and owed me a favor. My mind pictured a stage hidden behind heavy red velvet curtains. On this stage, a banquet had been set, and off to one side, as part of the scenery, there was a small room with an antique love seat carved from black ebony with red velvet cushions. Sitting on the seat, and patting the cushion beside her, was Fontanova. I mentally placed the cuscus next to her and awaited the outcome.

My creative entity responded well. She unbuttoned her blouse and gave the cuscus her breast, from which came a baptismal flow of milk. As I watched, Fontanova became the New Fountain, the goddess Isis, whose celestial milk flowed into the throat of the unhappy creature. Slowly I saw the cuscus dissolve and take on the form of the young man Jafar. I clapped my hands in glee, scaring them, and Fontanova vanished. Jafar leapt off the couch and ran to us, and we embraced him. I was, thus, enabled "to investigate and filter the emergence of seduction and devious treachery." As a result, I passed the test allotted to me by the King of Cups.

Page of Wands – Rules Ten and Nine of Wands.

Bidding farewell to the Royal Court at the Castle of Water, I rowed softly away, making my way along the shore of the Lagoon towards the Castle of Fire, which glowed brightly in the distance. The landscape between the two Castles changed rapidly from tropical plants, palms, hibiscus, and other moisture-loving plants to the edge of an arid plain. Giant geysers steamed and spouted, throwing unexpected fountains of white steam high in the air, while around them numerous mud pots were spurting disconsolately from time to time, burping up little gobs of steaming mud. In the distance, a wall of fire burned steadily, neither increasing nor decreasing. I was afraid it might be heading towards me until I realized there was nothing to burn out here. I decided to proceed on foot, so I moored the boat to a rocky outcrop that stank of sulfur.

As I stepped on shore, an armadillo clanked across the landscape, heading towards the desert beyond the Castle of Fire, his tail dragging in the dust. Suddenly he sat down, rolling himself into a ball with his tail pointing forward. I heard the heavy panting of someone running, and looked up as the footsteps slowed down and a tall red haired fellow appeared, shading his eyes and looking into the distance anxiously. I hailed him and he walked over to me, shaking his head.

There was something peculiar about him. I could see that he wore the garments of a Page, the leggings, tunic and short cape, although his feet were clad in pumps rather than the boots I had noticed on the other Pages. However, his skin looked very strange, for it had the fine unblemished luster of a baby, without a mark of any kind, and I wondered how he managed to keep it so perfect. Then I noticed a small strip of dry skin hanging down under his arm. It looked as if it had peeled off, like a snakes' skin. Was it possible that the Page had molted?

"Hello." I nodded to him politely. "I'm heading to the Castle of Fire, to take my next tests. Are you the Page of Wands, by any chance?"

"Well, yes, I am. I'm not going to the Castle right now. My quest is beyond it, in the desert on the other side. I am searching for myself, and the Goddess of Fire, Mahuia, has arranged for me to cross the burning wasteland on an armadillo that she has provided for me. Have you seen it anywhere?"

"It's over there, in a ball, pointing with its tail. It looks far too small to carry you, though, and I should imagine that its horny back would be very uncomfortable to sit on." I changed the subject and asked him. "What are you called?"

"My name is Ripskin. By the way, that isn't the right armadillo. It's the baby. Here we have giant armadillos to ride on, and they carry asbestos saddles that are quite comfortable and prevent one from catching fire. I have just completed my eighth molt. You may have noticed a pile of skin further back. I can tell you, shedding one's skin is no fun, especially when you have to take your clothes off so frequently to get rid of the shards. Now I don't have to molt any more. I'm done with that, thank goodness."

"Why is it necessary for you to shed your skin?" I pondered. "Most people don't have to do that."

"In fact, they do, it's just more gradual. Their skin just flakes off in very small amounts each day and grows anew from inside. In my case, I have reached the point where I can shed the entire skin in one fell swoop, as it were, and leave it behind. That's my last molt over there." Ripskin pointed to the flattened human shape lying next to a mud pot nearby, and continued. "I recently left the convent where I studied to become a molting monk. They actually threw me out because I wouldn't stick to their rules. They insisted on molting from the head down, and I prefer to start with the feet. I originally entered the convent because I have had mystical tendencies since I was a child, and my parents didn't know what to do with me, because I didn't fit in with their bourgeois lifestyle. They basically abandoned me when I was five, and the monks took me in, but I soon left and I've been on my own since then."

"That's hard, to be abandoned by ones' parents. Maybe it is better than being abused or having alcoholics to look after you, though. I have met some other Pages who have all had difficulties with their families. They are working on resolving their problems too. Do you have a test for me, by the way? I would like to hear it." I looked at him hopefully.

"Yes, I do. I'm glad I met you out here instead of having to go into the Castle to find you. It saves time, for my quest is to shed my outer self completely so that I can operate entirely by intuition. Your test is "**to liberate the oppressed by the interpretation of dreams.**" I think it sounds quite a nice one, for a change."

"Yes, it seems more philosophical and less traumatic, I must say. But how do you know about my other tests?" I was puzzled.

"I told you, I knew I was clairvoyant at an early age, and therefore I know what has passed for you, and what may lie in your future. Watch out for that toad in the bag that you insist on keeping with you, for example. Trouble there, mark my words. Then the Seven Shades. They are close by, watching you, and they plan to pounce at the opportune moment and capture you again." He nodded again, and a look of impatience crossed his face. "I must go. There is no time to be wasted. My armadillo is here. I will see you sooner than you expect."

Ripskin loped away, avoiding the mud holes, and leaped onto the back of a stout creature who immediately ambled off, its' scaly tail sticking out straight behind it. I wasn't sure what to do. The other Pages had remained by my side to help me and had accompanied me on my trials. I felt a little peeved, and thought about asking the Page of Wands to return, but decided I had better manage without him as he was, evidently, caught up in his own agenda.

Meandering along the shore, I came to a copse of short and scrubby bushes, half-scorched by the hot steam that came from the geysers. A snuffling sound below me attracted my attention and I spotted a black and white creature on a mound of earth in the center of the copse. It was the rear end of a badger digging furiously, the earth spurting from his paws, as he worked to create a larger burrow. I stopped to watch and the animal soon turned his earthy snout in my direction and gave a sharp bark.

"More rooms, more rooms, that's what I have to dig, dig. There is never an end to it. I get more requests every day, people are pouring in from heaven knows where. It's impossible to keep up." The badger shook the dirt off his nose. "Are you here now to order another room for your beliefs?" He asked querulously.

"No. I am on a trial. I don't have specific beliefs and I am without an escort, since the Page Ripskin is too busy to accompany me and has ridden off on his armadillo. I'd be grateful for any advice you can give me."

"Well, then, come on in and we'll talk. I know a few things around here."

The badger headed down the burrow, which enlarged as I followed him, so that I fitted quite comfortably. The smell of turned earth welcomed me and there were many passages leading off on either side, where the heady odor of incense and strange lights flickered down each corridor. We arrived in a larger central space, where I asked the badger who it was that requested room space in the burrow underground.

"It's the heretics. There are so many of them these days. Heretic this, and heretic that, some are Protestants fleeing from persecution by Catholics, others are Catholics who are requesting safe haven from Pagans. There are Moslems afraid of Jews; Rabbis hiding from the Aryan Nation; fighting Hindus and Sikhs; then there are Buddhists stabbing other Buddhists – I can tell you, it could be total anarchy in here. Fortunately, I am the only one who knows who people are and what they take cover from, and each group that arrives here gets a separate shrine room where they can worship at peace and without fear. It's hard keeping them apart, but because I insist on a vow of silence for all religious zealots who enter here, and I don't speak myself – at least, they can't understand me like you can – it works out quite nicely. Now, let me take you to meet our leader, the Priestess of Diurnal Hours. You will find her extremely intuitive."

The badger led me to a small room off the main hall, and up to a woman seated in the lotus position behind a stone altar on which a fire burned. Around her ten Wands were arranged in a semicircle, and as I approached, I recognized Semra, she who had been burdened by the wheel of ten Wands. Now she appeared serene, free of worldly problems, and obviously in charge of the tumultuous horde of people who arrived daily at her doorstep.

"Semra! How wonderful to find you here!" I exclaimed delightedly "I see you have made a home with the badger, and it looks very comfortable." I waited for her to rise, and she gave me a hug.

"Yes, after I handed back all the Wands that I had been carrying for other people that represented their problems, I got my own Wands back, and I was able to center my energy. I do yoga every day and meditate for many hours, in order to reconcile the mixed vibrations coming from each different group of zealots in this burrow. Without the calming effect of meditation, it would be mayhem in here. Many people disagree and oppose each others' beliefs, and they would set upon each other violently otherwise. It's crazy, this situation. People would kill each other for no good reason. Now, as you know, the Wands are intuition, and a person can reach their intuitive core by paying attention to their dreams. You will be passing through the School of Lucid Dreaming when you reach the Island of Yesod. That is a difficult learning process. In the meantime, you can practice with some easy dreaming while you are here."

Semra glided out of the room and I followed with the badger.

"Can you help me with my test?" I asked her hopefully. "You know what it is, don't you?"

"Yes, I do. That is why you are here. The heretics that we shelter here are all fleeing from persecution by other religions. Nobody understands that their beliefs are, basically, no different from anyone else, yet they are steeped in priestly dogma and can't see the truth. It is only through dreams that they will be able to lift the oppression under which they live on a daily basis. The land of dreams is common to all, and the symbols used by the dream masters are designed for everyone to understand. I advise them during the day, and my other half, Qamra, the Priestess of Nocturnal Hours, is on duty at night."

"Oh! Qamra is here too - that's wonderful. I was hoping to see her again and find out whether she has recognized her soul mate – her other half from the dream world with the cat necklace."

"Yes, she will be coming in at twilight to take over, as we have a particularly interesting case here at the moment. He is in the Catholic sector and imagines himself to be the Pope. Of course, that's ridiculous! He is a hideous little monster like a scaly red monkey, with bag-like fleshy wings that he flaps at you. More like the Devil, if you ask me." Semra shook her head and pursed her lips glumly. "He's the one whose dreams I'd like you to use for your test, though. I hope you can handle it."

I wasn't too pleased, and felt a little guilty at meeting the Father again in his new guise. However, if the test had to be passed and the results satisfactory, I had no choice. Remembering the time that Einerline and I had robbed his library, I was glad that he was too conservative to have set up surveillance cameras there, or his guards might have recognized me. As soon as I thought about that, the figure of Einerline, my intellectual entity, was by my side, his transparent brain whirring away furiously. He pulled behind him a wheeled contraption with which I was familiar, for it was the dream machine he had used for me to astrally locate my lost kayak.

In the morning, I was ushered into an anteroom with a small love seat that had red velvet cushions and a black ebony frame. On this seat lounged the red monkey, flat on his back, for he was quite little, and almost disappearing into the red cushions.

"Can I offer you a pillow?" I asked him. "There is a spare one here."

"Oh! Murder and farting damnation, NO! There is only one pillow I need, and that is lost. It is a gold velvet cushion with red tassels, and dear to my heart. A charlatan who passed through, claiming to be a Navigator, stole the cushion. Well, that person didn't know right from left, let alone be able to take a star sight or calculate set and drift."

Here the monkeylike figure raised himself, bared his teeth in a hideous grin and shrieked at the top of his voice.

"It was a fraud, and took my cushion, and I WANT IT BACK!" Then, suddenly calming down, he murmured almost inaudibly. "I am sorely oppressed and seek release from my dreadful state. Help me!"

As I leaned forward to catch his words, the red monkey fell back on the couch exhausted.

"You will have to be wired up for dreaming." I announced as I thought hard about the research that my entity Einerline had done regarding dreams, and he soon reappeared with his dream machine.

The creature shrank back on his couch.

"I am his Highness! You can't attach me to anything, you know. I'm free to make laws and do what I want, and everybody listens. In fact, they can often be persuaded to donate, if they can be tricked into thinking it will solve their sinful state" He continued, muttering under his breath. "Of course, they are complete fools, but that's how I make money for my church. Now, leave me alone."

I decided to play along with his supposed illusion that he was the Holy Father, although I knew it was the truth. "Dear Sire, I know who you really are," I said quite honestly, although Semra giggled and thought I was just playing him along. "We want to get rid of this uncomfortable costume you have on. It will be easier to take it off if you relax completely, for then we can unzip it, as it's very tight." Here I lied smoothly. "I suggest a light tranquillizer to get that done. You will merely feel dozy."

"All right then, if you think this is a costume. I thought it was me. I'm tired, so I'll take the draught." The monkey held up his head and I slipped a strong dose of lithium down his throat. It was not enough to kill him, of course. In a moment, he passed out, sinking still further into the red cushions until he was almost invisible. Just then, a bell rang for twilight and my friend Qamra stepped lightly into the room.

"Here is the Priestess of Nocturnal Hours. It is time for me to retire – we can't be on duty at the same time. Qamra, you know our Navigator here, don't you?" Semra indicated me, and Qamra ran forward to embrace me, as Semra departed quietly.

"I'm here to assist you with the dream analysis of the red monkey," said Qamra. "When we have completed that, we will talk, and I'll tell you what's been happening with me. Please go ahead."

Now Einerline and I quickly set up the dream machine, attached it to the monkeys' head, making sure he was still asleep, and were about to record the results when Einerline suddenly slumped to the floor. I hovered over him anxiously, keeping my thoughts on the dream research to try to reach him, but he remained in a dead faint, spread out in an ungainly fashion on the rushes strewn over the floor of the anteroom.

I struck my hand to my forehead. That was it! Einerlines' philosophical brain could only function in the everyday, practical world. Here in the anteroom Qamras' powerful nocturnal vibrations had overcome him, and his brain mechanisms had shut down. I motioned Qamra to reduce her dream energy level and asked around for a can of oil, and someone handed me an oil lamp. That would have to do. I bent down and poured some of the lamp oil into his right ear – the one that activated his left brain – and in a moment he sat up, shook his head, and asked where he had been. I lied and told him that it was a little stuffy down here, but that someone had opened a tunnel to bring in fresh air. That seemed to satisfy him, and we set to work, making sure the electrodes were firmly stuck to the monkeys' ears.

It was surprising, since the monkey was actually unconscious, that vivid dreams still came through from a deep level on the machine. It was clear that the subject was carrying an enormous amount of baggage from the past, far more than any other subject that Einerline had ever tested. Terrible scenes flashed across the screen that included incidents from the Borgia poisonings; the robberies of famous Pagan libraries; the torture of Giordano Bruno for his righteous beliefs; pages of Foxes' Book Of Martyrs - riffled through slowly; the atrocities of the Inquisition; the Nazification of a certain Pope; the useless clinging to old fashioned ideas which caused such suffering to his flock; the perversity of certain priests; and finally the terrible recent battle that ensued between the Haves and Have Nots outside the papal palace, during which thousands were mistakenly sorted into the wrong categories with disastrous results. Our subject twisted and turned uneasily as we recorded his dreams. He was obviously deeply oppressed because he had a lot to answer for, but since he had made the choice to rise in the hierarchy, perforce he had accepted the burden of all the previous deeds associated with his position, and I felt no sympathy.

We now had all the evidence before us, which we could corroborate historically, and so Einerline removed the apparatus and we left the red monkey to emerge from his unconscious state. When that occurred, we played back the recording by the dream machine to him, and he understood in horror the burden that was weighing him down. The guilt of ages was upon his brow, and I earnestly advised him to repent and cast off his current profession in favor of life as a mendicant beggar, during which he could make amends for the sins of the Father.

"Do I have to? Oh, all right. You told me you were going to take off this costume. Why is it still on?" He asked fretfully, struggling to ease his arms out of the tight sleeves, and trying not to show his distress at the replay of his unconscious self, which had picked up scenes from the collective unconscious of the papal past.

"You are within the power of the Castle of Fire." I said sternly. "All those who pass through here must shed their outer skins and learn intuition. A pilgrimage in the desert is the only way to get rid of the suit. We unzipped it but we couldn't get it over your shoulders. You must find the Page of Wands and ask him to assist you with the shedding process. He is very experienced, having completed his eighth molt, and is now a Nine. With determination, you can also become a changed person, and I wish you the best of luck. Now, you must leave the theological safety provided here, and go out into the real world and search for the Page, Ripskin. He is mounted on a large armadillo."

Taking him by the arm, I marched him out of the burrow and pushed him through the undergrowth, watching as he set out forlornly on his journey across the dusty plain, dragging his fleshy wings behind him.

Returning to the burrow and bidding Einerline goodbye, I made my way to Qamras' chamber, which had a beautiful circular rose-colored carpet on the floor, surrounded by nine Wands that burned gently, giving off a delicate light. On a small stone altar lay a necklace in the form of a cats head, marvelously carved.

Overhead a colony of bats were squeaking and fluttering their leathery wings, and then, with one accord, they streamed down from the ceiling and silently flapped their way out of the burrow on their nighttime foraging excursion.

Qamras' voice interrupted my musing. "When the moon rises, he will come," she said softly. "While we wait, I will tell you my story and how I gained the title of Priestess of Nocturnal Hours, for which I am extremely grateful."

We passed a pleasant couple of hours talking, and then the chamber slowly lightened, and I saw that a full moon was rising right inside the room itself. It was as if we were sitting outside and looking at the sky, so vivid was the effect. The moon was larger than usual, and as I gazed at it, I saw a shadowy form cross in front of it. It was Qamras' male entity, who could only show himself at night. I saw that a thin silvery cord attached him to her belly, which seemed as if it was made of a misty vapor, and a low and vibrating whisper came to me.

"Oh! You, who gave her the cat necklace! I bow to you, for you made her aware of me, her dream lover, and how she may reach me. She studied hard, and filled a dream journal in the daytime, and gradually I was able to show more of myself, which she wrote down. When she understood that I always appear as a male, but that I am capable of shape-shifting into different male figures in her life, she became aware that I was her male counterpart. We dreamed together for many months until she mastered lucid dreaming so that we could always be together as soul mates. When the dreaming was complete and we stood together, the Enochian Anchorites gave her the title of Priestess of Nocturnal Hours." He wavered in a slight puff of air from the doorway, as his cord stretched and contracted in response.

"Yes," said Qamra, in a reverie. "Now we can always be together. He is my soul mate. He is not an illusionary soul mate from the world of day, but real as the night. Together we watch over the pitiful heretics who have found refuge here, in the hope that their illusion of separateness from each other can be resolved in peace."

The knowledge of lucid dreaming and its path into my intuitive center was very valuable, and I was grateful to Qamra and her lover for letting me into their secret. I knew I would never be alone, for I also carried that secret soul mate within me at all times. Besides, I had my Guide – remembering suddenly that the old man had not shown himself to me for some time. I didn't realize that I would be needing his counseling desperately within the next few weeks.

We went late to bed and the following day broke blustery and hot. A searing wind from the zone of fire blew across the plain, and dust covered every part of the burrow interior, sending everyone into a silent frenzy of eye-rolling, gesticulating and coughing. The zealots moved in and out of their separate rooms mopping their brows, frowning at each other and obviously ridden with anxiety, which increased as the fire-driven wind rose to a howl outside.

With a sense of dread, we faintly heard the wail of the wind joined by the derisive hollering of some creatures that were digging and ripping at the entrance to the burrow, their activities partly masked by the ferocious wind. We hurried towards the entrance, grabbing whatever objects we could find as weapons on the way, and prepared for battle. The heretics had to be kept quiet and restrained from excitement at all costs, or they would turn on each other. We had to get rid of the interlopers quickly!

To my dismay, on reaching the entrance, I saw several dark figures in ragged cloaks hopping and scurrying around, wielding pickaxes and spades with which they were destroying the outer edges of the entrance. I counted six of them, and then I knew who they were.

It was an attack by the Seven Shades! But, where was the seventh? I counted again, but there were only six. Then I remembered that one was in a dungeon at the monastery, under the watchful eye of Damalis' monk.

The dissonance within the burrow, due to the different views of the heretics, had attracted them, for they had a nose for negativity. With this knowledge, my anger rose to boiling point and Bazoom, my angry entity, was soon fighting at my side along with the two Priestesses and some of the silent heretics, while the badger evaded the Shades by keeping low and nipping at their heels. Bazoom threw himself at each Shade in turn, as he dodged about to get a clear shot. He battered the attackers on their heads, sometimes getting entangled in their hoods, but managing to free himself ready for another strike, while the Shades shrieked and tried to fend him off. Soon their faces and heads were pouring black, sticky blood as if they had been flung onto a nest of spikes. Puffing loudly, but unhurt because of his incredible speed, Bazoom stopped for a moment and drew me aside, speaking between gasps.

"We need the toad, Oojo. He can vanquish the Shades, for he is also accursed, but by a different spell, and thus he will be the antidote. I'll dart and get his bag from the boat." Bazoom disappeared and I was careful to remain angry until he returned with the toads' bag, which he quickly dropped into my hand. I opened the bag and took out Oojo, who sat looking at me with an accusing stare.

"I need you to dismiss these six Shades before they get into the burrow and cause a conflict between the heretics who are sheltering here." I glared back at him. "Once the religious ones are set off, they will fight each other to the death. We can't allow that, for we're trying to convert them to irreligiousness. See what you can do, now. I'm relying on you, although with your record, you don't deserve it."

Oojo looked meek, and glanced at me obsequiously, but I knew it was an act. "I do have a plan. I'll see if it draws them off."

The toad hopped off through the dust and out of the burrow, where he sat until his loud croaks caught the attention of our attackers.

"Shades, my dears, come and listen to me. I will tell you of the red monkey who is your true enemy. Those idiots in the burrow are small fry, indeed, you demean yourselves by attacking them while the real perpetrator sits laughing at you nearby. Yes, the red monkey awaits you over there."

Oojo pointed vaguely with a sweep of his front leg and the Shades looked out across the plain. Then, one of them gave a shout. "Look! Over there! I saw a flash of red. It must be the monkey he's talking about. Come on, let's get him!"

The Shades formed into a tight group and made off in a shambling run, leaving a most distasteful odor behind them and several scurrying bugs that we swatted as they headed for the safety of the burrow. The toad ate their corpses with glee and then turned to me.

"Was that clever, or what?' He puffed himself up. "I have thrown them off our scent. I deserve freedom for that, at least."

"At least our scent is more tolerable than theirs," I quipped as I held my nose. "It's not over yet. They will return. Maybe not here, but somewhere along the way, for they are always following us. You are still under your curse, for you have been disobedient and worse than a loose cannon with your antics in the past. I have to be sure that you are a changed toad, and the curse lifted before that can happen. Now, back into your bag, and shut up."

I grabbed the toad before he could leap away and imprisoned him one more, feeling that if he had been a little humbler, he might have earned my respect for once.

I still had to consider the liberation of the Father in his monkey guise out in the desert, as he was searching for the Page and at the same time being shadowed by the six remaining Shades. It was time for me to leave the comparative safety of the burrow and go in search of Ripskin, in order to warn him of the double danger at his rear. I kept Bazoom in my pocket, just in case, although his prickles banged against my thigh as I ran.

A cloud of dust with the bobbing heads of hooded shapes showed where the six Shades were hunting over the plain, and gaining on the red monkey. He remained oblivious of them as his distant red figure, that alternately ran and then flew clumsily for a few yards in a zigzag fashion, showed that he had not picked up the Pages' trail, and I crouched low and kept behind the dry bushes as much as possible to avoid being seen by them. There was no sign of Ripskin, but I soon picked up the footprints of his armadillo and followed them. After tracking him for an hour I came up with him and, taking his arm as he dismounted, pulled him down into the bushes near a mud hole.

"You are being followed." I said in a low voice. "It is the red monkey who thinks that you will show him how to molt, for he has much shedding to do before he is purified. Beware, for he is tricky and, on top of that, he is traumatized by viewing the ghastly past of his predecessors in his dreams, which he now bears on his shoulders. Metaphorically speaking, that is."

"What is red? Who on earth is the red monkey? I have never seen one." It was hard to shake Ripskin out of his questing mode and his eyes had a faraway look.

"Red! Red, the color of fire. You have seen fire. Monkey, monkey! That is a man who is hairy, has not grown up yet and cannot speak. But this monkey can speak, for he is in disguise. He is really a man who thought himself very important until his clothes were stripped off by a couple of party revelers. He is in disguise, and he wants to be absolved and renounce his religion. You must strike while the iron is hot – he is ripe for conversion to agnosticism."

"Ag-nos-ticism, agnosticism? What is that? Where is the hot iron? Where is the fruit that is ripe?" I realized in desperation that Ripskin, having shed his entire outer eight skins, was unable to retain ordinary mundane facts. This could be a problem. He was relying entirely on intuition and his ego was fast fading. I stamped hard on his left foot, at which he shrieked and grabbed at his toes.

"Ouch! How dare you do that!" Ripskin looked at me with fury as his ego returned abruptly to defend him.

"Ah! That brought you around. Come down to earth, idiot! You have a job to do. The red monkey is looking for you. In fact, I am going to get him and bring him here, to save time, for I can see by looking into your eyes that nobody is home anymore. You can't go out like that! You have to retain some hold on the material plane. Stay here for now. I'll be back shortly."

Racing off over the plain to where I could see in the distance the flapping red shape of the Father, I saw with dismay that the six robed figures, who were also heading towards him at great speed, howling and gesticulating as they ran, were gaining on me. I urged myself to the utmost and reached the monkey a few yards in front of them, slinging him on my back, but before I could run away with my burden, they were upon me.

I fought hard and long, the darned monkey weighing me down. Bazoom again did his best, but the Shades were more numerous and sought revenge for our treatment of them at the burrow. Finally, they tied me up in a bundle with the monkey still astride me, and carried me off across the plain, immobile, with Bazoom hidden in my pocket again. I could feel he was shivering slightly so I tried to retain my irritability to keep him warm.

We journeyed for seven days and nights, finally reaching a small fishing village where squat, whitewashed houses rose from a cobbled street that led up to a green door with a grille across the front. Outside the door, one of the Shades spoke in a sonorous voice.

"Who has the key? Give me the key. We will slide these irritating monkeys down the tunnel and into the lower regions of our territory and leave them there for now. Hurry up and get this door open."

One of the hooded figures shuffled forward and unlocked the door. I was bound so tightly that I couldn't move, and the red monkey was attached to me like a vise. Immediately they heaved us through a trapdoor in the floor and we slid down a long narrow passage until we landed hard on the floor of an underground cavern. At first it was pitch black, but my eyes discerned a gleam of light from a crack in the cavern ceiling. As my eyes became accustomed to the faint light, I knew I had been there before.

"Bazoom! Bazoom," I whispered tetchily in order to activate him. "Sever our bindings with your sharp prickles. I know of a way out of here."

This might have been over-confident on my part. As soon as Bazoom cut the knots, I shook the heavy monkey off my back and, signaling him to follow, felt my way towards the gradually ascending tunnel that we had traveled with the Knight of Swords. It seemed a long time ago that the Knight had led us up the very same slope. We climbed up to the place where the opening to the outside should have been, Bazoom flying ahead. I began groping in the dark, but my heart sank when I found that somebody had blocked the hole with a huge boulder. We were certainly trapped this time!

The red monkey and I sat down by the boulder. I had to think. How could we get out? We had already been without food for seven days and little water, and I felt light headed. The monkey didn't offer much support, as he started pulling at my sleeve and complaining that his wings had been squashed during the journey.

"I can't help that," I rejoined irritably. "We are going to end our days here, at this rate, and I would rather not end them with you by my side. At least, let's do something constructive and try to get this suit off you."

No matter how I struggled, the zip on the suit was stuck open and I could not pull the suit off him. I was angry, frustrated, and very scared. Soon I felt the thin little arms of Paragutt around my waist, sucking in my stomach, and my mouth went dry. Bazoom sat on my shoulder and looked down curiously. It was the first time they met.

"Who's that measly little fellow behind you with the yellow streak? He doesn't look as if he's much use in a situation like this," mocked Bazoom.

"You may be wrong," I retorted. "This is Paragutt and he is my fearful entity. Paragutt came into my life before you, in fact, he is your parent, in a way, so be respectful. Fear is the goad that makes one look for a way out of a serious problem and activates adrenalin. That induces anger, born from fear, and when one gets angry, one is determined to succeed. You two can work well together. In fact, we should return to the cavern and there we can send you out, as one, through the crack in the ceiling, for you are both small. You must go for help. Forget the Page of Wands. He is totally out of it. His armadillo has more sense. Find someone, anyone, who can get us out of here."

We returned slowly to the cavern and I picked up Paragutt and put him on Bazooms' back – which was very uncomfortable and made Paragutt wince - and then I flung the two of them as hard as I could into the air, and they reached the crack, and held on, and were soon wriggling through it. I hoped they would find help, as we were getting weaker by the hour. The red monkey had collapsed, and he lay in a heap by my side, ominously silent. I soaked a rag in the water that seeped down the walls of the cavern and held it to his wide lips, but he refused to drink, so I sucked at the wet rag myself. I certainly wasn't about to give up yet.

It was getting cold in the cavern, and I went in search of something to burn. In the dim light, I found a few empty wooden boxes stacked in a corner. They were sent from the witches' department in New York to the Shades, and the contents were listed on the lids. Six kilos of bats' wings; seventeen large poisonous toads in aspic; twenty pounds of oversized cockroaches folded in two; a dozen goats' heads; and fifteen gallons of infants' blood. I dragged the boxes over to our position, breaking them up and stacking them for a fire. Then how should I light the fire?

Ah, yes! The magic matches that Eeleye Fastlever, the penguin, had given me in Merry Birdland. They were still in my pocket, and in spite of my repeated dunkings, were miraculously dry. I quickly had the fire burning, and with its bright glow I was able to explore our prison more thoroughly. There was absolutely nothing to eat, which was a problem. I reckoned I could last out for two more weeks without food, then it would be closure time. At least the fire made things brighter, and there was plenty of wood.

I looked at the red monkey. I didn't like the look of him, and shook his scaly shoulder. There was no response. Could he be dead? I felt his pulse, but couldn't find it. I picked him up and shook him hard, and one eye opened slightly.

A faint moan escaped him and he attempted to say something, as his thin lips moved slowly, trying to form the words. I put him down, laid his head on a rock, and bent over to hear what he had to say.

"It's….. all over for me. I'm going…. to my maker, whether he be above or below." He began to gasp, but persisted. "Please do …..something for me. A last favor. You can absolve me. There is a way….. I am offering my…… body as a sacrifice. To… to atone for the sins of all the Fathers before me." His head dropped back, and I moved to support him better. "Please…… eat me…. That way I can be immolated….. raw or cooked…… it doesn't matter……." The voice trailed away.

What a situation! I thought quickly. Fortunately he was still in monkey form, which I had heard was quite tasty. If he had been a man, it might have jolted my morals a little too fiercely. I raised his head towards me and looked deep into the fading brown eyes as I promised.

"I will eat you. It won't be very appetizing as I prefer monkeys marinated and roasted, and there is no marinade available. But never mind, that will, indeed, absolve you from all the sins you have taken upon yourself. I promise to do that." I was nearly in tears.

"Make sure….. I'm dead first……" were the last words he said as he took his final gasp and went limp.

I laid the body on the floor sadly. He had not been a great person, but his suffering had made him whole. I wondered what the red suit would taste like, probably horrible, and hoped that it would be easy to peel off when he was well cooked. I should wait for at least 48 hours, I thought, to make sure he didn't come around. Perhaps it would be a good idea to hang him by his toes, to tenderize the meat. I used my belt to hoist him up to a snag in the rock and left him there for a couple of days. He didn't show any further signs of life.

Two weeks passed and I was just stripping the last of the meat off the red monkeys' bones when I heard a loud rumbling noise. I ran up the slope towards the great boulder, and found that it was moving. Someone was pushing it aside! I managed to squeeze through the gap, and found, not Bazoom and Paragutt, for they had vanished, but Ripskin on his large armadillo. The animal was heaving and pushing at the boulder, his armored tail sticking out straight behind him. Sensibly refusing to mount the horny armadillo, I insisted that Ripskin lead the way and we finally returned to the Castle of Fire. The Knight of Wands, Ignitia, was able to inform me that I had passed the test, which was "to liberate the oppressed by the interpretation of dreams," and that my decision to devour the red monkey had liberated the Father from his subjugation to the demands of his faith and allowed him to progress in future incarnations.

Wandering thoughtfully down to my rowboat, I picked up the mooring line, untying it from the rock. But, what was this? The boat that I was pulling in was no longer the little rowboat, but a beautiful double scull with shining varnish and two pairs of oars, and in it sat the old man I loved so much, and he was laughing.

Knight of Wands - Rules Eight and Seven of Wands

Greeting my Guide with apprehensive delight, my words tumbled over each other as he stepped out of the shining scull.

"Oh! I'm so glad to see you! It has been horrible. I have come through so far, though. Where were you? I needed you badly sometimes. You didn't come! Why did you leave me?"

"You never called me. Even when you were starving in the Shades' cavern, you didn't think of me. That is perfectly OK. It means you are relying more on your own instincts and experience to get out of these situations, and that is essential, especially since you are now under the influence of the Wands in the Castle of Fire, for intuition can be tricky and sometimes mislead you. You will see that the Knight, Ignitia, always carries a ball of thread with her, to get out of mazes, which are all over the place here, and it's easy to lose yourself once you get disoriented in one of them." The old man chuckled.

"I haven't seen any mazes yet." I acknowledged. "I will be sure to look out for them. Now, what is the story of this boat, and where is my rowboat? I had gotten used to it."

"As before, when I took away the punt and gave you the rowboat, it is another step forward." My Guide announced. "This is to be your new boat. There are two pairs of oars because you must row with another person now. It is practice for the crew you will have to pick when you set out across the Mystic SEA, for you cannot yet handle the sailboat you will receive alone. Teamwork is important now – learning to work with the entities you possess. You have managed to nullify some of them, and the others must be brought into line and learn to get along with each other, for you cannot face the dangers on the Islands in the Mystic SEA if you're not centered. At the Castle of Fire, the lessons on concentration are going to be very important. Now I must leave you. Go ahead and pick a crew for your new boat. Who will it be?"

"Don't leave yet!" I begged him as I looked at the long, narrow scull with its tiny sliding seats. "It's scary to think I have to balance that vessel – it's more demanding than the kayak I had. I won't be able to do it!" A spasm of fear shook me.

I looked around. Oh! No! The old fellow had suddenly disappeared, and in his place stood my entity, little Paragutt, holding a pair of oars and shivering lightly. What a fool I was! I had become scared and invited him into my boat. Now there was nothing for it but to take him along, until I could swap him for someone else. I thought about the other entities. Globdinig was too heavy and clumsy, and in any event she had recently been sucked up into the Water Goddess' Cup and was imprisoned underwater. Bazoom was too wild and had no arms – how could he row? Suckersie had disappeared, although I felt she would come back soon. Swollup was dead; Pompeybou missing; Endevvy reformed; Little Laboria had lost an arm; Einerline wasn't physically strong and Kracklewergen would be sure to upset the boat the minute he touched it. There remained Bardogian and Fontanova, both involved in their own creative work and probably very reluctant to take to the water. Besides, I was a little nervous about putting them together after their wild performance at the Tantric Mass. I would have to put off any final decision for now and take the entity that presented itself.

Paragutt and I climbed into the boat. He was very lightweight, which was an advantage, but he had never done any rowing and so I seated him behind me to start with so that he could follow my strokes. We rowed around for several days, and I had to keep remembering to be a little anxious or he would have vanished. Eventually he picked up the stroke and I felt less nervous. The odd thing was, as my fear disappeared, Paragutt seemed to change color, turning from greenish-yellow to a vibrant gold, and he grew in height until he was about the same size as me. I moved him in front of me as he improved and took the rear sliding seat myself, rejoicing at the disappearance of the bright yellow streak that formerly ran down his back.

Now we were in tune and the boat skimmed over the water at incredible speed. When we had mastered the art of sculling, we rowed swiftly to a part of the lagoon where the water was on fire, to inspect the phenomenon. Blue, flickering flames rose up and disappeared mysteriously and beyond them, the vague outline of a black throne rose above a small islet. The rocky shore seemed to split in two, as great cliffs arose and were bisected by a large cataract of glowing fire which came from somewhere in the interior of the kingdom and, hissing, disappeared under the surface of the lagoon. We approached through the swirling steam and tied the scull up nearby, climbing up to the top of what appeared to be a flat mesa overlooking the wide crevasse in the landscape.

The sound of rapid hoof beats came faintly from across the plain, where we could see a Knight on a galloping horse riding full tilt at the abyss, urging her mount to utmost speed as they took off in a massive jump to reach our side of the mesa. As she sped towards us in mid air, her body armor became loose and fell into the flames below, and she reached up and grasped a flaming Wand that floated above her head, landing safely on the ground in front of us. Overhead, two hawks fluttered down to land on her shoulders.

The Knight of Wands addressed us. "I am Ignitia and this is my horse Smokey. I have come with the message for you – your next test. It is **"to seek the union and obliterate the division."** My hawks understand this, for as I jumped the abyss, they came together and mated as one. Now they will bear fruit. An egg will be born, and inside that egg is the potential of the whole world, for the two hawks are Suroh, he of the sword makers' forge, and his partner Horus, hawk of the Egyptians."

I immediately objected. "I know Suroh well, for we have adventured together. Suroh is a male bird. Horus is a male too, isn't he? How could they fertilize each other and produce an egg?"

"Suroh is the earthly counterpart of masculine Horus – inverted, as it were." Ignitia responded. "Horus is capable of androgyny, and can therefore become male or female. That is how Suroh received the fertilization of the material aspect of herself. She will bear the egg in due course, never fear."

Suddenly a shriek from Paragutt interrupted our conversation. As I was aware, he had metamorphosed in the scull and he was no longer driven by fear, though still extremely cautious.

"A snake! A snake over there! It's...it's a copperhead, I'm sure. They're very poisonous!"

Paragutt raised his oar, which he was still clutching, over his head and advanced towards a coiled copperhead snake that lay on the edge of the abyss that the Knight had just crossed.

"I will kill it before it bites one of us!"

"No!" I lunged in his direction but before I could stop him, Paragutt slammed down his oar on the snake and swiftly cut it into seven pieces that writhed for a few moments before falling over the edge into the abyss, leaving one piece teetering on the brink. I picked it up and stamped on it, flattening it, and then ran over to the rim. To my dismay, the other six pieces were changing rapidly into six very familiar shapes as hooded robes enveloped them, and the deadly six Shades soared over the flames, their garments flickering in the heat, landing further up the bank and running off across the plain, where they disappeared from view. I was horror struck.

"Paragutt! My intuition told me that the snake was a combination of all the Shades! When they were one, we could have killed that single creature with one blow. Why did you cut them into seven?"

"I know fear, for I am the personification of Fear." Paragutt stated calmly. "As one, the Shades would have seven times the power they possessed as seven separate entities. Would you rather face an enemy whose power is that of seven, or one-seventh of their strength when they are apart? I tell you, we must deal with each one of the seven when it is disconnected from the others, for if we faced that snake alone, we would not survive the conflict."

"That may be all very well, but I remember we thought that we had killed one of them already on our river journey. That didn't work, because he came back." I said. "What's more, one of them is still supposed to be in prison now. I caught his section and stamped on him to stop them from rescuing him. How can we get rid of them if they don't die?"

The Knight Ignitia interrupted. "Each one of the Seven Shades inhabits one of the seven sentient Paths in the Mystic SEA. They represent the evil side of that path, for they have both a good and a bad side, and that is something you will have to deal with on your journey into the Mystic SEA, which draws nearer. Now, we have work to do. The Shades are swiftly overtaking the runner Gofer, who carries the next bundle of eight Wands to the Shaman Reeve. If he is slain, Reeve and his clan will never pass on the blessings of intuition. They are the beginnings of humanity, which will not be able to progress without the art of intuition."

Instantly objecting, I complained. "Gofer has already delivered the eight Wands to Shaman Reeve. I was there when that took place, and I helped him outrun the Shades. Why is he bringing more Wands now?"

Ignitia responded impatiently. "Alas, early man has to develop slowly. Gofer must deliver more and more Wands, as they burn out in the cavern where early humans live. The clan is slow to learn, for they are in the childhood of humanity, and take time to progress. Let us not waste time. Ride pillion with me on Smokey and we will catch them up. Now, before I leave, I will bid Paragutt rest, and will award him the Order of the Nonexistant Empire, or ONE, for he has shown courage and foresight, thus becoming absorbed in your center. He will never be separated from you again." At this point, she bent over Paragutt, giving the sign of the Ankh, and Paragutt looked up at her adoringly, then turned and slowly walked away in thought.

"Does that mean I won't ever be afraid any more?" I asked the Knight, as Paragutt faded from view.

"Not exactly. It means that you have overcome fear on a personal level and absorbed your fearful entity. Together you can now face the greater fear, Universal Fear, which is the dregs of the Cup that each of us has swallowed at birth, the Cup of Lethe, or forgetfulness."

"So we are all born with Fear? How can that be?" I demurred.

"When we are born, we leave behind the beautiful life and agree to reincarnate into the lower worlds, where fear rules. We cannot let go of fear until we return to the place from which we came, but must fight it continuously. It is the sadness that man carries with him in Malkuth. Come now, we must leave and go to save Gofer, who is hard pressed."

I galloped with the Knight, mounted pillion on Smokey, as we cut across country and quickly overtook the six Shades, who cursed and shook their fists at us as we passed by. We were soon riding alongside Gofer, who was close to the glacier where the clan of Shaman Reeve lived in the ice crevasse. He was nearing exhaustion, so we relieved him of six of the Wands before arriving at the entrance to the crevasse, where I dismounted, leaving the Knight to ward off the Shades' approaching attack. Gofer and I swiftly entered the passage to the ice cave where the clan lived, carrying the eight Wands, and the passage closed behind us.

Light from the Wands shone on the dim interior of a large ice cave and on the faces of a handful of rough-looking people, dressed in furs against the chill of the glacier. There was a revolting acrid smell from unwashed bodies and dense smoke from cooking fires. The Shaman and his clan were busy sewing blankets from lemming skins. In front of an altar of ice where the remains of a small sacred fire smoldered, a Black Dog lay licking his paws beside two bowls, one red vessel and one of gold. The dog yawned and composed himself for sleep as the crowd passed around the new Wands and quickly relit the dying fire.

The Shaman, who was naked except for a headdress in the form of a cave bear and an ermine cloak, his hairy body emanating raw masculinity, drew Gofer and I into a small, narrow cave that led further under the glacier.

"This is not for the ears of those who are, as yet, unworthy. Therefore, I speak secretly to you. As Gofer is aware, the Shades have captured several loads of valuable Wands that he was conveying to us. Our Eternal Flame nearly went out. I am thankful that you saved these intuitive Wands. Our task now is to banish the Seven Shades back to the Islands in the Mystic SEA from which they came, bringing great evil to our world. I am a sorcerer and know the ways. I have hesitated to perform what is necessary until now, but the clan must be saved, for we are the only humans that exist in our world at present, and we need to propagate in peace."

Leaning closer, I lowered my voice. 'What do you suggest, then? It is very difficult to get rid of the Shades, because I've tried, and thought I had killed one, but he wasn't dead after all. Then I just stamped on one piece of the snake, but I feel sure I did not kill it."

"There is a method." Reeve spoke quietly. "It takes the combined energy of three witnesses, and we have three of us here now. We must form seven figurines with winged feet from the black clay under the glacier and then we will bake them in the Eternal Flame. When they are cooked, we will set them in a row facing the west, where lies the Mystic SEA, and place a wick in their …. excuse my explanation….arses. We then light the wicks. While the figurines get hotter and hotter, I will perform a magic ceremony, and when they are glowing hot, we will throw bowls of ice on them from the glacier. The figures will explode, and their spirits will be banished from our land and flee to the west. I know this will work. The three of us will perform this deed as follows. We will all make the figurines together. Then, Gofer, you will light the wicks while I perform the ceremony, and our Navigator will collect the bowls of ice and fling them at the right moment on the figures. We will get rid of them once and for all, at least from our world. They will be forced back to the deep unconscious from whence they came to torment us."

I was extremely interested in this procedure, as we began to scrape the dark clay into a container for the figurines. Soon I noticed that my poetic entity, Bardogian, was busy by my side.

"Who is this person?" Reeve was irritated. "We should have three only. Four is a bad number for spells. Send him away!"

"I can't do that." I admitted. "As long as I am interested in sorcery, he will stay, for he is a part of me. Gofer will have to go instead."

Gofer was considerably upset by my insistence that he leave, but Bardogian already had his hands deep in the clay and was shaping some marvelous manikins from the dark mass. Gofer reluctantly walked out to the main cave and we hastily completed the making of the figurines, carrying them out and laying them in front of the altar of ice. The Black Dog woke up and growled, baring his teeth, and snapping at us. I jumped aside as one of the clan came forward and grasped his golden collar, leading him away to the back of the cave. A hush came over the chattering crowd and one of them spoke.

"The Black Dog - he is angry. Why is that?"

"Quiet! You know not what is going on." The Shaman said sternly. "Cover your heads with your blankets and look no more. I demand silence. We are doing a banishment." We placed the manikins in the fire and they began to bake.

The blanketed group huddled into a corner. I thought how picturesque the scene was with the dark shadows in the ice cavern and the clustered group, their silhouettes dancing on the wall behind them, shivering under their covers.

At that very moment, another person appeared in the cave, as if from nowhere. It was Fontanova! Now I had both my poetic entity and my creative entity together in a most awkward and dangerous situation. I struggled to get rid of my inventive imagination, but Fontanova, instead of disappearing, stepped forward angrily and swept the seven molten figurines from the fire, where they shattered onto the floor.

"What do you think you are doing?" She cried angrily. "Bardogian! You again. Up to no good once more, I see. Your obsession with sorcery will be the death of you one day. Can't you understand that when the Black Dog is angry, it bodes no good! You must never ignore the message that the Dog sends – are you out of your mind?"

Bardogians' eyes shot fire. "Watch yourself! Always interfering, you are. Get lost! I'm sick of your moral indignation. You're always so right, aren't you?"

"Yes, I am. You know you're going down the wrong path. I've been through it myself, and I know. I had to change my ways, and you need to do the same. Bardogian, I really love you. Can't you see that I'm trying to save you?" Fontanova was almost crying as she spoke.

"You're just a control freak. You want to change me so that you can say you've won. I won't bow down to that. I'll do what I want, and if you have to freak out, that's your problem. Now, look what you've done with your meddling habits. The Seven Shades should be proud of you, indeed!" Bardogian turned his back and began to sulk.

My interest in the magical spell was crushed by Fontanovas' outburst, although I still admired her ferocity and thought of painting a portrait of her in a rage. The creative impulse was followed by a great feeling of guilt, during which Fontanova stormed around the cavern, pouting and swiveling her hips. I had allowed my two conflicting entities to destroy a very important spell casting. Now we were stuck with the Seven Shades, since they would by now have caught on to the experiment and built up defenses against it simultaneously. On top of that, Shaman Reeve, whom I greatly admired, was growing increasingly disturbed. Waving his hands in the air, he quickly muttered an incantation. A cold mist immediately slid from the walls of the cave and crept over the ground, gradually obliterating my arguing couple. Their shivering bodies dissolved in the mist and when I looked up, the vapor had dissipated. The pair standing next to the altar were no longer my two entities, but my friends the twins Kerry and Kerri, they who had vanquished the shark that was in the wave during my adventure with the Seven of Wands, and around them shone a warm halo that resembled the brilliance of the morning sun.

Although I was somewhat disconcerted by the Shamans' ability to instantly dissolve my warring entities, I was still delighted to see the twins who, I felt, had achieved a singular victory over division. But Shaman Reeve was frantic.

"My incantation has gone wrong. Who are these two, now? They must leave immediately! They are too hot. Their glow will melt our cavern – I can see water running down the stalactites already. Out! Get out! You are ruining our home. We will be without shelter."

Kerry spoke sternly to the Shaman. "No! You made us come here through the fog. We always like to use fog as a medium to travel, and our bright Sun disperses it when we arrive. Your nascent intuition created this situation without you realizing it, for you are a beginner, learning of the higher forces in man. It is time, time to melt the glacier, which has protected you and your kind for ten thousand years, and send you out into the wilderness to live in the real world. The sun welcomes you, so do not fear it."

As they spoke, the ceiling of the cavern lightened under the gentle radiance of their Sun, and with a mighty crash, it broke and cascaded down upon us, soaking us in freezing water. Great chunks of ice were crashing from the walls and the clan rushed hither and thither, ducking in an attempt to avoid them. There was little time. Reeve had to gather his people and hurry through the corridor to the outside world before the entire glacier could collapse on top of them and bury the remnants of early human life forever.

Our group hastened out in semblance of order with the Shaman leading. Kerry, Kerri and I followed with Gofer and the Black Dog, who was not forgotten in the panic. As I glanced back at the entrance to the corridor, I saw the Eternal Flame doused by a sheet of descending water, and the altar became a melting mass of broken ice. I rushed back and picked up the two dogs' bowls, feeling they might be important, and narrowly escaped being stunned by a huge block of ice. We hurried along the passageway, following the acrid body scent of the clan, and emerged on the icy plateau outside, where the terrified cave people were huddled, gazing around them with wild eyes.

Setting to work with the twins, Reeve and Gofer, to build a temporary shelter for the clan while they sat in stunned silence, I knew they were unable to visualize their next move. However, soon we had a brush house erected and a fire going. We herded them into the house, leaving one to tend the fire and three to look for more driftwood.

I was then able to turn to the twins, Kerri and Kerry, and ask them whether their union was complete, as they had been on the point of merging when I last saw them. I had not expected to meet them again until I reached the Mystic SEA, and I was surprised at their appearance here, of all places.

"I remember, I brought the Wand that matched yours, and the two flames were exactly alike. As one flame moved, the other copied it, like a flock of birds flying as one." I reminded them. "Then you were going to experience your epiphany and join together, since you look exactly alike, although you are male and female. There was a prophecy, I believe. What was that?"

Kerri smiled and spoke. "Yes, we did go through a ceremony and were joined as one. We became inhabitants of the Sun, and shed its light on all humanity. I'm afraid I cannot tell you about the prophecy, for that is still in the future. We will meet again on the course of the Sun in the Mystic SEA, for we are the twins in the Sun. And now, farewell, for you have much to do to lead this group of people onwards to an understanding of their intuitive abilities."

The twins bowed, holding hands, and then, to my amazement, the glowing ball of the Sun surrounding them rose up into the darkening sky, enveloping them, and slowly dropped below the western horizon.

In all this excitement, I had forgotten the brave Ignitia, who had kept the six Shades at bay outside the cavern, where they were trying to hack their way into the ice, for the crevasse had closed up behind us as we entered. The Knight looked exhausted and she was suffering from many cuts about the head, where the Shades had tried to dislodge her helmet to finish her off.

"Thank goodness I have retained my helmet. I was ready to gradually let go of the rest of my armor on my journey, which I started as I took up the burden of the Knight of Pentacles; rationalized as the Knight of Swords; expressed as the Knight of Cups; and finally understood as I am now, the Knight of Wands."

Ignitia groaned as I pressed a damp cloth to her wounds, then she continued. "The Shades fought fiercely, but suddenly broke off our battle and began to exult, jumping in the air, shaking their fists and yelling aloud the words "Halfa, halfa, evil seod rats evif!" Then they ran off – over there – across the icy plain."

I thought for a moment. Inversion – inverted words. "I think I know what they said, for they are the roots of the dark side. If you turn their words around, you will get the phrase "Five star does live, Aflah, Aflah.!" When you invert the five-pointed star, it becomes the sign for the devil. The Shades know much of sorcery, for they brought occult wisdom to humanity through the desert many aeons ago. We were in the process of banishing them with Reeves' help, when I allowed two of my entities to appear at once. It was a disaster, for these two are madly in love but constantly disagreeing with each other. They started a fight, destroyed the clay manikins, and caused the spell to fail. The Shades knew that the Shaman had botched their banishment, and they rejoiced. Now they live to attack us again, and it is my fault."

The Knight laid her hand on my shoulder. "Do not blame yourself, for when one approach fails, there is hidden success behind it. The argument between your two entities will lead them to greater understanding of their differences, and will begin their reconciliation. That is far more important. They are certainly deeply disturbed at the moment, and from that they will begin to change their attitude."

Ignitia paused, gravely proceeding. "Regarding the Shades, as Paragutt explained, they have to be tackled one by one, and that cannot happen until you reach the seven islands in the Mystic SEA where they hide. There your final battle will take place with each one, and as each is conquered, you will move to the next, and so vanquish each in turn."

I appreciated Ignitias' words, but my heart sank. "Do you mean I have seven battles to fight in the Mystic SEA? Seven. That is too many. I won't go to the SEA – I'll stay here. I have enough troubles at the Lagoon, but I can deal with them. The problems sound much worse over there. I won't go any further."

The Knight gave me a sympathetic glance. "It is your Destiny that you must complete your journey, and however long you decide to turn back or abandon your quest, you are merely delaying the inevitable, for you must, eventually, go into the Mystic SEA. So it is written for all. But do not fear, for the strength that you have gathered as you travel from one Castle to the next along the Lagoon will enable you to face the dangers. The Aces, who rule over the White Pyramid in the center of the Lagoon, will encourage you and spur you on to complete your mission during the twelve tasks they will give you there. Now, tomorrow, when the clan is rested, we will go to find the right maze and we will help them to understand the puzzle of the maze and the disappearance of their totem, the cave bear."

The following morning, which was very cold, we flushed the reluctant clan members out of their temporary shelter, formed them into a line, and led them away from the melting glacier. In some places, as we progressed towards the Castle of Fire, we were wading waist deep through flooding streams as the frozen land behind us quickly thawed in the heat of the fires of intuition that burned around us. Eventually our struggling group reached the dry plain that surrounded the Castle, the clan beginning to discard their lemming blankets and revel in their newly discovered warmth.

I had been looking out for a maze for some time when I noticed in the distance what appeared to be a long stone wall that stretched for several miles along the plain. Ignitia led us in that direction and I saw the wall was about ten feet high and had an arched gateway in it, with a wrought golden gate barring the way. Once we stopped outside the gate, I could see through it a series of other stone boundaries that ran in every direction, with several stone-flagged paths disappearing between them. The whole construction glowed in the fierce heat.

The Knight gathered us together and explained that we had to open the gate. We would then enter the maze and continue on our path until we reached the center, where an enigma awaited us. We entrusted Shaman Reeve and his clan to solve the enigma and Gofer and I would accompany them, as we were the only people capable of intuition at present.

"Aren't you coming with us?" I asked Ignitia anxiously. "We need your guidance. How can we solve the enigma without you?"

She looked sad. "That is up to you, I'm afraid. Like my three forebears, I cannot help you solve this test, and I must step back and let you continue without me. I will return to the Castle. I wish you luck and I hope that you will be able to reach the center of the maze and then find your way out again, for it is extremely difficult. Many have entered this maze and they have never been seen again. There will be bones scattered about."

Here she became silent and, wheeling Smokey around, abruptly set off at a gallop to the south, her cape swirling behind her. I watched until she disappeared, remembering that the other three Knights had all let me down at some vital point during my adventures with them. Now, there was nothing for it but to try the gate, in order to discover the enigma. It was firmly locked with a large gold padlock.

On my belt were a number of small bags containing useful items from my travels. They included an uncut Janus key that was presented to me by the parrot Arty Weight. One half was black obsidian and the other half was white agate. The key was surmounted by twin heads that looked in opposite directions. I took the key out of its bag and approached the gate, inserting it easily into the padlock. Immediately there was a grinding sound, and the padlock opened. I withdrew the key, which had been blank, and saw that a toothed pattern had been cut into it that was not there before.

The gate was now open, and Gofer and I ushered the reluctant clan inside, followed by the Shaman. The gate clanged shut behind us as we contemplated the endless stone barriers that diverged in every direction from our position. There seemed to be several paths that we could take, so we discussed whether we should all stay together as a group or split into smaller parties and take different routes. We decided to break into three groups, one headed by Gofer, another by Reeve, and the third by myself. Each group consisted of about ten clan members who meekly followed behind us as we took three different flagged paths into the maze.

After walking for some five minutes, I paused and glanced behind me at my bewildered and straggling group, who gazed up at the high surrounding walls with awe. One old woman edged up to me and spoke in a grating voice.

"The bear. Where is the bear? We look for the cave bear, our totem.

Reeve is our Shaman. He is incarnation of the bear. We will find the bear soon, won't we?"

I told her I was not sure. She dropped back with a worried expression as we moved on, the walls of stone hemming us in. We had turned several corners with no sign of other paths leading off when we came to a crossroads. Four paths led in different directions. Which one should we take? I was for continuing forward, but some of the group scurried off to the right, and although I tried calling them back, they quickly vanished around another corner. I decided to press straight on with the remainder, but after several more bends we found ourselves at a dead end, and had to turn back. Reaching the crossroads again, I had to decide whether to follow the group that had split, or take the path to my right. I reckoned it would be a good idea to go down that route, and turned right, followed by the rest of the group.

The path led to a sharp turn to the right and then another right hand turn that ended in a t-junction. I had a choice, to the right or to the left? If I went to the right, I would be backtracking and believed I would end up close to the crossroads. I went to the left and walked for about ten minutes, and then the path turned once more to the right. As we rounded the corner we stumbled upon the skeleton of a giant bear, still standing against one of the walls, its paws forever stretched up, clawing at the barrier of stones, a hideous snarl on its face from which the remains of dried furry flesh dangled horribly. The clan shrank back and clutched each other, and the old woman began to keen. The group then turned and ran frantically back the way they had come, screaming and wailing.

I looked at the skeleton with dread. Something was dangling out of its mouth, still gripped by the white teeth. I stepped forward and pulled at the object. It was a small bone cylinder that appeared to be hollow, so I popped off the top and drew out a tiny clay tablet, on which were written some strange hieroglyphs that I couldn't make out. I slipped the cylinder into my pocket, hoping that Shaman Reeve would be able to decipher it. Now I was alone as I retraced our steps back to the crossroads, expecting to find them waiting, but there was no sign of anyone.

I called several times. "Hallo! Hallo! Where are you? Call back if you can hear me."

Only the light whisper of the hot wind as it blew prairie dust over the maze answered me. I had lost all the members of my group already, which was upsetting. These early people were defenseless against the complexities of the maze, and they now risked their lives, wandering without a leader in the vast labyrinth. There was little I could do but set out again, hoping to find them. This time, since I didn't want to trip over the bears' skeleton, I went down the path that the earlier group had taken. I trotted along for some fifteen minutes, taking one turn to the left, before arriving at another crossroads. I again turned to the left, thinking to keep myself close to the center of the maze, and then negotiated a t-junction, where I turned to the right.

I hadn't thought of counting my steps, but I began to do that now. I soon lost count. From time to time I felt sure I heard voices, but the sound of the wind had increased to a low moan and brought with it the smell of the surrounding fires, and I couldn't be sure. How many times I turned to the right, or the left, or crossed a junction, I don't remember. Thirst began to bother me, and the light was failing. I had to turn back several times from dead ends. There was no sign of any of the other groups, since the maze was so big they could have been miles away by now.

Sitting down exhausted, I considered my next step. I had lost track of the way I had come, so there was no sure way of getting back to the gate. I decided to sleep there and reconsider in the morning, as I would gain nothing from trying to navigate at night through the endless pathways. I tried not to think of water as, my mouth dry, I curled up at the side of the path and fell asleep.

"I'm setting out in a small boat from a dock in a large bay. I know that I have to clear the headland under sail, but as I approach the entrance to the bay, it gets narrower and narrower, and eventually closes up. I can't find a way through. I sail along the cliffs and choose a gap, tacking into it. I find myself in a narrow channel that branches out into other channels in a bewildering way. It seems that I have been sailing for hours, but there is no open water. I feel claustrophobic and desperate. Finally I abandon the boat and dive down into the dark water. There is a set of submerged steps, and I am swimming down them. A figure that I can't see clearly takes my left hand and squeezes it. A voice comes to me out of the darkness. "Go back to your boat. You need a vessel to survive. Take the next turn to the right and the one after that. Then turn left, and left again. Follow the path for three miles – it is straight. Turn to the left, and when you come to a dead end, you will find steps hidden in the wall. Climb these steps as I tell you and you will see, over the wall, the center that contains the enigma. Go now, with my blessing......"

I awoke suddenly, striving to remember the instructions from the dream. I had to take the next turn to the right and the one after that. Then turn left and left again. Follow the path for three miles, and then turn left.

At the dead end, climb the steps and the enigma will be visible. I felt my drying tongue and knew I had to struggle on, or I would die. I replicated the dream information, arriving at the dead end and climbing the scarcely perceptible steps in the wall, fearing to look over the top, yet knowing I had little time left.

Hearing the sound of whispers, I peeped over the wall cautiously. Before me stood Shaman Reeve, Gofer, and the thirty members of the clan. In the center of the group was a large egg.

Primitive howls of delight greeted me as I climbed down from the wall and joined the group. They danced around the big egg and clapped their hands. Someone handed me a skin water bottle, and I drank with relief. Then I reached into my pocket and brought out the bone cylinder, handing it to Reeve as I explained where I had come across it. He took it with a sign of recognition.

"Many generations of Shamans before me have searched for this. It contains a message from the cave bears. Now we'll be able to find them at last. I hope there are directions to their lair from here."

As he spoke, he opened the cylinder and took out the little tablet, screwing up his eyes to read it. "This is the message. Oh! My Forebear!"

Here he glanced upwards with a ravaged look on his face, and then continued. "It says. "I am the last and final bear. All of our kind have now been extinguished by starvation, since the heat of the fire and the cold of the ice killed the plants and little animals that we used to eat. I have come here to the maze to die. Someday a passer-by will find my remains and rescue this cylinder. My message will reach the Shaman. It is thus - that the time of the worship of the cave bear is over, because humans do not want him as a totem any longer. In the future, many gods will come to the clan, and some people will embrace one god, and some another, and yet none of them will be any better than the cave bear. It will be in the name of progress, yet false and empty. I can do nothing. Fare thee well, my clan. I go now to die."

At this point, the Shaman began to weep, and the clan sat down in a circle and sobbed, beating their breasts until they were finished with grieving. I waited quietly and sadly, for the cave bear had been a magnificent animal in his time, and represented great power. I wondered if the gods that took his place in the future would be adequate to the task, for he had been a close and real part of the clans' life.

After about an hour, we all filed silently out of the center of the maze and wound our way back to the entrance, which they found easily, because the clan had taken the trouble to blaze marks on the walls showing us the path. Leaving marks was a practice that I had – stupidly - forgotten, but that they used regularly on their way through new territory. We traveled slowly over the plain to the Castle of Fire, carrying the egg tenderly, and watched over by the two hawks, Suroh and Horus.

Queen of Wands - Rules Five and Three of Wands.

We all reached the Castle of Fire after a days' march, Gofer carefully carrying the large egg. Crossing a burnt wood bridge that led over a moat of blue fire, we knocked at the Castle gate and Ripskin, the Page, admitted us, pulling back the curtain of fire that concealed the entrance, and directing us towards a great forge that stood in the Castle courtyard.

Ripskin sounded regretful as he spoke to me. "Your instructions are to leave Gofer and Shaman Reeves' clan and continue alone with the egg. Gofer will stay with us as the Queens courier. Go into the forge, burn off the dross that covers you, then bathe in the steam bath and clothe yourself in this fireproof suit." The Page handed me a thin body suit made of some fluorescent material. "When you are ready, you will be ferried out to the Queens' throne by her attendant and will learn where you are to take the egg for incubation."

I reluctantly said goodbye to my comrades, as they were ushered towards their quarters on the other side of the courtyard, wondering what the future held for the clan. They were just getting over the loss of their totem, the cave bear, and beginning to learn speech, which would lead them to new gods. I strode into the forge, where six blacksmiths were busy making swords, wrought gold cups, platters and finely-crafted wands. I recognized the similarity between these and the four Magical Weapons that my guide had taken from me in the sanctuary.

"Why do you create all four of the Magical Weapons?" I enquired of one blacksmith. "You all represent the suit of Wands, not the other three suits."

"Ah, yes." He responded. "I will explain. The suit of Wands, once understood, contains all the other suits, Pentacles, Swords and Cups, for intuition acts on all four of the suits. That is why we can manufacture all the suits in pure gold. Now, allow me to burn you off."

He picked up a large blowtorch, clicking on a blue fire, and aimed it at me. I shrank away, twisting my body to hide from the blaze and raising my arms in alarm. The blacksmith, undeterred, held the torch steadily as I writhed under its scorching heat. I could feel my outer skin beginning to blister and peel away. I gasped for mercy, and he finally lowered the torch.

"Go straight to the steaming tub near the furnace, duck down into the water and douse yourself. You will find that your outer skin will float off and you will feel a new sense of purpose."

I did as he asked, and although the water was hot, it felt good after my burning. I washed myself thoroughly and saw flakes of old skin floating to the surface. My new skin was smooth and soft, but strong. I felt exhilarated, and jumped from the tub waving my arms and dashing the water from my face. Then I stood ready while the body suit was carefully drawn onto me by three of the blacksmiths. I looked down. The suit was skintight and shone with many flickering colors as I moved my limbs. A surge of confidence came over me and I raised my fist in triumph.

"I am ready to deliver the egg!" I shouted. "Take me to the Queen, who will give me the next task I must accomplish."

The blacksmiths all cheered and clapped, and escorted me from the forge to my boat, moored by the shore. They pointed across a stretch of blue, shimmering water that seemed on fire, towards a small islet, where the Queen of Wands sat on a black throne. I stepped into the front seat of the scull and began to paddle away from the bank, only then realizing that I needed another person to maneuver the craft. I drifted for a few minutes, and then felt a slight bump as the boat began to move forward on its own and the splash of a paddle came from behind me. I tried to look behind to see who was sitting in the back seat, but could not.

We covered the distance to the islet quickly as on all sides blue, flickering flames rose from the water of the lagoon. Nosing gently against the isle, I jumped from the scull, looking behind me in time to see a small fire salamander slither over the gunwale and climb up the skirts of the Queen, who reached down to grasp the little amphibian with a smile. She held a great Wand that trapped the rays of the sun and turned it into a shining lamp that glowed above her throne.

The Queen of Wands was a freckled redhead with a determined manner. She appeared confident, and had a broad brow over an elegant and intelligent face. Her green eyes indicated her warmth and charm, and it was clear that she could see into the depths of a person and discern their secret intentions. I felt that she could be obstinate and even tyrannical at times, and so I was careful not to cross her.

"I am here, Ma Dame, to receive my next test, and to deliver the egg to the destination you desire." I knelt on the rough black basalt in front of her throne.

The Queen spoke in a quick, concise tone. "My name is Amferna, and you may call me that. Your next task is **to understand isolation as the requisite of coordination**. You must undertake a long journey by land, and your boat will remain here under our care. If you look over there….."

Here she pointed towards the desert shore, where two or three camels were drinking.

"…..you will see the mount that will carry you. I must remain here, for I am the mother of an only child, a daughter who is fierce and volatile, and who needs my attention now. The camel will take you part of the way towards the island in the north where the recluse Hugh has his temple, but beware of hazards along the way. He awaits the egg that you will be delivering, for he is the one who incubates it for us. When the egg hatches, I am hoping it will allow Shaman Reeves' clan, who are staying here, to take a mental leap forward and reach a far greater understanding of their potential as human beings. That is what we would wish. We have chosen you to bear this fragile load because we feel that you are capable of succeeding in this important task. Go now, and my attendant salamander will help you row to the shore and introduce you to your camel."

I could not contain my joy as I got closer to the shore and recognized one of the camels. "Lemig!" I called. "Is it you?"

My eyes squinted against the sun as one of the camels raised his head and spat a stream of water towards me, grunting happily. He looked like the camel I had ridden before. I noticed that he had drunk his fill of water, and he wouldn't need to be scared into drinking more. I hoped he would be my chosen mount, for we had a close and loving relationship in the past.

Bounding from the boat, I ran towards the camel as he whirled around and began to lope in my direction. We met and I flung my arms around his neck, while he nuzzled me softly and spat a little more. It was Lemig, of course. Walking behind him came a familiar figure, the camel driver Tabansi who had helped us up the river with the parents of Rivula, the Page of Cups, and had taken Lemig home when he became sick with bronchitis in that humid atmosphere.

"Tabansi! I am so glad to see you. It looks as if Lemig has completely recovered. Was he sick for a long time?"

"It is good to meet you again. Yes, I had to nurse him for over a month. We thought we might lose him, but my mother the crone Ediug knows all the herbal remedies. She gave him baths in Epsom salts, which relieved the catarrh. Now he is well again and ready for your journey, which I knew about when Ediug admitted to me that she had a vision of you crossing the mountains with a large object in a sack. What would that be?"

It was a pleasure to see that Tabansi had still not dropped back to his former habits and taken to drinking again.

"You are right about her vision." I agreed. "I must make a long journey to the isles in the northwest with my burden, a large egg. The mountains stand between us, and we must cross them by the pass where the hospice lies. I hope that Lemig can cope with the high altitude, Tabansi. What do you think?"

"I am not so sure." The camel driver looked solemn. "There are high mountains in the desert too, but there is no snow. We must make sure that Lemig has a blanket to cover him and keep him warm. I can cut a hole in one of ours for his hump, and then it will fit."

"Well, I expect he will be all right, because we should get going as soon as possible."

I was reluctant to leave so abruptly, but the egg waited in its padded sack. The camel knelt down and we slung it onto Lemigs' back along with the rolled up blanket and some provisions, and I mounted gladly, giving a gentle pull on the rein. He rose, I waved goodbye, and we set off at a fast lope across the intervening desert, winding our way between cactus and scrubby creosote bushes.

A day passed, and then another, and gradually the mountains grew closer until on the seventh day we began to climb the foothills. As it got colder, I put the blanket on Lemig at night and when snow began to fall, he wore it in the daytime as well. Although the going was hard, we reached the top of the pass after three days of travel, the snowdrifts getting deeper as we gained altitude, and Lemigs' breath coming in short gasps, which worried me, so that I eased him back and allowed him to take his time.

Gradually the ground flattened out as we came over the pass, and I was about to give a sigh of relief when Lemig stumbled and fell, rolling over-and-over and landing in a deep snow drift up to his neck. The ropes holding the sack containing the egg became loose and it bounced off and lay a short distance away. Hoping it was not broken, I tugged at Lemigs' rein, but he was buried too deeply and could not move. I had to get help! I remembered the hospice at the head of the pass. It was only a few hundred yards away. I struggled through the snow to reach it, and hammered on the door, over which hung a sign saying "The Hospice of the Holy St. Ida." A grille opened on a pale nuns' face and I explained my mission.

"A camel! Up here? That is very strange. We have a donkey that might be able to pull him out of the snowdrift. His name is Mandrake and he is very docile. I will get him and find a strong rope."

Thanking the nun profusely, I begged her to hurry. Within a few minutes, several heavily clad female figures clumped around the corner of the building, leading a small donkey, who winked at me. It was Mandrake, the little mount who I had ridden many times. I patted him as he brayed a greeting and we all made our way to the drift where Lemigs' snowy and forlorn head was wagging. We had to dig the snow away from his forelegs and under his belly to tie a rope around him, and then Mandrake bent his shoulders into the harness and the rope came taut. Slowly we eased Lemig out of his burial mound and finally he stood before us, wet and shivering.

One of the nuns was obviously in charge. "Hurry up! We must get him into the stable and rub him down. Get hot mash and a tot of brandy."

We rushed Lemig into the hospice stables and a large red-nosed abbess poured a liter of brandy down his throat, while some of the nuns brought in a steaming dish of mash, and others rubbed him down with straw and put dry blankets on him. After a few minutes, the camel began to roll his eyes and went into a fit of hiccups. His feet slid from under him and he dropped to the straw beneath, already snoring. We tiptoed away and, leaving the nuns to dry out his soaking blanket, I went to look for the egg.

I must have scoured that pass from one end to the other, but the sack containing the egg had disappeared. I was sure of the place it had landed, for the depression in the snow was still there, but dragging marks leading away from its landing place were plain. I followed the trail, which petered out where the wind had blown the snow off the bare glacial moraine, and then I became frantic with worry. Hurrying back to the hospice, I informed the abbess of the eggs' disappearance.

"Aha! That must be Dolf." The old crone hooted. "He's always up to something. A damn nuisance, having him hanging around here. I'd be glad to get rid of him. He's probably taken your sack to see what's inside. It gets pretty boring up here and there aren't that many sacks to investigate."

"Oh, dear!" I moaned. "He might break the egg by mistake. Where do you think he has taken it?" I felt ridden with anxiety and extreme guilt for Lemigs' accident.

"We know where Dolf is. One of us will lead you to his hideout. You must get the egg back by making the sign of the Hermetic Cross and saying 'By the name of Holy St. Ida, I command you to return this sack and its contents.' He will give in immediately, for he knows that St. Ida was his poor mother, who died of a heart attack after he threw her out of her house. We embalmed her and sanctified her. You must come and see the body when you return. It is very lifelike. Dolf is still suffering from guilt and shuffles around holding his crotch, for a very nasty person punished him by hurling a prickly ball at his privates, and they have never healed." Here the abbess cackled and bent over with laughter.

It was just as she had said. When we tracked him down, Dolf, holding his crotch with one hand, gave up the sack with the unbroken egg inside. He had not had time to open the sack and investigate what was inside with the other hand, so the egg was safe. I asked the nuns if there was anything I could do for them in return, for Lemig would have to stay with them until they could get word to Tabansi to come and fetch him once more.

"There is something you can do for us. Take Dolf with you when you leave for the isle in the northwest. He is strong and can carry the egg. Then we will get rid of him forever. Maybe he will be able to use the journey to repent of his foul deed and receive absolution. Will you do that?"

I agreed with some trepidation. Dolf was huge, with broad shoulders tapering down to narrow hips, and wore a sullen expression when I went to talk to him about the proposed trip.

"I am sorry about your sack," he admitted gruffly. "I get very bored up here. I feel tied to this spot when I remember how I caused the death of my mother Ida by ordering her out of her home. That happened here and I would like to be able to move on. Maybe this is my opportunity to break with the past, for nothing will bring back my mother. I will go with you."

"That is good. I need a companion to carry the sack with the egg, for I must leave my camel Lemig behind. He is too fragile to complete the trip, and I need him to be well for our long quest across the desert when we reach the Black Island of Binah. Let's go to the hospice and ask the nuns for some provisions."

We walked to the hospice, where the nuns greeted us gladly.

"Ah! Dolf will go with you?" They asked slyly. "That is a very good idea, for he is strong. Before you go, we will take you into the sanctuary to view Holy St. Ida in her glass case."

The abbess gestured towards a small side door and Dolf shrank back.

"I don't want to see her. That was my mother." Suddenly he burst into tears, sobbing and shrieking "Mummy, mummy, forgive me! I love you still."

Two nuns insisted and gently escorted him through the door, which was a squeeze. The abbess calmed him. "It will be good for you to see her. She is very peaceful. She has absolved you. Please, look at her. We have taken great trouble to preserve her in perfect condition, first embalming her, and then wrapping her limbs with linens soaked in myrrh. After a few months, we unwrapped her, laid her in a shroud and she has emerged as a perfect mummy. Accepting her as who she is now will help you to move on and resolve your feelings of guilt."

Dolf swept away his tears with a clumsy hand and gazed down on the glass case. Inside rested the tiny figure of an old woman, her face serene and glowing as if an inner light shone from it. As we watched, there was movement from the corpse, and a thin hand reached out, tugging at her shroud. Then St. Ida sat up and blew a kiss in Dolf's direction. She smiled, sighed, rearranged her shroud and lay down again. Then, all was still once more.

Dolf collapsed to the floor, moaning softly and burying his head on the feet of the abbess. In a muffled voice, he whispered. "I know now she has forgiven me. She is greater than I am. I will make myself worthy of her. I will fight demons and monsters, and even wrestlers, in her memory, for she was truly an amazing lady and I never understood it." He rose to his feet. "Let us leave soon on our voyage to the western isles, and I will be a faithful companion to you." Here he took my hand and gently kissed it. Emotion overcame me, which I fought back by sternly focusing on the organization for our trip.

The skies were clear when we left early the next morning. Dolf had slung the sack across his shoulders and secured it, leaving his hands free. He was no longer holding his crotch, which was a relief as it might have seemed strange to anyone we met on the journey. The way led down from the pass, and a couple of days later we were below the snow line and making rapid progress towards the islands across a level, wooded plain. Wild boar rustled in the copses and we were able to trap and cook one over an open fire. The fresh meat was nourishing and sorely needed and we dried the remainder over the smoldering embers and packed it away for future use.

Several days passed uneventfully and we then arrived at the shore of a rough channel of water, across which we could faintly see white cliffs arising on the other side. We boarded a large craft that took off and skimmed across the water with a loud roaring noise, depositing us on the beach next to the cliffs. From there, we took a tandem bicycle to complete the next leg of the trip. Dolf pedaled behind me, so that the sack would not be in my way, and I navigated in front. We made several stops and spoke with many people, and everyone admired Dolfs' gigantic strength and meek demeanor.

Finally, we saw in front of us the vision of the blessed isle where Hugh, the recluse, had his temple. A boatman rowed us across the narrow strait and left us on a stony beach near a small group of dwellings. The surroundings were bleak and a low wind moaned through the narrow alley separating the huddled cottages. Beyond the little village I could see, further away, a dark temple that stood at the apex of a jutting headland, looking out to sea. The small tavern in the center of town seemed to be a social hub for the few inhabitants, so Dolf and I made our way over to it.

Stooping under the low door, we found a cozy interior and the barmaid, a bustling and friendly soul, called out to us. "Welcome, visitors! Look lively, folks, we 'ave callers. Make room for our new guests at the table, now. Whatever be you wanting around these parts, for heav'ns sake?"

"We are bringing an important item for the person occupying the temple on the cliffs. Hugh, his name is, I believe. I was here a while ago, and I couldn't get a word out of him. Yet he is renowned for incubating eggs, and we need his services."

An old yokel spoke up. "He bin come here nigh 35 years ago come Christmas now, I reckon. D'yer wantter hear th' story?"

"Thank you, but I already did. I met you three years ago, here in this tavern, and you told me Hughs' story. He came from the continent, didn't he?"

"Yes'm, 'e did. We's afeared on him, too. It were a month ago come Sunday he hatched an egg bigger'n your head, by far. An' then there were trouble, I c'n tell ya. We's'n daren't go over that side o' the isle, fer there were a strange scaley thing come out o' that egg 'n it went 'n fell down th' cliff t'other side an' maybe its swam away, I'm tellin' ya. They'm out there seaward, waitin' on us, that thar crowd o' monsters. Me, I'm jus' about ready ter quit this weird land, like our young folks, and head fer the big citty, it ain't safe here no more, I reck'n."

Here he sucked on his pipe and spat a stream of tobacco juice towards a spittoon that stood nearby, missing it by several inches.

"He did hatch an egg recently, then?" I was excited at the news. "It seems we have come at the right time. Dolf, we should take our egg straight over to him. There is a narrow path across the sheep pasture to the temple. Let's go right away."

The barmaid looked surprised. "You only jus' came in! Ain't you goin' to have a beer, now?"

"Save the booze for when we get back. It shouldn't be too long. Then I'll buy a round for everyone." The Queens' valet had supplied me with a small pouch of cash to cover the cost of egg transport.

A frisson of fear ran through the company when we announced our departure for the temple. "Yer doan' wantter go there, I'm tellin' yer," said a wizened old fisherman from the fireside. "I've seen 'em, the monsters, when I took off ter go fishin', I'm tellin' yer. They'm swarming over the oggin an' darn near upset me boat."

"Well, we'll deal with that very soon." I was a little disbelieving with him in my hurry.

Dolf and I ducked out of the low door and set off across a stony, barren sheep pasture towards the black temple. The wind cried like a wounded animal as it battered the eves of the temple, and brought the scent of fresh seaweed from the cliffs below.

The building was quiet as we approached, then a vibrant groan broke the silence, and repeated itself several times. My hair stood on end as we crept around the closed walls to the entrance at the top of the cliff. On the narrow and precipitous path, I looked down to the distant, foaming sea beneath, where the endless white waves broke on a cold, rocky shore. We reached the open pillared terrace and peered into the gloom.

In the center of the floor, which was striped in different colors, stood a strange three-tiered pedestal of finely sculpted ebony, and beside it huge pieces of an empty eggshell were scattered. A trail of odorous burnt scales led away towards the cliff edge, where a slithering mark showed something had fallen while trying to take off. A small, huddled figure sat motionless, his head in his hands, under the pedestal. Three flaming Wands were propped against the empty stand. Pulsating groans came from this figure, which I recognized as Hugh, and I went towards him carefully, as he had not observed our approach. Dolf tiptoed after me with the sack.

I put my finger to my lips for silence, and then signaled to Dolf to deposit the sack on the floor by Hugh, and back away quietly. Without a word, we crept away, leaving Hugh to find the next egg for incubation by himself.

We were scarcely around the corner when a piercing whistle and a fiendish cry came from the temple, the like of which I had never heard before and that sent prickles of fear down my back, We peered around the corner and saw that Hugh was on his feet and untying the sack hurriedly. He took out the great egg, held it fondly, kissed the surface, and placed it gently on the pedestal, then arranged the Wands around it to begin the incubation.

We had no idea how long the process would take, and I could not ask Hugh, for he had been silent for many years. We returned to the tavern and I ordered beer all around. The locals raised their mugs in a toast.

"You'm brave!" Announced the spitting yokel. "None of us'n go near that there place. That bloke – he sum sort'a allychemmist wi' all his'n bottles and flasks. Why, yer might fall all th'way to th' ocean, where th' monsters be, 'n oi be not surprise iff'n he give a feller a little push, ter 'elp 'im on 'is way, as't were." He took a long swig of beer, the liquid coursing down his chin onto his filthy shirt front.

We caroused with the locals for some considerable time and shared some jolly rounds that left us quite drunk. After a close inspection of the taverns' facilities, which were less than acceptable, we decided to sleep in a sheep pen. Since I did not know how long I would have to wait for the hatching, I arranged for Dolf to leave the next morning. He had decided to become a professional wrestler and I wished him the best of luck. I was going to return to the lee side of the island, where I knew there was a small sod house, which at least was clean. I would collect my thoughts there and try to find out the incubation period for the egg now that Hugh had begun the process.

Reaching the sod hut after bidding Dolf goodbye, I sat down in a dry corner, drawing my fur cloak around me, and fell into a reverie. I don't remember much of the next two weeks, as I waited for news of the incubation. I was fraught, uptight, and unable to eat anything except a few berries and some roots that I found close to the hut. I felt isolated, unable to leave the place but longing for the human contact of the world outside and beyond the island. None of my entities appeared, either. I missed them and my interaction with them, my moods, and experiences in my life that had changed me. Now, it seemed as though I was in a coma – a sleep of sorts - that left me numb and unable to move. The world outside had gone on without me. I continually wondered what was in the egg and imagined it hatching all kinds of things, but mostly fearful ones.

After a couple of weeks, which I had marked by scratching on the wall of the hut, I was half-asleep when one night I became aware of a sibilant, gentle breathing from the other side of my retreat that penetrated the foggy thoughts in my brain.. I shook my head and listened carefully again. There it was – someone was in the corner of the hut. I was not alone! I tried to make out a shape in the dark, but could not, and a cold shiver gripped me as I remembered the Hoodwinker, she who had bound and dragged me from that same sod house, tied me to her horse, and ridden over the cliffs. On the other hand, it might be my Guide, and I badly needed his advice. I had been saved by the intervention of my Guide on that occasion, and taken to his hut, where my wounds were healed. Rather than strike a magic match, I decided to wait, in some trepidation, for daylight to see who was there.

The night seemed long, but I dared not sleep, as the slow breathing seemed to gradually creep closer. I didn't want to know what was there, next to me, and I drew my feet close under me as I hunched close to the angle in the mud walls, for fear my legs would be bound by a tight cord, leaving me helpless as before. I regretted coming back to the sod hut, but it was the only available shelter. The idea of sleeping in the tavern, where the beds were swarming with bugs and fleas, nauseated me.

I must have dropped off to sleep from exhaustion, for I woke with a start to feel leathery claws on my left leg, trying to pass a line around my ankle. I kicked out furiously and hit a bony mass with my right foot, whereupon a muffled curse caught my ears. Taking advantage of that attack, I leapt up and tore from the sod hut, stumbling over tufts of grass in my panic to escape the thing that was following me. I could hear short gasps of breath behind me interspersed with foul curses as the Hoodwinker – for it must be her – hunted me in the dark.

"Goddam it! Missed my mark. I only wanted to communicate. But the fear and denial is too great. I am not trusted. Never mind, I must stalk the Navigator and stop the hatching, for if the beasts get out, they will maim, putrefy, and kill, kill, kill…"

A spate of virulent blasphemies followed this outburst, forcing me to clap my hands over my ears and run more quickly into the black night. I didn't want to hear that language, ever. I rushed on wildly, somehow intuitively avoiding obstacles in the dark that loomed in front of me and dodging from side to side to avoid pursuit by the shadowy figure.

Slowing my desperate race as the dawn light began to filter through, I came up suddenly close to a little paddock with rough walls constructed of the local grey stone. Stopping for breath, I saw a beautiful light dun mare grazing in the paddock. She nickered as she saw me, swung her head, and walked over for me to pet her. Glancing over my shoulder, I saw no sign of my pursuer, and began to relax a little. I plucked some grass and held out my hand to feed the mare, looking into her soft brown eyes.

As she lipped the grass from my hand, I suddenly saw her eyes change maliciously, but it was too late! The mares' teeth clamped down on my arm like a vise and held me, while a sly cackle came from an invisible source. I struggled to free myself, as before my eyes the animal began to shape shift, and its head became the face of the Hoodwinker, who drew me towards her with glee. I stared in horror into her scheming eyes, black and glittering, and cursed my stupidity. I had forgotten that she could change shape at will, and she had trapped me into thinking that the horse was real.

"Listen, my dear." The Hoodwinker gazed at me pointedly as I struggled to get away and lowered my head, avoiding her piercing eyes. "My, you can run fast! What are you afraid of? I mean you no harm, for if you remember, I persecuted you before because you had not looked after your inner child, Suckersie. Now, I am aware, for I know all things about you as your Shadow self, that you sought out the baby and reconciled with her before you were able to pass through the veil into the sanctuary at the end of your river journey. So, why would I still be mad at you?"

The Hoodwinker paused and sighed. "No, I caught you here to warn you about the contents of that egg. It contains unborn creatures that mean to harm you. I know them well. They are from the age of the cave man and are deadly evil, and they incubate quickly. When they hatch, they can enter your mind and make you lose confidence and feel unsure of yourself and your decisions. You will lose your power and give in to them. They will teach you to foster hatred and revenge towards all those you meet. Even now these devilish contents are beginning to heat up, and the egg will give birth to who knows what fiend, within the next three days if we do not stop it."

She nodded and squeezed my hand, then let go. "Now, we must make a plan to outwit Hugh, whose mind has been drawn into the grip of these same demons of the Qliphoth, and he shall never return to sanity. He meddled once too often with dark forces, and does their work now, and he recently birthed a burnt scaley bird, a phoenix that failed to escape its own inner fire, and crashed down the cliff as it attempted to fly."

I tried to stay calm. That was where the burnt scales and the empty eggshells on the temple floor had come from, then. This was a big turn of events. The Hoodwinker, my inner Shadow, was asking me to trust her. She, who I feared most! I had to accept her message and understand that my confidence in Hugh, whom I had assumed was benign, was misplaced and he was deceiving me at that moment. After a moment of indecision, I turned to the Hoodwinker.

"We must ride swiftly to the temple and stop him," I cried decisively.

As I did so, I saw that the Hoodwinker was already saddling the dun mare, and we mounted, whirled her around, and took off over the paddock wall in the direction of the temple.

At a furious gallop, it did not take long to cross the island to the weather side and arrive close to the temple, where we dismounted and tethered the mare to a dead tree. The Hoodwinker drew me into the bushes, whispering in my ear.

"I am going to shape-shift again, so don't be alarmed. I will become the leader of the group of alchemists. That is the group that Hugh betrayed, by separating from them and taking with him occult secrets that were part of their heritage. He will react in guilt, seeing his leader here on the island when he thinks him far away, or dead. Yes! That's it. I will pretend to be the ghost of the leader – that will terrify him and distract his attention from the egg on the pedestal." She paused, wrinkling her bony nose for a moment. "We will coordinate our attack. Now, you will take the egg from the pedestal and roll it to the edge of the cliff, then push it off. That which is inside is not quite ready to hatch, and will perish on the rocks below. Hurry, now, for we have little time."

Silently we crept around to the narrow cliff path, where the Hoodwinker, with a puff of smoke, changed her appearance to that of an old, frail man with a long beard whose body wavered in the cool sea air that flowed over the edge of the cliff. The ghostly figure moved forward silently and stood behind Hugh, who was intent on arranging the Wands around the pedestal under the warming egg.

"Boo! Booby!" The apparition howled.

I could not help admiring the effect on Hugh, who whirled round and gave a shriek of terror. The old man pointed a finger at him and slowly spoke. "You are damned, Hugh, for breaching our holy vows and betraying our secrets for your own benefit. The time has come for you to die, Die, Hugh! Die!"

Hugh backed away screaming, his hands over his eyes, and I leapt forward, seizing the egg from its pedestal and rolling it swiftly towards the cliff, where I pushed it over and watched it bounce down and begin to break up as it smashed from rock to rock. Pieces of the shell broke off and a glutinous mass fell out and began to separate into monstrous unborn bodies of every shape and size, which became more bloody and battered as they crashed towards the bottom of the cliff. At last they all disappeared into the sea below, and the waves were red with the blood of the unborn.

The Hoodwinker had vanished, and, as I watched, I knew that the progress of the clans' humanity had been saved, for their lives would have been dark and fraught with conflict if this particular egg hatched They needed to find another egg - an egg with positive potential - I knew not where, but I would give them all the help I could in the search.

The wind moaned through the thin pillars as I turned back to the temple, which was the more appealing for a series of pretty, curved arches that framed an uncluttered area of floor striped in colors of green, pink, and grey. The wide space was empty, save for the skeleton of a man that had been tossed into a corner, and a broken pedestal that lay scattered across the floor.

King of Wands - Rules Four and Two of Wands.

My journey back to the Castle of Fire was long and arduous, but I felt wonderfully light and free from cares. I had finally made contact with the Hoodwinker, the Shadow within me, and found that she was not as terrible as I had imagined, and that she could become my ally. At the top of the pass, I stopped at the hospice, exhausted, and the nuns allowed me to take the donkey Mandrake so that I could ride down to the Lagoon in relative comfort.

It was good to be sitting on Mandrakes' bony rump again, his long ears wagging in front of me, and his nimble hooves finding their way along the rocky trail. We arrived at the oasis in time to see Tabansi and Lemig, where I left Mandrake. The camel seemed none the worse for his snow bath, in spite of his tendency to bronchitis. I had to report to the Queen of Wands, Amferna, and her salamander was waiting patiently for me with the scull, so I took up my oars and we rowed out to her throne.

Amferna welcomed me as the salamander snuggled into her lap. Beside her, and resting her hand on the Queens' shoulder, stood a beautiful strawberry blonde, her daughter, now evidently reconciled. I related the story of the egg and its vile contents to them, and Amferna did not seem surprised – in fact, she nodded sagely.

"Now, regarding the clan. I will inform Shaman Reeve that it was the wrong egg. It had to be destroyed so that mankind would not be overpowered in future by the demons it contained. When you get to the Mystic SEA, you must search for the right egg, one that contains positive power. Alas, I fear that egg is kept under lock and key in the Island of Yesod. You will be told where to find it when you contact the dream master there. In the meantime, we will keep the clan here, in a mental holding pattern, and teach them farming and animal husbandry, for they know nothing of these abilities. They will be waiting for word that you have hatched the right egg in Yesod, and you must let us know as soon as that happens."

Amferna continued thoughtfully. "You now understand isolation as the requisite of coordination. It was vital for you to spend time alone in the sod hut because, until now, you have tried to avoid any encounter with the Hoodwinker, whose home is below the tower of Belvedere. While you were visiting the three castles of Earth, Air, and Water, you were not obliged to activate your sense of intuition, and had other tests to pass. At the Castle of Fire, however, intuition is very important, and connecting with that side of your Self is vital before you can move to the Isle of the White Pyramid, for there you will prepare to move onto the Bar where you will find the first vessel that will take you across the Mystic SEA."

The Queen paused and smiled. "You have passed the test I set you, and now you must meet our King, Cinarburn, who awaits you in the desert yonder. The fireproof suit that you wear will protect you against the great heat that the King emanates, for he is Fire of Fire, and is constantly exploding. This is sometimes a great ordeal for me, since he always seems to find an initiate to join these experiments with him. However, I wish you well, and I know that you will succeed in the next trial. Listen to your gut and be strong always."

I bade farewell to the Queen and her daughter Rachel and returned to the shore by the oasis, where Tabansi, holding Lemig and Mandrake, awaited me. Both animals greeted me with great joy. Tabansi looked over the shimmering desert to the far horizon, where I could see a mushroom shaped cloud rising from the barren ground, which shook and undulated as the blast reached us. It was difficult to keep ones' balance in the tearing force of the gusts.

"The King is over there. He is in the process of another nuclear blast. This may alarm you but do not worry, you are protected by your incandescent suit and your intuitive knowledge, which will aid you as you interact with him. Now, you must choose one of these animals to ride into the desert. One will carry you safely, and the other may fail and collapse under you as you approach the King. Which is it to be?"

Looking from the eager faces of Lemig and Mandrake to the fiery desert, where rocks and cacti were scattered, and the ground looked very uneven, I reluctantly decided that would favor the donkey. Besides, I had twice used the camel as a mount, and each time he had become sick. I was concerned that Lemig might not be strong enough to undertake this mission, and I would have great need of his talents later on, so I chose Mandrake, mounting him swiftly and trotting off in the direction of the cloud far away, to the disappointment of the camel.

In a while we were very close to the dark cloud, which seemed to be dissipating. I reined in Mandrake and made out a dim figure emerging from the cloud, his headdress ablaze with light. It was the King, who now walked towards us. He was a mature man with a bronzed and muscular physique and auburn hair. Tough and wiry, his green eyes seemed to pierce mine as I stood before him holding the donkeys' rein.

"You arrived at the perfect time." Cinarburn told me. "A moment too soon, and you would have been engulfed in my latest explosion. A moment later, and Mandrake would have collapsed from the heat. I will give you the test you must pass. It is "**to nurture contradiction and formulate cohesion.**"

He gazed at me fixedly, and I thought I noted in his eye a more than passing interest, which unnerved me. I swept aside unwelcome memories of another, who had attracted my attention and proved to be unworthy, and the uncomfortable circumstances surrounding that attempted seduction.

"Come with me," said the King, taking my hand in his hot grasp. "You may leave Mandrake here. He will wait. I want to show you something." Cinarburn drew me some yards away towards two large and prickly cacti, and sat down on one of them, indicating that I should take the other for a seat.

"Mi Lawd, this seat looks awfully prickly." I protested. "Do you mind if I sit on the ground instead?"

"That will not solve the problem," the King said gruffly. "You can no longer turn your back on thorny issues. Sit, and you may find it is not so uncomfortable after all."

I eased myself gingerly down, and found that, in fact, the spikes did not penetrate the skintight suit I was wearing. I relaxed a little and Cinarburn patted my thigh, a little too fondly, I thought.

"Now, your test is rather enigmatic, for nurturing contradiction must seem strange to you. Everyone in the mundane world tries to resolve contradiction, always choosing one side or the other, which creates a dichotomy. Hence, the world is always split into two camps, contradicting each other and believing themselves to be correct. The truth is that contradiction itself is essential to nature and should be accepted intuitively as the only path towards true understanding."

Cinarburns' voice rose excitedly. "I am going to begin another explosion, which is essential for the learning process, and I want you to experience it with me. Are you willing to risk death? For, if the force goes wrong, which it sometimes does, only I will survive. You would be drawn up in the magnetic cloud and dispersed over the land as atomic dust."

"Well, I would be wearing my suit, wouldn't I? That would protect me, I would have thought." I spoke defensively as I felt a little nervous.

Cinarburn looked grave. "I am afraid you must remove the suit for this experiment." He said. "To benefit fully from an explosion, one must be naked and unencumbered by any sort of clothing. Let me help you, now, and we will take off the suit."

He slid his hand up my arm and gently took hold of the neck of the suit, pulling it down. I leaned from him and, pushing away his hand, resisted his suggestion, but he was adamant, and soon the suit was on the ground.

We now stood naked in a circle between the prickly cacti in the middle of the desert, holding hands. A jolt of desire shot through me at the thought of my strange circumstances. Cinarburn was intensely attractive and I wanted to participate in the explosion, but I was afraid that I would die. I closed my eyes and waited, with a beating heart, to see what would follow.

The earth beneath my feet started to roll gently in waves, which resembled the ripples on a pond and came increasingly close together, rising to a fever pitch as the King and I stood in the center of the ring. A dense smoke rose underneath our feet and, taking us with it, formed a column snaking up into the air. I held the Kings' hand tightly for fear of falling as we ascended at a fast pace. We rose into an impenetrable black cloud and intense feelings shook me. I heard the rumble of thunder nearby, and then a huge flash of lightning, followed by closer thunder, and then a series of flashes that seemed to engulf me. The body of the King jerked spasmodically as he hung in the center of the storm, and then a giant explosion shook us and tore us apart.

My body was rocketing upwards and the wind tore at my face and hair as I strained to keep my bearings. I couldn't see around me because a thick dusty fog billowed into my lungs, forcing me to cough and choke. I held out my arms and attempted to swim through the cloud and retain some sort of control, and then I started to fall. I shot downwards like an arrow, fortunately unable to see the ground below, into which I would surely crash and die. My travels flashed before me, including all the different people I had encountered and the situations in which I had been involved.

Only a moment must have passed, when my descent slowed down imperceptibly and I floated into the Kings' arms. He lowered me to the ground, smiling ecstatically.

"That was good! Did you enjoy it too?" Cinarburn laughed as I hastily put on my suit. "See, you are still alive, brave one. Never fear to take a risk, for therein hides the real meaning of life. Now, you must be on your way. Do not think to find your friends Isleta and Galeno, for they have already taken ship for the Mystic SEA, where they will prepare an important royal wedding on the Path of the Lovers. You will attend this future marriage, for you know the couple well. Just wait and see. Now, farewell, may you go safely to meet Cosmo, the priest of my temple and Guardian of the First Crossing, who will prepare you for your trip to the White Pyramid."

The King slung his cloak around his shoulders and waved goodbye as I mounted Mandrake, who had patiently waited for me, and wound my way back to the oasis, where I met the Queen. As I handed the donkeys' rein back to Tabansi, I was glad that the explosion had not killed my faithful ass.

My journey onwards would be by boat, and so I looked around for a second rower for my scull. The Queens' daughter stepped forward and offered her services, saying that she wanted to share my adventure. I hesitated, looking towards Amferna, and she nodded her assent.

"Rachel is her own woman and may go with you if she chooses. Just watch out, she can be moody and a little controlling, but I think you can handle that. She is maturing fast and a trip to see Cosmo and feel the veil would be very beneficial for her. I wish you well, go with Pan."

Rachel took the seat in front of me in the boat and proved to be, not only an experienced rower, but possessed of incredible and untiring energy. It was not until we had passed the half way mark of our journey that I realized her true nature. We hit bad weather during a canal passage, and the heat became intense. I found myself whimpering and complaining, and Rachel became increasingly agitated as I collapsed into the bottom of the boat, refusing to row any further. Burying my head in the bag with my cricket, Joana, I did not look up until I heard a familiar voice above me.

"You must go on – row. I your daughter, your baby, don't leave me to go on alone. That's not fair. Get up and get going, or I leave you and return to the Castle of Fire."

It was the voice of Suckersie, my inner child, who spoke. I looked up to see the beautiful young woman who sat before me. Then I understood that the Queen had tricked me, pretending that Suckersie was her daughter, Rachel, when, in fact, she was mine. Suckersie was all grown up, though, and I had not recognized her.

I got up abruptly and moved to embrace her, but the scull tipped to one side and water began to flow over the gunwale. I was afraid it would capsize, so I saluted instead and resumed my seat. As I began to row once more, a great joy filled me, as I knew that my childlike self had returned. We soon covered the remaining miles to the island of the bull-king, and reached the remains of a white temple that stood on a knoll by the waters' side. Behind the temple lay many ruined buildings that had once been the great palace of the bull-king before the waters had swept it away.

We entered the temple, walking down a red carpet that led in a straight line to a low dais of three steps with a whalebone seat upon it. The priest Cosmo and his consort Adonia sat upon this seat, with their son Dysis between them, and behind them hung the veil decorated with harps and bulls heads.

"Welcome, travelers. We meet again. You are here to undertake the trial of the bulls and the harps, the two images that appear on the veil. If you pass this test successfully, I will be able to instruct you and prepare you for your initiation on the Isle of the White Pyramid. Come, and I will show you what to do."

Cosmo rose from his seat and led us through a small side door in the temple that gave onto the old palace, where rubble from the once great building lay scattered over a wide area, and weeds grew thickly between the stones, while brambles trailed over quaint statues with broken noses and other parts.

"Alas, the labyrinth is no more, for when the great wave came, the roof of the palace collapsed onto it." Cosmo looked sad. "The Minotaur fled and took with him the sacred harp of the heavens. The harp is hidden somewhere on this island, and the Minotaur, who is the bull-king, may be concealed in the same place. You must find the harp and wrest it from the grip of the bull-king, then bring it here. Beware, for the Minotaur, although of great age, is dangerous still. What is more, there are four bulls on the island and three of them are clones, or imitations. Only one guards the real harp. Is it the bull in the forest, the bull of the hills, the bull that lives on the plains, or the bull from the sea? You must pick the right one and bring the animal to the temple with its harp. Then you may lift the veil once more and enter the Ring Pass Not. I will give you this lamp to guide you, and then I will await your return."

Rachel and I looked at each other. We did not know where to start. The island was large and there were mountains, forests, beaches, and large tracts of grassy plains where we might find the four bulls. We reckoned that maybe the bull of the hills lived in a cave, and so we set out for the hilly center of the isle to the North. We made camp and cut branches for a shelter near the mouth of one of the caves, and decided to explore the following morning when, lighting the lamp, we entered the cavern and began a long trek downwards through a damp and slimy tunnel. Parts of the tunnel appeared to have been hewn out of the rock by hand and enlarged to make an easier passage. Now and again the pathway became wider and we found ourselves in caves of different sizes, some of which had strange hieroglyphs on the walls and arrows that pointed ever downhill.

After traveling for several miles, we reached an enormous cavern where shadows on every side, dancing in the light of the lamp, seemed like giant, menacing demons. It was hard to see in the flickering light, so we made a close round of the cavern, finding many natural sculptures and formations of great beauty. Then we rounded a corner and froze!

In the shadows, the head of a giant dun colored bull with a large ribbon around its neck was stealthily moving, and we strained forward, holding out the lamp, to see the body. There was none, instead, the bulls' head was attached to a large harp that stood in an alcove of the cavern. To our horror, the head moved again, wagging slowly from side to side, and then spoke.

"Help me! I am the Bull from the North, trapped in the power of this harp, which is out of tune, for its strings became crossed when it was carried away by the great flood, and made me a prisoner for all time. Can either of you tune a harp? It needs restringing, and that might take some time, but if you can then play the correct tune, I will be free at last. Please save me, for I have been here alone for many aeons."

The bulls' head wept openly, and raised piteous eyes to plead for his freedom. We could hardly refuse such a request as we understood that this was one of the tests that Cosmo had arranged for us, so we carefully pulled the harp out of the alcove and set it down on a flat section of the cave floor.

I was not musical, but Rachel seemed to know what to do, and began to unthread the strings that were in the wrong position, laying them carefully in order beside her on the floor. Several strings remained in the harp, twenty-one in all, that were still in the correct positions. The bull explained that he had loved a moon woman, a famed harp player, who had been swept away by the flood. If we could reproduce her favorite tune, we would all return to the temple safely. Meanwhile, Rachel had quickly restrung the harp, and struck a tremulous note on it.

The head of the bull shook and a frown crossed his face. "That is not it – try again. Her tune was as sweet as honey and as strong as a lion. You must get it right."

My child plucked the strings again and again, but could not find the exact note that introduced the tune. It was hardly surprising, as we had not heard the song before. The moist air in the cave gradually sank into our bones, and after some hours, I began to shiver.

"Rachel, we have to leave," I whispered to her out of the bulls' earshot. "It's so cold we will get hypothermia if we stay here any longer. This can't be the right bull. He must be one of the clones that is endowed with the power of automatic speech. You have tried hard to tune the harp correctly, but the chance of finding the right tone, when there are a million choices, is virtually impossible. Come now, and bid the bull farewell."

When the bull heard that we were leaving, he wept openly, tossing his head in a strange, mechanical way. Then he became extremely angry, lowering his horns and roaring loudly. As the clamor of his rage rose to a crescendo, his head suddenly split open and a welter of springs, screws and cog wheels spun out and clattered to the floor. The harp instantly crumbled to dust before us, and with a terrifying din echoing around, we fled, zigzagging through the tunnels away from the cavern.

Back at our camp, I knew how close to danger we had been, for if Rachel had struck the right note, the magical spell it invoked would have trapped us in the cavern forever. We had a lucky escape and night was drawing in, so, after catching and roasting two marmots for supper, we decided to start out the following day for the forest to the West, where the next bull might be hiding.

The day broke and we doused our fire and descended the hill country towards a dense pine forest. The giant trees blocked out all but a dim light, but we could still make out the springy ground underfoot and we progressed rapidly. After a while, the evergreens began to thin out and deciduous trees, such as birch and cottonwoods, replaced them, interspersed by cool, grassy glades. We found a clearing where a small pool reflected the dancing sky overhead, and made camp as a base, cutting willow branches for a shelter. The next day we ventured out, and spent three days searching the forest near our camp, but it was not until the fourth day, when we decided to break camp and head further to the west, that the land began to rise and form a hillock. At the top of this slope, the distinct shape of an overgrown ditch formed a circle that contained a small pool, and in the center was a cairn of stones with a door in the side just above the water level.

We could not see any other hiding place, so we waded out and pulled at the door to open it. Our first attempts failed, as it was very rusty, but Rachel worked up a frenzy and tore it open with all her might. Out splashed the tiny plastic statue of a bull, that floated away on the limpid surface. At the back of the cairn we could see the shape of a harp covered with moss, and we pulled it free. It was dripping with moisture and the paint came off in our hands, damaging the exotic design of dancing maidens.

The little bull, who was black, bellowed softly. "Lift me up. My harp needs to be restrung and, when that happens, I can return once more to my normal size. I am the Bull from the West, and I have been shut up in this cairn for years, since that overblown entity Belvedere swore to oust me from his life. Please fix my harp, for I need my freedom."

Here the bull wept copiously, his pleading eyes turned towards us as he regained the bank and scrambled up it. Personally, I was a little suspicious, but Rachel impulsively reached towards the harp and began to unravel the mixed-up strings that were damp and slimy with disuse. Working fast, she had the harp restrung within an hour, and plucked at the strings, only to hear a dismal booming sound that reverberated through the surrounding woods and made the bull shiver as he shook drops of water from his tiny flanks.

"That is not the right note." The bull said in disgust. "Keep trying, for I must regain my full size as soon as possible. Then I can punish that pompous Belvedere, the idiot who put me here. Hurry, now."

Rachel turned to me in desperation. "The strings of this harp are ruined, because they have been damaged by water and stretched beyond their limit. I fear this harp will never sing again."

She dropped her hands from the instrument and stood up. Just then, the little statue of the bull shook convulsively, and water poured from its eyes and mouth. In horror, we stood above it as it slowly disintegrated before our eyes with a bubbling hiss, and sank into the ground. A strange rustling came from the trees around us, almost like a sigh of relief. We replaced the dud harp in the cairn, and left the area, knowing that we had only found another cloned bull.

The following day, we changed direction and began to head due east towards the great plains that lay beyond the forest. We traveled for three days, and then came out of the trees and moved swiftly across a rolling sea of grass towards the rising sun. It grew hot, so we rested under a bush and wondered where to look for any cattle that might be around. Towards evening, as it grew cooler, we continued east and soon the shades of night rising from the horizon enveloped us, yet we moved on through the darkness.

About midnight we were crossing a dry riverbed when I heard a snort ahead of us, and the dull thud of hooves reverberating on the hardened ground. At the same time, the gentle wind that was blowing from the east began to strengthen and soon we were facing a stiff breeze that threw dust in our eyes. With the darkness and rising wind, it was hard to see, but I caught a glimmer of white moving in front of us, and warned Rachel to take shelter behind a boulder.

The pale blur moved towards us and the figure of a gigantic white aurochs emerged, pawing at the dried watercourse to seek a drink. The wind blew his bovine scent in our direction, so that he was unaware of our presence. As he came ever closer, I made out a brand on his flank in the shape of a harp, and I motioned to Rachel, pointing out the brand and whispering.

"This must be the right bull. He's awfully big. I don't know what to do. This harp is only a design. How can we get hold of it?"

"We must kill the bull and cut the brand out of his flank." She murmured softly. "Let's wait until morning comes, then we can devise a method."

The bull had found water, drank, and then moved on. We cautiously followed him, keeping downwind so that he wouldn't spot us, until the dawn came and the animal paused to rest. There we crouched behind a tired looking mesquite bush, covered by a creeping vine that I recognized as deadly nightshade. Knowing its properties, I suggested to Rachel that she took some of the vines' leaves and ventured to feed the bull. Having great courage, she undertook to do this for me, moving slowly towards the animal with an armful of leaves.

The bull snorted, lowered his head, and, pulling the leaves into his mouth, commenced to munch on them. Soon he lay down, closed his eyes, and began to breathe in short gasps as his body gradually stiffened from the poisonous plant. When he was dead, I told Rachel to wait until his skin sloughed off from the effects of the deadly nightshade. We would then be able to cut out the section with the harp brand and take it with us.

Since the bull was already dead, I thought there would be no need to restring the harp on this occasion. Then I remembered the aurochs I had shot at the beginning of my journey, and how my Guide had told me that the bull was ever renewing, and was impossible to kill. As the magnificent beast rested before us, a portion of his skin containing the brand fell to the ground, and I picked it up. Looking at the design, I noticed that the strings of the harp were crossed. Should we re-draw it? That might restore the bull to life, which would be dangerous for us, but might be essential for our quest.

The animal that lay in front of us was so beautiful that I felt a pang of guilt. I wanted to see him alive, roaming the plains in all his magnificent strength. My desire must have struck a chord, for I thought I saw a shadowy movement behind the mesquite bush. A strange bird emerged, strutting forward on lanky legs, its head adorned with a burst of small black quills that wavered in the strong breeze, while it regarded us with a reddish eye and a menacing curved beak. I was certain that here was the secretary bird I had encountered on my river journey, and I felt that it was signaling to me.

With a squawk, the bird placed one of its quills in my hand. "My name is Isa Real Gardy, late secretary to the Crow, who you met on your previous adventures. He will soon reappear, but for now, you need to redesign this harp. Throw away the piece of skin with the brand, and take a fresh piece from the Bull of the East. Use my quill to draw a new harp, put the strings in the correct position, and then run your fingers across them, and you will restore life to the bull. By the way, you still have the talisman I gave you, I hope?" The secretary bird cocked its head on one side and looked at me quizzically.

"Yes, I do. I still haven't deciphered the sigil, but the talisman is in a pouch, safely stowed in my current boat. I have been moving it from boat to boat as my Guide changes the vessels that I am using on my travels." I assured the bird.

"That is good. You will need the talisman for protection when you reach the Island of Malkuth. The Qliphoth, or evil ones, are rampant there. I will meet you on the Island and help you to activate the talisman and explain the sigil thereon." Isa Real Gardy preened his feathers. "It will not be long now. It remains for you to undertake the four elemental tasks at the Isle of the White Pyramid, to prepare you for the crossing of the Mystic SEA. I will be there to greet you amongst the Islands, along with the other six strange birds you have met, who will help you. Now, goodbye, and we will meet again soon."

With that, the secretary bird flapped his wings and ran away across the plain, leaving the quill in my hand. I began to draw a new harp, the strings all in the correct position. When I had finished, I asked Rachel to play the instrument symbolically. She gently plucked at the piece of skin with the drawing on it, and a magical tone arose, a combination of notes I had never heard before on my travels, yet dreamed of hearing in eternity.

Suddenly the skin we were holding slid out of our hands and, before our eyes, the white coat of the dead bull was complete once more, and he opened his eyes, which glittered in the hot sun strangely. We backed away, not daring to look behind us, mesmerized by his gaze. There was nowhere to run, no hiding place, as the enormous animal rose to his feet, shook himself, and faced us. The knowledge that we had poisoned him made my heart sink, and I clutched at Rachels' arm, pulling her closer to me as we slowly backed away.

It was no use. The bull came at us with a terrifying snort, scooping up the dirt with his wide horns, frothing at the mouth and bellowing with a thunderous roar. We dodged to one side as his hot breath scorched us, tried to run, and twisted away from the fearful prongs, but the bull caught Rachel with a ripping sound and, tearing her away from my side, tossed her into the air high above his head. She screamed piteously and flailed her arms, shouting for me, but I could do nothing and remained transfixed with horror as the mouth of the white bull opened wide, like an enormous trench, and swallowed my child, my baby Suckersie. She, who had grown up to be Rachel was suddenly gone, and the bull turned towards me, his glaring eyes red with rage.

How I escaped, I will never know. The bull might have been satisfied with his meal. In any case, I ran and the animal did not follow, but turned away into the gathering twilight and headed back to the east. The wind moaned and shrieked for me as I turned south towards the coast of the isle, traveling all night alone in despair and a deep feeling of guilt. There only remained one bull to find, and I expected that to be one of the clones, as I was convinced that the white bull was the one for whom we searched, the genuine Minotaur. Nevertheless, I must complete my search for the bull from the sea without my child. I reached the southern coast of the island after only a days' march, and lay down on the beach, where I cried myself to sleep.

I'm watching the tide come in, worried that it might overwhelm me while I sleep. I know I'm asleep and that I am dreaming. I understand that I can manipulate the dream I am having. I focus my gaze on the wavelets as they whisper into the sand at my feet, for I am standing up and looking out to sea. Shading my eyes from the noonday sun, I look out across the ocean stretching far into the horizon, and I see emerging from the waves the head of a great red bull, which swims towards me. There is a figure in white perched on his back. Who is it? This woman peeps from under a bridal veil of pure organdie, while her bright lace gown ends with a long, long train that floats like phosphorescence in the water behind her, and in that train vague forms appear. As she grows closer, and the bulls' shoulders breast the foam, I see within her train, as it undulates with each wave, the outlines of all kinds of sea denizens which materialize and dissipate without ceasing, ghostly wraiths of extinct ammonites, antiarchi and even tiktaalik, sharks and coelacanths, including modern fishes that are familiar to me.

The red bull plunges to the shore, water streaming from his flanks, and I look up into the face of the bride, and it is Rachel, and she is laughing. Now the bull stands on the shore and she slips from his back, touching the sands of the beach and leaving no footprints there. The bull snorts, lowers his head, and prepares to charge. I am transfixed – a jolt of terror hits me and......

.....I awoke with a violent jerk. The red bull stood on the beach a few yards from me. He was pawing the wet sand and spraying it in great chunks behind him, his little eyes showing evil intent. I remembered the bride in the dream, but she was not there any more. The bull was real and he spoke in a voice trembling with rage.

"I am the Fire Bull, and I live in the South. You have violated a sacred trust by killing the white bull. That was not in the contract. If you had waited and tracked him, he would have led you to his lair, where he keeps the real harp, the one for which you were searching. As his ally, I must take revenge on you for the harm you did him by your impatience. You will never reach the Isle of the White Pyramid, traitor!"

Backing away hastily, I spoke softly to the animal in an attempt to calm him, but in his rage he charged and pierced me in the groin with a razor thrust, tossing me aloft like a rag doll. I landed with a stunning thump on the sand, winded and halfway into the water. The universe whirled about me and I had no time to collect my thoughts before I saw the snorting animal above me, straddling my body, and then his sharp hooves thudded into me, again and again, as I twisted and turned, frantically trying to avoid them.

I felt no pain, only the bare attempt to survive, but my mind was blurring fast. With a last effort, I grabbed a rock from the beach beside me and smote the bull between the eyes as his head came down to finish me off. A white film came over his gaze as he fell to the ground near me, and his body was instantly consumed by flames and reduced to charcoal. I closed my eyes as weakness overwhelmed me. I quickly lost consciousness and remembered no more.

Ace of Pentacles – Rules
Six of Pentacles.

The soft swish of oars in the water came to me as I regained consciousness.
I tried to lift my head, but weakness overwhelmed me, and I dropped back
onto what felt like a narrow plank that rocked gently forward and back.
I could hear the clack of the sliding seat on the scull on my left side. This
did not make sense. Every bone and sinew in my body moaned in agony,
as I recalled the attack from the Bull from the South.

With an effort, I turned my head to the left and saw the familiar face
of the old man who was rowing the scull. It was my Guide! He smiled at
me and shook his head fondly as the boat grated on a cold, snowy shore.
Picking me up in his arms and shielding me from the freezing wind that
blew flurries of white crystals onto our skin, he carried me up the beach
towards a great white triangular shape looming above us. A buzz of activity
immediately surrounded us - many people talking; waving their arms;
glancing around and sniffing dried blossoms that they held in their hands.

My Guide lowered me onto a soft stretcher, which the crowd trampled through the snow to a door in the side of the white triangle, followed by the old fellow. Once inside, wafts of strange scents, musical trills and strange flashing colors assailed my nose, ears, and eyes as they laid me down in a comfortable bed in a corner.

"Where am I?" I croaked weakly. "I can smell, I can hear, I can see, so I know I am not dead."

My Guide leaned over me. "I have brought you to the Isle of the White Pyramid. I found you lying on the beach unconscious, after the Bull from the South attacked and trampled you. Of course, one can hardly blame it, these bulls are very loyal to each other. He has been consumed by fire now, for he was made of wood and was a carved clone. As for the white bull from the East, when you redrew the harp on his flank, he became the real Minotaur that Cosmo asked you to find."

"Cosmo told me that I should bring the real Minotaur and its harp back to him. I must return to find the white bull, and complete his test." I struggled to rise, but fell back as my bruised and battered body cried out. A belated thought struck me. "The Minotaur – that is half bull, half human. The white bull was a full sized animal!"

"Why do you think it swallowed Rachel? It needed to absorb a human to regain its psychic shape as a Minotaur. Your daughter is now half-bull, but don't worry, that will be resolved in due course." The old fraud went on. "Cosmo, the Guardian of the First Crossing, has come over here to the Temple of the North, and you will meet him soon. This side of the White Pyramid is dedicated to the element of Earth, and ruled by the archangel Auri-el. Sensawaria, the Ace of Pentacles, who is the Root of the Powers of Earth, is the manager here. That is why you are noticing so many sensual impressions around you, for this is how they live in the element of Earth. Rest now, and I will dispose of your scull and prepare the new sail boat for you, which will be moored at the Bar. When you are ready you will use this vessel on your journey into the Mystic SEA." He patted my shoulder. "Now, I will leave you for a while. Try not to get into any more trouble!" The old fellow chuckled as he waved goodbye.

The Earth people treated me kindly and tended my wounds carefully with their knowledge of healing herbs, and after a week or so, I was able to walk around inside the Temple of the North. I found that everyone in the temple was engaged in some sort of sensual activity. Some tended gardens of cypress and narcissus, thumbing the moist earth as it ran through their fingers; others were making musical instruments, testing their strings and playing sweet songs; a third group copied eye-catching patterns of color with paintbrush and spray can. There was no doubt of their technical abilities, but I did not see anywhere the inspiration that might create the perfumes or the designs that the artists were reproducing, nor the composers of their serenades.

I understood from those I met that the interior of the temple was disposed of a triangular base that rose to a peak far above, through which cold northern light filtered. The interior was divided into nine three-sided spaces in three sections, the first being the five outer rooms that I had entered, in which the activities I had noted were carried out, namely, the garden in the central space with music and cooking on the left and art and textiles on the right. Farther in were three more rooms, composed of a school for musical culinary work, a central stock room where the plants for perfume were dried, and a tapestry weaving section on the right. Beyond these three rooms was the ninth room, whose secret nobody would discuss. Yet I knew instinctively that Sensawaria resided behind its closed door.

Wandering in the garden, I saw many molehills and sometimes caught a glimpse of velvety whiskered faces pushing aside the earth as they worked. I wondered why the gardeners didn't place traps for the moles, as they were undermining the flower beds, but evidently the moles had some sort of divine presence here, for I saw the gardeners bowing to the animals when they appeared and feeding them with earthworms. The feeling of the place, in spite of continuous noise from the murmur of many voices, the strumming of instruments, and the clang of cooking kettles, was static rather than dynamic, as the people moved slowly about their tasks, seemingly indifferent to their surroundings and lacking motivation.

A small dwarflike figure detached itself from a group of gardeners and came towards me. "We were just talking about you. Can't resist a bit of gossip! I hear that Cosmo is closeted with Sensawaria in the ninth room, and they are discussing the Art of Generation. I suspect this may be your subject in the Temple of the North."

I gazed closely into his eyes, brown as clay, and he gave a distinctive wink. "So I am here to learn something! I have already discovered many things on my journey, and I am ready for whatever the White Pyramid asks of me."

"Then, follow me." He announced as he moved through the garden and into the drying room where the scent of mixed blooms lingered, and struck once on the gremlin knocker on the great door of the ninth room. Shuffling came from inside, and lowered voices, and then the door swung open on to a space I could never have imagined. Dozens of round pentacles hung on the walls, with the design of the pentagram upon them. A clay throne, set on a dais at the apex of the room, was backed by a large woven tapestry on which the form of the angel Auri-el emerged from a large transparent oval. There sat the Guardian of the First Crossing, Cosmo, clad in robes of deep brown decorated with white snowflake patterns, on his head a crown shaped like the dome of a cathedral, with long icicles falling below his ears. He greeted me, and I genuflected. Beside him stood a short female dressed entirely in white skintight clothing, her generous, powerful figure covered with white gold and diamonds in strange patterns, and wearing a gold belt across her breast. This was Sensawaria, evidently, and she stepped forward and addressed me smartly.

"Welcome to the Temple of the North. We are glad to hear of your recovery from the trampling of the Bull from the South. Your courageous actions purged the Land of the Bull-king from the three cloned bulls, and the white aurochs, who is the Minotaur as you suspected, found his way back to Cosmo alone. Then the priest knew that you had achieved your final task at the Castle of Fire and we arranged for your Guide to rescue you and bring you here balanced on a board athwart your scull."

The stocky Ace paused. "I represent the Root of the Powers of Earth, being the apex of the suit of Pentacles, and a mundane representative of our Lord Kether, in Whom be Glory. Here you will learn of the different potentials of Generation, essential to the earth functions. To begin at the beginning, you must become a mole, for only then can you fully appreciate the value of earth. Watch out for the owls, though!"

She raised her hand, and, picking a pentacle off the wall behind her, threw it towards me. Instinctively I reached out to catch it, but as I touched it, I sank to the floor and found that I was virtually blind, although a thin membrane protected my eyes from dirt. My arms and legs shriveled into short stumps, my two forepaws armed with powerful digging claws. My cone-shaped nose elongated into a sensitive pink snout that probed the earth in front of me, as I found myself in a flower bed in the garden.

This was a great shock, and I was glad that I was allowed to retain the brain of a person, for I knew that the owls would make a meal of me if they could find me. I found I was possessed of a sensation, which received impulses from the earth around me as I slowly nosed my way forward. I was able to interpret vibrations without their cause being visible to me. There, a quick scurrying meant a black beetle; here, a curling sensation told me of a group of nematodes; and there, yes, there, a heaving and pushing in the dirt nearby was a gopher! I nosed my way steadily in the opposite direction, munching on small beetles that I found. I was aware that the soil surrounding me consisted of hundreds of different elements that made up a vital and interesting whole. I thought to myself – this is what it's all about – nothing can exist without this rich nourishment on which everything depends for life.

Inching my way along and downward, I dug skillfully through the earth, which slid aside from my long claws, as my probing nose wriggled its way through the darkness. After a while I felt the earth growing thin underneath me, and, before I could save myself, the last clod gave way and I felt myself falling, hot air rushing past me, at which I curled into a ball to save myself. I landed with a pile of loam above me, on the top of a burning hot metal surface that shook and wobbled in time with a regular clanking. I managed to twist and turn my body to one side, falling still further, but away from that terrible heat, and found myself on top of a slippery rounded surface that smelt of shoe polish.

Since I could see very little, although I was aware of bright lights around me, I relied on my sense of vibration to ease my body so that I slid off this unstable platform and rolled under something dark and moist. It felt safer under there, away from the owls. My sensitive nose picked up the smell of earthworms, and my stomach gurgled at the thought of a delicious meal. A voracious appetite assailed me as I thought of the worm softly sliding down my throat.

I found that, although I could not see clearly, I could hear the voices of two people talking above me.

"How many pyramid tops do we have now?" A snarling voice asked. "Is it time to organize another shipment to Fakoor?"

"I have counted them, and we have six hundred and sixty six. We need one hundred and eleven more before we need to ship them." The voice had a crackling sound, as of machine gun fire. "Those Bullet Casings aren't putting out their full capacity. They are too excited about the new Casings that are arriving with news from America. Many people are being shot there, which is good, for we need more workers here."

"What about the Bomb Shards from the suicide bombers?" The deep voice continued, sounding like a cannons' boom. "Have they been put to work yet?"

"We have them in training over by the boxes of rendered gold. Our overseer, the Atomic Fallout, is whipping them into shape, for they are convinced that there are 72 virgins waiting for them somewhere here, and they won't accept the reality of their situation." The rattling voice continued. "I don't know why their leaders feed them that false information, but it certainly benefits us down here."

"May they long continue to destroy each other." Said the dull, thudding voice. "Our industries down here need the extra Shells, in whatever form they come down to us. Let us hope for a major war, which would fill our coffers to the brim, for the fools up there will have to manufacture more weapons to replace those that they used in the fight against their "enemies." I, personally, am glad I don't live up there. Humans are crazy. Give me the peaceful unrest of the Qliphoth any day, its quieter down here." Here a mirthless laugh walloped across the room and disturbed me as I lay quietly in my damp spot.

Their conversation sickened me, and I thought of my beloved Earth, and how it was being slowly torn apart by the greed and ignorance of humans. I was deeply ashamed of my human brain, and resolved to change things when I emerged from mole form. I wriggled cautiously out of my hiding place and, avoiding the vibration of trampling feet near me, managed to reach an earthen wall, into which I burrowed hastily. I worked my way upwards and soon broke through the dirt into the garden at the Temple of the North again.

I felt myself picked up by two hot hands, and heard an incantation over me. I sat up, and looked down at my bent legs and my hands, covered with earth, in my lap. I had returned from my passage through Earth, and was again in my own body. Something was different, though. Disturbing thoughts pervaded my mind after the conversation I had overheard underground. I knew I had been down in the realm of the Qliphoth, and, dismayed by their heedless attitude, I felt the urge to do something to help the environment before it was too late. No sooner had I firmly reached this conclusion, than I found myself back in front of the clay throne on which Cosmo sat, laughing.

"So, you avoided the owls! It's not so difficult, after all."

He went on, without observing how deeply perturbed I was by my encounter with the Qliphoth. "Now, there are different forms of Generation. The most obvious for you humans is that of reproduction of your kind. Naturally, everything reproduces, but there comes a time when, for one reason or another, they fail to reproduce, and become extinct. However, the spirit that animated them cannot die and assumes another form, thus passing through a succession of generated manifestations. There are also other forms of Generation, such as producing electricity, a useful tool; or inventing a product, which is a birth of sorts; or initiating a significant move forward. Now, I would like you to perform three tasks connected to Generation - a Production, an Invention, and an Initiation of some kind.

You may summon help if you need it. Your body will remain in this room while the three tasks are completed, and you may travel astrally if you desire."

Sitting down, I thought for some minutes. A Production. That might mean a play, for example. When the theater came to mind, my creative entity, Fontanova, was soon sitting beside me, nudging my elbow.

"A play. What a good idea! I know exactly what we can put on. We will need some actors, of course, and I have a couple with me here. May I introduce Ailis and Quigley, from the Six of Pentacles?"

Two handsome people clad in deep yellow and green colors, adorned with gold and topaz jewelry and holding stalks of wheat in their hands, stepped forward. I recognized them from my adventures on the river, and greeted them warmly.

"The play we produce will be reality based, for Ailis is now near term to deliver a child, which will change the balance between them that they have been trying to achieve." Fontanova pointed out. "Since this is all about a new Generation, it will be singularly appropriate. I have engaged a camera man so that we can video their lives as a reality show for the next few weeks. This is Worley."

Here she looked down and, following her gaze, I saw a large mole with a video camera strapped to his shoulder. He was having difficulty with the controls, for the length of his digging claws impeded his movements. A mole photographer? Impossible! But, here Worley was, nevertheless.

We arranged to use the cooking room as our scene, because Ailis would now have to become more domestic, and Worley set up the video. We did not have long to wait, for she went into labor the very next day, and things immediately started to go awry. Suffering with labor pains, Ailis became irritable and impatient, begging for the birth to be over, and I could see that Quigley was utterly confused. Worley followed their arguments diligently, although they cursed the media for filming them. Evidently they had not planned or practiced for the birth, and had not thought about Quigleys' role as coach, because they had been so busy focusing on their relationship as a twosome. Now, as I had warned them before, a third was to be born, and that would radically change their equilibrium.

As Ailis whimpered and moaned, writhing on a cushioned couch that we had set up, she called out, saying that she had changed her mind, and did not want the baby after all. Meanwhile the whirring of the video camera operated by the mole distracted Quigley from his vital task as coach and he tried to kick Worley out from under his feet.

I stepped forward and whispered in his ear, calming him, and he gently held Ailis from behind, his hands under her arms, and synchronized his breathing with hers, which helped her to relax a little. Fontanova directed the scene from behind Worleys' camera. It was not long before the baby's head crowned and Fontanova stepped forward to act as midwife, catching the tiny boy as he emerged and cutting the cord.

A loud and magnificent wail from the babe split the air as Ailis fell back onto her cushions. Quigley looked bemused.

"What do I do now?" He asked.

"Well, for heavens sake…here - hold the baby! Wrap him in this cloth." Fontanova was bustling about, organizing everything, while Worley steadfastly recorded the scene.

"What will you call him? You must have chosen a name already." Quigley looked blank, but held out his arms stiffly as she placed the baby in them. Obviously, he had never held a child before. He was afraid of dropping him, so he hastily placed him by his mother on the couch.

Ailis did not respond to her new son, but lay back, moaning and complaining of pains in her abdomen as the afterbirth was delivered. She ignored the little boy.

"We have made a terrible mistake." She groaned. "This is a bad idea. Quigley - it's all your fault. You forced yourself upon me even after I had told you the time was inappropriate. Now, look at the result. What are we going to do?"

Quigley, who was at the end of his tether, became angry and, shaking with rage, confronted her. "No, it's not my fault! You are always so seductive, running after me and acting provocatively. I couldn't restrain myself. I never wanted a child. Our relationship was perfect the way it was – just the two of us. Now we will have to make some hard decisions. Maybe it's best for the child to have him adopted right away."

Profoundly shocked by this interchange, I had always known them as two very spiritual people who were striving to achieve a perfect relationship. Suddenly I saw that it was a complete sham. Adding one further element to their uncertain balance had finally upset the apple cart. I could not allow the Production to continue, so Fontanova stepped forward and called out "Cut!" and the mole shut down the video.

We were deeply ashamed. The video was a complete failure, and had not turned out the way I had anticipated, with the perfect couple happily welcoming their firstborn into the world. Alas! The video was all I had to show Sensawaria as my first test. We could not remake it. In the meantime, I asked Fontanova to arrange for Ailis and Quigley to take parenting classes, and to support them until they got used to the new triangular situation with their child..

My next task was to invent something, and it was not long, as I searched for ideas, that the strange, bent figure of my intellectual entity Einerline was by my side, an absent-minded expression on his grimy face as he muttered to himself in a dry, rustling voice. The whirring cogs and wheels of his transparent brain created visible flashes as the activities of neurons lit up his skull. His eyes were surprisingly liquid and had a softness that was hard to describe.

"Ah! Yes. An Invention, let me see. Well, how about this?" Einerline gave a crooked smile. "Since the mole, denizen of earth, is sacred to the Temple of the North, why don't we create a robot mole that will help them with their gardening? I noticed that they are using some very antiquated tools. The robot mole would be a great gift and amuse them as well. Shall we try it?"

"What a good idea!" I responded, relieved that he had come up with something exceptional, as usual. "I will look for the parts that we need."

"You won't find them around here. Remember, these people are Pentacles – back in the stone age. They haven't developed emotionally or intellectually yet and they aren't capable of Invention. That is why they call in advocates such as yourself." Einerline scratched his chin thoughtfully. "I will have to manufacture the parts for the robot myself. Let me see, it won't need eyes, for they are blind, but claws, ears, nose and mouth – for eating earthworms." Here he gave a wry grin. "Leave me alone for a while and I will work on it."

Going over to one of the points of the triangular room, I sat down, keeping my mind on intellectual matters. I couldn't resist a sly glance over in his direction, and I saw that Einerlines' thin mouth was hanging open and, emerging with a clatter onto the floor beneath, were various small objects – a set of claws, a pointed metal nose, coiled springs for the ears, small back feet and a velvety body made of some sort of polyester. He looked up.

"You can come over now. We'll put the robot together and see if it works." He blinked softly. "I haven't used clockwork, but a system of laser beams that can be controlled optically, when a person moves their eyes. They can sit and direct the mole to mow, plough, and harrow their garden without doing a thing. Here, take this piece and screw it to this section."

We had the robot mole built in less than an hour and placed it on the floor. Einerline moved his eyes, and the robot responded, moving slowly and precisely up to his foot, where it turned around, as if in a swimming pool, and came over to me. I bent down and picked it up, stroking its' soft fur. It looked very realistic and it could easily have been mistaken for a real mole. I was pleased. Sensawaria would like this invention, for sure. I put the mole in my pocket and bade goodbye to Einerline, who returned happily to his research in the library.

The third task that lay before me was to Initiate somebody through an evocation. A simple ceremony could take place in the tapestry room, I felt, so I walked over there. Now, who should I choose to initiate? It must be someone who wasn't too important, in case the ceremony went wrong and the aspirant was swallowed by the ether. I considered some of my entities. Pompeybou, my boating companion, simply would not do. He was too mundane to follow the procedure. Besides, I would need his skills when we took ship at the Bar – if I ever got there. Bazoom – no, he might get angry and wreck the ritual. I finally settled on Bardogian, my poetic self, who already had spiritual leanings, so I composed a quick poem.

'Now you have mastered skills which are profound. Cast wide the disk toward the way you choose, and if it falls upon some fertile ground, intelligence will be the plant that grows.'

Bardogian immediately walked towards me and offered me a joint. I took a small toke as I explained what I wanted him to do. He stood in the middle of a circle that I made on the floor and we went through the Pentagram Ritual in order to banish any evil spirits and clear the air. I then went into an ancient Chaldean initiation ceremony during which I chanted the various evocations, closing my eyes in ecstatic dreams and visions.

I saw myself witnessing a chariot race outside a great city wall, between Bardogian in a white chariot and an unrecognizable figure in a dark cloak that came from behind and whipped up its horses in an attempt to overtake him. They were pounding the hard earth at full gallop, as the dark figure edged its black chariot closer and closer to Bardogian, who struck at it with his whip to keep it at bay. The two chariots were within feet of each other, at high speed, when I noticed the whirling scythe blades on the wheels of the black chariot. Before I could stop them and return to the circle of protection, the blades cut into Bardogians chariot and sliced through its wheels, and the vehicle crashed to the ground, pulling the two horses down with it, where they rolled about convulsively.

A choking scream rudely interrupted my mood and I quickly opened my eyes to see Bardogian sliding slowly out of the sacred circle, pulled by a leathery claw that clasped his ankle tightly. I had to think fast. My shadow self, the Hoodwinker, had evidently been hiding in one of the tapestries that covered the walls of the room – a reproduction of a Bosch painting – and had grabbed him while I had let down my guard! I leapt forward and grabbed Bardogian by his arms, and pulled back fiercely. To my horror, his body began to split apart before my eyes, and he dissolved into a thin mist, which rose into the air and dissipated into the three corners of the room with a faint howl.

The Hoodwinker gave a snarling laugh as she crept up to me. "At last! Those chariots are useful weapons. I've rid myself of one of your entities. You constantly surround yourself with them and they are nothing but trouble. They prevent you from becoming aware of me in my totality. Now one is gone for good. Ha! Ha! HA!"

With that she swept from the room, leaving me alone and terribly afraid that I had lost my sense of poetry and my favorite hippie, Bardogian. The Initiation ceremony had been a failure. With the Production also in jeopardy, it only remained to hope that my Invention, the robot mole, would save me from utter disaster at the Temple of the North.

Having completed my obligations as best I could, I approached the door of the ninth room cautiously, the robot mole heavy in my pocket, and raised the gremlin knocker. A curious sigh came from inside the room, as of many peoples' disappointment. This sound was not encouraging. The door peeked open and an eye appeared.

"What do you want?" It asked.

"I have completed the three tasks that were set. I would like permission to move on to the Temple of the East. I have an Invention to show you." I added brightly, hoping that they would not ask about the other tasks.

"Under the circumstances, we already know about the other two tasks. You must be aware that you have failed dismally. However, we agree to look at your Invention and determine whether the possible success of this may redeem you. Please enter."

I walked slowly up to the throne apex and genuflected, bringing the robot mole out of my pocket and addressing Sensawaria carefully. "Your honor, this Invention will speed up your gardening and make it much easier and faster to prepare the earth for planting. Would you care to come out to the garden, where I may activate it?"

They agreed and we all trooped out to the garden room, where I placed the robot on the ground and, flashing my eyes before receiving their answer, in order to forestall a denial, set it in motion. The little mole ran up to their feet, turned, and went around the garden beds, plowing neat rows in preparation for planting. I was pleased with the effect and did not notice the deep frowns of disapproval that crossed their faces.

"How do you like it?" I looked up at them and the smile vanished from my face. I saw that Cosmo and Sensawaria were evidently furious. The latter stepped forward and fixed me with a withering glare.

"Blasphemy! Denigration of our sacred god, the mole! You have made an idol of his image, and set it to work like an ordinary manual laborer. That is sacrilege. The mole as god must only turn the earth from below. Your..." here she paused for effect... "devilish object is turning the upper earth, that which our dedicated laborers are trained to do. You have made a joke out of our most devout beliefs!" She turned, and with one blow, kicked the little robot out of the ground, where it fell some feet away.

However, to the surprise of everyone, the robot did not break apart. Instead, it sat up on its rump and bravely addressed the assembled group.

"You call me evil, a blasphemy. You are fools! I am useful. I am not a replica for idolatrous worship, but made in the image of your god for practical purposes. I am angry that you do not understand my true calling, which is to help you. Now, I curse you, for you have insulted me, and never more shall you have the opportunity of Invention. I wish you goodbye, for I am leaving to find those who can appreciate my talents." With that, the robot mole stormed out of the garden and disappeared.

The people in the group gave a stunned gasp. After a few minutes silence, Sensawaria stepped forward. "I am sorry. Maybe we were wrong. In view of this fact, we are allowing you the equivalent of passing the other two tests, since it was not your fault that Ailis and Quigley received their child with indifference, nor are you to blame for not seeing the Hoodwinker hiding in the tapestry, for she made herself flat with stitching, and matched the background very skillfully. Please accept our apologies with this gift of the Pentacle, your first Magical Weapon."

She handed me the magnificent silver platter decorated with moonstones, which my Guide had removed from my collection before I began the tests that the Court Cards set me. "You may pass on to the Temple of the East with out blessings." She sheepishly backed away, and I saluted, then turned and left the building, making my way out into a fierce blizzard that blew from the north.

<u>Ace of Swords - Rules</u>
<u>Six of Swords.</u>

I fought my way through the blizzard outside the Temple of the North, the snowflakes biting at my cheeks and eyelids as I turned to the right at the corner of the White Pyramid. Immediately snow stopped falling, although the wind continued to blow with vigor. I must be on the East side now, I thought, and looked for an entrance to the Temple of the East. This face of the pyramid, scored by wind action over many aeons, looked barren and the door was only accessible through a windproof barrier, as the air was constantly in motion. Having recovered from the injuries caused by the bull, I was able to walk into the Temple with its nine rooms on my own feet, carrying the moonstone platter safely wrapped in my cloak.

A tall, thin figure approached me, the air-conditioning inside ruffling his fading locks.

"Can I help you?" He asked with stiff politeness. "This is the domain of the Ace of Swords, Root of the Powers of Air, and his name is Braimind."

He took a closer look at me, peering into my face as if to distinguish some recognizable feature. "You must be the person we are expecting, for our astrologer Aurelio arrived from the great city of knowledge not long hence, and he informed us that he was waiting for a pupil to join him."

My heart gave a leap of joy. Aurelio, the Six of Swords, was exceptionally intelligent and had remained in the city of learning to study after we parted. I was pleased to note that he had picked astrology as his passion.

"I believe I am that pupil. I have recently come from the Temple of the North, where I performed three tasks for them. I have been rewarded with a beautiful platter for my pains." I didn't mention how miserably I had failed in two of the tasks, for although I had been forgiven, I still felt guilty.

"Come this way, please. I will show you through the eight rooms on our way to the ninth, where we will meet Braimind and Aurelio." We stopped in an exceptionally well-stocked library as the thin man indicated two rooms to the right. "In this room here we have the printing presses for journalism and literature, and beyond that, the grammar and logic rooms. On the left, you see the photography studio and a sound proof room for composers of both music and lyrics."

We moved further into the pyramid, and I saw a room on the left where people were busy creating collages from photographs. To the right, figures were bending over a long table, drawing up blueprints.

The thin man explained. "My name is Stamper. I review all the blueprints and then stamp them with my approval." He sighed. "Some of them are very difficult to deal with, and cause me much grief."

"Why would a blueprint affect you emotionally?" I was puzzled.

"They aren't the usual blueprints. These are patterns created by careful consultation amongst the Enochian Anchorites and their applicants. They are the blueprints made up before birth, which foreordain the clients' future life on earth. We have to draw up some of them with significant difficulties to overcome, due to bad karma. When I see what some people will have to go through, I am filled with sorrow. But there is nothing I can do to help them."

"How curious! I do believe in Destiny, but I had no idea that it would be carefully arranged before one was born. Now, what are these people doing over here?" I turned towards the collage room.

"These collages are made up of photographs that the applicants have taken during their current lifetime. Each person must work in this room to make the most of their memories in this way before they die, and try to produce a beautiful design. If they fail, that increases the bad karma, which will influence their blueprint for the next life."

"I understand that the Temple of the East is a step further forward in thought than the Northern people. Does that mean the flowering of intellect in humankind?"

"Yes. We are Air people, under the influence of the sphere of Hod, and those of the Earth are living in the sphere of Malkuth." Stamper explained. "The Malkuthians don't use their rational powers very often, as they take things as they come and tend to remain in a rut. Of course, we are not yet exactly in either of these immense spheres, which are vastly more complex than our basic systems here, but you see the idea. Now, problems do arise when we consider the Temple of the West, ruled by the Water sphere Netzach. They are very emotional and uncontrolled. We are probably too tightly reined in. It is only in the dream world of Yesod that our two opposing spheres, Hod and Netzach, can reach equilibrium."

"Are you saying that only in dreams do we know the real truth about the connection between our rational world and our emotional state? No wonder dreams are so important. Where do we learn about them?" I remembered my encounter in the vault with the sleeper Qamra and her dream soul mate, and our test of the red monkeys' dreams.

"That will be in the Temple of the South, where intuition rules. They deal with the dream world and the Fires of inspiration. Now, I will introduce you to Braimind, and he will arrange a shape-shifting for you before Aurelio will consort with you for your next three tasks."

He knocked on the great door of the ninth room with a knocker in the shape of a hawk's head. I heard a cough from within and then the door opened and across the floor came a tall man dressed in a white robe, who saluted me in a friendly fashion. I recognized Aurelio, and recalled how we had read the hieroglyphs on the pillar together that had given him the clue to his Destiny. He shook my hand warmly, drawing me towards Braimind, who sat a little behind him on a throne, which swung to-and-fro on an airborne carpet. Above them hung a large computer printout of the archangel Gabri-el, blowing a trumpet. The Ace of Swords, a serious and dedicated man, stepped down from his throne. He was dressed in a skintight white suit with a peaked helmet and a long, narrow necklace, and held a bare sword in his right hand, pointing downwards.

A large hawk perched on his left shoulder. The bird looked at me with recognition in its brilliant yellow eye, cocking its head to one side and giving a small, shrill cry. Then I recalled Suroh, my avian advisor during the grave situation between Yevgeny and Yaroslav, the swordsmiths.

"Bring me my jesses and embroidered hood." Ordered Suroh, with authority. "We have a mission. In fact, we have three missions connected with rational thought. The first is to train a spy to Infiltrate the deadly group of the Seven Shades, to bring them down and destroy their training ground. The second is to Aspire to become familiar with the art of astrology," ….here Aurelio bowed in mock solemnity…. "and the third to clear ancient and worthless thoughts by the method of Respiration, taught by our friend Braimind here with the help of your inner child, Suckersie."

A pang shook me. I remembered that the white bull had swallowed my child and become once again the Minotaur at the center of the labyrinthine complex.

"Suckersie is gone." I faltered. "She has been immolated. I fear she will not be able to help us."

"We know about that unfortunate occurrence. Try not to grieve. It is hard to destroy ones inner child – they have a tendency to return. Let us proceed rationally and see what happens." Suroh became silent.

Braimind stepped forward and took up the instructions.

"Before you leave to perform your tasks, I would like you to get a first hand experience of the element of air. Therefore, you must become a bird. You may choose any bird, so give it some thought. Let me know in the morning and we will activate you in your air element."

The following morning I went to Braimind and told him that I would like to be a dove. He took down a short sword from the wall collection and touched me on the shoulder. I flapped my arms and found myself rising easily into the air, where I hung fluttering for a moment over his head. He looked up at me and nodded approval. "You look good in those white feathers. Now go and explore."

Flying low towards the door, I managed to negotiate the opening by banking a little to one side, then swooped through the rooms out into the wind on the East side of the Pyramid. Strong gusts of air caught me and nearly flung me against the sloping sides of the structure, but I managed to swing myself around the corner, where I found an eddy that allowed me to pick up speed into the wind and move away from the pyramid. It was hard work, flying against the wind, but I never thought of turning and leaving the wind at my back, for then I might not be able to return to the Temple of the East.

As I fluttered across the Lagoon, the wind eased, and I began to enjoy my new shape. I had always wanted to fly, and here I was, lighter than air, soaring up with the gusts and gliding down in a well-executed sweep that made me feel good. I spent a few hours flapping my wings, which felt strangely light, and practicing turns and banks. During this time, I moved farther southeast, and a strange land beyond the four Castles lay below me where two armies were drawn up, facing each other and ready for battle. Heralds were galloping back and forth between the tents of the combatants, carrying messages. I drifted down towards a beautifully embroidered tent, where several officials stood outside, discussing the latest information. They were so busy they failed to notice me as I folded my wings and perched on the back of a chair next to the doorway of the tent, then hopped lightly to the ground and slipped inside.

"I personally can't understand why we are fighting this war." Said a man decorated with the stars of a colonel on his shoulder. "The King has already lost his previous battle with the Viceroy of Muckabad. He is just hurling himself against an implacable enemy, and bankrupting the Court once more, with his demands for more and more armaments."

"He doesn't have enough to do." The speaker lowered his voice and glanced towards the doorway, where I perched inside next to the sleeping King. "He's too stupid to have any intellectual pursuits, and he isn't interested in creative projects, like cathedral building. Fighting passes the time for him."

"Well, I have information that the Viceroy is bringing up a new weapon, an eagle that he has been training to peck out the eyes of the King, and although I warned him yesterday, I would be glad to see it happen, personally. The King has heard of the danger but he will have none of it, and refuses to wear his visor. Hark, he is waking."

The official stepped towards the tent doorway. "Good morning, Your Highness. How are you today? Ready for the battle?"

King Compos growled a little, then rose from his bed and called for his armorer. While he was getting dressed, I crept under the side of the tent and flew over the battlefield towards the Viceroys' multi-colored marquee, where I saw a large eagle sitting chained to a perch outside. I narrowed my wingspan and landed on a tree branch a few feet away, not wanting the huge bird to attack me, for I would make him a tasty meal.

"Good morning, your Eminence," The words slipped easily off my pointed tongue. "I hear there will be a battle today." I cocked my head on one side, scratched behind my hidden ear with one claw, and edged closer.

"Yes, it really is a drag. I'm so tired of pecking out eyes I don't think I could face another pair, even if it is the King of Pentacles. The Viceroy doesn't want to fight. Although he won last time they went to battle, he feels this will be a hollow victory for him, as the King is badly under manned, and he has run out of Knights. Many of his followers have quit and are living in the forests around here, eating boar meat and relaxing in their hammocks." The eagle shifted a little on his perch and carefully aimed a squirt of shit at a foraging lizard. "Personally, I am hoping they call it off."

"What if the Viceroy refused to fight and retired from the field?" I asked chirpily, chipping at an ant on the branch with my beak. "Would he lose face? I understand that his officers don't want to join battle either."

"H'm, that's interesting. I didn't know that." The eagle thoughtfully shredded the corpse of a mouse that he held in one claw. "Yes, I'm afraid the Viceroy could not lose face. That's the problem."

"I'm supposed to be a peaceable sort of bird. Do you think I might be able to persuade the King to cancel the battle appointment, or maybe divert his attention?"

"I would say, if you can divert him, that might work. I wish you luck." The eagle blinked solemnly as I took off and flew back to the Kings' army. I had an idea.

I flew straight into the nearest forest, following its winding paths until I came upon a herd of wild boar feasting on some corn that someone had spilt on the ground. I landed on the hairy back of the largest animal, and several of them looked up, wiggling their dirty snouts at me. Since I was now communicating with an animal, there was no need for words, and I was able to send a message to the boars by telepathy, telling them that the King longed to see them and that he was waiting impatiently in his tent for them to arrive.

They grunted approvingly, and without more ado, the whole group set off towards the position of the Kings' army. I flew ahead of them, and reached the Kings' tent just as he was mounting his charger and gathering his forces. To slow him down, for the boars sometimes got sidetracked by the smell of truffles, I perched between his horses ears and gazed at him with my limpid eye.

"What a beautiful bird!" Cried the King, leaning forward and trying to catch me in a gloved hand. I fluttered a little out of reach, perching on a nearby twig. The King dismounted and walked towards me, but I slipped away from him again, leading him towards the forest. This went on for some time, as I kept ahead of him, always leading him towards the herd of boars. After a while he started to get angry, and slung his bow from his shoulder, reaching for an arrow. This was not good! I hoped the boars would soon arrive.

"If I can't have you, my dove, nobody will." The King shouted in a rage.

He raised his bow, drew back the arrow, and let it fly. As I jumped off the branch, deflecting the arrow downwards with one foot, a loud shriek below me announced that the arrow had found its mark, and a large boar fell to the ground in its death throes.

The King was absolutely delighted and called off the battle, sending a messenger to invite the Viceroy to a grand feast, and so, as I flew back to the White Pyramid, I knew that I had saved the day.

"Do you have an entity that you would like to train as a spy?" Asked Braimind, when I had resumed my human shape. "It must be someone who is very level-headed and practical, and capable of smooth organization."

I thought for a moment. "Yes, I do have that part of myself. His name is Endevvy – for endeavor, you know. He is idle at the moment, because he mistakenly cut off the right arm of his manual laborer, Little Laboria, and she has retired, unable to work any more. Endevvy would welcome something to occupy his mind. Shall I summon him?"

"He sounds very suitable. Let's see him." Braimind responded.

Turning my mind to visualize a teeming spy organization, I imagined telephones ringing, computers whirring, and reports coming in from all corners of the world. Endevvy then stood before us, a gleam in his eye.

"We have a very challenging task for you, Endevvy. You will help us to defeat the Seven Shades, for they are constantly in pursuit of me, attempting to capture me and tear down my defenses. Will you join us and form a spy organization to infiltrate their ranks?" I requested.

"By all means. When do we start?" Endevvy braced himself, shaking his head with its selected tools. "Where can we work?"

"I suggest that we take over the photography studio, since we will be using overhead photos to track them down. Since we have not yet invented the airplane or the unmanned drone, I think that Suroh would be happy to undertake that task."

The hawk nodded as we assembled in the photography studio. It took several days to work out a plan to undermine the Shades, and when we were ready, I set out with Endevvy and Suroh, perched with a small fisheye camera on my left shoulder, to a prearranged location.

Above us, squat, whitewashed houses rose from cobbled streets that twined their way upwards to a building with a round dome at the top of the hill. After several minutes upward climb, we came to a battered green door with a grille across the front. I hid in a narrow alley across the street with Suroh and bade Endevvy knock seven times on the door. Two suspicious, bleary eyes were soon visible through the lattice and a guttural voice spoke.

"Are you friend or foe? Speak your mission." This remark was followed by a fierce bout of coughing and hawking, as phlegm was cleared.

"This is friend. I bring news of the missing sword with the emerald. Let me in." The door opened narrowly and Endevvy squeezed through the opening. I crossed my fingers in silent prayer and waited.

Half an hour passed before the door reopened and Endevvy came out. I studied his face hopefully, but it appeared from his expression that he had failed to infiltrate their defenses and it was likely that our ruse had not worked. It was a wonder that the Shades had let him go, but his innocuous demeanor may have quieted their suspicions. I asked him what had occurred. He explained that he had told them the sword they were searching for lay hidden in the center of a stone maze, guarded by a crazy man wearing a mask made up of two finely crafted obsidian eyes, a nose of pure quicksilver and an iron mouth full of tiny jagged bloodstone teeth, somewhat like a coarse saw blade. I knew then that Mablevi, the sneaky camel driver to whom I had bartered the eyes and nose in exchange for my camel Lemig, must have obtained the remaining part of the mask – the mouth – from an unknown source. Now that the mask was complete, Mablevi was capable of great power, as long as he wore it. But - where did Endevvy get that story?

"How do you know about the eyes, and the nose and mouth? You weren't with me when I obtained them. What is going on?" I was a little miffed.

Endevvy looked offended. "I am a part of you, remember. Of course, I would know about them. The story is true, for I have been infiltrating the activities of Mablevi for some time, knowing that he cheated you and sold you the camel Lemig twice. I am supposed to look out for your mundane problems, you know."

"So you are. Now Mablevi has also stolen the jewel-encrusted sword from the armory at the Castle of Air, is that it? I left it with Typhona, the Knight of Swords, whom I trusted. Now she has betrayed me again! Well, we don't know yet how Mablevi obtained the sword and there is no use wondering. Now it's time to move to the next phase of our plan."

I knew of a desert hideout where the Shades regularly practiced their subversive military attacks. Once every seven days they progressed, in giant leaps, from the small fishing village where they lived to this spot, near the stone maze in the land of the Castle of Fire. I remembered what the Knight of Wands, Ignitia, had told me. She insisted that I could only destroy the

Shades one by one, never while they were in a group, and that I would have to face each one when I reached the Islands of the Mystic SEA. I swept this thought aside. Surely, a simple bomb would settle the matter? We could drop something on them at the very moment they were in consultation, for they would huddle close at such times.

We traveled at high speed from the village to the desert, where Endevvy suggested that he manufacture a killing device from the available resources. I had my doubts, as there wasn't much bomb making material to be had, but he went off and was soon collecting dung balls that had been made by the numerous scarab beetles that scuttled around us. He manufactured one enormous dung ball out of them all and bored a small hole into it, where he gingerly placed seven asps that he had found under the rocks, sealing them in and leaving a tiny breathing hole.

"There is one asp for each of them!" He laughed. Then he became serious. "H'm, I only noticed six Shades when I was in their house. I wonder where the seventh Shade is?"

"You should know, since you are a part of me," I teased. "It is still in the dungeon of the monastery where we left it, of course. Unless Damalis has screwed up again, and let it out."

We made camp, hidden behind the stone wall of the maze and waited for the day that the Shades would arrive. They came in due course – six of them – and gathered about the arched gateway where the wrought golden gate barred entrance to the maze, but they could not open the gate - however much they rattled and swore. I had the Janus key in my pouch, and that was the only key. Finally they backed off, took a run at the gate and attempted to leap over it, but smashed against some invisible obstacle and fell like stones to the ground, as if a secret barrier existed over the walls of the maze. They were temporarily bruised and defeated. But then, how had Mablevi gained entrance without the key? Another enigma to solve, I thought.

The six Shades, grumbling amongst themselves and scratching under their filthy robes, which were swarming with fleas, made their way to their military camp, and set about training. They somersaulted, leapt in the air, drilled with lances, practiced with pecking birds and renewed their technique for running takeoffs over the desert, although suffering from the bruises they had received. We hid behind a large boulder with the giant dung ball and waited for them to finish and get together for their consultation.

At last they gathered in a group and began their discussion. It was about springing the seventh Shade from the monastery dungeon. They discussed several approaches, which were extremely useful for us to hear, and when they were almost done, I gave Endevvy the signal to roll out the ball, which was fast drying out and threatening to collapse. The giant ball bounded towards them, towering over them and, although they tried to avoid it, the ball fell apart right in the middle of the group. The seven asps slithered out, and each made for one of the Shades.

The last asp hesitated.

"I have no Shade to bite!" It complained in a singsong voice. "There has been a mistake. Wait a minute. Come back here. We must review the situation, for there has been a slip-up. Where is my Shade?"

The six asps stopped in their tracks, turned, and gathered around the seventh. Unfortunately, this allowed the six Shades to take off at a run, and they were soon disappearing over the horizon with cackles of laughter. Our plan had failed!

Endevvy and I returned to the Temple of the East feeling mortified. We gave a poor explanation of the attempt to Infiltrate their group, and Braimind shook his head.

"Disappointing, but we'll have to go on to the next task. There is no time to waste, for you and Aurelio need to return to his city. When you have finished studying astrology through triangulation, you may return here and we will assess your grades. I wish you both well. Go in the name of Eos!"

Aurelio, it appeared, was an adept leaper, and normally leaped every morning before breakfast to keep in trim. We progressed through the dry regions in leaps and bounds towards our goal, although several times I tripped over boulders and on one occasion fell into the entrance to a musty underground vault, which seemed familiar. I didn't have time to reflect on that as we traveled along a low coastline with the towers of a magnificent port city visible ahead of us. We soon approached the high walls that surrounded the city and joined a stream of donkey carts, peasants and chariots that were driving in and out of the gate.

It was a wonderful sight. Tier upon tier of white marble colleges, libraries and lecture halls, surrounded by landscaped walkways between flowerbeds, ponds and trickling fountains met my gaze, and ahead I saw the curved dome of a huge observatory. We walked inside and I gasped with amazement, for the foyer, between blue streaked marble pillars, had a granite floor in mosaic laid out in a glittering display of stars and planets, and each panel between the great pillars was decorated with a scene from the twelve astrological signs.

Aurelio motioned to me. "You will be studying here with me for a while, and so I've made arrangements for you to stay at the observatory. Come, I will show you to your room."

Together we walked up a long, gently curving staircase and Aurelio opened double doors at the top. I gazed above me with spellbound intensity. The room looked directly up into the heavens through a huge curved glass skylight that was the only window. Under this skylight, a vast round bed was made up with pale blue satin sheets, and two maidens and two youths stood waiting with hot water for a bath and scented garments to dress me after my journey. There was even an attendant holding my little friend Arbil, the mongoose, the protagonist of many happy snake hunts in the nearby desert.

Suffice it to say, I remained in the observatory for nine months, snake hunting in my spare time and climbing the long staircase of the massive lighthouse, to observe the state of the sea when storms arose and the waves dashed against the solid foundation of the Pharos. At the end of this time, I graduated with the degree of Court Astrologer. I obtained an unparalleled knowledge of the zodiac and of the youths and maidens also, which was very satisfying.

This very pleasant interlude was rudely shattered as I learned that I must leave. Aurelio had one final test for me. I must make out my birth chart, which would show me the areas of my personality that needed further work. By a method of triangulation we found the constellation Libra and my rising sign of Scorpio.

Aurelio shook his head. "This is going to cause difficulties for you. You have three planets in Scorpio, the death sign. Here, Pluto is in your twelfth house – that is the house of Karma. You must overcome many negative obstacles, yet you are protected by your Guide in this house, so do not fear. He knows that you must let go of old behavior and past habits in order to move forward with your life. The breathing exercise you will learn from Braimind will help with that. Now, my friend, I will bid you goodbye, until we meet again during your crossing of the Mystic SEA, where I await you once more." Aurelio bowed and kissed my hand, then stepped back into the shadows of the darkened lobby.

Returning alone across the desert, I wandered in a mental fog until I found myself by some mysterious means inside the ninth room of the Temple of the East.

Braimind, the Ace of Swords, welcomed me. "Your body has been cared for here while you were in astral form for, in order to return to the city of learning with Aurelio, you had to travel back in time." He sighed. "That city is no more. It was destroyed by the followers of a dangerous cult called Christianity, and now nothing remains of the libraries and temples but dust, where transients roam and frequent whores in dark bars. Only the chosen have been able to carry the teachings of the city forward into our time, and even now they are spat upon."

I was devastated. The city annihilated! "What about Aurelio?" I questioned anxiously. "Did he escape the attack?"

"Aurelio is the Six of Swords, and therefore outside time and space. He exists in your imagination, just as Endevvy and your other entities do. Aurelio is safe in your mind. You will meet him again, and you will be amazed at his progress, so do not worry. You have one more task, and I have made special arrangements for you to begin the process in the morning, so rest now. I will take you to your corner bed."

The following day I woke and Braimind led me outside. I was astonished to see the great white bull, the Minotaur that Rachel and I had poisoned, standing in front of the Temple of the East. The bull snorted and pawed the ground, and I hid behind Braimind in a cowardly fashion.

"Come out!" He ordered, pulling at my tunic. "Don't be feeble, now. You've faced this bull before. It is time to conjure the return of Rachel, who is your inner child Suckersie. We need her for the breathing exercises. I will tell you what to do. Go up to the bull and stroke him between the horns. He will lower his head and prepare to charge. You must back off, then turn and run towards him, grabbing him by the horns, and somersault over his back. That will break the spell."

I had heard tell of the art of bull jumping in the land of the bull-king, but this was ridiculous. I hesitated, and the bull glared at me malevolently.

"Don't waste time thinking about it. Thoughts will only cause you to rationalize, and when you do that, you will know logically that this is not a good idea. However, it is the only way to show mastery of the Minotaur and to regain your child. Don't hesitate. Run towards the bull now." Braimind looked me straight in the eyes and his voice was firm.

Reluctantly I stepped towards the animal as it lowered its mighty head. I was just able to reach up to the crest between the six-foot long horns, and I rubbed the coarse hair. The bull grunted, backed off and scraped the earth with a forefoot in annoyance. I took a fast run and, as he lowered his head to charge, grabbed the massive horns, my arms outstretched as far as they would go, and flung myself over his back. The somersault landed me hard on his rump, and I slid off, rubbing my butt ruefully. I had just managed to vault the bull, but it was close.

Braimind laughed loudly. "OK. You win. I expect you'll have a bruise or two. Now, see what the bull is doing."

He pointed at the animal that was kneeling on the ground, choking as if something was caught in his throat. Foam poured from his mouth and his eyes stared wildly. Then, with a fierce hacking noise, his mouth opened cavernously wide, and out stepped Rachel, foam free and unhurt, and ran towards me, where I opened my arms for her as the bull rose to his feet and backed away.

As I embraced my daughter, she seemed to shrivel, and instead of holding an adult, I found myself with a young child of about seven in my arms. It was Suckersie, and she admonished me.

"Why did you make me stay inside the bull?" She pouted. "It was very dark and horrid. I wanted to come out and be with you, but when I tried to squeeze up his throat, it was too tight, and I had to wriggle back. That is not fair!" The child glared at me and made an attempt to smack me, but I caught her arm as she swung.

"Calm down, Suckersie. You are here now. I couldn't let you out before because I wasn't ready. The bull knew that. Now I need your help with the breathing exercises. Will you stay with me?"

"I don't want to. It will be boring. I want to play over there." She pointed to an area where young children from the Temple of the East were throwing and catching some birds that seemed to enjoy their games. "I want to play with them, not do some boring silly breath thing with you. I don't like you. You made me stay inside the bull too long."

"Suckersie, I need you with me for these exercises. I'm very sorry I didn't let you out before. That is my fault – sometimes it is hard to face you, because you accuse me of nasty things, like the time when you were buried in the sand. Now I am concentrating on my relationship with you. Please give me a little while to work out my problems with you, and you won't regret it."

"All right. I suppose so. But when we have finished, can I go and play with the birds?" She looked yearningly over at the other children. "That would be much more fun."

"I promise that you can do that." I caught myself, remembering that I should not make promises that I may not be able to keep. I made a note that I must keep this promise. "The exercises will not take long and I think they will be finished today, OK?"

Suckersie gave me a curious glance, then slid her hand in mine and we walked into the ninth room of the Temple.

Braimind told us to sit cross-legged, opposite each other and touching hands, so that there was a pulsating current between us. We closed our eyes and he began to count breaths, which we followed, starting very slowly at first, and gradually increasing the pace. As the time between my breathing accelerated, I began to feel lightheaded, and Suckersie became paler. I knew that we were crossing the threshold into hyperventilation, but there was no stopping, and soon the fast rhythmic breaths took over, and I seemed to be floating in space above the floor with my inner child opposite me, her face transfixed by longing as fleeting fear glinted in her eyes. I held her gaze and took myself back to my childhood, and became her. Then I knew the beginnings of her fear, her uncertainty. It seemed that I was able to review what had happened to separate us, the trauma that had occurred as our parents fought and that I had forgotten.

Her eyes grew softer as I understood the memory, and I knew that I was not to blame. I had banished Suckersie, because she was associated with the many conflicts that I had witnessed, but the person I was now had grown beyond that upbringing, and it was no longer relevant. Our breaths were coming so fast now that sweat poured from us, and our hands were hot and sticky. The stickiness became worse and worse, and I tried to withdraw my hands from her grasp for a moment. Strangely, try as I would, I could not release myself from her grasp. We were glued together, and soon I saw our hands begin to dissolve into each other, and the melting ran up our arms into our bodies, until the moment that I fell into a dead faint.

When I woke, Braimind was cooling my brow with a damp cloth. There was no sign of Suckersie. "Where is my child?" I asked him plaintively, feeling exhausted. "Is she going to be all right?"

"Suckersie is perfectly all right. In fact, she is perfect. You have absorbed your inner child into your own body, and you understand now that you are united, and there can be no more separation, for the past, your memories of unhappiness, no longer exist in the Now. You are finally free!" He patted my shoulder. "Now, go out and play with the other children. They will show you how to throw the birds so that they aren't hurt. Have fun!"

Getting up, I ran lightly out to the grassy courtyard. I no longer felt tired, but much younger, and I caught a beautiful thrush as it fluttered towards me, kissed its feathered head, and threw it to a young boy opposite me, who laughed and held the bird softly.

The following morning the request came to join Braimind in the ninth room, for a guest had arrived who wanted to see me. As I walked into the room, I was delighted to see the old fellow who was my Guide talking to Braimind. He turned and I went up to him gladly.

"I have something for you, even though sometimes I think you don't deserve it." My Guide laughed as he held out a parcel about twelve inches long, which I took and unwrapped. Inside was an elephant skin sheath decorated with five-petaled Tudor roses, patterned after the Celtic manner. I drew out the Dagger inside, its engraved handle set with rubies, that Kracklewergen had given me, telling me that it represented my willpower in its shortened form. I was overjoyed! This was the second Magical Weapon that I had regained, for I already had the platter from the Temple of the North.

"Don't get too excited," warned the old man. "You did not do well in your first task, which was your botched attempt to destroy the Seven Shades. Ignitia told you that you could only take them on one by one, and I am reminding you of that, for they can't be destroyed in a group. Besides, now they have revenged themselves on you by springing the Seventh Shade who belongs to Malkuth, out of the monastery dungeon." He nodded sagely. "You enraged them, and that gave them the added motivation to break through the rock walls that imprisoned their comrade, and release it. Its' head is somewhat squashed, because you trod on it, but it has survived and harbors great hatred for you. Now, they await you amongst the Islands of the Mystic SEA, and they are plotting even now to obliterate you. Never fear, for I will fight by your side. They must be overcome, for there is no other way through the Mystic SEA. Take this Dagger now, as a symbol of the element of Air, and I will show you the route through the center of the pyramid to the Temple of the West."

He stepped towards the inner corner of the triangular room and I bade Braimind goodbye and followed him. As we moved into the darkened corner, the apex of the wall seemed to give way in front of us, and a gentle mist, undulating in hues of purple, enveloped us. I looked above me and saw a spiral stairway that curved upwards into the starry night without end. Then, peering down from a great distance, I could just make out what I thought was a face – the face of someone I had met before in the amethyst tower – the face of Belvedere, my ego. I felt drawn towards him, but the old fellow took my arm and hurried me forward.

"Not yet, my friend!" He admonished. "You are passing through the influence of the sphere of Yesod, the dream world. It's true, this is also the seat of your ego Belvedere, who is at the top of the stairs. Your battle with him is not yet met, the war remains undeclared, but he will be there in the Mystic SEA and he will summon the Shades and the Hoodwinker to aid him, for they do not want you to desert them, but stay with them for ever. Beware their cunning strategy to hold you in their grip, for it is subtle. Believe in me, and I will see you through. Come now, for there is the door into the Temple of the West."

The spell was broken and the dream of mystery vanished as we opened the door into the ninth room of the Temple of the West, where stood Liquilim, the Ace of Cups.

Ace of Cups - Rules Six of Cups.

We found ourselves immediately in the ninth room of the Temple of the West, where a cascading waterfall took the likeness of the archangel Raphael. I watched as the liquefacient, shimmering form of the Ace of Cup, Liquilim, seemed to melt and coalesce with astonishing rapidity, as if the fluid falls shed their plumes over her. She was a beautiful blonde, slim and graceful, and moved with sinuous poise The old man, my Guide, bowed and went back the way we had come, and I heard his footsteps as he climbed the spiral stairs to Yesod.

Liquilim beckoned to two shadowy figures in one corner of the room. As they stepped forward, I recognized the couple from the Six of Cups - Princess Marijusha and her lover, Govinda, who had been striving to balance their relationship for a long time.

The Ace spoke directly to me."As your first task under the laws of Immersion, I would like you to negotiate between these two and try to resolve their emotional differences one way or another. This cannot continue. They love each other, but Marijusha is torn between her worldly love for Govinda and her love for the muse that directs her – the Bride. Maybe you can do something to help. Besides, someone stole her gold velvet cushion recently, and she is distraught without it, for it is an aid to meditation."

Carefully ignoring the mention of the ubiquitous cushion, I replied. "I recall their difficulties. Govinda could not see the door of the palace, because he was not sufficiently aware. He had to break the bars on a window to climb in. It doesn't work when a person forces themselves on you." I sighed. "I feel I can help them reach an understanding, but two things must happen first. Govinda needs to move away from the relationship and focus on his own spiritual development. He is a fine man and, although a commoner, worthy of the Princess."

I turned to Marijusha. "I understand the conflict you are going through. I feel it is a mistake to commit yourself totally to the worship of the Bride of Malkuth, for that takes you away from real life, and it is only through your interactions in real life that you can grow towards the Bride, who is life itself. Do you understand me?"

"I haven't looked at it that way. I suppose that's true - about the Bride, I mean. You have met her, haven't you? So, you are aware of the attraction that she gives out. She is very compelling." Marijusha wiped away a tear. "Do you mean that if I make a commitment to Govinda, I won't lose my connection with the Bride? She will not go away?"

"Govinda is a part of the Bride, and so are you. How can the Bride ever go away? She exists in you, and you exist in her, as her manifestation. There is no other explanation." I made a suggestion. "While Govinda is doing some work on his emotions, you can serve the Bride by serving her people. I have had a dream in which I saw a dam above a western city that is about to burst. It is being undermined by erosion, and will inundate the towns in the canyon below very soon and drown many people. Go there, and try to save them before it is too late. I prophesy that the dam will break very soon. Will you do that?"

"If it serves the Bride, of course, I will leave now. Will you come with me? I may need your help to negotiate with those in harms' way who do not believe me."

"That's true. You will need to convince them, for they do not think ahead. They are reluctant to leave their houses and place of trade, their tourist shops and restaurants. Come, we will go together."

Marijusha and I left our physical bodies in the ninth room and traveled instantly in astral form to the narrow canyon below the great dam, where signs of weakness were, as yet, barely visible. Yet I knew that, within a week or two, disaster would strike, for we were able to foretell the future while in our astral bodies.

We made our way to a local printer and soon had placards in place all over town, warning of the impending dam break. Many people gathered around the notices, reading them, looking at the dam, and then shaking their heads. Some laughed, while others shrugged their shoulders and pointed at their foreheads cynically. They did not believe us.

After a few days, it was evident that the placards would not work, except with a few of the more intelligent folk. We had to think of something else, and so we paid a visit to the mayor of the town, dressed as Water Board officials. Our suggestion was to arrange with him to have a fake dam burst test exercise on the day that we were expecting the real break. It didn't take long to convince him that it was a good idea, because we told him that we were concerned about the levels of erosion around the dam, and wanted to arrange a repair party to shore up the eroded areas along with a practice evacuation of the population.

We set the date one week ahead, and preparations went forward. The mayor printed new placards announcing the exercises that were to be held in the city park, urging all the villagers to attend. I was somewhat concerned that he had chosen the low lying city park for the exercises, but I felt it was too late to make a change. We settled down to wait, spending our time getting to know some of the people and hiking in the hills around the dam, where we saw further evidence of erosion.

The day of the predicted dam burst arrived and my heart was pounding as the mayor started the exercise and evacuation. Sirens went off, doctors examined people with fake wounds lying on stretchers in the park, and the roads were filled with people heading for higher ground, their carts jamming the highways. As the exercise proceeded, the roads out of town became impassable, and everyone was at a standstill. People were getting angry and frustrated, and many started to return to their homes.

I ran amongst them with Marijusha, urging them not to turn back, for we knew the danger was imminent for those with low-lying houses.

"You have to pretend that this is a real threat!" I shouted, waving my arms. "Do not return to your homes until the exercise is over, but head for higher ground."

"That's rubbish!" An elderly resident complained. "We know this is just a practice run. The dam will not burst. It has been there for ages, and I've lived here 45 years with no trouble. Besides, it's hard to walk uphill."

"You never know. It is better to be prepared." My words were lost as, with a great roar, we heard the dam give way. "Run for your lives," I yelled.

"The dam has burst!" I shoved the nearest group of people in the park towards the side of the canyon, but the throng barely moved, as the path was still choked by those who were uncertain of which way to go.

A sarcastic voice beside my elbow spoke. "I have to congratulate you. That recording of a dam burst was very realistic, and added to the confusion. How did you do it?"

"It's not a recording, you fool. The dam has burst! Save yourselves, for here comes the water......" My voice was smacked from my lips as a huge wall of water overwhelmed us and swept the crowd away downstream, with all those around us in a welter of flailing arms and legs.

Our carefully planned negotiations had been a colossal failure. The Princess and I found ourselves hanging from a large dead tree, with more than half the population of the town lying drowned around us.

A lone voice wailed. "Why did the mayor make us come to the park by the river? My family would have been safe in our house up on the hill. Now all are dead. Why did he do that? I don't understand."

The sound of choked sobbing and burbling groans was broken only by the bells of the remaining doctors' carts, come to bring bodies back to the morgue. Three-quarters of the townspeople, whose homes were above the water line, perished needlessly, and the remaining few found the mayor and committed him to the water torture, after which they hung, drew and watered him.

Marijusha and I returned to our bodies in the ninth room and awaited the fury of Liquilim. To our surprise, the Ace of Cups remained calm, like the surface of a frozen lake. She explained the situation carefully.

"I cannot condone what you have done in theory. The park next to the river was not a very smart choice for the exercises. However, in practice you have unwittingly released a large number of people from their collective bad karma, for all of those who died in the onrush of water were condemned to do so by past lives. They were the occupants of a village who collaborated with the Inquisition during the age of witch hunts, when they witnessed and encouraged the cruel water torture of many innocent women and young girls. Therefore, although you feel you have failed, you have actually succeeded. You have my congratulations." She smiled. "Now we must wait until Govinda is ready, and then we will reunite Marijusha with him, and see what they have learned."

Marijusha and I watched as Govinda came through the door. He walked straight and exuded confidence. She ran to him, and he enfolded her in his arms. "My dearest one, I have discovered the secret of finding the door to your palace, and I need never break in again. Do you believe me?"

"Dear Govinda!" Marijusha was sobbing softly. "I understand now that ordinary actions in the world can free any stranger at your side from karma, if they are rightly directed. I know now that the Bride is not only the source of creation, but also the destroyer. Destruction must come before creation, mustn't it? So there were worlds before ours came into being, and there will be worlds after us, and we will be interacting with all the souls around us who long for completion."

"Yes, I have learned that it is so. We will both be doing the work of the Bride, our muse, in her manifestation as World. Will you be mine, now?" Govinda gazed deeply into her eyes, and saw her answer, as she said "Yes."

After the happy couple left to plan their wedding, Liquilim gave me my next instructions. Before I continued with my remaining tasks, I was to shape-shift into an underwater creature, a fish, an octopus, or anything else I chose. I slept on it and then returned, asking to become a marlin. I felt that this fish was a noble example of the water world. Liquilim took up one of the many Cups that formed a continuous frieze around the ninth room, and splashed some water on me. I dropped to the floor, gasping, and her attendants hurriedly picked me up by my fins and ran with me to the Lagoon, where they threw me in and I was able to breathe once more. I flicked my tail, and immediately shot forward through the water. It was amazing! I could see clearly in the shallower water of the Lagoon, but I could not maneuver very well, and I wondered if I could find an outlet to the sea, where I would be able to test out some of my best jumps.

Searching methodically along the seaward side of the Lagoon, I headed south, probing the soft sand of the Bar with my sword. It felt strange to have a long rigid object in front of me, attached firmly to my head, it felt powerful, it felt as if I could run through any predator in front of me with the sword, or slash sideways and cut my enemy to pieces. Towards evening, I noticed that the sand was gently sliding away into deeper water, and I swept the water with my left hand fins to turn west, heading out to sea.

It was a dangerous move. I had not thought clearly about what I would do out there in the Mystic SEA, and I should have remembered the stories that the yokels had told me about the monsters in the eggs that Hugh had incubated. Now Hugh was dead – killed by a ghost! What could that mean? My human brain within the powerful body of the marlin was still conscious and capable of reminiscences.

I swam for some time in the limitless sea, enjoying my ability to leap out of the water, turn, and dive deep to catch the plump tuna I found swimming in shoals around me. The feel of water on my tough skin, rushing past me as I sped through kelp forests, was as if I were flying. As the daylight died, and the water grew dim, I came to an outcrop of rocks about sixty feet down, and began to investigate the crannies to find a tasty moray eel, for I fancied a change in diet. I stuck my sword into a small hole in the rocks and hit something soft – maybe an eel - that gave way as I pushed harder against it, trying to impale it and pull it from its hideaway.

Alas! It was a foolish idea. I found that I could not pull my sword out, no matter how I back-flipped my fins, thrashed my tail and struggled to free myself. Whatever was in the hole had me firmly in its grasp, and would not let go. Several hours passed and this was turning out to be a serious problem. Should I wait to see if the creature would get tired? If I went on struggling, I would deplete my energy, and trapped without food, I would die. That did not seem a comforting thought, even through I knew I was in astral form. What would happen if my astral form remained stuck underwater and could not return to my waiting body in the Temple of the West?

I was thus contemplating my fate, my sword ignominiously caught in the rock cranny, when I heard the sound of a motor boat approaching, and a fishing line with a very large and delicious looking object hooked onto it slowly trailed across the surface above me. I could not, at first make out what sort of bait was on the hook, until I got a better look by screwing my head sideways and getting one eye facing upwards. Then I got a terrible shock!

The bait was a young girl of about twelve or thirteen, her long blonde hair floating in the water as she flailed her arms and rose to the surface to get air, and then sank down again, her mouth crumpled into a sad but resigned grimace, and her legs trailing behind her. A strong, delicate scent blended with the seawater as the boat circled around my position. This odor filtered down towards the crevice and I felt the creature relax its grip on my sword. With a short tug I was able to pull free. At the same time, out of the crevice oozed a truly hideous monster, indescribably ugly and ferocious looking, and swam in little jerks, pushing its body towards the attractive bait.

It was clear that someone was sacrificing young women to sea monsters around here. I gave a mighty swish of my tail and rushed towards the young girl, intercepting the path of the monster and slashing angrily at it with my sword. A fierce fight ensued, the monster twirling itself around me and sinking a row of very sharp teeth into my neck, while I attempted to turn and hack at it, and the water turned red with our blood as we fought. Soon both of us were exhausted by our lacerations, and the monsters' grip on my body grew weak, as its grip slackened and it fell away limply into the deep, spiraling round and round and trailing parts of its broken body.

Swimming feebly to the young girl and faint from loss of blood, I felt the life draining from me. With a last effort, I unhooked her with my sword, allowing her to swim free towards the Bar and safety. I took the hook in my own mouth and tugged fiercely to alert the fisherman above, for I felt darkness closing in. As the line grew taught and I was pulled inexorably towards my fate as a marlin, my last thoughts were of the beauty of the young girl I had rescued, and I closed my eyes in joy as I was pulled over the stern of the boat.

I woke up in the ninth room of the Temple of the West, with the Ace of Cups, Liquilim, bending over me, an anxious look in her gentle eyes. As my gaze slowly focused on her, she gave a sigh of relief.

"Bravo! Well done, my friend, I'm so relieved you're all right. You would not know it, but I am the maiden you saved in your past life as a marlin. Without your sacrifice then, I would never have been able to reach my goal of becoming the Ace of Cups. Now I am able to lead all those who drown in their emotions to safety through my abilities as the Root of the Powers of Water. You are in my debt for evermore, and as a strong Water sign, Scorpio, is in your Ascendant, you have my protection from all fluid dangers you must face in the Mystic SEA, to which you will travel very soon."

Liquilim dipped her hand into a font of water close by, and the clear liquid ran between her fingers as she spoke.

"You may have noticed that all elements are flexible, and water is the most flexible of all, for neither earth, nor air, nor fire, can change itself into as many different forms. Clouds, snow, seas and ice sheets, all are forms of water. Therefore, flexibility is a key element of water. You must learn to be more flexible, for the Sword of your Will power, forged in the interaction between the spheres of Hod and Netzach, must be both strong and supple, like the sword of the marlin. In time, you must face the challenge of the Path of Art. You will need to perfect your Will during your travels in the Mystic SEA."

Liquilim paused. "Family ties are the best way to learn flexibility and compromise, just as water flows around obstacles rather than trying to batter them down. Even the waves of a stormy sea break and fall apart as spray when they hit an object. You will place yourself astrally as the mother-in-law of a certain family to experience their conflicts, which result from your presence in the home of your son and daughter-in-law. That is your next test and I wish you well."

I found myself standing alone in front of the doors of a large mansion as the taxi drove away, with a suitcase at my feet. I knocked, and a starched maid with a supercilious glance opened the door and silently bade me enter, taking the suitcase. Without a word, the maid led me towards the stairs, and hurried up in front of me. I put my foot on the first step and found that I barely had the strength to push down on my knee and drag up the other foot, which I placed feebly on the next step. My body felt like lead. I clung desperately to the banisters and eventually managed to pull myself to the top of the stairs, the struggle leaving me completely exhausted. Through the door at the top I spotted a bedroom lined in pink brocade with flounced pink curtains around the four-poster bed, lace obscuring the windows, and a pink chamber pot seated fatly under the commode.

The maid placed my suitcase on the luggage stand.

"I will run a bath for you, Madam. Then I will unpack and lay out your clothes for the evening." She looked disdainful. "Dinner is at eight in the floral dining suite. The elevator has been out of order, but we have arranged a special wheelchair for you that can climb the stairs. You won't have to face that ordeal again as the chair should be here shortly." She smirked and hurried into the bathroom and I heard the sound of flowing water as I pushed the lace curtains aside and looked out of the window at the formal, beautifully tailored gardens that stretched on every side of the mansion.

My legs were very tired, so I sat down on the bed. The maid helped me out of my clothes and into a bathrobe, then went downstairs as I walked slowly into the steamy bathroom. Dropping my robe, I paused to wipe off the haze from the mirror, and peered into it.

Horrors! That was not me! The face that molded itself vaguely in the mirror was that of an old woman, probably near 90 years of age, seamed and cracked, with sagging jowls, turkey neck and wispy non-existent hair. I hastily looked down at my body.

No wonder I had trouble climbing the stairs! I saw a shriveled pair of thin legs ending in distorted lumpy feet, the flesh hanging off them, and above the scraggily thighs were the remains of two outstretched breasts that lay disconsolately on the furled skin of a grayish stomach. I had become senile!

Cautiously climbing into the bath, I lay there, thinking. It came to me that I was in my astral form, and that my younger body was waiting for me in the ninth room of the Temple of the West. That was a relief! Evidently I had come to live with my son, who had done well for himself, because I could no longer live alone, and I understood why. I slowly sponged myself down and then grasped the bar to raise myself out of the bath, which seemed abominably slippery. Dragging on the bathrobe, I dried myself and dressed slowly, then rang a bell for the maid. She soon appeared with a very extraordinary wheelchair, and I sat down in it, feeling humiliated. The trip downstairs was quite interesting, however, as the chair took over and made its way down the steps with alacrity, and I was duly impressed.

I remained in the chair for dinner, at which I met my new daughter-in-law, for my son had remarried for the fifth time. She was a stupid-looking blonde with excessively pouting lips, and the smell of her coated make up, as she bent to politely kiss me, was overpowering. Dinner proved to be a meal fraught with red flags. The woman gossiped incessantly about their neighbors and contradicted me when I tried to join in the conversation. I was not going to like it here, I could tell, and when I studied my sons' attitude, I saw boredom and irritation alternately crossing his face. I felt a great sense of powerlessness overcome me that crushed me inwardly, and I sagged forward in the chair and fell into my dessert plate. The butler rushed forward and mopped the rhubarb pie off my face, and I could hear a suppressed titter of laughter from the blonde.

You will be laughing on the other side of your face, I thought privately as I tried to look dignified. War had been declared, and I had lost the first battle. However, I did have the advantage of knowing my mind was as taut and finely tuned as that of a younger person, although I was literally hiding in a decrepit body. I had the advantage. I must play it well.

The following morning the patronizing maid came to take me for a constitutional in the grounds. I could not help envying the situation my son was in, for he had succeeded financially, and had done much better, in a worldly sense, than I had. I admired the tidy privet hedges around the rose beds, the abundant kitchen garden, and the stables, where he kept several beautiful Arab horses. I wished fervently that I owned it all myself.

Then I noticed the wheelchair suddenly gain speed. I tried to look around to ask the maid to slow down. Out of the corner of my eye, I saw with surprise that she was not there, and someone else had taken her place. A strange figure was pushing my chair. This mangy looking woman had a pale green face and tightly pursed lips, and she was speeding along, bumping over stones on the path and steering around corners like a madwoman.

"Who are you?" I managed to croak out. "Slow down, for God's sake!"

I shouted as I was hurled to one side while the chair made a violent one-wheel swing around a corner. I gripped the arms of the chair and ordered her to stop. "What is going on? Are you crazy?"

Rising from the chair with difficulty, I supported myself on the arms and faced her. She sneered at me. "I am Covvymor, your envious self. You summoned me, because you covet your sons' material goods and chattels. Especially the Arabian horses. You can still have it, you know. Your son has made a will, leaving everything to you, because he doesn't trust his new wife. We can get rid of them, and then you will have this estate for your own. I have a plan."

Covvymor leaned forward and whispered in my ear. It was a good plan, and so we moved forward with the arrangements. The blonde woman could go, she was of no use to the human race, but my son – it would be emotionally wrenching to get rid of him, for I still had some lingering feelings regarding his happy childhood. However, he had made some bad choices, especially with his five marriages, and I felt it was time for him to bite the dust.

It was my son's habit to ride early in the morning on his Arab stallion, a handsome dun horse with a flowing black mane and tail. Sometimes his wife accompanied him on a pale colored mare, but she was a poor horsewoman and merely in the learning stages. We picked a morning with the promised threat of a storm, and watched as the two of them rode out along a leafy drive towards the woods.

Heading quickly into a thicket close by, Covvymor and I timed our attack to coincide with the approaching storm, and put up a very tall lightning conductor rod with two thin wires that led from it across the path about five feet high. We knew that this was the route they would take, to return to the stables.

The storm came rapidly closer, and soon we were pelted by rain, but I did not care, for I would soon be mistress of the mansion, wouldn't I? I cackled and rolled around in my chair with glee. The sound of galloping hooves came towards us as the rain slashed down and thunder rolled nearby. We could hear the crackle of lightning, and I felt sure that our conducting rod, which was much higher than the surrounding trees, would be struck. I did not have long to wait.

Two soaking wet riders appeared around the bend in the path, galloping at full tilt, the blonde hanging onto her horses' mane and bouncing around in the saddle uncontrollably. The thunder cracked, the horses, their ears laid back, leaped on, terrified, and then!

I was back in my body in the ninth room, with Covvymor by my side. Where were the two riders?

Liquilim explained, her eyebrows raised suggestively.

"You are a fool! The lightning strike killed you, instead of your son and his wife, for you had allowed one of the wires to fall across your wheelchair while you were wriggling around. It's lucky you were only in astral form, or that would be the end of you. How careless! You allowed your emotions to get the better of you and did not plan cautiously. Besides, you failed the flexibility test because you were too rigid in your attitude to your daughter-in-law, and mentally condemned her before you had given yourself a chance to get to know her."

Liquilim shrugged. "The only redeeming fact in this sorry tale is that, when your son saw your dead body slumped in the chair, he began openly weeping and took the corpse into his arms, carrying it to the mansion, where he laid you out in a fancy coffin. Furthermore, he changed his ways, got rid of the blonde and sold the mansion to a speculator, and now he has joined an ashram in Poona and vows to devote the rest of his life to good causes."

At the news of the mansions' sale, Covvymor ran from the room, crying out in despair, and threw herself into the Lagoon, where she drowned swiftly, for she could not swim, being unfamiliar with water.

It was now time for my third task, but before that began, Liquilim decided to show me the other rooms in the Temple of the West, since I had come straight into the ninth room through the center of the Pyramid, instead of the outer door.

"Why did I arrive in the ninth room here?" I asked. "I thought I should come around the pyramid and enter from outside. It doesn't make sense."

"The Temple of the East is under the influence of the Hodians, and we are from the sphere of Netzach. The path between the two is fraught with peril, and the name of it is Death. To step outside the Pyramid would risk losing your mind to madness, therefore the passage through the dream world in the center helps to balance you. You know what happens to people when they are not allowed to dream – they go crazy. This path is about transformation, and traces out the s-curve that you follow during your time on the Isle of the White Pyramid." Liquilim opened the door towards the West. "Come, and I will show you the other eight rooms."

The three rooms we entered consisted of a central room which appeared to be a chapel, dedicated to a strange god, for stained glass windows on each side, which were back lit as they received no outside light, showed cavorting figures in woodland surroundings, playing Pan pipes and drinking from large wine casks. Circles of dancing figures, brilliantly costumed under the moon, were especially well drawn and the artwork was truly spectacular.

On the left of the chapel was a darkened room with rich red velvet hangings and a large central table on which a crystal ball stood. Around the table wispy forms seemed to float, and letters on the table condensed into words, and then shifted position to form other words. I was unable to make out any definite individuals. They all seemed to flow in and out of each other as they sang in low, crooning voices.

On the right, a red light announced the presence of an exotic brothel, from which arose the odor of incense and cries of earthly delight, prompted by the soft skirling of Pan pipes.

We moved on towards the outer five rooms, where we found on the far right a cosmetic surgery operating room where people were able to look exactly alike by altering their original looks through surgery. A large number of hair stylists and makeup artists scurried around, working on the final touches of fakery on several beautiful women. This room, dedicated to Venus, was the Center for External Beauty. Next to this room was a gym, furnished with stationary bicycles, treadmills, exercise machines and weights. A number of both men and women stood in front of a mirror and flexed their abdominal muscles, admiring each other.

The room on the far left was dedicated to psychic research and thought transference. Several people lay on cots with wires attached to their heads, while attendants monitored different screens placed around the room. To the interior of this room, the Center for the Study of Dreams existed, where many people slept in beds or sat at desks busily writing down the dream they had the night before. An instructor walked around the group, interpreting the dreams as the sleepers related their nocturnal adventures to him.

The lavishly decorated outer room, which led to the outside world, contained a large fountain in the middle with a surrounding pool of water. Young nude people were bathing in the pool, splashing each other, laughing and wallowing in the bright water, without a care in the world. It seemed a truly delightful place to me.

I was disappointed when Liquilim explained that these people were group-oriented and had not yet reached the stage of knowing themselves as individuals. They were under the influence of the Pan principle and had no desire to question their existence in intellectual terms. This was an advantage in some ways, but was a dead end for humanity, as only those with inquiring minds would be able to carry on the torch of human progress.

Now that I had visited the nine rooms of the Temple of the West, Liquilim gave me my last task. She warned me that the task would be dangerous, for I faced further conflict with my inner shadow, the Hoodwinker, who had recently stolen my poetic self, Bardogian during my failed initiation. The Ace of Cups would not elaborate further.

"You must recover the Mask that is made of the obsidian eyes, the quicksilver nose, and the bloodstone teeth. You know where it is, Mablevi wears it in the center of the stone maze. You will have to find out the true nature of Mablevi, the evil camel driver, and the way to do that is to open your emotional side through the practice of morphing. To help you, I will call forth my little allies, the two newts from the pool beneath the eternal waterfall, and they will guide you. Go now, and may Anahita, the Goddess of Spring Waters, guide you."

I set out alone, glad that my envious entity Covvymor, who was truly unpleasant, had not been able to swim. Reaching the pool by the spring, I called forth Anahita, who rose from the depths to greet me, accompanied by two adorable newts, their tiny frilled gills like lace ruffs on each side of their heads.

"You have come for help from the newts. Morphing is not easy, but you have some idea of the process from your previous experiences. The newts will show you what to do."

The two newts obviously worked together on this process and were eager to demonstrate their technique. One newt quickly rolled the other into a ball and, taking a grass stem from the bank, steered the rolling ball towards the edge of the pool, balancing it on a rock. The newt then whipped the ball forty times until it began to exude a frothy substance. I felt like leaping forward to rescue the poor creature, but Anahita held me back.

"Morphing demands sacrifice. Let them be, and simply watch."

The glutinous ball lay still for a few seconds after the whipping, and then a plume of clear liquid spouted from the top of the ball, forming itself into a large toad. I gave a start. It looked remarkably like my wretched toad Oojo, the enemy of my favorite cricket, Joana, but I hesitated to acknowledge him. His habit was to appear and disappear without my authority as he was completely out of control. The other newt dropped the grass stem and darted back in consternation, to disappear under a rock.

"Oh! Dear." Anahita muttered to herself as Oojo, for it was him, leapt into the pool. "It's happened again, he has escaped. You never know what a body will morph into – that's the problem. Never mind. You can see how it's done, so roll yourself into a ball and we'll just give you forty lashes and see what comes out. Lie down and put your head between your legs. Yes, that's it. Now, bend your back as far as you can and roll towards that flat rock by the pool."

Reluctant to perform this feat, I was, on the other hand, curious to see what the experiment produced. In any case, my task was to salvage the Mask, and that was vitally important, so I rolled towards the rock and waited there while Anahita picked up a long willow switch, cutting the air sharply as a test.

Holding my breath as the switch landed repeatedly over my shoulders, after the first few blows I went into a sort of trance. I couldn't feel the lashes any more, but drifted in a frothy game of bubbles that wafted past my nose in myriad colors. One of the bubbles popped against my nose and then I found myself swimming in the pool, moving my legs and streamlining my body when I dove down. I had morphed into an enormous newt. This was singularly inconvenient, since I was under the impression I would need long legs to cross the desert and reach the center of the stone maze to beard Mablevi in his den.

As usual I was wrong. There was Mablevi, wearing the Mask I desperately wanted, by the side of the pool with a bucket in his hand. He had come down for drinking water, and bent forward to dip the bucket into the pool.

It took only a single swish of my powerful tail to reach the bucket and the hand that held it, and sink my jaws firmly into his flesh. He shrieked at the top of his voice as I turned, yanking him off the bank and into the water, where a desperate fight ensued.

I had to let go of him to get a better grip on his legs to pull him under, but as soon as I released him, he swam with all his strength and made for the bank with great speed. I came after him, but I was rebuffed by a blow to my snout, which stung and made my eyes water, temporarily blinding me. It was imperative to stop him leaving the water, so I lunged at him again, this time catching him by the elbow.

He was half out of the pool, and I was shaking him like a rat and hoping that the Mask would fall off. He screamed, but held on to the Mask, for he knew what I wanted, and I had to drop him. This time he was slightly wounded, and moved more slowly, so I was able to get a good grip on his thighs and drag him to the bottom of the pool, where he passed out and let go of the Mask, which sank into the mud.

Immediately releasing the unconscious figure, which drifted to the surface upside down, I dived for the Mask to save it, nosing around in the mud. Fortunately, it had no time to sink further, and I was able to pull back gently with it in my mouth and deposit in Anahitas' underwater cave. As I let go of the Mask, water began pouring into my mouth and I choked. I felt myself losing consciousness. I was drowning. What a stupid way to die! My last thoughts were that I had morphed back into human form before reaching the safety of the bank.

I turned over in the bunk and opened my eyes. My gaze fixed on the back wall of a small hut, on which was a shelf with various flasks, pipettes and bottles containing strange objects. Below them hung clothing made from animal skins with fur trimming and lining for warmth. There was a delicious smell of simmering stew, and the figure of an old fellow stirring the pot brought a huge sense of relief. I was in the hut where my Guide lived!

He saw that I was awake and came over to the bunk.

"You nearly got lost that time." He chuckled. "A newt, who is less primitive than a marlin, finds it impossible to breathe underwater. You were very thoroughly drowned and full of water. I had to pump you out for an hour. The Mask is safe, for now. We will pick it up later, for you will need it in the Mystic SEA. Now you can rest, and I will bring your supper soon."

"What happened to me?" I asked weakly. "I was a newt – they don't drown, do they?"

"You are wrong. Newts can only breathe underwater before they become adults. Then they lose their gills. You made the mistake of staying down too long while you fought for the Mask. That cut off your oxygen supply, and you were unable to retain the newt form. Luckily, I was watching, of course, and was able to save you."

We ate a tasty supper and then the old man shyly presented me with a strange shaped parcel. "This is your reward. You succeeded in unmasking the Hoodwinker, even though you did not complete the other two tasks set for you correctly. You showed great bravery, and I now present you with your third Magical Weapon, the Cup. Use it wisely."

I unwrapped the parcel carefully. Inside was the gorgeous copper goblet, encrusted with a design of gazelles and doves entwined in jade around the edge, given to me by Little Laboria, who was now retired and working as head of the nursery for the Queen of Pentacles. I was delighted.

"Now I have three of the Magical Weapons!" I paused for a moment. "Why did you mention the Hoodwinker? I haven't seen her for a while."

"Oh! Yes, you have. The enemy that you fought in the pool was not Mablevi, for he doesn't exist in reality. Mablevi, the camel driver, is just one of the forms that the Hoodwinker can manifest. Mablevi, the cheater, is gone. Your friend Tabansi is looking after your camel, Lemig. But, beware the Hoodwinker, for she has other forms at her disposal – even the form of a toad!"

Ace of Wands - Rules
Six of Wands.

The magical Platter and the Goblet were now tucked into the pockets of my cape safely, and the Dagger in its sheath by my side. I said goodbye to Liquilim and left the Temple of the West, turning to my left and rounding the corner of the White Pyramid, where the rain soon stopped and gave way to a scorching heat. The ground was almost too hot to walk on, and I hastily hopped towards the door of the Temple of the South, that was covered by a sensible heat shield.

Once inside, I knew I was in the center of the first tier of rooms, and I looked around me. The main room seemed to be an interchange of connections between the two side rooms, for rows of metal towers on each side received and sent out flashing signals, rather like an electrical grid. I walked through a room on my left filled with machines of every shape and size, from which came incessant crackling, hissing and fizzling noises. Experiments of many sorts were in progress, and equations written on a blackboard on one side showed that calculus was one of the pursuits of the Fire people. In the farthest room stood a large telescope, trained on a revolving window, and I put my eye to it and saw to the depths of the universe, where galaxies whirled and stars gave off sparkling light shows.

On the right of the central area was a room with maps covering the walls, showing the position of every wild fire on the earth currently burning, and below the maps were calculators measuring the amount of smoke in the atmosphere. Beyond that, experts were at work on processing new methods of using fire for the benefit of mankind, including the first intuitive sketches of an elevated flying cart powered by solar fire that dispensed with the use of wheels.

Returning to the central room, I passed into the second tier of three rooms. I could hear chanting coming from the right hand room, and peeked around the door. To my amazement, I saw several bearded men and women, their legs crossed in the lotus position, jumping around the room, hanging upside down, and sticking to the side walls, their lengthy beards hanging below them.

I quickly withdrew and looked around the central room, where several robed figures were sitting wordlessly gazing into crystal balls and pools of reflecting water. The hushed silence was palpable. Tiptoeing, I moved farther to my left, where I found a heavy steel door. I turned the handle, but the door was locked, and a quiet voice spoke behind me.

"What are you looking for? Not snooping, I hope?"

A tall figure in a shining gold suit, sporting a large breastplate with an equal-armed cross in the center, his head wreathed in laurel, addressed me. "You should have waited at the door for someone to accompany you. Instead, you barged in and stuck your nose into our business. That is not a good start, for Percepto is aware of your intrusion, and he is the one to give you the three tasks you must perform."

Feeling ashamed, I immediately apologized. "I became fascinated by the atmosphere in here the minute I walked in. It was so intense – beyond anything I have experienced in the outside world."

"That is because this is the domain of Intuition, the Fire Within. I am Feroz, the Six of Wands, five times champion of the balancing Game of the Cross. If you remember, I rescued the babe in the transparent egg for you. I know that the child has now grown by seven years, and that you have succeeded in absorbing her into your own psyche. That is not easy, and I commend you, but take care you don't get burned here, for the power of Intuition is very deep. Now, come with me into the ninth room, and Percepto will give you your first task."

"What is in the room on the left?" I asked guilelessly. "Why is the door locked?"

"That is the Chamber of Ceremonies. Only those who have won all four Magical Weapons may enter there, for any false ritual or conception can destroy their physical bodies. You have three of the Weapons. Now, let us see if you can win the fourth weapon, the enchanted Wand. Then you will see that room."

Feroz led the way and we entered the ninth room. I saw before me a wall of fire in the form of the archangel Micha-el, and through his body a gradient that seemed to stretch ever upwards to an unknown place at the top of the pyramid. Far above us stood a figure in shining white on a mountain peak, holding a great wand above his head that sucked embers from the ground below a burnt tree. We began a blistering climb, and I paused for breath halfway up. Once I sat down, a great lassitude overcame me with the heat and I no longer wanted to continue. A faint sigh by my right elbow prompted me to turn around, but there was no-one there. I thought of my lazy self, Spredaloth, and how she had sunk under the mud at the Castle of Water. No, she could not return. I got up and pressed on determinedly.

When we finally reached the Ace of Wands, Percepto, I collapsed onto a pile of rocks and wiped my sweaty brow. His firey red hair was pushed under a curious tight skull cap and he wore the emblem of a fetus on his left thigh band. The Ace spoke in a voice that gave off the roar of an uncontrolled wild fire.

"I am the Root of the Powers of Fire. I give life back to the burnt embers, so that they may flourish again, and the Tree of Life that I nurture will burst forth, sending out new buds during its cycle of life. People carry the gift of Intuition hidden in their auric cocoons from one existence to the next, so that they can gradually become aware of the budding of their Magical powers and live fully within the Destiny that they have chosen."

"Intuition is hard to fathom, but I would like to learn the secret." I murmured. "What tasks do you have for me?"

"We have lost a great ally, the human perception, in our efforts to rouse up the intuitive abilities of the world population. Unfortunately, they invented a thing in a box that has attracted their attention and now rules over them night and day. This thing shows pictures of catastrophic events; happenings collected by other people; and stupid stories; to persons sitting on couches. The sitters aren't participating in these events, but they feel as if they are. Therefore they don't have to have any imagination, because the mental work is done for them. They are like huge sponges, absorbing event after event endlessly, because the information never stops coming in. Sadly, this means that many people aren't using their intuitive and imaginative powers any longer, but have become automatons."

The Ace continued. "When this began to happen, after a few years our representative, the Phoenix, went into decline and refused to squawk any more. Then he disappeared and it took us several aeons to find him asleep inside a great furnace, which you call the Sun." Percepto looked grave. "Your task is to persuade the Phoenix to arise and come down to us again, for I do not know what will happen to mankind without its presence, which touches the lambent flame in each of us. Feroz will accompany you, for he is five times champion of the Temple of the South, and has proved his courage by jumping the banner of the Phoenix into the unknown."

"I will be very glad to have him with me. Should I put on the suit that I wore during my trials with the King of Wands?"

"That would be a good idea, for as you approach the sun, you may otherwise get seriously burnt by the fierce glow."

The task of raising the Phoenix seemed dangerous and did not appeal to me, but after I had donned my suit, Feroz and I set out in my scull, which the old man had left tied up at the shore. We rowed along the shores of the Lagoon in a flat calm, our oars the only sign of movement in the still water, looking into the sun through some tinted glass, but there was no sign of the great bird. I looked down at the water, where the reflection of the sun glittered on the surface, and that gave me an idea.

Shipping my oars, I turned to Feroz. "Why not deal with the sun through its reflection, rather than risk a closer encounter?" I suggested. "We can catch the reflection in this canvas bucket, take it back to the Isle, and work on it there."

Feroz seemed doubtful. "That wouldn't be the real thing. Besides, even if we try the bucket idea, we can't allow the Phoenix to birth near the White Pyramid, for it might scorch the exterior and would certainly alarm those in the other three Temples."

"We can take the bucket with the sun in it to the shore beyond the Castle of Fire, where nobody is living between the Castles and the Bar. That would be much safer. If the plan fails, we still have the far more dangerous option of venturing close to the sun itself. It's worth a try, don't you think?"

Feroz hesitated, finally agreeing to my plan. Carefully edging up to the suns' reflection in the water, which was hard as it seemed to drift away, we finally caught it as it fled close inshore, before the reeds broke up its purity. We carried it in the bucket to a safe place, and gazed into the reflection for some hours, as the water gradually evaporated and the image of the sun eventually lay in the bottom, dry as a bone. I was afraid we were going to lose it, but Feroz said some magic words over it in Arabic and it began to shimmer violently as we drew back.

To our astonishment, a small bump grew in the center that formed itself into a beak. Then a head appeared, two large wings, and the body and feet of a great red bird. It fluffed out its feathers until it filled the bucket, squeezed over the edge and then, uttering a loud squawk, flapped towards our position with a fierce glint in its eye, growing bigger by the minute.

We were terrorized and about to take shelter when the great bird, which must have been nine feet in height by then, suddenly squatted and, with a loud groan, laid a large transparent egg on the ground in front of us, then rose and flew off towards the bright sun, where it disappeared from view. We kicked ourselves for our stupidity, for we had not thought how to control the Phoenix once it was born from the reflection, and now it had escaped. I hoped that it had not gone back to its nest in the sun.

Leaving the capture of the bird until later, we decided to focus on the egg it had laid. We crept up to the egg cautiously and looked inside. Something with a long, spiked tail was wriggling inside. Tiny spouts of flame made the egg blister, and a horned face appeared. It was a baby dragon!

"What do we do now?" I asked Feroz. "I don't think it's a good idea to let it out, do you? The bird is a good sign, for it represents rebirth, but the dragon, well, that must have been hidden inside it – in the egg. Does that mean the Phoenix repressed its dragon nature?"

"That is possible. But look!" Feroz sounded excited. "The little dragon is beckoning and trying to communicate. Put your ear to the side of the egg and listen. Maybe we can catch what it is saying."

I bent toward the wobbling egg, placing my ear against the jellified mass. A disembodied voice spoke in a faint croak. "Let me out! I have something to tell you," it insisted. "Break open the egg."

"If I open the egg, will you promise not to escape?" I asked, as a faint memory chased itself across my mind and was gone before I could grasp its significance.

"I won't escape." Came the smooth response as the little dragon smiled, showing a large number of very sharp teeth. "Don't waste time, now. I have a mission."

Feroz looked stern as he replied. "Don't let it out. We have enough trouble as it is. It will remain safely imprisoned in the egg until we return, for we must find the Phoenix. That is the task that was set for you, remember."

I remained obdurate, for I had no idea where we could begin our search for the bird. "I think it's important to deal with this first. Maybe I should go inside the egg, rather than letting it out. I will remove my protective suit. Facing it inside will be risky for me, but safer for the people in the Temple of the South."

"Go ahead, then. Your attitude is admirable if foolish, and even though I don't agree with you. I will watch over you during your encounter."

Feroz stood beside me as I made a tiny nick in the surface of the egg and squeezed inside, finding myself crouched by the dragons' tail. Feroz closed the slit as the baby swiftly turned and hissed at me, and I felt the scorching of its breath on my face. Before I could utter a word, the creature flung itself at me, knocking the wind out of me, and scratching and tearing at my torso as I lay encased inside the egg. I fought back wildly, poking at its eyes and trying to wriggle onto its back, where I could get a grip on its throat from behind. The creature lashed me with its tail and the spikes tore down my left side as I scrambled over its shoulders and got a grip around the leathery neck.

The little dragon tried to shake me off, but I clung fast, and pressed up on its windpipe with my thumbs, pinching into the soft tissue under its neck. It began to gasp for air, and its struggles grew less as I maintained my pressure, until finally it lay still. I looked through the perimeter of the egg and saw Feroz on his knees, his face raised towards the sun, with eyes shaded against the glare, pointing at something in the sky. I eased myself out of the transparent egg with difficulty, for I was badly hurt, and looked up as a shadow crossed the face of the sun and came towards us.

Feroz gasped in amazement as the great Phoenix landed near us with a flurry of dust, closing its wings, and proceeded to address us.

"Now I can come with you to the people of Fire, for you have vanquished the dragon that dwelt in me from long ago, when mankind began to distrust the messages from Intuition, and became prisoners of their rational mind. I was burdened by the dragon that lay repressed inside me, and now I am free."

Turning to me, the Phoenix continued. "You have shown much courage and insight. To release the dragon would have been a huge mistake, even though it begged you to let it come out. It would have grown bigger and caused havoc for everyone, instigating the desire for conflict, and eventually a dreaded war between the four elemental people of the White Pyramid."

The bird paused, preening itself gently. "Now I will come with you to Percepto, and a new era will begin. We will teach the people how to get back in touch with their intuitive selves, and move humanity forward again. Come, now, and let us go."

The bird allowed us to climb onto its back, and we flew to the Isle once more, where the Ace of Wands received us with great joy. Soothing compresses soon healed my wounds and scratches, and I quickly recovered from these injuries and was ready for my next task, thanking Feroz for his help and bidding him goodbye.

I was surprised to see Percepto come forward with a long black gown made of charcoal ashes, glued to an underlay of sackcloth. "Please put this on. You are ready for Initiation in the Chamber of Ceremonies, since you vanquished the dragon hiding in the egg of your potential. Furthermore, you cannot build the bridge that will support you across the water from the Isle of the White Pyramid to the Bar, where your vessel awaits you, without the fourth Magical Weapon, the Wand, to assist you. That will be awarded to you if you succeed in passing the initiation task that the Master of Ceremonies will give you."

Putting on the gown was most uncomfortable, as the sackcloth scratched my back and arms and tangled in my legs, and the dust from the ashes caught in my nose and mouth, making me cough harshly. However, I was prepared to go through the initiation. Percepto unlocked the heavy door to the Chamber, and made the sign of the Hermetic Cross as we moved into the room beyond. Once I was installed, he retired.

In front of me in the center of the room was a round white table with nine chairs, while the walls were lined with red satin drapes. At the center of this table lay a black, right-handed swastika, surrounded by several strands of barbed wire. This swastika vibrated continually and seemed about to break apart as I felt the evil emanations coming from it, and I drew back nervously. I forced my gaze from the swastika and noticed, at the apse of the triangular room, a lone figure wearing a grey fur mantle that stood in silhouette facing a small cubic altar on which burned a single candle. The person turned towards me, and at the same moment seven additional figures mysteriously formed themselves out of the satin drapes and moved forward, taking seven of the chairs around the table. The person in the fur mantle indicated the eighth seat at the table for me, as he occupied the ninth chair.

We sat facing each other across the white surface of the table. I looked at each of the entities, for one could not call them human, trying to decipher their intent. From the left of the person in grey, I saw a figure in black that looked like a female. Next to her in order were those indistinguishable others, clad in blue, red, yellow, green, orange and purple robes. They were silent and their faces hidden beneath hats of the same colors. I looked down at my gown, and saw that the black remained only on one part of the garment, while three quarters of the color had changed from black to a mixture of citrine, olive green and russet triangles.

The figure in grey addressed me. "Your task is to take the swastika that you see before us, and restore it to its rightful position, which is left-handed. How you accomplish this is your problem to solve. Now, go and place your left hand on the swastika and observe what happens." There was a murmur of agreement from the seven figures.

The table was large, and to reach the swastika I had to crawl ignominiously across it, my multicolored gown trailing under my knees and catching on the barrier as I attempted to reach across the barbed wire. Each time the wire seemed to undulate and grab me before I was able to touch the object, and my hands became scratched and my gown torn in repeated attempts to overcome it. I became angry and, still kneeling in a most uncomfortable position, grabbed the wire with both hands, tearing it from its position around the swastika. Throwing the wire aside, I clutched the swastika tightly.

There was a loud bang and a puff of smoke, and I found myself outside the Temple at the top of a steep hill holding the swastika. It vibrated ceaselessly, causing my arms to become numb. I could no longer feel anything, so I dropped it and it began rolling like a cartwheel down the hill. I watched, fascinated, as it picked up speed and, bouncing from rock to rock, careened downwards until, coming to a ledge below me, it leapt into the air and vanished from sight.

Oh dear! I thought. I hadn't even begun to work on reversing its direction before I had lost it. Now I would have to go and look for it. I began to descend the steep hill cautiously until I got to the ledge, where I lay on my stomach, being intimidated by heights, and looked over. A vast chasm lay below me, the sheer rock walls descending for several thousand feet, and the floor was scarcely visible except for a whirling cloud of dust that rose up from the depths.

Drawing back, I wondered how to get down to the bottom of the chasm, for the swastika must be down there, if anything was left of it. That might be to my advantage, for if it had been broken, maybe I could rearrange the pieces in the left-handed direction without further trouble.

I will not describe my descent into the terrible chasm, for it took many days of criss-crossing tiny paths cut into the rock walls, that even a mule would have jibbed at. I tore my gown on prickly bushes and tripped over it several times before I had the good sense to remove it, my incandescent suit still being underneath. I found no food, but drank from small rivulets in the rock walls, the unfriendly bushes at least providing hand holds for me in the more challenging places. The light grew dimmer as I descended, darkening until it became almost pitch black as I reached the floor of the chasm, utterly exhausted. I immediately lay down to sleep, and I began to dream.

I'm clambering down a vertical rock wall that changes into a flight of steps. These steps are so steep that it is impossible to get a foothold on them, and I am clinging to a rickety handhold that seems about to give way. I've become stuck, and can go no further. Suddenly the rail breaks, and I am plummeting swiftly down, my fall arrested by the hand of a strange figure that appears beside me. We swoop up and fly low over the choppy waves of a great bay where, in the distance, are two jutting headlands on each side of a narrow channel leading out of the bay. My companion sets me down on a jetty where a boat is waiting, bobbing in the rough water, and I know I have to get into the boat alone.

I am rowing out into the bay now, standing up, without anybody in the boat with me. A vague figure wearing a bulls hide, and with a speckled bird head dress blowing in the stiff breeze, walks across the water and gets into the bow of the boat in front of me. I can feel the craft sink down with his weight, yet when he sits on the thwart, the prow of the boat is visible through him. I continue to row, unable to see - through the thick fog that has suddenly gathered - how close I am to the opening of the bay, for I know that a storm is looming and I fear the open sea.......

Waking to a dim light, I perceived a figure with a bulls' hide thrown across his shoulders and a speckled bird head dress over his brow. He walked forward and took me by the hand silently. We moved along the sandy floor of the chasm in the gloom, ahead of us the glowing, leaping flames of a large bonfire.

There were moving figures around the great fire, they whirled and swayed, they danced and cavorted in a circle, throwing objects onto the flames, singing and shouting, waving their arms and shaking their fists. The dust rose from their thudding feet and spiraled upwards towards the night sky. They resolved themselves into a group of maniacal Druids, and behind them in large heaps were all kinds of objects in boxes and crates, round and rectangular shapes, made of metal and another strange substance that melted in the flames, for they were rapidly hurling these items into the fire, which grew bigger every moment.

I recognized these objects, for they were similar to the boxes Percepto had described as TVs. The boxes that switched on and off and had taken over the minds of humanity, leaving them bereft of imagination and the knowledge of an inner god. A large Druid, shrieking high, held in his hand the object I was looking for – the battered swastika that I had dropped from the top of the chasm. He was about to throw it into the fire when I leapt forward, catching his arm.

"No! Don't burn it!" I shouted above the din. "I need to reverse it for my initiation. I won't be able to pass through the ceremony without that swastika." I tugged at his arm, but he laughed in my face, and with a mighty toss, threw the swastika into the flames.

"So much for your foul emblem!" He yelled. "The sacred sign of the Celts has been defaced for ever by Nazis. All we can do is to destroy it and its malevolent associations for it is no use to us any more."

Sprinting to the fire without thinking, I hurled myself into the flames, searching frantically for the swastika before it burnt away. There it was! I bent forward to pick it up, as the closer flames licked at it, not noticing the tremendous heat of the fire and the fact that I could be burning myself. I turned, trying to jump clear, but it was too late. I stumbled, falling into the burning embers, uttering a cry such as I had never heard before in all my travels, and lost consciousness.

I found myself back in the Chamber of Ceremonies, with the eight colored figures sitting solemnly around the white table. In my hand was the swastika, still warm from the embers of the fire.

The grey elder addressed me. "You have indeed passed our initiation test. You will observe that the swastika you are holding is now left handed. You withstood the heat of the fire until it twisted the material from which it was made, and reversed it. I know you will not remember that, for you thought you were burning up. In fact, you had forgotten that you were wearing the fireproof suit, and that saved you. Your sacrifice has made it possible for the sacred left-handed swastika to resume its former importance as our spiritual symbol, and you have been recommended most highly by the nation of Druids for your courage."

He paused, raising his hand, in which was a shining Wand that sent forth iridescent fire, and throwing back the mantle that he wore to reveal his face. It was my Guide!

I humbly received the last of the four Magical Weapons, the Wand of Fire, from my beloved mentor and master, and passed from the Chamber of Ceremonies to learn of my last task.

Percepto was there to greet us as we regrouped in the ninth room. The old man, his mission apparently complete, abruptly vanished, as the Ace of Wands explained that I must now gather all my forces together to build the bridge that would carry us from the Isle of the White Pyramid over the waters of the Lagoon to the Bar.

Instantly objecting because I did not fancy the idea of a big engineering project, I quickly proposed an alternative. "I have my scull moored nearby. I can easily row over to the Bar with one other entity, then I can ferry the others over. That would be faster than spending days to construct a bridge, with all the tools and materials we will need, for there is little available on the Isle."

"I am sorry." Percepto shook his head. "Your boat has been taken away, for all twenty of your entities, or at least those who survive, must accompany you over the bridge to the Bar, where you will choose three of them to crew your new vessel. Choosing your crew is very important, and demands intuition, for you must know inwardly which entities can work together. There is no room for dissent on a small boat, only discernment."

I felt overwhelmed by the task set before me. First, I had to summon all the entities that were still available. When I had gone through the list, out of roughly 22 entities, if I included Oojo the toad and Joana the cricket, at least six were dead or absorbed; three were in prison and three either too frail or too slow to pitch in with manual labor. Mithinkky had reluctantly been released by Persephone in the spring, when the world was new again. Therefore, only eight remained that might be of any use in bridge building. They were;-

    Bazoom – for his energy through anger
    Endevvy – adept with tools
    Fontanova – good at organizing
    Pompeybou – engineering abilities
    Kracklewergen – strong - although unreliable
    Pupidoro – the unknown entity, management
    Mithinkky – vague, though good ideas
    Numbyling – mediator and calming.

I therefore decided to form a team out of the remaining eight. I would put in charge a new entity that had not appeared before, but seemed to be pressing forward to be of service, Pulpidoro. The main team would consist of the foreman Endevvy, who understood the use of tools, Bazoom, Pompeybou, and Kracklewergen. I would bring in Mithinkky, who had been released by Persephone, for consultations. Fontanova would do the organizing and act as nurse in case of need, and Numbyling would deal with any conflict between the parties and desensitize psychological problems.

In order to call the team of eight together, I had to express all eight of the necessary qualities at once, and maintain those aspects of myself until we had completed the bridge. This would demand tremendous effort. I first found a large rock that I climbed, and stood in a commanding position on top. I then called for order while the other seven entities milled about below, and soon Pulpidoro, the eighth, stepped in and demand silence. He then launched into a long sermon about the value of manual labor, and how it benefited and humbled a person who had become too prideful.

Pompeybou - who was known to be pompous - and Kracklewergen did not like the sermon, and the trickster began to make catcalls and throw small pebbles at the speaker. Meanwhile, Endevvy was listening intently, while Bazoom buzzed angrily in disagreement. The three feminine entities stood silently in the wings.

Shushing Kracklewergen, I then spoke to the entity Pulpidoro, privately telling the latter to finish his oration and shut up. Snapping my fingers, I caught Bazooms' attention and glared at him. He immediately looked subdued, for once.

Pulpidoro lectured on and on and would not stop, expressing his moral and ethical views ad infinitum, and so I had to drag the reluctant fellow down from the rock and shut him in a small office with a lot of paperwork to do. Then Endevvy and I organized the tools, while the other three scrounged around for materials, which were thin on the ground. I sent the three female entities out to hunt for wood, rocks and wire around the Island. They came back empty handed, for they had found that, unfortunately, the four Aces were very tidy, and only on the West side where the Ace of Cups lived, were there any piles of useful materials, such as mill wheels, grinding stones for flour and dam building supplies. The Swords had plenty of books, and the Pentacles compost, straw and mounds of pumpkins, while the Wands could produce nothing of any use on the material plane except junk radio masts.

The length of the bridge had to be 500 cubits, and although the Lagoon was not deep at this point, the bottom was shifting mud and sand and would not support pillars, so a suspension bridge was out of the question, and there were not enough rocks to build a Roman arch type. Steel was missing for a trestle, and the wood we found was mostly twisted driftwood and unusable for planks. I was in despair until the dumpy Mithinkky, followed by the other two women, came to me with an idea. Their arms were filled with books and they carried piles of books on their heads. Mithinkky spoke slowly, her sagging lips mouthing the words.

"I think.… I think I'm Mithinkky. I have, maybe a stupid, um, had a thought. I don't know very much and I can't read. But someone, um, told me that books were made of paper, which was made from trees. I don't know how trees can turn into a book, but there are piles of used books outside the Temple of the East. I think they are exercise books from their schools, because the Ace of Swords likes everyone to study a lot. Then they throw the books out." Mithinkky licked her lips. "There should be enough books to cross the gap if we sink them into the mud, and keep piling them up, do you think?"

I had to explain to her gently that books disintegrated in the water. "They will turn to pulp and fall apart, I am afraid. That is a nice idea, but we must think of something else. Numbyling, what do you suggest?"

Numbyling, a tall, sad-looking woman with half-closed eyes, had extremely smelly feet. "I'm not really interested in the bridge." She sighed. "It's too much work. Why can't we just stay here and hang out?"

"You know that is not possible. We all have to leave the Isle, because my tasks are almost finished and I need to move on. Whether you like it or not, you will have to come with me and the rest of my entities. Now, make an effort. I know you are very clever, so use your brain for once."

"I will make an effort to think." Sighed Numbyling, and sat down.

Turning to the third female entity, I entreated. "Fontanova, you are the creative one, come on now, what can we do?"

"I think that we should make a raft. It should be big enough for all nine of us. The missing entities are not here anyway. The raft can be made of tightly bound bundles of straw from the Pentacles temple. We can tie them together with wire and lay books on top to make a platform. Then we can push the raft with a spare Wand. I'm sure that Percepto would loan us one."

That seemed like a good idea, and we set to work building the raft, which was soon ready. We pushed it into the water and were set to climb aboard when Percepto came out of the Temple and held up his hand.

"I am sorry. The raft will not do. I asked you to build a bridge. That is the only way you can cross over to the Bar. Now, I will give you a hint. Use your Intuition and imagination, and see what you can do." He turned and went inside, leaving us baffled and disillusioned, after we had completed a great deal of useless work on the project.

Now I racked my brains, but I could not come up with an answer, while the eight entities stood around, looking irritated and upset. It was becoming increasingly exhausting to maintain eight attitudes at once, and I felt like giving up. I curled myself into a ball, acknowledging failure, and wondered why Globdinig, who was the only one to fully empathize with my depression, could not be there with me. I felt suicidal.

After three days, during which I could neither eat nor drink, I reached the limit of my possibilities. I had visited all four Castles and succeeded in passing their tests, and I had performed, as best I could, the eleven tasks given me by the Aces. I had also shape shifted in my astral form into three of the elemental creatures, to learn understanding of their plight. Now, after months of effort, I had failed the last task - to cross to the Bar. Since this was where it would end, I gathered together my eight entities and told them I could no longer maintain them as one, and that I was going to die. I asked them to dig a grave and place me in it, with the addition of suitable tools such as paint brushes and scrapers, a jar of vodka, and some coconut macaroons, and bury me for ever.

They began to dig, sobbing and wailing continually, for they knew they would have to die too, if I was no more. They were very attached to me, and could not contemplate life without me. When the grave was finished, they tied me in a fetal position and dropped me in, then began to toss earth into the hole. I lay there, my orbital sander close to my nose, and felt the earth thudding on my body and gradually becoming heavier. I knew, when my nose and mouth was covered, that would be the end, and my life a catastrophic fiasco.

Their sobs grew louder, and they choked continually as they saw the earth reach my nose and mouth and cover my face. I felt myself suffocating, but strove not to panic and claw at the mass over me. Instead, remaining torpid, I sank into oblivion.

I'm in the rowboat, finally heading out of the great bay. I see a figure with the head of a hawk standing in the bow, for I am rowing Greek fashion upright and facing forward. As we pass out of the bay, the figure points directly overhead to the headland on the left, and I see a strange blue light, in the shape of a woman, that seems to elongate and stretch itself farther and farther outwards, reaching over us towards the other headland in a great shining arc of electric blue. As we pass below it, the figure in the bow turns, and I see that it is my Guide.

He chuckles. "Stop the boat before it clears the headland! There is your bridge, you idiot. When you took up the fetal position, you became Hadit, the dot in the circle that is your monad. As soon as you discover that you are the dot Hadit, you can center yourself and look outwards, and you will see that you are surrounded by the circumference of your own circle, which is called Nuit, the blue one who bridges the heavens before you."

The old fellow continues. "Now, take the Intuition you have learned in this dream, or rather, your state of suffocation, and use Nuit as your bridge to the Bar, for she is willing. Go ahead and absorb her now, and dig yourself out of that stupid grave before it is too late......"

With a remaining flash of consciousness, I frantically clawed away the earth over my face, and thankfully took a huge gasp of air. The entities stopped spading earth into the grave, and I called them to help dig me out.

"I have the solution!" I assured them with relief. "Get me out of here, and we'll go. I know how to build the bridge."

They quickly dried their tears and helped me from the grave, and I stood on the shore of the Island, gazing towards the Bar and becoming Hadit. From my center, the sky goddess Nuit extended herself in a beautiful arch over the Lagoon, and my eight entities danced over the shining bridge and grouped themselves on the shifting sands of the Bar, where I quickly joined them. I fell to my knees in thanks to Nuit, who smiled insightfully and faded from my view.

<u>Epilogue to Gulftide.</u>

We found ourselves safely on the sands of the Bar, which was about thirty feet wide. On one side stretched the limpid waters of the Lagoon, with the Isle of the White Pyramid rising majestically in the center, while behind it, in the distance, loomed the far eastern shore where the four Castles of the Elements were. I could just make out each Castle, as I knew what they looked like. On the far left was the Castle of Earth, its adobe brick walls standing stalwartly in the distance. Next to it, to the right towards the south end of the Lagoon, was the Castle of Air, with a dense mist swirling around its delicate spires. Then came the Castle of Water, and over its shining battlements waterfalls cascaded, so that it was visible one moment, and gone the next. The Castle of Fire was furthest to the south, as the land grew drier and turned from the lush green of a tropical climate to a vast desert. This Castle was unmistakable with its bright glow and the flickering flames behind it. I thought of all the Court Cards I had met, of the tests I had taken, and of the adventures that challenged me there, and I was grateful.

I turned towards the other side of the Bar, where a sailboat of about thirty feet was moored in a small inlet, with stacks of provisions waiting for us to stow on board for our journey into the Mystic SEA. Beyond the boat, which bobbed cheerfully on the choppy waves, a vast ocean stretched into the distance westwards, with nothing visible until the horizon drew down darkly on the unknown that lay ahead of us. A fresh breeze of about 10 knots made the waves scurry up the sand, and further along the beach was a small fishing hamlet with a ramshackle bar sign swaying in the wind above it.

I gathered the eight entities about me, and noticed that I no longer needed to focus on their attributes to keep them with me, for they seemed to have taken on a life of their own. We knelt in a circle, thanking the goddess Nuit for her help, and dedicating ourselves to our mission, yet to be. Then we walked to the hamlet and stopped outside the bar, which was called The Purple Prince, and they waited while I peered into the darkness, seeing several old wooden bar stools and cracked tables, but no sign of any local topers.

The barman beckoned to me and whispered. "He's in the back, taking a nap in the hammock. Approach slowly and gently, for he hates to be disturbed."

He pointed to a door at the rear of the building and I stepped outside, my heart pounding joyfully. There was a large bulk swinging in a hammock between two withered trees at the far end of the yard, and so I went towards it. As I got closer, I observed a foot with a dirty buckled black shoe dangling from the hammock, and a sleeve of purple satin was visible through the mesh, while a shock of curly red hair stirred in the breeze.

I shrank back instantly. I knew who it was – Belvedere, my Ego. How stupid of me! I had thought that the person waiting for me would be my Guide, for I expected him to be on hand to give advice and answer my questions, now that I had reached the Bar. Hiding behind a shed, I thought for a moment. My instinct was to hurry back to the tavern and warn my eight friends that their boss was sleeping out in the yard, for they were entirely beholden to him, I believed.

I was half way to the back door of the bar when a loud, raspy voice addressed me. "Just a minute. Where are you off to? I've been waiting here for you a long time." Belvederes' voice gave way to a dull, booming laugh. "Ha! Ha! I'm not stupid. You expected your dear, darling Guide to be here, didn't you? Well, he's away on an errand, a long errand. He won't be here until you're ready to put to sea, and now you must select your crew on your own. Out of my eight manikins, you can only take three, and the other five will have to return with me to my amethyst tower and hang up on the poles until you get to the first island in the Mystic SEA, Malkuth."

He gave an evil guffaw. "Yes, you will have to cross the sea between the Bar and Malkuth now, and it is populated by the monsters of the Qliphoth in their hundreds. See how well you manage to battle with them, smart ass! Better, far, to stay here with me and forget about your plans. I'll offer you a good life – we can go to the thrift stores and buy clothes, sort through the bargains in the grocery store, and scrape together the money for your transport, feed for the horse, and a second hand wagon. You can never survive the challenges in the Islands of the Mystic SEA! But if you are stupid enough to go, I will be looking on and manipulating the three entities you choose for your crew, so beware."

The Qliphoth! A shock passed through me as I remembered spying on them with the Page of Pentacles, and hearing their evil words during my trip underground as a mole. They were terrifying. I wasn't going to show my fear, though, and I whirled around angrily.

"Don't challenge me, you dirty pig! I know what I'm doing. I've passed all the Royal Trials that the Court Cards set me, including the 12 tasks of the four Aces, and even building the bridge. I can easily deal with anything that crosses my path."

"Oh! My little one thinks it knows all about everything, does it? Well, snotty face, see if you like this!" Belvedere reached into his pocket and pulled out a huge black tarantula, thrusting it into my face.

I shrieked with all my might and darted backwards, afraid to touch the waving hairy legs, and Belvedere laughed again, louder and louder, and I knew my touch of bravado was nothing but a hollow joke. Hastily I dived into the bar and ran out into the street, where the eight entities stood, looking very nervous.

I pulled myself together. "Come on, you guys, let's get the provisions stowed on the boat. You can all help, but only three of you can go with me on this part of the trip. Belvedere has said so."

Their faces fell. I hastily explained that the remaining five would, if they proved worthy, be able to join me later on, and that the sail boat was too small for nine of us.

"Who will you pick?" One of them asked nervously.

"Pick me, pick me." Cried another.

"You will really need me." Said a third. "Don't leave me behind. I've worked hard for you."

It was heart rending. I was only thankful that the missing twelve entities had dispersed, and I was not sure how many of them were still alive. I wouldn't find out until I needed one of them desperately.

With all of us working, the boat was loaded in about three hours, with food, sails, safety equipment, navigation instruments and all the other useful items I would need on the trip. I stayed inside and put everything in the correct place while the others handed me each item. Once the boat was stowed, I jumped down onto the sand and gathered the eight around me. I explained to them that I would be taking my cricket, Joana, to give me the weather forecasts, but I would leave Oojo the toad behind because he might cause trouble. They all nodded in agreement. "That toad, he's a nuisance. You never know what he'll do next."

I then went on to say the three entities I would pick had to be useful to me on the trip. I needed one experienced sailor to be my mate, in case something happened to me. Then I needed a person who could cook and who could, also, take the helm. That would be someone who was willing and eager to learn. The third person should be exceptionally strong, to help reef sails, and have the ability to make repairs when the gear gave way. I looked at the eight, and I knew that Pompeybou would be the best person for the mate. I beckoned to him, and he stepped forward, carrying his old and faithful hand bearing compass. Next, I picked Numbyling, because she was very calm and unlikely to disagree with anyone else, and she would do as she was told – and that meant cooking. The third person would be Endevvy, because he had mechanical and engineering abilities and the stamina to face bad weather.

The remaining five showed their disappointment, and Pulpidoro became very angry. "Why didn't you pick me? I'm good at everything and I can tell people what to do."

"It isn't about telling people what to do. The crew is a team and we all work together. I am the captain, and we can't have anyone on the boat that might countermand my final decisions and run us into trouble. I'm sorry, Pulpidoro. I am sure that I will be able to use you in due course. Each one of you, provided you have conquered your bad habits, will come to the Islands of the Mystic SEA and share my adventures. For now, please go to the Purple Prince bar, where Belvedere will meet you and take you back to his amethyst tower."

They trooped off reluctantly, waving to me, and the four of us climbed aboard the boat and prepared to leave the following morning.

There was a fair breeze as we moved gently out of the inlet and began to feel the boat buck to the swells. We set the sails and I put Numbyling on the helm straight away, giving her instructions on sailing points, so that she would soon be able to manage by herself. We set a course due West, 270 degrees, and soon the Bar was fast vanishing behind us and the Mystic SEA surrounded us on all sides. What would we find out there? Which of us would survive to vanquish our enemies? Would we meet strange and terrifying creatures on the Islands? Where would we finally arrive? I knew not what lay ahead for us, and so we sailed west into the glow of the setting sun.